Praise for Angela Marsons and Detective Kim Stone

LOST GIRLS

"*Lost Girls* was yet another brilliant read…[A] gripping and addictive read, hard to put down." —Off the Shelf book reviews

"Angela Marsons has written a tightly woven thriller that will keep the reader riveted to the last page." —The Book Review Café

"This is one author that stands out from the crowds…*Lost Girls* will keep you hooked and anxious until the last page."

—Bye the Crime

"Another superb, thrilling novel by Angela Marsons.…every book keeps getting better and better!"

—Reading Corner for Book Lovers

"Compelling, addictive and frightening. *Lost Girls* is a book you can't afford to miss." —A Bookseller Blabbering

EVIL GAMES

"*Evil Games* is a fabulously dark and chilling read…[I] can't recommend this series highly enough."

—By the Letter Book Reviews

"Yet again Angela Marsons has written a five-star crime novel. I loved *Silent Scream*…*Evil Games* is certainly as good as the first, if not better, and I wish I could give it a higher rating than 5/5."

—Off the Shelf Book Reviews

SILENT SCREAM

LOST
GIRLS

Also by Angela Marsons

Silent Scream
Evil Games

Angela
MARSONS

LOST
GIRLS

Detective Kim Stone

Book Three

GRAND CENTRAL
PUBLISHING
New York   Boston

Grand Central Publishing
Hachette Book Group
1290 Avenue of the Americas, New York, NY 10104
grandcentralpublishing.com
twitter.com/grandcentralpub

First published in 2015 by Bookouture, an imprint of StoryFire Ltd.

First Grand Central Publishing edition: October 2021

Grand Central Publishing is a division of Hachette Book Group,
Inc. The Grand Central Publishing name and logo is a trademark of
Hachette Book Group, Inc.

The publisher is not responsible for websites (or their content) that are not
owned by the publisher.

The Hachette Speakers Bureau provides a wide range of authors for speaking
events. To find out more, go to www.hachettespeakersbureau.com or call
(866) 376-6591.

Library of Congress Control Number: 2021939705

ISBN: 978-1-5387-0417-2 (trade paperback)

Printed in the United States of America

LSC-C

Printing 1, 2021

DEDICATION

This book is dedicated to Mary Forrest whose love and generosity touched so many, including myself.

Mary, you taught us all so much and those lessons stay with us in our hearts.

PROLOGUE

February 2014

Emily Billingham tried to scream through the hand that covered her mouth.

The fingers were thin but strong against her lower jaw. She forced out a sound that bounced back off his flesh and threw back her head to try to prise herself free. The back of her skull met with something hard, a rib.

"Knock it off, you stupid little bitch," he said, dragging her backwards.

The pounding in her ears almost drowned out his words. She could feel her own heart beating hard against her chest.

The fabric across her eyes blocked out her surroundings but she felt the gravel underfoot.

Every step took her further from Suzie.

Emily bucked again. She tried to force herself away from his body using her upper arms but he just pulled her closer. She tried to squirm away from his grip but his arms tightened. She didn't want to go with him. She had to get free. She had to get help. Daddy would know what to do. Daddy would save them both.

She heard the creak of a door. Oh no, it was the van.

She summoned the strength to scream. She didn't want to go in the van again.

"No...please..." she cried, trying to squirm out of his grip.

He kicked her hard in the back of the knee.

Her leg buckled and she stumbled forward, but he stopped her falling to the ground by grabbing a handful of hair.

Her scalp stung as the tears broke free from her eyes.

In one movement he launched her into the rear of the vehicle and slammed the door shut. It made the same tinny noise it had days ago when she'd been walking to school.

Her classroom seemed so far away now and she wondered if she would ever see her friends again.

The van reversed quickly, launching her against the doors. The pain shot from the back of her skull like a firework.

She squirmed to right herself but the van was moving fast, throwing her onto her side.

Her cheek crashed against the wooden floor of the vehicle as it bounced along at speed. She winced as the skin on her bare calf snagged on a nail. A trail of warm blood trickled down to her ankle.

Suzie would tell her to be strong. Like when she'd sprained her wrist in gymnastics. Suzie had held her other hand and squeezed strength into her heart, telling her it would all be okay. And she'd been right.

But she hadn't been right this time.

"I can't do it, Suzie, I'm sorry," Emily whispered as the tears turned to sobs. She wanted to be brave for her friend but the trembling that had started in her legs was now travelling the length of her body.

She pulled up her knees to her chin, tried to scrunch herself tighter, into the smallest of balls, but the shaking wouldn't subside.

She felt a drop of urine slip from between her thighs. The trickle turned to a stream that her body was powerless to stop.

A terrified sob was torn from her body as Emily prayed for the ordeal to end.

And then, suddenly, the van came to a stop.

"Please M-Mummy, come and get me," she whispered as the sudden ominous silence settled around her.

She lay against the door, unmoving. The trembling had paralysed her limbs. She had no more strength to fight him and awaited whatever came next.

The fear formed a lump in her throat as her captor opened the door.

CHAPTER 1

Kim Stone felt the rage burning within her. From the ignition point in her brain it travelled like electricity to the soles of her feet, then surged around again.

If her colleague, Bryant, was beside her now he would be urging her to calm down. To think before she acted. To consider her career, her livelihood.

So it was a good job she was on her own.

Pure Gym was situated on Level Street in Brierley Hill and ran between the Merry Hill shopping centre and the Waterfront office and bar complex.

It was Sunday lunchtime and the car park was full. She drove around once, spotting the car she sought before parking the Ninja right outside the front door. She didn't plan on being there long.

She stepped into the foyer and approached the front desk. A pretty, toned woman smiled brightly and held out her hand. Kim guessed she was looking for some kind of membership card. Kim had a card of her own to show. Her warrant card.

"I'm not a member but I do need a quick word with one of your patrons."

The woman looked around as though needing to seek advice.

"Police business," Kim stated. Kind of, she added to herself. The woman nodded.

Kim looked at the directions board and knew exactly where she was heading. She took a left and found herself behind three rows of machines on which people were stepping, walking and jogging.

She looked along the rear views of people expending energy on going nowhere.

The one she was looking for was stepping up and down in the far corner. The long blonde hair tied back in a ponytail was the clue. The fact that her phone was in front of her on the display screen was the clincher.

Having found her target, Kim became oblivious to the sounds of people's limbs lifting and striding or the curious glances she received as the only fully dressed person in the room.

All she cared about was one woman's involvement in the death of a nineteen-year-old boy called Dewain.

Kim straddled the front of the machine. The shock on the face of Tracy Frost almost pierced her rage. But not quite.

"A word?" she asked, although it wasn't really a question.

For a second the woman almost lost her footing and that would have been just too bad.

"How the hell did you...?" Tracy looked around. "Don't tell me you used your badge to get in?"

"A word, in private," Kim repeated.

Tracy continued to step.

"Look, I'm happy to do it here," Kim said, raising her voice. "I'll never see these people again."

Kim could feel at least half the eyes in the room upon them already.

Tracy stepped backwards in a dismount, then reached for her phone.

Kim was surprised at the height of the woman and guessed her to be five two at best. Kim had never seen her without six-inch heels, whatever the weather.

Kim barged through the door to the ladies' toilets and pushed Tracy against the wall. Her head missed the hand dryer by an inch.

"What the fuck did you think you were doing?" Kim screamed.

A cubicle door opened and a teenager scarpered out of the room. They were now alone.

"You can't touch me like—"

Kim stepped back so that only a sliver of space existed between them. "How the hell could you break that story, you stupid bitch? He's dead, now. Dewain Wright is dead because of you."

Tracy Frost, local reporter and all-round pond scum, blinked twice as Kim's words found her brain. "But...my...story..."

"Your story got him killed, you stupid cow."

Tracy began to shake her head. Kim nodded. "Oh yes."

Dewain Wright had been a teenager from the Hollytree estate. He'd been in a gang called the Hollytree Hoods for about three years and wanted to get out. The gang had got wind of it and stabbed him, leaving him for dead. They thought they'd killed him but a passer-by had performed CPR. That was when Kim had been called in to investigate attempted murder.

Her first instruction had been to conceal the fact that he was still alive from everyone except his family. She had known that if word got back to Hollytree the gang would find a way to finish him off.

She had spent that night in the chair beside his bed, praying he would defy the prognosis and breathe on his own. She had held his hand, offering him her own energy to find the strength to come back. The courage he'd shown in trying to change his life and battle the fates had touched her. She had wanted an opportunity to know the brave young man who had decided that gang life was not for him.

Kim leaned in close and speared Tracy with her eyes. There was no escape. "I begged you not to break the story but you just couldn't help yourself, could you? It was all about being first, wasn't it? Are you so bloody desperate to get noticed by the nationals you'd throw away a kid's life?" Kim screamed in her face. "Well, for your sake I hope they do notice you—because there's no place for you here any more. I intend to make sure of it."

"It wasn't because of—"

"Of course it was because of you," Kim raged. "I don't know how you found out he was still alive but he's dead now. And this time it's real."

Confusion contorted her features. The stupid woman wanted to speak but couldn't find any words. Kim wouldn't have listened anyway.

"You know he was trying to get out, don't you? Dewain was a decent kid just trying not to die."

"It couldn't have been because of me," Tracy said, as the colour began to return to her face.

"Yes, Tracy, it was," Kim said emphatically. "The blood of Dewain Wright is on your grubby little hooves."

"I was only doing my job. The world had a right to know."

Kim stepped in closer.

"I swear to God, Tracy, I will not rest until the closest you come to a newspaper is driving the delivery—"

Her words were cut off by the ringing of her mobile phone.

Tracy took the opportunity to step out of Kim's reach.

"Stone," she answered.

"I need you at the station. Now."

Detective Chief Inspector Woodward wasn't the warmest of bosses but he normally took the time to offer some kind of curt greeting.

Kim's mind worked quickly. He was calling her on Sunday lunchtime after insisting that she take the day off. And he was already pissed off at something.

"I'm on my way, Stacey. Get me a dry white wine," she said, hanging up the phone. If her boss was confused because she'd just called him Stacey, she'd explain it to him later.

No way was she going to reveal an urgent call from her boss while standing within spitting distance of the most despicable reporter she'd ever met.

It could be one of two things. Either she was in a shitload of trouble or there was something big kicking off. Neither scenario would benefit from this lowlife hearing the conversation.

She turned back to Tracy Frost. "Just don't think this is over. I will find a way to make you pay for what you did. I promise," Kim said, opening the bathroom door.

"I'll have your job for this," Tracy shouted after her.

"Crack on," Kim tossed over her shoulder. A nineteen-year-old had died last night, for nothing. These weren't the best days she'd ever had.

And she had a feeling that this one was about to get worse.

CHAPTER 2

Kim parked the Ninja at the rear of Halesowen Police Station.

West Midlands Police served almost 2.9 million occupants, covering the cities of Birmingham, Coventry, Wolverhampton and the area of the Black Country.

The force was divided into ten Local Policing Units, including her own area of Dudley.

Kim reached the office on the third floor. She knocked, entered and froze.

Her surprise was not because Woody was seated beside the imposing figure of his boss, Superintendent Baldwin.

It wasn't even because Woody was dressed in a polo shirt instead of his normal white shirt complete with epaulettes bearing force insignia.

It was because even from the doorway Kim could see beads of sweat on the caramel skin covering his head. His anxiety had nowhere to hide.

Now she was worried. She had never seen Woody sweat.

Four eyes rested upon her as she closed the door.

She was unaware of anything she'd done to piss off both of them. Superintendent Baldwin hailed from Lloyd House in Birmingham and she'd seen him often. On the television.

"Sir?" she said, looking at the only man in the room who meant anything to her. It was impossible to view her boss without also seeing the framed photo of his twenty-two-year-old son wearing full Navy uniform. Woody had received his dead body back from the Navy two years after the photo had been taken.

"Sit down, Stone."

She moved forward and sat on the single chair, abandoned in the middle of the room. Now she looked from one to the other, eager for a clue. Most conversations that took place between herself and Woody were preceded by his need to strangle the stress ball that rested at the front of his desk. Normally, it was a reassuring sign to her that all was well between them.

It remained on the desk.

"Stone, an incident occurred this morning: an abduction."

"Confirmed?" she asked, immediately. Often people went missing and were found within a couple of hours.

"Yes, confirmed."

She waited patiently. Even with a confirmed kidnapping Kim was unsure why she was sitting before the DCI and *his* boss.

Luckily Woody was not a man given to unnecessary intrigue or suspense, so he got straight to the point.

"It's two young girls."

Kim closed her eyes and took a breath. Ah, now she understood the escalation along the food chain.

"Like the last time, Sir?"

Although she hadn't been part of the investigation thirteen months ago, every member of the West Midlands force had been interested in the case. Many had helped in the subsequent search.

Kim knew many things about the old case but the most resounding fact came straight into her mind.

One of the girls hadn't come back.

Woody brought her attention back to the present. "At this point we're not sure. Initially it appears so. The two girls are best friends and were last seen at Old Hill Leisure Centre. One of the mothers was due to collect them at twelve thirty but her car had been immobilised.

"Both mothers received a text message at twelve twenty confirming that kidnappers have both girls."

It was now only fifteen minutes past one. The girls had been taken less than an hour ago but the arrival of the text message meant there would be no enquiries to friends and neighbours, no hope that the girls had simply wandered off. The girls were not missing, they'd been kidnapped and the case was already live.

Kim turned her gaze to the superintendent.

"So, what went wrong last time?"

"Excuse me?" he asked, surprised. Clearly, he didn't expect to be addressed directly.

Kim studied his face as his brain formulated a response. Police media training at its best. There were no furrowed lines or beads of sweat at the hairline. Hardly surprising. There were many levels of culpability beneath him.

Baldwin offered her a dead stare in response to her question. A warning to keep her mouth closed.

She stared back. "Well, only one child came back, so what went wrong?"

"I don't think the details—"

"Sir, why am I here?" she asked, turning back to Woody. This was a double abduction. This was a matter for force CID, not local. The management of a case like this would be divided into many different sections. There would be the search for clues, background, door to door, CCTV and press. Woody would never put her in charge of press.

Woody and Baldwin exchanged a look.

She sensed that she was not going to like the answer. Her first guess was that her team was being seconded to assist. Forget the current workload of sexual assaults, domestic violence, fraud and attempted murder cases they were working as well as the finalising of statements for Dewain Wright.

"You want my team on the search—"

"There is no search, Stone," Woody said. "We're issuing a media blackout."

"Sir?"

This was virtually unheard of in an abduction case. The press normally got hold of it in minutes.

"Nothing has been transmitted via the radio frequency and at the moment the parents are not saying a word."

Kim nodded her understanding. If she recalled correctly the same had been attempted the last time but the news had broken by day three. Later that day the surviving child had been found wandering along the roadside and the other had not been found at all.

"I'm still a little confused as to what…"

"You've been requested to head this case, Stone."

Ten seconds passed, during which she waited for the punchline. None came.

"Sir?"

"Of course, that's impossible," Baldwin said. "You are certainly not qualified to head an investigation of this magnitude."

Although Kim didn't disagree she was tempted to mention the Crestwood case where she and her team had captured the killer of four teenage girls.

She turned in her seat so she faced only Woody.

"Requested by?"

"One of the parents. She's asked for you specifically and won't even speak to anyone else. We need you to take the initial details whilst we assemble a team. You'll report back here immediately and hand over to the Officer in Charge."

Kim nodded her understanding of the process, but he still hadn't fully answered her question.

"Sir, can I have the names of the girls and the name of the parent?"

"Charlie Timmins and Amy Hanson are the girls. It's the mother of Charlie that has requested your involvement. Her name is Karen, says she's a friend of yours?"

Kim shook her head blankly. That was impossible. She knew no Karen Timmins and she definitely had no friends.

Woody consulted a sheet of paper on his desk.

"Apologies, Stone. You might know this woman better under her maiden name. Her name was Karen Holt."

Kim felt her back stiffen. The name lived safely in her past; a place she rarely visited.

"Stone, your expression says you do indeed know this woman."

Kim stood and aimed her gaze only at Woody.

"Sir, I will go and carry out the initial questioning to hand over to the appropriate Officer in Charge, but I assure you this woman is no friend of mine."

CHAPTER 3

Kim steered the Ninja through a line of traffic to the front of the queue. As the amber light promised to illuminate she spurred the machine into life and roared across the intersection.

At the next island her knee air-kissed the tarmac at forty miles an hour.

As she travelled south she left the heart of the Black Country, named due to the thirty feet of thick iron ore and coal seam outcrops in various places.

Historically, many people in the area had held an agricultural smallholding but supplemented their income by working as nailers or smiths. By the 1620s there were twenty thousand smiths within ten miles of Dudley Castle.

The address she'd been given was a surprise to Kim. She hadn't envisioned Karen Holt living in one of the finer parts of the Black Country. In fact, she was marginally surprised the woman was still alive at all.

As she headed through Pedmore, the properties began to recede from the road. The plots grew longer, the trees higher and the houses further apart.

The area had originally been a village in the Worcestershire countryside but had merged into Stourbridge following extensive house building during the interwar years.

She pulled off Redlake Road into a driveway that crunched beneath the tyres of the bike. She rolled up to the property and whistled in her head.

The detached house was double-fronted and Victorian, perfect in its symmetry. The white brick looked recently painted.

Kim stopped the bike at an ornate portico entrance supporting a balustraded balcony above. Bay windows protruded on both sides.

It was the kind of house that said you'd made it. And Kim had to wonder what the hell Karen Holt had done to get here. If Bryant had been with her they'd have played their usual game of "guess the house value" and her opening bid would have been no less than one and a half million.

Parked beside a silver Range Rover was an unmarked Vauxhall Cavalier. A brief assessment confirmed the house was not overlooked from any direction. As she went, she made mental notes to pass on to whomever Woody nominated as Officer in Charge.

The front door was opened by a constable Kim recognised from a previous case. She stepped into a reception hall boasting a Minton tiled floor. The centre of the space was dominated by a round oak table supporting the tallest vase of flowers she had ever seen. A reception room lay on either side of the hallway.

"Where is she?" Kim asked the officer.

"Kitchen, Marm. The mother of the other child is here as well."

Kim nodded and headed past the sweeping staircase. A woman met her halfway. The recognition took some time to register on Kim's behalf but was instantaneous on the face of the woman before her.

Karen Timmins bore little resemblance to Karen Holt.

The slashed jeans that had once melded to every available curve had been replaced by a stylish pair of slim-leg trousers. The low, tight tops that had barely contained her breasts had been replaced with a V-neck jumper that whispered at the body beneath instead of screaming it out loud.

The dyed blonde hair had been allowed to return to its natural chestnut and was cut stylishly around a face that was attractive but not striking.

There had been surgery. Not a lot but enough to significantly change her face. Kim guessed at a nose job. Karen had always hated her nose and there'd been a lot there to hate.

"Kim, thank God. Thank you for coming. Thank you."

Kim allowed her hand to be clutched for a whole three seconds before she took it back.

A second woman appeared beside Karen. The terror in her eyes gave way to hope.

Karen stepped aside. "Kim, this is Elizabeth, Amy's mum."

Kim nodded to the woman whose eyes were blackened with smudged mascara. Her hair was a sleek bobbed helmet of auburn. She carried a few more pounds than Karen and was dressed in cream chinos and a cerise jumper.

"And you are Charlie's mum?" Kim asked.

Karen nodded eagerly.

"Have you found them?" Elizabeth asked, breathlessly.

Kim shook her head as she ushered them back into the kitchen.

"I'm here to collect the initial details for the..."

"You're not going to help us find..."

"No, Karen, a team is currently being assembled. I'm only here to take the initial details."

Karen opened her mouth to argue but Kim held up her hand and offered a reassuring smile.

"I can promise you that the very best officers will be assigned to work with you with far more experience in this kind of case. The sooner you give me some details, the quicker I can pass them along and get your children back home safely."

Elizabeth nodded her understanding but Karen narrowed her eyes. Oh yes, that was a look she recognised.

And just as she had when they were teenagers, Kim ignored it. "You were sent messages?" she asked.

They both thrust their phones towards her. She took Karen's first and read the cold, black words.

> There is no need to rush. Charlotte will not be home today. This is not a hoax. I have your daughter.

Kim handed the phone back to Karen and took Elizabeth's.

> Amy will not be home today. This is not a hoax. I have your daughter.

"Okay, tell me exactly what happened," she said, handing it back.

The two women sat at the breakfast bar. Karen took a sip of coffee then spoke. "I dropped them off at the leisure centre this morning—"

"What time?"

"Ten fifteen. The class starts at ten thirty and ends at twelve fifteen. I'm always there to collect them at half past."

Kim could hear the emotion in her voice as she fought back the tears. Elizabeth covered Karen's free hand and urged her to continue.

Karen swallowed. "Right on time, I left the house to pick them up. They always wait in the reception area until I get there. My car wouldn't start—and then I got the message."

"Do you have any CCTV on your house?" Kim asked. She had to assume that the car trouble was deliberate and had been achieved by access to the property.

Karen shook her head. "Why would we?"

"Don't touch the car again," Kim ordered. "Forensics might be able to lift something." It was possible but not probable. "The kidnappers knew your routine well."

Elizabeth lifted her head. "More than one?"

Kim nodded. "I would think so. Your girls are nine years old. Not easy to handle together. A struggle would have been difficult to contain with one adult and two children. There would have been noise."

Elizabeth made a small sound but Kim couldn't help that. Crying would not get their children back. If it would, she'd summon a few tears herself.

"Have either of you noticed anything strange recently? Familiar faces or cars turning up; perhaps the feeling of being watched?"

Both women shook their heads.

"Have your girls mentioned anything different, perhaps being approached by a stranger?"

"No," they said together.

"The girls' fathers?"

"On their way back from golf. We managed to contact them just before you arrived."

That answered all her questions. Clearly both fathers were in the picture so any kind of custody battle was unlikely. It also told her that the two families were very close.

"Please be honest with me. Have you contacted anyone else, friends, relatives?"

They both shook their heads but Karen spoke. "The officer we spoke to told us not to until someone had been in touch."

It had been good advice, and given because the snatch was confirmed. They were not missing. They'd been taken.

"What should we do, Inspector?" Elizabeth asked.

Kim knew that their natural instincts would prompt them to be searching, moving, walking, acting, doing. The girls had been gone for around an hour and a half. And it was going to get a whole lot worse than this.

She shook her head. "Nothing. We can now assume this is a planned kidnap by people who know what they're doing. They know your routines and have watched you closely. The girls will most likely have been lured away from the entrance of the leisure centre in one of three ways. The first is by a person they know. The second is by a person they perceive to be trustworthy and the third is with a promise."

"A promise?" Karen asked.

Kim nodded. "Your girls are too old to be persuaded by sweets, so more likely a puppy or a kitten."

"Oh, Lord," Elizabeth breathed. "Amy has been begging me for a kitten for months."

"There are few kids that can resist the temptation," Kim offered. "That's why it works." She took a deep breath. "Listen, there's going to be a media blackout on this."

At this point they didn't need to know why. The less they knew about the previous case the better.

Kim continued. "So, there'll be no search. There's no point. We're not going to find them in a manhunt. The crime has been planned and they've already made contact. Your girls are not in a field somewhere waiting to be found."

"But what do they want?" Karen asked.

"I'm sure they'll let you know but until they do you have to keep quiet. Not even family members are to be told. There are no exceptions. If the press get hold of this it will make a difference to the investigation. Hundreds of people scouring the area is not going to get your girls back."

Kim could see the indecision on their faces and that would be someone else's fight soon but for now she had to urge them to remain silent. At least until she got back to the station and it became someone else's problem.

"It may be your natural reaction to want everyone you know on the lookout, just as you'd like to be out there searching yourselves, but it won't do any good." Kim stood. "The Officer in Charge will be here soon. You should take that time to make lists of people you might need to contact over the next few days to explain the absence of your children or yourselves."

Karen looked stunned. "But I want … can't you—?"

Kim shook her head. "You need someone with more experience in abduction cases."

"But I want—"

Right on cue a child started crying from the next room. Elizabeth pushed her chair back. Kim followed, heading for the front door.

Karen grabbed at her forearm. "Please, Kim–"

"Karen, I can't take the case. I don't have the experience. I'm sorry but I promise you that the assigned officer will do everything possible—"

"Is this because you hated me back then?"

Kim was stunned. The words were not untrue but Kim would not let that influence her when the lives of two girls were at risk.

Kim felt the frustration grow at her inability to help the desperate woman but her superiors had made her position perfectly clear.

"Why, Karen, why me?"

Karen offered a half-smile. "Do you remember when we were placed with the Price family and Mandy's trainers wore into holes? You asked Diane for a new pair and she said no."

Mandy had been a shy, quiet child who rarely spoke. The soles of her feet had been grazed and sore with a hint of gravel rash.

"Of course I remember," Kim said. For her it had been foster family number seven. Her last.

"I remember what you did. You found out how much they were paid each month to take care of us. You then wrote down what they spent on grocery, bills and rent."

Yes, Kim had watched what they unloaded each Saturday morning and then walked around the supermarket totting it all up. She'd stayed up late one night and gone through the household bills.

"And after a month you presented them with a sheet of paper you were going to post to social services."

The family had been career carers and had always taken the older kids for the highest pay rate.

"I still remember what happened after you confronted them," Karen said, with a smile that didn't even come close to her eyes. "It was new trainers all around." She shook her head. "We knew nothing about you, back then, Kim. You wouldn't speak to a soul about your past—in fact you rarely spoke at all—but there was a determination in you."

Kim offered her a brief smile. "So you want me to head this case because I got you a new pair of trainers?"

"No, Kim. I want you to head this case because I know that if you decide to help us, I will see my daughter again."

CHAPTER 4

Woody was alone when Kim knocked and entered twenty minutes later.

"Sir, I want it," she said.

"Want what, Stone?" he asked, sitting back in his chair.

"The case. I want to be the OIC."

He rubbed his chin. "Did you not hear the superintendent when he said—"

"Yes, I heard loud and clear but he's wrong. I will bring those children home, so if you just tell me whose arse I need to kiss to—"

"That won't be necessary," he said, reaching for the stress ball.

Damn it, she'd already lost and she hadn't even started her sales pitch. But she had clutched victory from the jaws of defeat in the past.

"Sir, I am tenacious, determined, driven..."

He sat back and tilted his head.

"I am persistent, stubborn..."

"Oh yes, you're that, Stone," he offered.

"I will not eat, sleep or drink until..."

"Okay, Stone. It's yours."

"No one will work harder than...umm, what?"

He sat forward and let go of the stress ball. "The superintendent and I had quite a conversation after you left. I used many of those words. Amongst others. I assured him that if anyone can bring these girls home, you can."

"Sir, I…"

"But both of our necks are on the line for this one, Stone. The superintendent will not be held accountable for any failure. Especially after the last time. There is no leeway on this case. One wrong step and we are both out. Do you understand me?"

Kim appreciated the level of faith that Woody had placed in her ability and she would not let him down. She tried to picture the conversation that had taken place between her boss and the superintendent. The man before her must have presented passionately to win over Baldwin.

"What do you need?" he asked, reaching for his pen.

She took a deep breath. "The complete files from the last case. That'll tell me everything I need to know about how the investigation was conducted."

"Already in progress. Next?"

"I want the FLO assigned last time."

This request he wrote down, and would be tricky but to her it was imperative. The family liaison officer would have been with the families the whole time and would be able to offer an insight into events and advise her on any similarities.

"I'll get on it. Next."

"I intend to set up base at the Timmins' house. I'll run the investigation from there."

"Stone, that's not really—"

"I have to, Sir. I need to be available. The first message came by text. We don't know if that's how they will continue to communicate and I need to be there at all times, ready to action any developments."

He thought for a moment. "I'll need to get that cleared by Superintendent Baldwin but that's my concern, not yours. I expect to be kept properly informed and that's *my* level of appropriate communication, not yours."

"Of course," she agreed and stood, looking towards the door. "I need to call my team."

"They're upstairs, waiting for you."

Kim frowned. "Sir, I only just asked for this case?"

"I called them in as soon as you left. They don't have any idea why so I'll leave it to you to fill them in."

She tipped her head. "How could you have been so sure?"

"Because you were told you couldn't have it—and you don't like that one little bit."

Kim opened her mouth and closed it again. For once she could not disagree.

CHAPTER 5

Kim entered the squad room and closed the door behind her. Immediately she had the full attention of her team. The door very rarely met the frame.

"Afternoon, Guv," they all said together.

She briefly appraised her team. Yep, Woody was right when he said he'd called them all in.

DS Bryant still wore the rugby shirt from afternoon practice together with a dirt smudge beneath his left eye. Although his natural build suited the game of rugby, he was now on the wrong side of forty-five to walk away from the pitch uninjured. As both Kim and his wife had pointed out numerous times.

DS Dawson looked as perfect as ever. Of the opinion that one was judged by one's attire, Dawson ensured his five-eleven height was suitably clothed at all times. Even on a day off, his impeccable clothing showed off the results of gym membership. If Kim had to guess, she'd say he'd played squash earlier, showered and then changed before preparing to take a liquid lunch with his mates. Never mind.

Unlike the others, DC Stacey Wood was dressed for work in navy blue trousers and a simple white shirt, signalling she'd probably been at home engrossed in her computer, fighting warlocks and goblins on the game *World of Warcraft*.

Kim perched on the edge of the spare desk that butted up to Bryant's.

Dawson glanced at the closed door. "Shit, Guv, what did we do?"

"In your case I'm sure I can come up with something but on this rare occasion it's not us."

"Hallelujah," Bryant said.

"Bostin," Stacey added.

"Okay, firstly, what's the alcohol situation?"

Yes, it was Sunday. But now they were at work.

"Dry as a bone," Stacey offered.

"None," Bryant said.

"Almost," Dawson groaned.

And Kim herself hadn't touched a drop since she was sixteen, so they were good to go.

"Right, I know Woody kept you all in the dark but there's a reason." She took a deep breath. "A couple of hours ago two nine-year-old girls were snatched from Old Hill Leisure Centre. Confirmed. The girls are best friends, as are the parents."

She paused to give everyone a chance to digest the information.

Bryant glanced at the closed door. "Press blackout *and* force blackout, Guv?"

Kim nodded her head. "Only four people on site know and they've been sworn to secrecy. Nothing is to be transmitted over the radio. We can't risk this getting out."

"Confirmed how?" Dawson asked.

"Both mothers have received text messages."

"Bloody Nora," Stacey whispered.

"No search, then?" Bryant asked.

As a father to a teenage girl his natural instinct was to get out there and look.

"No. We're dealing with professionals. So far we know that the girls were due for collection at 12:30. The text messages were received at 12:16 and the car of the collecting parent had been tampered with."

"Guv, this is sounding awfully familiar."

"I agree. We all know that whoever was behind the abduction last year was never caught. It could be the same people or a copycat crime."

"What do we hope?" Stacey asked.

Kim wasn't sure. If it *was* the same people they would have learned from the last time. Their skills would be refined. They would have back-up plans, exit strategies. But on the plus side Kim would be able to see how they had performed; study their methodology from the case notes of the previous kidnapping.

"Guv, what went wrong the last time?" Bryant asked.

"I don't know but I'm sure we're gonna find out." Kim took a deep breath. "Listen guys, this is going to get heavy. We'll be working out of the Timmins' house amongst distraught parents for as long as it takes to get these girls home."

"Isn't that 'if' we get the girls back, Guv?" Dawson asked.

Kim turned her gaze on him. "No, Kev, I mean when."

He nodded and looked away.

She would not contemplate defeat before they'd even started. The last team had achieved fifty per cent success—and even that had been by default. The kidnappers had let the girl go. Kim would not have any member of her team entering that household feeling they had already lost.

"All the family members will want something from you. They'll think you know something they don't. They'll want to know everything.

"We have to keep our distance. It's not our job to be their friends or extended family. We're not counsellors or priests. We are there to find their daughters." She looked directly at Dawson. "Both of them."

Dawson nodded his understanding.

"Okay, Stace, I want you to make a list of remote and mobile equipment. Include everything you think we might need and get the list to Woody. He'll make sure we get it."

Stacey nodded and started tapping on her keyboard.

"Kev, I want you over at Lloyd House making a nuisance of yourself until we get those case files. Woody has requested them but we need them as soon as possible."

"Got it, boss."

"Bryant, for God's sake go home, shower and change. Pick up a lock and a drill, then come here to help Stacey with the equipment."

Bryant stood. Stacey and Dawson burst out laughing. Kim followed their gaze with horror.

"Bryant, you have got to be joking."

He stood away from the desk displaying black shorts and legs that belonged in a zoo.

"Woody said to come into the office right away, Guv."

Kim hid her smile and looked away. "Please, Bryant, go now."

He reached the door before she spoke again.

"Oh, and I shouldn't need to remind you that you tell no one about this case. You all know what I mean."

They each acknowledged her warning. Sometimes even their own family members had to be kept in the dark about work.

Kim stepped into The Bowl, a wood and glass structure in the right-hand corner of the room that was supposed to be her private office. It was barely the size of a decent lift and was used only for the occasional bollocking. For the most part Kim spent her time perched at the spare desk, amongst her team.

She turned and glanced as her colleagues galvanised into action. There was no room for uncertainty in her team members.

Any doubts would be all hers.

CHAPTER 6

Kim arrived back at the Timmins' house as darkness was threatening to fall; a development that would not help the state of mind of the parents. The early March days were struggling to leave the February temperatures behind. Every day was offering a long goodnight from mid-afternoon.

Kim knocked and entered. The constable was seated behind the door.

"Anything to note?"

He stood as though addressing a sergeant major. "Husbands have come back. There's been shouting and a lot more crying."

Kim nodded and headed towards the kitchen.

Karen appeared before her in the hallway. Her hands were clasped tightly to her breast.

"Kim, you're..."

"The Officer in Charge of this case," she finished, with a half-smile.

Karen nodded gratefully and led her into the kitchen.

"It's about fucking time, Inspector. Have you found my daughter?"

"Stephen," Karen protested.

"It's okay," Kim said, holding up her hands. There would be many emotions for the families to work through and anger would be high on the list.

She quickly shook her head.

Two totally separate time zones were operating within one room. The last few hours had sprinted by for her but had been a lifetime to the parents.

She expected frustration and rage. There would be accusation and mistrust and Kim was happy to accept it all. To a point.

She faced the man who had spoken. His hair was as black as her own and showed no signs of grey. He carried around twenty pounds of excess weight and his hands were nicely manicured.

Karen sent a withering glance as she introduced him. "Kim, this is Stephen Hanson, Elizabeth's husband, and this is Robert, my husband."

Kim hid her surprise. Robert Timmins was an inch over six foot. She knew Karen to be thirty-four, the same age as herself, but Robert looked considerably older.

Not an unattractive man, he appeared to take care of himself. The grey at his temples suited his face, which was open and honest. His right hand rested on Karen's shoulder protectively.

This was not the kind of man Kim had envisioned Karen making a life with. As a teen she had gone after bad boys. Their criteria had included tattoos, piercings and possession of an ASBO.

There had been one in particular for Karen. Another care kid whose orbit she'd been unable to escape. The two of them had separated and collided numerous times during their teen years. And each time he thumped her she vowed never to go back. After the fourth or fifth time, no one was listening.

"Pleased to meet you both. Now to update you. I've met with my team who will all be arriving over the next few—"

"Where the hell is the search? Where are the teams, the helicopters?" Stephen Hanson cried, moving towards her.

Kim didn't move an inch and he stopped on the safe side of her personal space.

He looked her up and down. "For fuck's sake, this is what we get."

Although Elizabeth had the grace to lower her eyes, Kim sensed the hope within them all that his shouting would somehow precipitate the return of the girls.

"Mr. Hanson, there is a press blackout on this story. Only a few people know that your daughter has been abducted."

His eyes blazed in the face of her calm, measured tone.

"So, nothing is being done?"

"Mr. Hanson, I urge you to calm down. Having the press all over this is not going to get your child back."

The other three watched the exchange between the two of them. Every moment that passed explained the dynamics of this group better.

Stephen Hanson was casting himself as the hero of the hour. Kim understood that his caveman instinct was to protect and take charge.

"How the hell can a search not be beneficial? If the public know, they'll come forward with information."

"Such as?"

"A man bundling two young girls into a vehicle," he said, as though speaking to a child.

"You don't think that would have been reported anyway?" Kim replied, raising one eyebrow.

He hesitated. "That's not the point. People don't think about what they might have seen until you make it public."

"The best we could get from a witness appeal is a sighting of them close to the snatch point. That information is useless to us now because we already know for sure that they've been abducted. Unless they can offer a registration number, offender description and known direction of travel, that information is not worth the consequences."

Stephen Hanson shook his head. "I'm sorry, but I couldn't disagree with you more. I intend to get my daughter back if I have to call every news outlet in the country."

He took out his mobile phone.

"I can't stop you from doing whatever you feel is necessary, but once you make that call you will probably seal the fate of your daughter," Kim said, in a measured tone.

He hesitated for a moment as the two women gasped.

Robert Timmins took a step forward. "Stephen, put down the phone." His voice was calm, quiet and authoritative. It bit through the tension that had filled the room.

Stephen turned to his friend. "Come on, Rob, you can't agree—"

"I think we should listen to what the inspector has to say. Once you make that call there's no going back, but it may be something to consider later."

"By then they might be fucking dead," he exploded. Stephen clearly didn't like being told what to do by anyone. But he hadn't yet pressed a button.

"They might be dead now," Robert said calmly.

Elizabeth and Karen cried out. Robert squeezed his wife's shoulders reassuringly. "I don't think they are but I can't imagine any scenario whereby we gain benefit by having Sky News parked up on the lawn."

Kim could feel the controlled rage emanating from Stephen.

She stepped in. "Listen to me. Your daughters are alive. This is not some random opportunist snatch. This has been planned and there will be contingencies.

"Do you remember last year when two little girls were taken from Dudley?" The two ladies nodded. "So far this is very similar to what happened then. We don't know the full details but only one girl came back. The body of the second girl was never found.

"A press blackout was issued but the news broke on the third day. The publicity may have spooked them into doing something rash. That's not what we want this time. The kidnappers have already made contact. You know they've been taken for a reason and not by some random paedophile."

Kim ignored the horror on their faces. They had to know the truth and unfortunately hers didn't come with tea and sympathy.

"They will be in touch. They want something from one of you or all of you. The most logical assumption is that we're talking money but we can't rule out other things."

Finally, she had the attention of them all. "Do any of you have enemies that you can think of? Disgruntled employees, clients, family members? Everyone should be considered."

"Do you know how many people I piss off each week?" Stephen Hanson asked.

Probably not as many as I do, Kim thought.

"I'm Crown Prosecutor for Organised Crime."

Had this been another situation, she would have said that he didn't piss off as many as he should.

Kim knew that the CPS division for which he worked was a separate arm of the service to the lawyers that presented the cases she worked on, which was why they had never met.

Regardless, the relationship between most police officers and CPS was strained at best. There was nothing worse than working a case for weeks, months, even years, to have prosecution discontinued on evidential grounds.

"How many of your prosecutions would have the resources to put something like this together?" she asked. "This isn't a brick through a window, Mr. Hanson."

"I'll make a list," he said.

His change in attitude came with the promise of proactive momentum. Kim made a mental note to keep Stephen Hanson busy.

"How about you, Mrs. Hanson?"

She shrugged helplessly. "I'm only a paralegal but I'll give it some thought."

"Mr. Timmins?"

His face was furrowed in deep thought. "I own a haulage company. I had to let a few people go around seven months ago but I don't think…"

"I'll need their names. They'll all need to be ruled out."

Silence fell.

"Karen?"

She shook her head. "Nothing at all. I'm a housewife." She shrugged as though that was enough.

"Anything in your past?" Kim asked pointedly.

"Absolutely not," she said, just a little too quickly. Realising the speed and decisiveness of her response, she added, "But I'll certainly think about it."

"And the last thing for now is to get your list of phone calls ready for tomorrow. Your stories for the girls will need to match so that no one becomes suspicious. Understood?"

They all nodded and Kim breathed a sigh of relief. They were all co-operative. For now. It wouldn't last. For the moment they had things to do, things to think about that might aid the return of their children, but as their emotions ran the gamut she and her team would be on the receiving end.

She stepped out of the lounge to take a breather. At that moment the doorbell sounded throughout the house.

The constable opened the door as Kim walked towards it.

She was greeted by a middle-aged woman with ash-blonde hair. Her build was slightly overweight but carried with authority. She wore light jeans and a thick Arran knit jumper beneath a heavy winter coat.

The woman smiled past the constable, directly at Kim.

"Helen Barton. You requested my presence here."

Kim looked at her blankly.

The woman offered her hand. "Family Liaison Officer."

"Oh, thank God," Kim said, taking her hand.

Finally, tea and sympathy had arrived.

CHAPTER 7

"Damn it," Kim said, as Bryant brought the car to a stop outside the darkened leisure centre.

They had left Stacey unloading the computer equipment and Dawson on his way to the house with the old case files.

Her natural urgency had propelled her out of the house to their first and as yet only lead.

She exited the car and turned to take in the surroundings.

A road ran alongside the building, cresting in a hill before heading down the other side. Next to the complex lay a construction site following the demolition of a local council building. To the right was the entrance to a park. A dirt road separated the two areas.

On the other side of the road stood residential properties set back from the pavement and elevated. A clutch of newer houses masked a road that led to a small council estate behind.

"Too many possible directions of travel," Kim said.

She suspected the kidnappers had parked on the dirt road between the building and the park. Close enough to effect a speedy exit but not close enough to the road to raise any suspicion if the girls put up a fight. A conveniently placed birch tree obstructed the view from the homes.

Bryant followed her gaze. "You think that's where it happened?"

"If they did their homework, yes."

Kim travelled the path towards the entrance door and placed her face close to the glass. There was no sign of activity.

"We need the CCTV, Bryant."

"Err... I think it's closed for the night."

"No shit," she said, examining the door frame.

"Yeah, Guv, just so you know, breaking and entering is an offence."

"Hmmm... Bryant, go back to the car and switch on the police radio."

"Oh shit. What are you—?"

"Just go," she ordered.

He huffed and headed back to the car.

Kim crouched down to inspect the bottom half of the door. An alarm contact was fitted to the side edges but no lock. She'd already established the same at the top. The locking mechanism was at the centre.

She kicked at the metal strip that ran the length of the bottom of the door. Nothing. She kicked again, taking care to avoid the glass panel. Still nothing. She threw back her right leg and kicked a third time. The alarm sounded a deafening wail and a strobe illuminated above her head.

She strolled back to the car and got in.

Bryant's head rested on the steering wheel.

"Guv, why couldn't you just—"

His words were interrupted by a radio message from their control room requesting officer attendance at a suspected break-in at the leisure centre.

She shrugged. "Call us in, Bryant. We're pretty close."

Bryant shook his head and confirmed their attendance.

Now all she had to do was wait. The alarm monitoring company had made their first call to the police. Their second would be to a key holder.

"Couldn't you have shown just a little patience?" Bryant asked.

Kim ignored him. It would have taken time to track down the appropriate person on a Sunday evening, further time in persuading them to return to work to assist with CCTV. No, she liked her way better. A key holder was now on the way and it hadn't cost her a single threat. Woody would be pleased.

"Patience? Come on, Bryant. Even you know me better than that."

CHAPTER 8

"That'll be him," Kim said, as a Volkswagen Polo pulled up beside them.

Bryant had already called the premises in as secure but the alarm would need to be re-set.

She got out of the car and came face to face with a man in his mid-twenties with bleached blond hair. She already had her warrant card in her hand.

"Manager?" she asked.

He nodded. "Brad Evans." He tipped his head.

"Attending officers. There's no intruder," she confirmed.

He smiled. "Well…umm…thanks, but why…"

She fell into step beside him as he walked towards the entrance of the facility. "Well, strangely enough we were on our way here when we got the call."

He turned towards her as he reached the door. The alarm had stopped but the intermittent blue light above showed both his good looks and his frown.

"Yeah, that is strange."

Bryant coughed behind her.

Brad unlocked the door and entered the foyer. The lights automatically illuminated the area. The second door was push button access.

Kim looked to the ceiling and spotted the camera.

She followed Brad into the reception area and inhaled the scent of chlorine.

The café area was open and spacious. Plastic chairs and tables littered the room. A row of vending machines sat against the left-hand wall. Beyond was the entrance door to the communal changing rooms.

At the furthest point was a partitioned glass viewing area that looked onto the shallow pool.

While she assessed the area Bryant explained that they'd been on their way to view the CCTV following a serious assault.

"Can't it wait until normal hours?" Brad asked.

"No," Kim said, simply.

Bryant shrugged his agreement.

Brad's face hardened. Kim was not concerned. His Sunday night plans would just have to wait a while.

"If you follow me," he said, walking away from the swimming facilities. They passed a gym room on the right and public toilets to the left. At the end of the corridor was a door marked "Private."

Brad keycoded himself in and sat, logging into the system. She was relieved the place had gone digital. That would make Bryant's job much easier.

"The system covers every inch of the premises," Brad said. "Other than the changing rooms, for obvious reasons, but there is a static on the changing room exit."

He steered the system to the front screen and lifted his arm to check his watch.

The pointed mannerism was not lost on Kim.

"So, what would you like to see?"

"Yeah, we can take it from here," Bryant offered. "We have a description of the possible offender."

Brad showed no sign of vacating the seat. "Ah, that makes sense. If you give me the description I can…"

Kim had no idea what made sense, but Bryant pressed on.

"We may be some time so it's probably best you get to work on re-setting the alarm," her colleague said, tapping the back of the chair.

Brad looked from one to the other before reluctantly getting up. "It'll take a few minutes to check the building." He looked pointedly at Kim. "But I imagine it's all in order."

"Better to be safe," Kim said, stepping out of the way.

Brad pointed to an internal phone and held up his mobile. "Zero will put you straight through to me, just in case you need anything else."

Kim offered him a smile. "Thank you, Brad."

Bryant took the controls while Kim instructed. "Go to the static camera on the changing room. I want to make sure there was no one else around when they came out."

Bryant typed in the date and time.

Nine windows filled the screen; all freeze-framed at the time point of 12:05 p.m.

"Top right and make it full screen until we identify the girls."

Bryant pressed the play button and the images spurred into life in real time. They watched silently. Two minutes later the girls came out of the changing rooms.

Amy was wearing pink jeans and a navy jumper. Charlie wore black leggings and a long T-shirt. Both were carrying their coats and backpacks.

"Go to camera five," Kim said. After a few key strokes Kim could identify the girls from a camera that watched ninety per cent of the common area.

The two of them walked across the space to the vending machines and dropped their belongings at the side. They perused the snack machines, pointing before making their choice. Amy took crisps, Charlie chose a bag of sweets and both selected a hot drink.

They sat cross-legged beside the Coke machine as though having a picnic.

Kim watched the immediate area to see if anyone was paying particular attention to the girls. She had the eerie sensation that she could be watching the last few moments of these girls' lives.

Her gut repelled the idea and, as it was normally the most reliable organ in her body, she had no choice but to believe it. Not even for one moment would she allow herself to think these girls were already dead. She would bring them home alive. Changed, but alive.

"Last few minutes of innocence, eh, Guv?" Bryant said, echoing her thoughts.

They both knew beyond a shadow of a doubt these kids would never view the world the same way again. Whatever the outcome.

At 12:23 they both stood. Charlie took their rubbish to the bin and they donned their jackets. Amy put her left arm through the shoulder strap of the backpack but with her coat on couldn't get her right arm through the other strap.

Charlie got hold of the strap and pulled it around, making a loop for Amy's arm. The dynamics of their friendship were clear even from this small gesture.

They walked towards the foyer and entered. For some reason Charlie looked back into the café area but didn't stop.

"Switch to the external," Kim instructed but she already knew.

"Damn, he's under the camera and it points down the path." Not along the trodden path through the grass.

"Pause, rewind, just a couple of frames."

Bryant did so and she saw the unmistakable lift of Charlie's head to look up into the face of an adult.

Something else caught her eye.

"Bryant, take it back again."

Now she was in no doubt. She picked up the phone and called Reception.

"Brad, I need you back in the CCTV room. Now."

CHAPTER 9

"That is you, isn't it, running through the foyer?" Kim asked.

Brad squinted at the screen and shrugged. "We all wear—"

Jesus, it couldn't be that hard to recall. "Brad, this was lunchtime and you were running."

"Oh, yeah, yeah, it was me. A woman had collapsed in the main area. It's my job to greet the ambulance and get them to the location quickly." He paused, looking at the screen. "But, what's this got to do with an assault up the road?"

Oh dear. God had blessed this guy with brains as well as beauty. Kim exchanged a look with Bryant. Before them was a man who had walked right past their kidnapper.

"Brad, did you get a look at the man who was speaking to these girls?"

His face hardened. "Oh, yeah, and I can tell you he needs bloody speaking to."

"Can you tell us what he looked like?"

He thought for a moment then looked her up and down. "About your height, maybe an inch taller. I'd say thirteen or fourteen stone. His face was kinda ordinary. Nose was a bit long but his voice was soft and quiet with no local accent."

Kim frowned. "How do you know how he sounded?" The kid had only been running past.

"I asked if he could lend a hand. I told him we had a first aid incident but he flatly refused. He wasn't unpleasant about it but I got a bit rude. You'd think—"

"Brad, could you get down to the station at Halesowen and work with a sketch artist. We need to know who this man is."

Brad frowned and offered a nervous laugh. "You're kidding?"

Kim shook her head as a sickness began to rise in her stomach.

"Can't you just track him through your own system?"

"Why would we know?" Bryant asked but Kim didn't need to.

"Because the guy I spoke to was a copper."

CHAPTER 10

"Thanks, Brad," Bryant said. "We'll call you again if we need to."

"Umm... is this going to take much longer?" he asked.

"No. We'll be done in just a minute."

Brad edged out of the room.

"Damn it, Bryant," Kim growled.

He knew exactly how she was feeling. Criminals impersonating police officers were abhorrent to them both.

"Are we done?" Bryant asked, pushing the chair away from the desk.

Kim opened her mouth to say yes but a thought occurred to her.

"Hang on, we spotted the girls leaving the locker room at 12:09 so go back to 12 dead but I want the camera that covers the viewing area."

Bryant tapped in the time and then selected the third camera. The screen sparked into action. Kim scrutinised the seating area that was closest to the small pool.

She studied each individual body, and a minute and a half in she found what she was looking for.

"Pause," she said, and the picture froze. Kim stabbed the top right-hand corner. "Press play and keep your eyes on her. I've got a feeling she's not going to feel very well in a minute."

They both watched the screen, looking predominantly at the back of a blonde head. Every twenty seconds or so the head would turn slightly.

"She's keeping an eye on the exit from the changing rooms," Bryant noted.

Kim nodded. "Keep watching."

The routine continued with a few quick lifts of the arm. Checking her watch. At 12:09 Kim saw the girls in the bottom left-hand corner of the screen leaving the locker room.

The figure turned away completely and covered her face for a couple of seconds by scratching her left temple. She then turned slightly in her chair so that she was side on to the viewing area but with the vending machines in her peripheral vision. Her hand continued to obscure her face from the view of Charlie and Amy.

As the girls stood up to leave, Kim watched the woman take a mobile phone from her handbag. She fiddled with it for a few seconds before putting it back.

As Charlie and Amy headed towards the exit the woman stood and left the viewing area. Three paces out, she folded to the ground.

From this second camera Kim noted that Charlie looked back at the commotion but she was too far away to see anything.

"Distraction," Bryant said.

Kim nodded. "And a good one. Everyone would have been looking in that direction. It's human nature. Spectators wouldn't have noticed the two girls simply leaving the building. Charlie looked back to see what was going on, but she didn't stop. She expected her mum to be waiting outside."

"Clever bastards," Bryant murmured.

Yeah, Kim thought. That's what she'd been afraid of.

"But you know something else, Bryant. As the girls came out of the changing area our woman raised her hand to her face so they wouldn't see her."

"Oh, shit," he said, shaking his head. He knew what this meant.

The woman deliberately causing a distraction was someone the girls knew.

CHAPTER 11

As Bryant spoke into the phone, summoning Brad back to the CCTV room, Kim knew they had a problem.

The case was top secret and she could not divulge the details to anyone.

The manager poked his impatient head around the door. "What now?"

"About that sketch," Kim said, pleasantly. "Any chance you could come with us now to make a start?"

His eyes widened and Kim sensed that his patience was already stretching beyond its normal tolerance.

He shook his head. "I'm sorry, that's impossible. I've got plans, Officer."

"Brad, I need you to come with us to the station. This is not an assault case, it's much more serious, and now you're involved."

He paled as he looked from her to Bryant and back again.

"But...I don't get it. That bloke was a copper."

Kim shook her head. "No, he wasn't. He was impersonating a police officer to get what he wanted and you can identify him. I think you're vulnerable."

Brad was now standing fully in the room. "What's he done? Has he killed someone?"

"Well...not that we—"

"Inspector, I'm over your cryptic answers. You can't tell me what's going on but you want me to cancel my plans?"

Kim was astounded at the drama of it all. Not going out for a few beers was hardly the end of the world. Not much of a sacrifice for the rest of your life.

"Brad, I can only ask that you—"

"Are we done?" he asked, as the colour returned to his face.

Kim reached into her pocket and handed him a card. "Okay, keep your wits about you and if you experience anything out of the ordinary I want you to call me. Got it?"

He put the card in his pocket without even looking at it and held the door open for the two of them to leave.

She paused as she drew level with him. "Brad, will you just listen to—"

"Officer, please let me lock this building and get on with my life."

She hesitated for another minute but Bryant nudged her forward.

"Damn it," she said, pushing the automatic door before it got a chance to open.

Bryant matched her step as she headed back towards the car. "Much as you'd like to, Guv, you can't protect 'em all."

True, but she could bloody well try.

She turned back as Brad locked the door.

"Sorry about this, but there's something else I need to look at," Kim said, offering what she hoped was a regretful smile.

His face darkened. "Is this some kind of joke?"

She stepped closer to him. "Please don't be rude, Brad. I'm not being rude to you. I just need—"

"I'm not being fucking rude. I'm just saying—"

She stepped forward again and frowned. "Please don't swear. That's an offence under the Public Order—"

"Is she for real?" Brad asked Bryant.

"Don't ask him, Brad. Speak to me. Unless you're trying to insult me by speaking to 'the man,' that is?"

"You're a fucking lunatic," Brad said, stepping back against the wall. He had nowhere left to go.

Kim took another step forward and crowded his personal space. Her face was an inch from his. "I've only asked for your help and co-operation..."

"Back off, Officer," he said, pushing her shoulder.

She turned to Bryant with a smile. "Okay, cuff him and read him his rights."

Woody was going to love her for this one, but it was as much as she could do to keep Brad safe. Even for just a little while.

She just hoped it was enough.

CHAPTER 12

"I hope you know what you're doing," Bryant said from the side of his mouth as he closed the back door.

You and me both, she thought, heading to the passenger door. "You drive. I'll call Ambo Control."

The temperature had dropped two degrees and was barely hovering above zero.

Being in a car after riding the Ninja always felt like trudging up a mountain with a twenty-pound backpack. The abundance of metal and trim was cumbersome. She drove her own battered Golf only when taking Barney to the Clent Hills or when the roads were icy.

"Detective Inspector Stone; I wonder if you can help me," she said into the phone.

"I'll try," answered the female voice.

"Paramedics were called to a female who had collapsed at a leisure centre in Old Hill. Around lunchtime today."

There was silence on the other end as the despatcher tapped a few keys.

"Yes, I can confirm that to be the case."

"Can you tell me where she was taken?" Kim asked.

"The patient was taken to Russells Hall hospital."

"Can you tell me her name?"

"No, I'm sorry but I can't give you that information."

"I understand the data protection issues but we really need to identify this woman."

"Inspector, I'm sorry but I really can't give you those details..."

Kim growled. They had to establish for certain whether that woman was involved but there were times when the legislation of data protection was like quicksand.

"Listen," Kim shouted at the phone. "We need to know—"

"I can't give you any information," the despatcher said, coldly, "because I don't have any details to give. The female in question never made it into the hospital. As soon as the ambulance doors opened, she bolted."

CHAPTER 13

Kim headed past the lounge and straight into the war room.

Stacey was connecting cables to two laptops and a network adaptor.

Dawson stacked a fourth plastic box in the corner.

"Is that it?" Kim asked, surveying the case notes from Lloyd House. She had expected more. They were talking double abduction and one murder.

Dawson nodded.

"Okay, Bryant will fill you in. I'm going to talk to the families."

Kim headed through to the informal lounge, which appeared to have become the gather point. They all looked at her expectantly.

"Right, folks, my team is now here and we'll be working out of the dining room. I have to ask that you stay out of that area."

Three of them nodded but Stephen just glared at her.

She glared back. "I will be putting a lock on that door, just to make sure. You may agree to it now but if we're still here in a few days you will not keep that promise.

"You're all acquainted with Helen, who will be with you most of the time, but the rest of us will be in and out. An officer will remain on the front door for the duration. Now, what are your stories?"

"Food poisoning," Robert and Elizabeth said together.

"We'll each call the school in the morning. It won't be much of a stretch. The girls are always together."

"What about family?"

"Same story," Stephen said. "I'll be taking Nicholas to my parents shortly and they'll be told the same thing."

Kim saw Elizabeth swallow deeply. Clearly it was a decision she didn't agree with and Kim could understand it. With one child missing, Elizabeth couldn't bear the thought of the other one being out of her sight, but it appeared that she had given in to her husband. Kim thought it was the wrong call. The child would have provided a small amount of distraction for them all.

It was not her job to disrupt the dynamics of these marriages but each hour that passed told her something.

"On the way back I'll collect clothes and personal belongings from our home. We'll be staying here," Stephen said.

"Good idea," Kim said. Having them all in one place would certainly make her life easier.

"Then we can support each other."

Kim found his qualification of the decision unnecessary and, to her ears, insincere. That might have been how he'd sold it to his wife but Kim guessed it was because he wanted to stay close to the investigation.

And if she were in his position she would be exactly the same.

"I'll go and prepare one of the spare rooms," Karen said, jumping to her feet. She appeared eager to actually do something.

"Wait, there's something else. We have reason to believe that there is a female involved in the abduction of your daughters. A diversion was caused at the snatch point by a woman feigning illness. I think she is known to one of you."

She took the still photo from her pocket and held it up.

Elizabeth gasped immediately and covered her mouth. Her expression showed shock and then disbelief. She stared at the photo and began to shake her head.

Kim looked to Stephen for clarification.

The colour had been sucked from his face. "There must be some mistake. She…"

"Who is it, Mr. Hanson?"

"That's Inga, our daughter's ex-nanny."

CHAPTER 14

Inga Bauer felt the crowd dying down around her. The last eleven hours had been the longest hours of her life.

The pub was emptying of couples and groups, satisfied they had squeezed the last few hours from the weekend before returning to their homes.

Inga could no longer return to hers.

Before being thrown out of the shopping centre earlier, she had watched the daytime crowds head home, weighed down by bags after an afternoon browsing and buying. They had talked and laughed, sipped overpriced coffees. They had lunched or snacked and they had spent. And then they had left.

Inga had been with them the whole time. Trying not to die.

She adjusted her position against the fruit machine. It was a spot that had enabled her to remain unnoticed for the last few hours, but safety was slipping away again. Only a couple of diehards remained at the bar, nursing little more than the foam in their glasses. Two male bartenders were busy washing up and stacking, clearing down for the night.

She couldn't leave yet. She needed more time. Her body was tired and only tension held it upright. She needed to sleep. She needed to relax. She needed to rid herself of the fear. Just for a while.

Instinct had told her to stay amongst crowds. But on Sunday night there were no crowds left to find.

They would already be looking for her. Of that she was sure. She hadn't stuck to the plan. She was supposed to have remained at the hospital until Charlie and Amy were safely hidden. And then they were going to collect her.

The two males at the bar exited the pub and now she was on her own. The shorter bartender stared at her pointedly. She got it.

She stepped out of the bar and braced herself against a cold wind that immediately paralysed her cheeks. Her heart missed a beat as a plastic bag skittered past her feet.

She headed for a multi-storey car park that would at least shield her from the wind and give her a moment to think.

A smattering of cars were lit by a few yellow spot lights recessed into the ceiling. It was a game of extremes, Inga realised, as she wandered around the space. Stay with crowds and light and chatter, or find a dark, silent corner.

She felt sure there must be a nook or cranny somewhere that she could fold herself into and remain out of sight. Just for a few hours, so she could rest and think.

She spied a lift shaft in the far right corner. From a distance it looked dark and eerie, a place any lone female would wish to avoid. Inga headed right for it.

As she neared the area she found that there was no corner. A walkway circled the shaft, leaving it too exposed. Danger could come at any angle if she dared to close her eyes.

She headed out of the car park, her eyes searching every structure, every shadow for a crawlspace.

The exit led on to a road that travelled between two car parks. At the edge of the car park sat an outdoor play area, surrounded by green mesh fencing that rose to chest height.

A sudden memory engulfed her. She began to head towards the colourful shapes. A white security vehicle approached. She ducked down.

She held her breath, pressed against the wall and waited for it to pass.

If the patrol vehicle was carrying out regular checks she guessed she had a good ten minutes until it came around again.

She moved amongst the shadows and crouched beside a bin.

She held still and listened for any sounds. The silence reassured her that it was safe to proceed. She climbed onto the bin and over the fence. Her foot met with a wooden bench on the other side.

The blood pounded in her ears. Now she was trespassing. If she was caught she might be held until the police arrived. The thought caused fresh terror in her chest.

But she'd come too far to turn around now.

She inched across the bark surface and headed to the wooden climbing frame. It was shaped as a castle with ropes, steps and ladders. And at its pinnacle was a turret; small, confined and safe.

She negotiated the apparatus and threw herself into the enclosure. The breath finally left her body as her back hit the wooden wall. The two-centimetre gap between each slat would not afford her much warmth but it would allow her a view.

She would know if anyone was coming.

She closed her eyes for a second. She felt safe. For now.

As the fear eased out of her body exhaustion moved in. She was crammed into a small wooden structure six feet from the ground.

They would never find her here.

That one single thought dragged the last bricks of tension from her stomach. She would worry about her exit strategy later. She had hours to form a plan but for now, just for a little while, she could rest both her body and her mind.

Exhaustion weighted her eyelids like roman blinds. She felt herself falling away from her own consciousness. Her thoughts broke away and floated outside her head.

The memory that had brought her to this safe place played in front of her eyes like a film.

Amy climbing up the structure. Amy swinging on the parallel bars. Amy waving to her from the rope swing. Amy getting her lace caught at the foot of the turret and falling to the ground.

Amy hugging her tightly.

With the dread leaving her momentarily, Inga was hit with the full force of her own involvement.

The tears rolled over her cheeks.

"Oh, Amy, what the hell have I done?"

CHAPTER 15

Will Carter sat back, satisfied.

Day one had gone to plan, except for a couple of tiny details but he had no doubt they would be resolved in the near future. Permanently.

Inga, the stupid bitch, should have waited at the hospital until they returned to pick her up. It was a simple instruction and now she would have to die. Sooner than originally planned. She was supposed to play along and spend an hour or two in the A&E department. Will had assured her that Symes would collect her as soon as possible and she could take care of the kids until the exchange was made.

That part had been pure fiction and Symes was supposed to finish her within minutes of leaving the hospital.

This problem was not something he had bargained on—but that's why he had Symes.

"Fucking send the text now," Symes said from behind.

Will ignored him and performed calibration tests on all three monitors. One camera outside and two inside.

The desk before him resembled the *Starship Enterprise*, although he was no Captain Kirk. Kirk was a weak, sanctimonious wanker whizzing through space saving species and universes. What he should have done was raped, looted and pillaged his way around the galaxy. Would have made for a more interesting forty minutes.

"Just fucking send it. Then we can relax."

"I'll send it on time. As per the plan."

Symes spat into the corner and Will felt himself heave. Really, there was no need.

"Who made you the fucking boss?" Symes grumbled.

A decent education, Will was tempted to respond but kept his mouth closed.

Symes was a goon; a hired hand. A henchman recruited for his natural gifts and abilities. He had no soul. And that would prove useful in the days to come.

Will understood Symes's frustration. He'd been promised a present and it had been taken away. But Will had a little surprise up his sleeve. All in good time.

For Will, it was about the strategy and planning. Almost two years and a failed attempt had led him to this point.

He craved the end result; could almost taste the freedom. He could hold his nerve to achieve maximum level impact. There was a schedule and he was sticking to it.

"Look, go and do the food run and then we'll be ready."

Symes hauled his bulk to a standing position and left the room.

Symes's complaints didn't mean anything. He was born to be a soldier, to be instructed and ordered around.

Will switched screens on the monitor to his left. Symes didn't know that area of the corridor was covered on CCTV. He thought the only camera down there was focussed on the door to the room that held the girls. Buffoon thought the small dome was a smoke alarm. Why the hell would they need a smoke alarm?

But the man needed watching. Yes, they had a deal, and Will had every intention of standing by it, but he didn't need the idiot getting impatient and taking his reward too early.

And so he watched as Symes completed his tasks. He was a man seduced by cruelty for his own entertainment and if he was honest Will didn't care all that much as long as it didn't affect the plan. But at this stage of the operation they could not deviate.

As he heard Symes mount the stairs he switched back to the screen that divided into a quad and displayed the perimeter of the building.

He would venture downstairs later once Symes was asleep. They all had their secrets.

And his secret was not known to anyone.

He stood and moved to the table in the corner. Ten mobile phones lay charging from a row of adaptors.

He patted the one in his pocket set to silent. That was the important one. That was insurance.

Eeny, meeny, miney, mo. His finger landed on the third from the left. That would be for message number two.

"Yer gonna send it now?" Symes asked, plonking himself back on the sofa.

Will was unsure why Symes was so eager. This was not the message that would change the lives of the families forever. This was not the message that would shatter their existence and cause irreparable harm—that would come tomorrow, and he couldn't wait.

"I'll send it at the agreed time," Will said, calmly. He turned to the idiot behind him. "Now, put your face straight. I have a job for you."

CHAPTER 16

"You set, Stace?" Kim asked.

A bed sheet had been placed over the glass dining table and Stacey had positioned herself at the furthest point from the door. The two computer screens were faced away from prying eyes.

All unnecessary furniture had been removed, leaving a six-foot-long dining table and six leather chairs.

"Getting there, Guv. Just searching for the best signal."

"The lock's on the door," Bryant said, standing.

There was a gentle tapping sound. Bryant pulled open the door. Robert offered a tired smile as he awaited permission to enter his own dining room.

Kim didn't offer an invitation. The household had to accept the area had been seconded by West Midlands Police and was out of bounds to them now.

"Umm...I thought this might be of some use," Robert said, pulling into view an easy chair covered in red velour that had graced the corner of the formal lounge. "It might be more comfortable."

Kim appreciated the thought. "Thank you, Mr. Timmins," she said, as Bryant began pulling the chair into the room.

"Call me Robert, please."

Kim nodded. "Robert, may we move the pictures from the walls?" It was a kindness. She hadn't planned to ask.

"Please, take them down. If you pass them to me I'll get them out of your way."

Bryant began to take down the coastal watercolours and paused at a family portrait of the three of them.

"I'll take that, Officer," Robert said, holding out his hands. "Drill what you want into the walls."

Kim nodded her thanks. That had been her next question.

"And Charlie's room...may we...?"

"Of course," he said, nodding, but his pain was obvious. "Fourth door on the right."

She thanked him before he took the pictures and moved away from the area.

She turned. "Well, you heard him, Bryant. Put that drill to good use."

"You know, if I'd wanted to be a chippy I would have been," he moaned.

"And if I'd wanted to be a school teacher..." she said, hauling one of the wipe boards into position on the wall behind the door. Strategically placed so that anyone standing in the doorway would not have a view of the case notes.

"Is that it then, are we unpacked?" Kim asked, looking around the room.

"One more box under the table," Bryant said, drilling a second hole.

Kim reached underneath and pulled it out. She took the lid off and smiled. The box contained a brand new coffee machine, a pack of mugs and four packs of Colombian Gold; her favourite.

"Bryant, marry me and have my children?"

"Can't do, Guv. Missus says I'm happily married."

Stacey stood and peered over the edge of the table. "Oh, yummy, I'll get some water."

Stacey left the room and Bryant turned. "How's the gut?"

She smiled. They'd worked together for almost three years. Consequently he was the closest thing to a friend she had.

"My gut is unnaturally quiet," she said, honestly.

"It'll churn soon enough. What do you make of this bunch so far?"

She shrugged. "There are some interesting dynamics in the group. Stephen's a bit of a blusterer but so far without any real conviction."

"Typical prosecutor," Bryant said.

"Robert seems nice enough but I think there's more to him than meets the eye. Elizabeth appears to bend to Stephen's will like Uri Geller's favourite spoon and Karen is nothing like I remember."

"Children's home?"

Kim nodded. "And foster family seven."

Bryant dropped the drill. "Jeez, how many were there?"

It was a stark reminder that the person closest to her in the world knew so little about her past. Perfect.

As was the timing of her mobile phone ringing right at that second. Until she realised who was on the other end.

"Stone," she answered.

Woody's voice boomed in her ear. "What the hell do you think you're doing?"

"Sorry, Sir?" she answered.

Bryant was quietly shaking his head.

"I have a kid in my station under arrest for assaulting you. Is that correct?"

"Yes, he put his hands on me."

"Do not insult my intelligence. The truth. Now."

Kim groaned inwardly. She had known this conversation was going to come but she'd hoped it would be tomorrow.

"Brad saw one of the kidnappers, Sir. I don't think he's safe on the streets."

"Did you suitably advise him?" Woody asked. Somehow the rage was travelling through the line directly into her ear.

"Of course."

"But you thought you'd engineer his safety at the station, anyway?"

"I don't think he understands the severity of the situation and I couldn't tell him."

"Be that as it may, Stone, I am not prepared to keep that young man here for a moment longer on your trumped-up charges and any subsequent lawsuits will be on your head. As soon as he is finished with the sketch artist I shall have him taken to wherever he wants to go with a profuse apology from West Midlands Police."

Kim closed her eyes for a second. "I know he's—"

"And if there are any further shenanigans of this nature, Baldwin will not need to remove you from this case, as I will be more than happy to do it myself."

The line went dead in her ear.

"Ouch," she said, throwing her phone onto the table.

"You had to know that was coming," Bryant offered.

She shrugged. Of course, but that didn't make it fun.

"Bloody hell, Guv," Dawson said, opening the door. "It's dropped to minus two already."

Kim waited for him to remove his jacket. He had been tasked to Inga's address, which had not been hard to track down after a general idea from Elizabeth Hanson.

Unfortunately that was all she'd been able to learn from them. The employers had known nothing of their employee's friends, boyfriend or family. If Inga had talked, they hadn't been listening.

Stacey had been unable to find any connection between the nanny and the previous families so that ruled her out as a link.

"Well?" she asked.

"Her place looks like a monster truck went through it. Twice. The door was open, and of course I had to see if she was in there. Whoever's looking for her is not a happy bunny. Everything was trashed and I mean everything: furniture, ornaments, pictures, plates."

"A warning then?"

"Oh yeah, she'd better hope we find her before they do."

"Either a warning or a man that can't control himself," Kim said, tapping her chin.

"Or both," Dawson said.

Kim nodded. "Any description of the male from the neighbours?"

Dawson rolled his eyes. "Old guy downstairs with dementia gave me an exceptionally detailed description. Said the guy was around five foot two, black curly hair, glasses and a navy blue shirt."

"And?"

"Then his son stepped out to see what I wanted and guess what? That's right, he was five foot two, black curly hair, blue shirt and..."

"Glasses," Stacey finished.

Kim groaned. "Okay, Kev, make Inga Bauer top priority in the—"

Her words ended abruptly as a loud, shrill scream filled the house.

CHAPTER 17

Symes sat in the shadows and waited. That stupid bitch, Inga, had swindled him out of his promised payday but he would find her and when he did she would be sorry. She would pay with added interest but for now he had been thrown an unexpected bonus.

He knew he intimidated people and he enjoyed every minute of it. His height and muscle mass were the first things that people noticed about him. Next they clocked the shaved head, then the tattoos and a picture was formed. And was probably quite accurate.

But it was more than that and he knew it. The expression in his eyes dared anyone who glanced his way to take him on. It let the world know he was ready for a fight.

Even now a group of men stood not too far away, fags in one hand, pints in another, but not one of them dared look him in the eye.

It hadn't always been that way. By the time he was ready to fight back his real enemy had been dead. Only while he was a child had his father dared to hit, kick and spit on him. Every ounce of the man's frustration at his wife's desertion had found a direct route to his son's flesh. If only his father had known that eventually Symes would come to hate his mother. It was something they could have agreed on.

As a child he had found that his pain was eased only by causing pain. There was a release, a euphoria like nothing else he had ever experienced. The power transported him to another place. It was beyond sexual, it was almost religious in its purity, something to worship.

A movement caught his peripheral vision. He looked the figure up and down.

It was time to say a prayer.

CHAPTER 18

"Another text message, Marm," Helen said, poking her head in the doorway.

Kim had guessed as much from Karen's scream and brushed past the liaison officer.

She found the four of them in the comfy lounge, as she now thought of it. The activity was completely at odds with the ambiance. Unlike the formal lounge across the hallway, this room was bathed in a beige glow with soft, warm furnishings and sofas gathered around a fire and a TV. Clearly it was intended as a space for a family to gather at night to relax. But now she felt the room might explode with tension at any minute.

Stephen paced the area behind the sofa. Robert stood at the window biting down on his hand. Karen and Elizabeth sat close to each other, staring at their phones.

"What the hell is that supposed to mean?" Stephen shouted.

Kim held out her hand towards Karen who relinquished the device readily. Kim immediately saw that the text message was from a different number than the first. She took Elizabeth's phone next and the words were exactly the same.

Your daughter is safe for now. The game will begin tomorrow.

"Tell us, Inspector. What does that mean?" Stephen raged.

Kim shook her head. At this point she had no clue what they were dealing with.

She couldn't help but wonder at the purpose of the text message. It asked for nothing. It told them nothing. It appeared to be a poke.

"Did you pre-empt this?" Stephen asked. "How do we react? What do we say?"

"At the moment we say nothing, Mr. Hanson. The message calls for no response," Kim replied calmly.

He threw his hands in the air. "Is that really how you intend to manage this investigation, Inspector? No response?"

She tried not to offer a reaction to what was clearly a fear-induced rant but it was becoming clear that every bit of his rage was going to be aimed at her.

Kim opened her mouth but Helen stepped forward.

"Try to focus on the first part of the message," she said, looking around the parents. "Your daughters are safe."

The ladies looked to the kindly woman who took a seat at the end of the sofa. Elizabeth tried in vain to stem the tears but Karen allowed them to fall freely.

Helen looked to Kim for permission to continue. Kim offered a slight nod. This was not her skill set.

"Look, consider the logic. Whoever these people are, they want something from you. It's not in their best interest to harm your girls in any way."

All eyes were on Helen. Her warm, comforting voice drew them in like a congregation. This was serious counselling training at work.

Robert took his place beside Karen and gently took her hand. Unconsciously she leaned into him. The tears slowed as they all focussed on Helen.

Kim edged out of the lounge and headed back to the dining room. She closed the door behind her.

"Okay, guys, there's nothing more to be done tonight so I want you all to go home and turn up fresh tomorrow. Six o'clock start. I can't promise there'll be no all-nighters while we work this case, but not tonight."

"You going home, Guv?" Bryant asked.

Kim shook her head. She would make her bed in this room tonight.

"Then, I don't see why we—"

"Because I said so, Bryant." Her voice left no wiggle room.

Slowly Dawson and Stacey collected their belongings and filed out of the room. They had a total of seven hours to get home, sleep and get back again.

Bryant took his time. "What about The Prince?" he asked, with a knowing smirk.

She raised an eyebrow. That was Bryant's pet name for her dog, Barney. So called because she treated the dog like royalty, apparently.

"I called Dawn earlier. She's moved in."

Kim had claimed Barney from the shelter after his owner had been brutally murdered a few months earlier. The dog didn't mix well, didn't like crowds and was unlikely to change. They suited each other perfectly.

But one person Barney had taken to was the receptionist at the grooming salon. He hated the groomer with a passion but he liked the nineteen-year-old girl who lived with her parents and loved the occasional freedom that came with taking care of Barney.

"Hope she passed all the relevant checks," Bryant said. "The only dog-sitter I know who has probably been put through the DBS."

Kim offered no reply but he wasn't far wrong.

"Bye, Bryant," she said, looking pointedly at the door.

He offered her a salute and took his leave.

Kim began to empty the contents of her rucksack. She folded the change of clothes neatly and placed them underneath the easy chair. She stacked her toiletries to the side but left the bike magazine in the bag.

A soft tap sounded at the door. It was Helen.

"I've persuaded them all to get off to bed, Marm. I'm not sure how much sleeping will be going on but they're in the right place if they can drop off for an hour or two."

"Thanks, Helen. Get off home now." Kim checked her watch. "Can you be back by about nine?"

Helen shook her head. "No. I'll be back at the same time as the others."

Kim smiled. "Six."

"I'll see you then," she said, backing away from the door. Suddenly the head popped back into view. "Try to get some rest, Marm."

Kim nodded and took a seat at the dining table.

She heard the front door close. Helen was going to be invaluable to her and the investigation. She would form the bridge between the team and families. She would provide the reassurance without the detail, freeing up Kim to focus on the case.

Kim made a mental note to ensure that Helen got enough time away. Otherwise she would drown under the weight of sadness, fear and expectation.

And, potentially, grief, said a small voice in her head.

She pushed it away and headed out of the room. Lucas nodded her way as she headed up the stairs.

As she passed along the hallway she could hear talking from one direction and soft crying from somewhere else. She headed for the fourth door on the right and entered quietly. She closed the door before feeling for the light switch.

A single bed jutted out from the left wall. A poster of five boys looked down on to a quilt cover and pillowcase from some Disney film. There was a slight indent in the bedding where someone had sat. A pair of monkey printed pyjamas were folded neatly on the pillow, awaiting Charlie's return.

Kim placed her own behind in the place she suspected had been made by Karen and looked around the little girl's space. The furniture was white antique with a distressed finish. A bookcase held ornaments, cuddly toys and a few books. A chest of drawers supported a small television in the corner. And a dressing table held a mirror surrounded by a trail of fairy lights.

Everywhere her eyes landed she saw the personality of Karen's little girl. Bracelets, rings and coloured hair inserts. A couple of hair scrunchies, a set of multi-coloured braces to be added to any pair of jeans.

In front of the wardrobe was a collection of trainers: a pair with lights, a pair with wheels and an assortment of colourful laces to mix and match.

Kim switched on the bedside lamp. Immediately a projection of the solar system began to rotate on the ceiling. She smiled at the effect. As she leaned across to turn it off her arm caught a photograph that faced the bed.

It was a simple silver frame and held a newspaper clipping of both girls with wet hair beaming into the camera. The lengthy piece was headed with a title that reported a double win at a national gala.

Clearly Charlie liked to look at that photo before she fell asleep. Kim placed the frame back on the bedside cabinet as the ringing of her phone came from beside her on the bed. The brittle sound fractured the peace and she wanted to silence it immediately.

It was a mobile phone number that she didn't know.

"Stone," she answered.

"It's Inspector Travis from West Mercia."

"Okay," she said, frowning. There was a time they had addressed each other on a first-name basis when they had worked together for West Midlands. Until the day she made inspector before him. He had transferred to the smaller, neighbouring force and taken his animosity with him.

"I have a body," he stated.

Kim found it amusing that he had never once addressed her by her rank. "And?" she asked. What did he want from her—flags and a party?

"It might be someone you know."

The dread that had been following her for hours finally settled in her stomach.

"Go on," she said, readying herself for what she knew was about to come.

"Male, blond, early twenties—and he has your card in his pocket."

CHAPTER 19

The engine of the Ninja died as it reached the cordon tape.

She removed her helmet and hung it over the handlebars. The Lyttelton Arms was a gastropub situated on the Bromsgrove Road in Hagley; barely a mile from the border where the two forces of West Midlands and West Mercia met.

The pub itself was the last property before the road narrowed to a lane with hedges on both sides. Fifty feet from the pub Travis stood in her way, obviously alerted to her arrival by the Ninja. The cars had been cut off at the traffic island so every sound travelled.

Only the light of his torch illuminated the immediate area between them.

"I need to take this case," Kim said, without preamble. Niceties hadn't existed between the two of them for more than three years.

"No chance," he said, shaking his head. "I remember saying the same to you not too far away from here and you shot me down because you were there first."

Oh yes, she remembered it well. It had been the body of Teresa Wyatt, which had kicked off the whole Crestwood investigation.

"Don't make it personal, Travis. This is not the time to get me back," she said, stepping to the side to walk around him. He blocked her path.

"Why's this kid have your card in his pocket?"

"His name is Brad and he has it because I gave it to him," she said, stepping to the left.

Again he moved in front of her.

"What the hell is your problem?" she growled.

"You're not getting it, Stone."

"For God's sake, I can hardly pick up the crime scene and run away with it, can I? Just let me take a look."

Somehow Woody's instructions to play nice appeared to have wormed into her subconscious. She hadn't called Travis one foul name yet.

"Five minutes, Stone. I'll give you five whole minutes at *my* crime scene."

She shook her head and stepped past him. Oh, the names were hovering at her lips.

"I'm still curious how you know this guy," he said, matching her stride.

"And I wouldn't want to spoil that fun by telling you," she said, as three torchlights shone her way.

She shielded her eyes and carried on walking. Two further torches shone down onto the body of Bradley Evans.

Kim took a few seconds to brace herself for the final expression this young face would ever make. Only hours ago he had been an athletic, animated young man, assisting her and Bryant before a night out with his mates. And now he was dead. The chill that ran through her had nothing to do with the temperature.

She could have done more to prevent his death. She knew she could. She wasn't sure what but somehow she felt there was more.

The keys of the leisure centre glistened in the torchlight. They had either fallen out of his pocket or been removed by Travis.

"No pathologist yet?" she asked.

"On her way," Travis said.

"What time was he found?"

"Twenty past twelve," Travis offered.

It was now after one a.m. and the pathologist wasn't here. As the Officer in Charge she would not have been standing around with a group of redundant police officers at this stage. She would have had the phone attached to her ear threatening to move the body herself if they didn't get here soon. For this short limbo period of time, clues could be getting lost, evidence destroyed, witnesses travelling further away. The investigation was stalled until the techies had arrived.

But, she had to remember this was not her crime scene.

She held out her hand to the closest officer. "May I?"

He passed his torch and she lowered it to the ground.

The single track lane lowered to a ditch on either side where the edge of the road surface met the soil beneath the hedgerow.

Brad's body was turned into the foliage and lay on its side. The torch travelled the length of his black-clad body, almost lost in the darkness, until it reached his shoulders.

"Jesus Christ," Kim whispered.

His head no longer held its shape. Gone was the tidy circumference of a normal skull. It appeared to have been replaced by a deflating football. As she shone the torch around she saw the trail of blood where Brad had been literally kicked around the road by his head.

Beneath where his skull now rested was a pool of blood and brain matter that had seeped from one of the many wounds inflicted. Had he not been wearing the same clothes Kim would not have recognised him. He didn't look like Brad any more. He didn't look like anyone any more.

"Someone didn't like this kid one little bit," Travis said, beside her.

She couldn't be bothered to respond. The person who had done this hadn't even known him. He had simply been in the wrong place at the wrong time and had dared to ask someone for help.

She handed the torch back to the officer on her right. She'd seen enough.

She took two steps away from the body and turned back up the road.

"Bloody hell, Stone, by my watch you've still got a minute and a half left," Travis sneered at her retreating back.

His snide comments were not worth her energy.

Travis would have to chase his own tail on this one. He wasn't going to find anything but as she walked away she made a silent promise that she would make Brad's killer pay for what he'd done.

As she neared the Ninja she groaned out loud as a familiar car extinguished its headlights.

She reached the cordon at the exact same second as Tracy Frost.

"What the hell do you want?" Kim asked by way of an opening greeting. For Tracy it was the best she had. Surely Woody's instructions of "play nice" didn't stretch this far. Even Woody knew she had her limits.

Truthfully, she was not surprised to see the reporter on the scene so quickly. She was sure the woman had a police scanner implanted in her ear.

"Just doing my job, Inspector," she said, removing a leather glove.

Kim looked behind her. "Yeah, and leaving a trail of slime as you go."

Tracy took out a Dictaphone and switched it on. "More importantly, Inspector, what are you doing here? This is West Mercia territory."

Kim approached the officer who was pretending not to overhear their exchange.

"Do not let this woman sneak past the barrier. In fact, shoot her if you have to." She turned to Tracy and looked at the machine. "Hope you got that."

She aimed to walk past the woman who fell into step behind her. Jesus, was there anything that would penetrate the rhinoceros skin?

"Give me something, Inspector," she said, smiling. Remarkable really, seeing that just this morning Kim had pinned her to the wall and threatened her.

"Don't tempt me, Tracy," Kim said, pulling the helmet over her head. Unfortunately it didn't block out the voice beside her.

"I wanted to talk to you about the other thing."

Kim turned. "By that I assume you mean the death of a young man named Dewain Wright and your contribution towards it?"

"Yeah, that," Tracy said, leaning against her car.

"I have nothing left to say."

Tracy smiled coyly. "You're going to feel very stupid when you realise you were wrong."

"I'm not wrong about you, Tracy. I know exactly what you are and how you work."

Tracy shrugged. "Have it your own way, but I warned you."

"Yeah, well, now I'm warning you. Get out of my way or I'll..."

Tracy stepped aside for her to pass. "Okay, but don't think you've seen the last of me."

Oh, if she had just one wish.

Kim threw her leg over the seat and waited for Tracy to approach the officer at the cordon. On this one she was the problem of West Mercia.

She looked back at the activity in the dark, narrow lane. What now held her attention was the thought that if the person who had done this to Brad was anywhere near Charlie and Amy, then God help them all.

CHAPTER 20

Kim tapped lightly on the door to attract the attention of the officer sitting just the other side.

It opened and she suddenly realised he had not been relieved from his post in over twelve hours.

"Go take a rest on the sofa, Lucas," she said, removing her helmet.

He shook his head but his eyes were squinty and red.

"Go," she insisted. "Your relief will be here in the morning."

"Don't take me off the case, Marm," he pleaded.

"I won't, but you can't work twenty-four hours."

He nodded and tiptoed across the hallway into the informal lounge.

Kim tiptoed too. All shoes sounded loud on the expensive tiled floor.

She reached for the key in her pocket as she passed by the door to the kitchen. A shadow stood out in the darkness and Kim's heart missed a beat.

"Jesus, Karen, I thought you were in bed."

"Where've you been? I tried the door," Karen said, taking a sip from a glass of water.

Kim switched on the light. "I sometimes take the bike for a burn late at night. It clears my head."

That was not a lie. She often did that. Just not tonight. But Kim was pleased that the key to the war room was safely in her pocket.

"Are you working on another case, because my daughter is the most—"

"Karen, I'm not working on any other case. This will be my only case until I bring Charlie and Amy home."

"Promise?"

Such a childlike request from a woman trying desperately to keep it together.

"Promise," Kim offered, then tipped her head. "What are you doing down here alone?"

"Got fed up with pretending to try and sleep. Robert is tossing and turning and I can hear Elizabeth crying down the hall. I came down for a glass of water and just...stayed."

She touched the screen on her mobile phone.

Kim wondered, to the nearest hundred, how many times she'd done that.

"I just keep staring at it, willing it to go off and dreading the fact that it might."

Kim took a seat on the opposite side of the breakfast bar. The rest of the house was silent around them.

"I keep thinking that if I concentrate hard enough I can turn back time and stop them from going to the leisure centre."

Kim suspected it would have made no difference. The snatch had been planned, the families chosen and it would have happened at some point.

"One minute I'm filled with rage that someone has my daughter and the next I want to offer them my life in exchange for my baby. In my mind I've pledged to every charity and vowed to be a better person. There's nothing I wouldn't give to get Charlie back. She's my world."

Karen reached behind her. She placed a framed photograph of two girls beside the phone.

"Do you want to take this next door, just so you know?"

Kim shook her head. She needed no reminders but she took a moment to assess them in detail. Charlie's skin was more tanned than Amy's. She was slightly taller than her friend and sported a mass of blonde, unruly curls. Her mouth was a moustache of ice cream. Her eyes were piercing blue.

Amy's hair was a dark helmet with an untidy fringe. They both looked into the camera, their necks stretched, hands gathered at their chests, their faces scrunched.

Karen touched the outline of the fair-haired child. "They were pretending to be meerkats. We were at the safari park. We couldn't get them away from the little creatures. Not even for the fair rides. They were trying to name every one of them but they wouldn't keep still."

"What's Charlie like?" Kim asked, staring at the mass of curls.

Karen smiled. "I think spirited would be a good way to describe her. See that hair, she's been singled out because of it since nursery school. She's been called 'mop head' and other less pleasant names but she refuses to get it cut or even trimmed. She loves her hair and that's all that matters.

"Don't get me wrong, she's not spoiled. Robert is indulgent but he's a stickler for manners. He allows her to express herself but won't tolerate mean or spiteful behaviour. He loves her more than anything in the world. He's the first one to roll on the floor or chase her around the garden making animal noises."

Kim was content to sit and listen. Sleep was not even a distant promise with the picture of Brad in her mind.

"Do you have children?" Karen asked.

Kim shook her head.

Karen looked sad and Kim chose not to correct her. For her it was a conscious choice. Her mother's genes would end with her.

"You're missing out, Kim. You don't know love until you're a mother. Every other type of love fades beside it."

Yeah, still not worth it to continue this particular bloodline, Kim thought. She said nothing. She could cite a hundred cases of child cruelty and neglect that didn't quite conform to Karen's spring meadow view. Hell, she could even quote her own, but she didn't.

"You didn't like me much, back then, did you?"

Kim was startled at the sudden change of subject matter. It was a dire understatement but Kim simply shook her head.

"Why?"

"Now isn't the time—"

"Please, Kim, talk to me about something else. I need a break from my own thoughts. The pictures being conjured in my mind are going to drive me insane. Tell me how you remember that time."

With more clarity than you, Kim thought. It was pointless going down that road. It was in the past. Unalterable.

Karen continued. "I know we weren't close but there was still a bond between us all. There was a sisterhood. We all looked out for each other."

"That's really how you remember it?"

Karen's open and honest expression was her answer.

Kim had seen this before. Some people rewrote their own past. They reinvented themselves completely to add distance to the facts. Kim chose to pack it in boxes and leave it there.

"Karen, there was no sisterhood and we certainly didn't look out for each other."

"I know I was a bit aggressive at times but that was just—"

"You were a selfish individual who wanted what everyone else had," Kim said honestly.

Quite frankly she'd have been happy to leave Karen's memories where they were, in a work of her own fiction, but she'd brought it up and Kim was not an enabler.

Those days had been hard for them all. Some kids had chosen to band together; to belong to something, forming a substitute family. Kim had not. She had formed no lasting friendships or enduring bonds with anyone. But she had hated bullies with a passion.

Intermittently from the age of six her path had crossed with Karen's and the interludes had rarely been pleasant.

But it wasn't until that last foster home that they'd spent any real time together.

"Do you remember a slight Indian girl named Shafilea?" Kim asked.

Karen searched her memory. "Oh, God, yes, she was a funny little thing, wasn't she? If I remember correctly she had a big head."

Yes, she'd had a big head and a very small body.

She'd been removed from the care of her parents who had starved her for months because she'd worn a pair of ripped jeans. Kim had overheard the foster parents moan about the strict diet and nutrition menu they had to follow to build up the muscle mass of the girl gently.

Kim had tried to speak to Shafilea a couple of times but even the three trips per week to a therapist would not induce the girl to open her mouth.

"Do you remember those drinks she had after tea?"

Karen smiled. "Yeah, we all wondered why she got a milkshake and we didn't."

Kim could barely contain her amazement at Karen's twisted recollection. Kim was unsure where she was on the day that house unfolded into a sparkly fairy castle awash with butterflies and elves.

In truth the foster home had been two council houses knocked into one, holding more bunk beds than Ikea.

"They were protein shakes formulated to strengthen her undernourished body."

"Oh, I didn't know—"

"I caught your best mate flushing the girl's head down the toilet until she handed it over."

Karen looked doubtful and began to shake her head.

"The girl was ten years old."

Karen looked horrified. Just a year older than her own daughter was now.

"No, you must be mistaken," Karen said. Although her words lacked the conviction of the righteous.

"Well, she wasn't plaiting her hair with pink, glittery ribbon," Kim snapped.

Karen's hand covered her mouth. "Oh my God. It was you, wasn't it?"

Kim didn't respond.

"You were the one who beat up Elaine. She never said anything and neither did you but I remember it. And now I come to think of it, she really did hate you."

Finally, Kim thought, some clarity.

Her actions that day were not something she was proud of but sometimes you just had to speak the same language as a bully.

Silence settled between them as they both filed away their own recollections of the past.

"You know, Kim, you might be right about back then but right now the only thing I care about is seeing Charlie again."

Kim nodded her understanding as Karen covered her mouth to stifle a yawn.

Kim checked her watch. "It's almost three. Go and try to get a couple of hours, okay?"

Karen nodded and touched her phone once more.

Kim leaned over and placed her own hand on Karen's. The frightened eyes implored her.

Their gaze held for a few seconds.

"I will bring your little girl home."

Karen nodded and squeezed Kim's hand in response. She yawned once more and headed out of the kitchen.

Whatever the circumstances, the body demanded rest and—although it could be delayed by stress, energy, fear, worry—eventually fatigue came knocking.

Kim was still waiting.

It was time to head back into the war room.

She reached out and took the photo.

CHAPTER 21

Kim emptied the old filter into the bin. The sodden coffee sent it to the bottom with a thud.

She placed a crisp, white triangle into the machine and added four generous measures of coffee and then another for good luck.

She sat at the table and waited, her eyes drawn to the photo on the wall.

She was entranced by the girls' purity. Both beamed at the camera, a snapshot of joy caught forever. Two young souls secure in the world built around them: their families, their friends, their innocence.

Kim wondered if there had ever been a moment in her own earlier life when such a moment could have been caught.

There may have been a time between the ages of ten to thirteen when the camera might have framed a smile. With Erica on one side and Keith on the other, foster family four had made her feel safe. And yet, even then her eyes would have reflected the sorrow inside. The kindness of the couple could not have erased her past.

She could not think of Keith and Erica without travelling to Mikey. The box in her mind marked "loss" held the memories of them all.

She closed her eyes for a second. How different would life have been if they'd had a mother like Erica?

Kim quickly shook the thoughts away. Delving into the contents of her mind was like a game of mine jumping. Stay for too long and she'd be blown to smithereens.

She hated to admit that Karen's words had unnerved her. The description of maternal love couldn't have been further from her own experience. That all-encompassing devotion of which she spoke was lost to Kim. She had no frame of reference and so couldn't comprehend the thoughts. There had been no magical bond with her mother. Kim had been too busy trying to keep herself and Mikey alive.

The chat with Karen had drawn her back to the past and now it was with her. Here. In the room.

Kim pushed the chair back and opened the door. She gingerly stepped along the hallway.

"You okay there, Marm?" said a figure from the corner.

"I thought you were sleeping," Kim said to Lucas, who had resumed his position.

"Had a couple of hours. Fine now until relief arrives," the young officer replied.

She nodded and pulled open the heavy oak door. The freezing temperature reached in and grabbed her bare skin. She happily stepped out to greet it.

She thrust her hands into her pockets and faced the cold wind head on.

It swirled around her head, numbing her ears, before pushing against a tree, which passed the movement along so that the entire row of conifers leaned to the right.

Kim thrust her hands down deeper as she walked to the tree line. The wind paused abruptly. The only sound was her feet landing on twigs made brittle by the ice and dislodged by the wind.

Kim turned as a sudden gust lifted the lid of the wheelie bin and threw it back down before retreating again.

She resumed her walk but a rustle reached her ears. No plants or trees moved.

Her body reacted instantly, senses switched to high alert. She froze every muscle in her body to listen for the sound again.

Silence.

No light reached her from the street lamps at the end of the drive. The only light from the front of the house was in the hallway, obscured by the heavy oak door that Lucas had pushed closed.

A scent wafted past her nostril. A hint of petunia but no flowers were in bloom.

She turned her head slightly in the direction of the rustle. A gust blew along the tree line, revealing a mass on the other side of the dense hedge.

The smell grew stronger as the shape moved slightly to the left. The two of them were now level but separated by the tree line.

The movement of her heart sounded loudly in her ears. If she retreated to the house she would never know who had been out here in the shadows, skulking and watching.

She was halfway down the perimeter line. Even if she sprinted up or down and round to the other side she would lose valuable time.

Kim stood still for one more second before thrusting her arm forcefully through the hedge.

Her hand met and curled into thick, coarse cloth. The wind lulled so that she heard a sharp intake of breath. And then a laugh.

"Who the hell . . . ?" Kim said, pulling the jacket through the trees.

Kim loosed the figure who was trying to brush tree cobwebs from her face.

"Up to your old tricks again, Stone. Keeping secrets?"

Kim's heart electrified in her chest.

Tracy Frost knocked Kim's hand away from her jacket but Kim stood firm. This was not going to end well.

"What the hell are you doing here?" Kim spat, but she already knew and it wasn't good.

"I could ask you the same question," Tracy said, tipping her head.

"Except I'm not going to answer and you know it."

Kim's mind was working furiously. She would not give this woman an inch.

"I know there's something big going on..."

"Yeah, feel free to file that in the *Dudley Star* tomorrow," Kim said, holding her ground. "And don't you have anything better to do than follow me around?"

"You would make a great story, though."

"You followed me from the crime scene, didn't you?"

Tracy shrugged but looked mighty pleased with herself.

"What the hell do you want?" Kim asked. She was quickly losing patience. Conversing with anyone in freezing temperatures at four in the morning was bad enough but with this lowlife it was absolutely unbearable.

"I reckon it's an abduction," Tracy stated with a smile.

Kim felt the disgust circulate around her body. Only this poor excuse for a woman could say that sentence with a smile.

"Good for you," Kim said, turning away.

Her heart was beating wildly. Kim knew she had a problem.

"Press blackout, Force blackout. Tells me you're scared of fucking it up again."

"Let's not go there, Tracy."

"Ha, you still think it was me, don't you?"

Kim gritted her teeth. "I know it was you. You broke the story of Dewain Wright and cost him his life."

Tracy shook her head. "It wasn't me," she said in a voice that said she was sick of saying the same thing.

Kim was just as sick of hearing it and she still didn't believe her.

"No, you keeping the truth hidden did that and you know it."

Kim turned away. "Tracy, get the f—"

"I'm going to find out what's going on, Stone. And when I do—"

"You'll keep it to your damn self, you heartless bitch, because if you don't you will live to regret it."

Tracy stepped forward into the challenge. "And if I don't?"

"Then I will leak a story of my own. I'm sure the public would love to know that you like a drink. I mean, *really* like a drink, and that one night you were so pissed you beat a man up for taking pictures of you, and only one of my officers being there stopped you getting arrested. Dawson should have booked you for drunk and disorderly, a few Section Five offences and a sexual assault."

Tracy stepped back.

"You really thought I wouldn't find out? Dawson may be a pain but he's also very loyal. I know that your hand found its way down his trousers during the scuffle. Be a great headline for a crime reporter, wouldn't it? Your editor would love to run it. Right after signing your letter of dismissal."

Tracy knew her well enough to know there was no bluff. Only one of them knew how much the threat needed to work. Although the press blackout was in operation, Tracy had a big mouth and Kim could do without her even voicing her suspicions.

"A few days. I'll wait a few days," Tracy said, backing away completely. "And then I'm digging."

Kim felt the relief flood through her body. The last thing she needed was Tracy sniffing around this case right now.

Tracy was ten feet away when she turned. "I know what you're thinking, Stone, and I'm not going to say it again. But instead of just instantly blaming me for what went wrong, check the timeline and see what you find."

Kim responded by turning away and entering the house. She didn't need to check a thing. Tracy Frost was responsible for the death of Dewain Wright and that's all there was to it. Tracy's crack about Kim's own culpability was no more than an effort to deflect blame from herself.

Damn it, she would check the records and prove herself right once and for all.

CHAPTER 22

Charlie Timmins sat with her back against the wall. It was one of the few areas she'd found that wasn't covered in cool, wet slime that smelled really bad.

The tops of her legs were cramping but she tried her hardest not to move. It was like playing the freeze game with Daddy, except when they played Mummy would stop the music and she and Daddy had to stay still for as long as they could.

Charlie loved the game but found that when she had to concentrate on staying still every part of her wanted to move. Suddenly she would be covered in tiny invisible itches but she would try to focus on something around her to distract her mind.

And that's what she was trying to do now as her hands absently stroked the hair of the head that had finally fallen asleep in her lap.

Charlie had no idea if it was night or day or how long they'd been in the smelly darkness.

The policeman said he'd been sent by Mummy because her car had broken down. Daddy had told her to never talk to strangers but he was a policeman.

The thought of her daddy made her throat ache so bad. She fought back the tears out of habit. Amy got more frightened if she got upset. Then Amy's face would freeze and she'd breathe funny. Twice now, Charlie had managed to calm her back down by playing a game.

She swallowed back the tears. They hadn't helped her yet. Mummy and Daddy hadn't come. At first she'd been angry but gradually she'd come to understand they didn't know where she was.

Charlie knew they would come if they could.

A shudder ran through the whole of her body but it wasn't the cold. It was a different kind of feeling to when Daddy had taken her ice skating. That day, her teeth had chattered and her flesh had been cool. But a minute away from the ice, and her trembling had stopped.

She swallowed the fear down deep into her stomach and tried to tell herself she wasn't afraid. Trying to think about everything that had happened kept the shaking away.

The room held one double mattress and a bucket. Charlie had realised just a few seconds before Amy what it was for. A single bulb hung from the ceiling, throwing a sickly yellow glow around the room.

She tried to focus on what she knew. There were two men. They didn't come into the room but she knew there were two because their footsteps were different. She and Amy had been fed twice and one placed the meals just inside the door and the other skidded them across the floor.

Both meals had been the same. A sandwich in a plastic package, a bag of crisps and a carton of juice.

Their last meal had been brought by the skimmer. Charlie had shushed Amy to listen as the footsteps on the stairs had been followed immediately by the opening of their door. The door had closed and the footsteps had moved away. Another door opened and closed not far away. Then the footsteps had passed by their door once more before going back upstairs.

It was something she'd think about more when she wasn't so tired. Maybe she could just rest her head back and sleep for a little bit. The sound of Amy's deep breathing was willing her into relaxation. Maybe for just a minute, while Amy was sleeping, if she could ignore the mattress spring digging in her thigh.

Her head fell back against the knobbly, cold wall. Even the coarse brick digging into her head couldn't stop the weight of her eyelids from drooping. She felt the heavy blackness descend. She liked it. She wanted to follow it. It looked safe and maybe when she woke up Mummy and—

"How are you doing in there, little girlies," said a voice from the other side of the door.

Charlie bolted upright. The fatigue had pulled her towards sleep and she'd missed the warning noises she was trying to learn.

"Charl...what's...?" Amy stirred and lifted her head, woken by Charlie's sudden movement.

"Shhh..." Charlie hushed.

"I've been busy tonight, little girlies. Do you know Brad from the leisure centre?"

Amy had grabbed her hand and held it tightly. The sound of the voice was almost nice. It was soft but not warm. Pleasant but not friendly.

"Who's Brad?" Amy whispered.

"He sometimes took our money at the front desk," Charlie whispered. And he had once put a plaster on Amy's toe.

"Answer me, girlies," he shouted.

"Y-yes," Charlie shouted back as Amy scooted into her.

"I met him today and we played a little game. I like to play games."

Amy sucked in a big breath and looked towards her. Charlie felt her eyes widening as she continued to stare at the door.

"The game was to see how many times I could kick his head before it exploded. It was so funny when his nose splattered beneath my boot. I kicked him again and his eyeball popped clean out of his socket."

"Charl…" Amy whispered. "Make him…"

"Put your hands over your ears," Charlie said. And she would do the same.

"I can't," she said, unwilling to let Charlie's hand go.

"Come here," Charlie said, lifting their joined hands between both their heads like a pair of shared earphones. "Now do this," she said, raising her free hand to cover her other ear.

"…cried like a baby and begged…to stop…kicked him again. A good…rugby kick and I…head might break away from…neck."

Although the voice was muffled, Charlie could still hear most of the words and it was enough to paint a terrifying picture in her head.

She squeezed her eyes shut, trying to block out the words and the images.

"…snapped and blood poured out of…ears…teeth landed…floor."

Amy gave a little whimper and Charlie pulled her closer.

"…brain oozed…over…"

"Charl…" Amy breathed.

Charlie was powerless to make it stop. She closed her eyes even tighter, scrunching up her whole face to block him out.

"…enjoyed it, girlies. I loved…second of it.…payment you see. Not interested…money…causing pain. I hurt…bad, my little pretties…"

Charlie was still hearing only parts and it was enough to make her tummy feel bad. But when the final sentence came she heard every word.

"And I can't wait to play a game with you."

CHAPTER 23

Kim was already sitting up straight at the dining table when the first member of her team arrived. This morning briefing would be a speedy one and she wasn't in the best of moods. She didn't like late-night visitors and she especially detested liars. Tracy was both of those things.

"Morning, Guv," Bryant said, removing his overcoat. The casual dress code had been discarded. It was Monday, their first full day of investigation, and he was a detective. That meant charcoal suit, white shirt and tie. The first two were not negotiable but on occasion the third offered a smidge of flexibility. For Bryant, plain clothes directive was not dress-down Friday. Although only forty-seven, there was a lot of old school inside him.

"Coffee's done," she offered.

He took a mug and poured a cup. "Helen's an early bird, eh?"

Kim nodded. The FLO had knocked on the front door at five forty-five sharp.

"Is that the same kid on the door since yesterday?"

"Yeah," she said. "There's a second officer coming to take the day shift and then Lucas will be back tonight."

"You talked to Woody already?"

"Sent him a text."

Bryant held his coffee with both hands and looked at the photo on the wall. "Pretty little girls," he observed. "And she is rocking that hair."

Kim smiled as Dawson and Stacey walked in together.

She noted immediately that Dawson had taken full advantage of their distance from the office and was wearing indigo G-Star jeans with a university sweatshirt.

"In a rush, Kev?" she asked, staring pointedly at his lower half. Of her team, he was always the one to push her just that little bit.

"No, Guv, I just…"

She stared at him, hard.

He held her gaze for five seconds before looking away.

"I don't expect to have to tell you again. Now, get the board."

Stacey sat at the head of the table and switched on her equipment.

"Okay, across the top of the board write 'Charlie and Amy.' On the left I want the date and time of the snatch. Next column I want the two text messages word for word. On the second board I want lines of enquiry."

Kim slowed. Dawson was doing his best to keep up with her but was still writing the content of the second text message.

"First line of enquiry is CCTV. Against that, note Inga. Second is phone numbers that sent the texts. Third is case files from last time and fourth is the list of possible enemies from family members. As a prosecutor Stephen's will be long and possibly most relevant. Next we look at any names from Elizabeth and then the list from Robert."

Kim waited for Dawson to catch up.

"Last heading is just the initials 'FM.' We need to tread carefully on this one. Investigating family members is going to cause a divide between us and them so I'd prefer they didn't know." She turned to Stacey. "I want you to dig around their friends, acquaintances, extended family and finances."

"But if they're not to know, how—"

Kim cut Dawson off. "That's where Helen comes in. She'll get some names and details without arousing suspicion."

"But, Guv?"

"Yes, Kev?" she said, giving him her full attention.

"What if this is the same MO as the last time? What if it's the same people as before? Doesn't that make all this a waste of time?"

"You know, Kev, I wish I'd thought of that. I know, scrub the board clean and when I next speak to the kidnappers I'll ask if it was them. Sit back, everybody, we're just gonna wait for them to call."

Kim knew she was being a little harsh on him but some days Dawson's manner just got under her skin.

"Kev, even if it is the same kidnappers, these two families were chosen for a reason so there has to be a link."

He nodded his understanding.

"So, I want you out there tracking Inga. Speak to neighbours, friends, anybody that might offer a clue to her whereabouts. We know she was involved and that's how they got the details of the routine. We also know she got scared and decided to bail. She is the priority."

"Got it," Dawson said.

"Okay. Stace, what can we get from the mobile phone numbers?"

Stacey pulled a face. "Not a bloody lot."

Exactly what Kim had been afraid of. She waited for Stacey to explain.

"We can't tell from the text messages which network each phone is connected to. I reckon he'll have a hoard of pay as you go phones with free credit that ain't registered. And if he's as clever as we hope he ain't they'll all be on different networks anyway, making it almost impossible for us to approach the providers."

"Can't we just track the mobile phone numbers?" Dawson asked.

For a detective he watched way too much television.

Stacey shook her head. "Mobile positioning is a technology used by telecom companies to approximate the location of a mobile phone."

She placed her own coffee mug and Bryant's about ten inches apart and placed her pencil between them.

"It's based on measuring power levels and antenna patterns, 'cos a powered mobile phone always communicates wirelessly with one of the closest base stations. Advanced systems determine the sector where the mobile phone resides and roughly estimates the distance to the base station, sometimes down to fifty metres in urban areas."

"Well, surely that's a starting point?" Dawson asked.

Stacey moved the mugs to the edges of the dining table and left the pencil where it was. "In rural areas there might be miles between base stations, so a hit on a tower can be pretty useless in terms of location."

"But we have the telephone numbers," Dawson said.

Stacey rolled her eyes and turned to Kim. "Guv?"

"Because the phones will be switched off, Kev. No tracking technology will work if the phone isn't at least powered."

"Do we know for sure...?"

"Checked them both last night," Kim said. "They're off, maybe even broken up and thrown away by now."

Bryant took his mobile phone tower and drank from it.

Dawson was unconvinced. There were days when his tenacity proved invaluable, but sometimes it was wrongly directed.

"But I read an article about accessing a mobile phone's internal microphone to eavesdrop on the conversation."

"Yeah, good luck with getting anyone to sign a warrant on that," Stacey said. "But it probably wouldn't do any good. I'm betting the batteries ain't even in the phones."

"But can't we do anything?"

Stacey sighed. "Oh Kev, we can get permission to position phones in emergency situations but it's pretty clear he's gonna use a different phone for every communication and the phone would still need to be switched on. All I can do is fire off emails to the four main networks with the numbers and see if they'll carry out a search—but we're talking days, if not weeks, and an invoice that will run into thousands from each of 'em."

Stacey looked to Kim for confirmation.

Kim didn't hesitate. "Do it anyway, you never know. We need every chance we can get on this one."

The room fell silent, enabling Kim to hear activity from the kitchen next door.

She pushed back her chair.

"Okay, any downtime is to be spent reading through the old case files. We may get lucky with something that was overlooked."

She hadn't yet assigned herself and Bryant a task.

Kim had a feeling they were going to be taking a field trip.

CHAPTER 24

Inga stumbled over a raised slab as she accessed the public walkway.

She had managed to exit the play area without being detected. The night in the wooden castle had been cold and uncomfortable but for a few hours she had felt safe. The conditions had prevented her from falling into a full, dense sleep but her body had stolen the occasional catnap, interrupted only by the intermittent glare of the security vehicle headlights during its passing patrol.

It was during the ambulance ride that she had realised how ruthlessly she had been used. Listening to the voices of strangers showing real concern about her wellbeing as she lay still, deceiving them. Tears had pricked at her closed lids and she had never felt so lonely in her life. Except maybe once.

She marvelled again at the skill with which she'd been seduced into doing something totally against her own beliefs. The manipulation of her own insecurities and fantasies had been easy. She had been no challenge.

Every one of Inga's weaknesses had been used against her. She had been given what she craved but she had given them so much more. She had given them Amy.

The movement of walking was injecting the sensation back into her toes. They tingled painfully as the warmth spread throughout her feet.

Her mind was clearer now that she'd rested for a few hours.

Her first priority was to change her clothes. She was still wearing the same outfit from the incident, making her instantly identifiable to anyone who might be looking for her.

Four miles stood between her and the small flat. She could take the back streets and alleyways and just go and get a change of clothes.

As the idea formed into a plan her pace quickened. If she could just get into her flat for long enough to change and grab her passport she could get to the airport, withdraw some money and get on a flight.

Yes, by using her cashpoint card she would put herself on the radar but by that time she'd be safely in the hub of a busy airport. Anonymous. And the very second she touched down in Germany she would make a call to the police and tell them what she knew.

She looked into her purse as she neared Cradley Heath bus station. Feeling more hopeful about the plan, she decided to spend what was left on a bus ride.

She ran in front of a bus just pulling out. The driver screeched the vehicle to a halt, offering her a filthy look.

She jumped on, grateful to be amongst the misery of the working crowd starting a new week. Oh, she ached to have their problems.

Twelve minutes later she jumped off the bus and headed into Dover Street, the main road that ran parallel to her own. If she turned the corner from the top end of the street she'd be able to assess quickly if anyone was hanging around.

She knew who she was looking for and he wasn't easy to miss.

She stood at the corner, her eyes searching every space. She saw nothing. She took a few steps forward, assessing every building as she went.

She jumped at the sound of a wheelie bin being pulled back into the garden after the weekly refuse collection, but made it to the Victorian house safely.

The keys jangled against each other as she tried to get the front door open. Inga cursed her own clumsiness as twice they fell from her hands. She finally closed the door behind her and leaned against it.

She felt the warm familiarity of coming home. Suddenly, she pined for the mundane drudge of normality.

Everyday life was not so far behind her that she couldn't remember coming home each night from work and moaning to herself about her employers or the crowded bus or the cost of groceries.

She put the key into the lock of her front door but it eased open. Her heart beat wildly as the door slowly displayed the carnage within.

Every piece of furniture she owned had been smashed to pieces. Her clothes were strewn and from the doorway she could see they had been ripped and cut. The clinical stench of bleach permeated the air.

She stared at the destruction before her and imagined Symes smiling as he destroyed her home.

The total devastation was meant as a warning and she'd received it loud and clear.

Inga turned on her heel and fled.

CHAPTER 25

Karen was alone in the kitchen when Kim entered.

She turned from her cleaning and offered the ghost of a smile. Kim noted that the jewellery worn yesterday had been removed and not replaced. No make-up covered her skin.

"Morning, Kim, hope last night wasn't—"

"Can we talk outside?" Kim asked.

Karen paused, mid-wipe.

"Is everything okay, do you have news?"

Kim shook her head and moved towards the French doors.

Karen wiped her hands and reached for a black shawl from inside the utility room. She offered a red one to Kim.

"I'm fine," Kim said.

It was almost nine and the temperature had reached one degree.

Karen closed the kitchen door and pulled the shawl tightly around her. "What's—"

"Tell me about Robert," Kim said, moving away from the back door. Karen followed, looking confused.

"He is a truly wonderful man. I didn't necessarily think so when we first met but he's persistent when he wants to be."

Kim nodded. This was Karen's one chance to tell the truth.

"I was working late shift at a luxury car rental place. Every few weeks he'd come in to lease a car for the weekend. He liked to drive different cars but didn't see the point in owning a whole fleet with only himself to enjoy them.

"We had a few short conversations. I was twenty-two and he was forty-one. The fifth time he came in he brought me a huge bouquet of flowers. At first I refused to take them and do you know what he said?"

Kim shook her head.

Karen smiled. "'Please don't think my attention is creepy, despite the age difference. I'm not a grubby old man; I am courting the woman I would like to be my wife.'"

"Smooth," Kim said.

"It was clever. All weekend I couldn't stop thinking about what he'd said and therefore couldn't stop thinking about him.

"I resolved to give him a piece of my mind the next time we met but then I didn't see him for almost a month. And I realised that I wanted him to come in.

"When he did, he was wearing a tuxedo. He looked so handsome and suave I couldn't tell him off. He acted as though nothing had happened and asked for the most expensive car we had. It was a Bentley convertible. I asked why the special occasion and he told me it was for a very important first date. Ours."

It was a move that could have been plucked from a romantic comedy but it had worked and Robert appeared to be a very nice man.

"We were married exactly one year later. It was beautiful."

This was not moving as quickly as Kim would have liked. She took the express route.

"Does Robert know that Charlie is not his child?"

Somewhere in this fairytale there had been deceit and Kim could no longer listen to the censored version.

Karen's head left the clouds and snapped towards her.

"How the hell . . . ?"

"Because I've studied that photo and there is not one feature in her face that remotely resembles your husband, especially those lips."

Karen's body crumbled as the sobs began. Kim continued to stare ahead.

"Oh, God, Kim, it's such a relief to finally—"

"Don't take your solace from me. I'm not a priest, Samaritan or counsellor. I'm a police officer and there's only one thing I need to know for sure."

"It was Lee," she mumbled, looking down.

Kim nodded. She'd thought as much. She'd seen it in the lips. For a mean, aggressive piece of shit, he'd had a very feminine mouth.

"It was just the once, I swear. I just couldn't—"

"Karen, I don't give a shit. What does piss me off is that you didn't think it was important to tell me the truth immediately. Do you not understand that every single piece of information is vital? Do you really think withholding this kind of detail is going to help me get your daughter back?"

Karen's hand went to her throat. "Oh, God, Kim, I'm so—"

"Does he know about her?"

Karen's face paled instantly. "You can't think—"

"I can't afford not to think, Karen. I have to rule him out."

Karen shook her head vehemently. "He doesn't know about Charlie. I never saw him again after… I don't even think of him being her father. To me her father has always been—"

"Are you going to tell Robert?" Kim asked, pointedly. She had to know if a distracting domestic situation was about to unravel.

Karen looked horrified. "God, no. I can't tell him now and neither can you."

Kim had no intention of telling Robert the truth. It was not her place but she had to investigate the possibility that Charlie's real father was involved.

She could understand Karen's refusal for full disclosure. Robert held the purse strings—and who was going to consider ruining themselves for a child who was not their own?

Karen took a step towards her. "Look, Kim, it really was just the one..."

Kim turned and walked away. There was an old adage that if you couldn't say anything nice, get the hell away before you said something very wrong. Or something like that. She wasn't sure of the exact wording as she'd never taken heed.

Personally, she hated deceit of any kind but in relationships it was unforgivable. If a relationship was over, kill it and move on but don't make someone you loved feel like a fool.

She entered the war room and rubbed her hands together.

"Stacey, start working on finding a Lee Darby. He'll be in our system and shouldn't be too hard to track down."

"Got it, boss," she said.

"Umm... Guv, just to cheer you up, Woody's been on the phone," Bryant offered. "He wants us to stop by."

Fabulous, Kim thought, reaching for her jacket.

Her day hadn't started well and she had a feeling things were about to get worse.

CHAPTER 26

"What the hell can he possibly want?" Kim grumbled as Bryant negotiated the town centre traffic around Halesowen. "He knows what we're working on and he summons us to a bloody meeting."

"Must be important, then," Bryant offered but she was not in the mood to be accommodating.

He pulled into the car park. Kim was already releasing her seatbelt.

"Wait here and keep the engine running. I won't be long."

Kim sprinted into the building and up the stairs. She knocked and waited for a second before entering.

Woody was alone.

"Sir, you called for me?"

She stood just inside the door.

"Stone, take a seat," he said, removing his glasses.

"I'm a bit pushed for—"

"I said sit."

Kim took three steps forward and sat.

"Where are we?"

There was no way in hell he'd called her in for a progress report. That he could have done over the phone. But she'd play along.

"The team is now ensconced at the Timmins' home. The Hansons have moved in also. Last night they received a second text message saying the game would start today. Helen is in place and we've viewed the footage at the leisure centre. The kidnapper posed as a police officer and, as I'm sure you know, Bradley Evans is dead."

Woody's right hand clenched around the pen he was holding.

"Exactly what were we supposed to do, Stone?" he asked, softly.

She knew he was right but Brad was still dead. "I don't know. I just wanted to protect him, somehow, Sir. It's our job."

"And I know you tried your best in your own way, but the death of Mr. Evans rests purely with the person who kicked his head around the road. Our focus has to remain with Charlie and Amy."

He put down the pen and reached for the stress ball.

Oh shit.

"Stone, you need to remember that what I'm going to say is not negotiable. You may shout and scream, stomp your foot and sulk as much as you want but it won't change a thing."

"Good news, then?"

"You will be assisted in this case by two key experts. One will arrive today and the other tomorrow."

"Sounds like a Dickens novel to me," Kim said.

"The first is a behaviour expert..."

"A profiler, Sir?"

"No, a behaviour expert."

Same thing, Kim thought. She had her own views on profiling, which she'd be more than happy to share with the "behaviour expert."

"Well, on the back of two text messages I'm gonna be all ears."

"The second is a negotiator..."

Kim dropped her head. "Is this some kind of wind-up?"

"...Who might prove useful once contact is better established."

"I can negotiate. How about this—as soon as I catch the bastards I'll negotiate a lifetime in prison without any possibility of parole and a best friend named Butch?"

"The negotiator was my idea, Stone."

"Oh...why's that, Sir?"

"Let's just say I feel your skill set lies in other areas."

She respected his judgement.

She raised one eyebrow. "Could we do a deal? I'll take the negotiator and you keep Cracker?"

Woody's mouth almost turned up in a smile.

"And I trust you will remain both courteous and professional at all times."

He placed the stress ball back on the desk.

Kim had learned to choose her battles wisely. "Of course. You know me."

His dour expression said it all.

She sighed, heavily. "Anything else?"

"No, I think I've brightened your day quite enough."

"Yes, Sir," she said, not trusting herself to say more.

She left the office and hurried back down the stairs. She paused for two seconds and made a quick decision. A detour to her office took no more than five minutes.

"We all getting a pay rise?" Bryant asked as she threw a folder onto the back seat.

"No, even better. We're getting a profiler and a negotiator."

"And a candlestick maker?"

"Not right now but who the hell knows later."

Bryant chuckled. "Umm... what's the point of that exactly?"

"Makes the brass feel better. So that if this case goes horribly wrong they can hang me out to dry and say that I had every available resource."

"But it's not going to go horribly wrong, is it, Guv?"

"You can bet on it."

Bryant smiled. "Am I resuming our journey to Featherstone?"

They had barely left the Timmins' driveway before Stacey had tracked Lee Darby down. He was currently residing at Her Majesty's Pleasure.

"Oh, yes," Kim said. It was not a meeting she was looking forward to.

CHAPTER 27

Karen was surprised at her ability to function normally when faced with a methodical task.

There was a part of her that thought if she carried on as normal Charlie would simply breeze back into the house. The logistics of this were not important. Karen knew that her child was being held captive and wouldn't just materialise but when she allowed herself to complete normal tasks it seemed possible.

Every few minutes she glanced longingly at the front door and ached to just run free. She wanted to shout, scream and search, sure that Charlie would hear her and appear. She would discover that the text messages had all been some kind of hoax and the two girls had been safe all along.

Karen blinked away the tears as the futility of the wish cleared the way for the facts. The fantasy was heaven for the few seconds that it lasted but she always returned to the truth. Twenty-four hours had passed and her child was still not home.

Preparing and cooking lunch had given her a rest from her own mind and the one thought that kept trying to surface. But she couldn't think it; *wouldn't* think it. If she did it would destroy her. Charlie was alive. She knew it.

Karen busied herself with cleaning the plates. Four were barely touched but that was okay. The purpose had been in making it, not eating it.

She filled the sink with hot water, bypassing the dishwasher. She didn't want the task of clearing up to take minutes. She wanted it to occupy her for hours. Until the very second that Charlie came home.

Each moment it grew harder to face Robert, knowing what she knew and what he did not. Although she had felt chastised by Kim, Karen knew the detective was justified. If she'd thought it would have any impact on her daughter's safety she would have shouted the truth from the rooftops. But it had no bearing. It couldn't.

"Can I help?" Elizabeth asked, entering the kitchen.

It was on the tip of Karen's tongue to refuse; if she shared the task it would be finished sooner and she would be left once again with her thoughts. One look at her friend's face changed her mind.

At least she had the luxury of being in her own home. She could cook, clean and generally try to keep herself busy.

"Grab that tea towel," Karen said. "What are the boys doing?" she asked. Hardly boys, but it was how they both referred to their husbands in the plural.

"They're both on their laptops. Robert is pretending to read emails but hasn't pressed a button for ten minutes."

"Stephen?"

"He's made a couple of calls. Apparently there are some things that can't be delegated. It's not his fault. His work is not so easy to hand over as mine," Elizabeth said, uncomfortably.

"Really?" Karen asked.

"No, I'm not nearly as indispensable as my husband. If I'm sick the next batch of queries simply goes to the closest paralegal. Not so for Stephen. Even a severe case of food poisoning isn't enough to stop the case queries coming through."

Karen pretended not to hear the edge of bitterness in Elizabeth's tone. She knew her friend had met Stephen at law school and when the relationship started to suffer as they'd both tried to attain their law degrees, she had put her own career on hold to support him. The general plan had been that she would resume her studies once Stephen became established. Then Amy had put in a surprise appearance, followed by Nicholas.

Karen would have liked another daughter or even a son. She hadn't yet given up hope that maybe one day she would bear Robert's child. She had never used contraception and Robert had no need to question his virility. In his mind he had fathered Charlie.

Karen knew Elizabeth didn't hold her career stall against her children. She was a wonderful mother but her buried animosity towards her husband was another story.

What had started out as a casual acquaintance due to their daughters meeting at nursery had grown into a deep friendship outside of the fondness their children held for each other.

A shared love of eighties music and Chinese food had formed the foundation of many interesting Friday nights. The relationship between their husbands was not as close, but they got on and endured each other's company for the sake of their wives and children.

Stephen, Elizabeth and Robert had made numerous calls to employers, colleagues and friends to explain their absence from work, meetings, social events. Their phones had tinged with constant acknowledgements, replies and get well soon wishes.

Karen had made no calls. Her circle was a very small one. And she had no issue with that. Elizabeth had been astounded at the absence of a housekeeper for such a large property and even though Robert had suggested it many times, Karen always refused.

"Have you checked on Nicholas?"

Elizabeth nodded. "He's having a fabulous time. I couldn't talk for long. The temptation was too great."

Karen understood Elizabeth's feelings. Something within her said that the more people who knew, the better it would be. A bit like rallying the troops. That someone would be able to offer something that would get their children back.

"Do you think we're doing the right thing going along with this media silence? I mean, maybe we should be getting people involved?" Elizabeth said, echoing Karen's thoughts.

A part of Karen wanted to scream it to the world. She wanted hundreds of people out looking. And if she felt in her heart that it would bring her daughter back she'd do it in a heartbeat.

But she could think of nothing worse than a trail of family, friends and colleagues in and out of her home offering well-meaning platitudes. She couldn't face the pressure of having to remain pleasant and courteous to people while Charlie was still missing. Once she was home Karen would throw a party and the whole world could come.

Karen concentrated hard on the utensils, ensuring she cleaned every surface three times.

"You know something, Kaz," Elizabeth said with a tremor in her voice. "Wherever our girls are, I hope more than anything they're together."

Karen felt the emotion gather in her throat. There were times when she felt she could cry no more.

But as she looked at the tears falling from the eyes of her friend she realised there were always more tears.

They fell into each other's arms and cried as though their lives depended on it, sharing the pain only they could understand.

Karen whispered into her friend's shoulder. "I hope they are too."

A moment later Elizabeth pulled away and dried her eyes.

"Do you trust her?" Elizabeth asked.

Karen nodded without hesitation, knowing Elizabeth spoke of Kim.

Their paths had crossed a few times throughout their childhood years. Initially, Karen had been intrigued by the girl's black hair and dark features. There was something exotic about her looks.

Kim had always been a loner, which had made her all the more interesting. Karen couldn't remember one single friend of Kim's. She had not sought close relationships and had shut down all efforts to befriend her. She didn't want to belong, or affiliate to make her life easier. She'd just wanted to survive.

Elaine had been Karen's best friend and had hated Kim with a passion. She had tried to recruit her into their group and it had failed. After that, she tried to manipulate Kim with hard stares and the occasional push and shove.

Karen recalled the day Elaine had been playing a cruel game of Shadows. She'd spent the day mimicking Kim's every movement, staying no further than two feet behind. Many of the other kids had thought it was a great game and by tea time the audience to the antics had swelled to include most of the children's home.

Karen had gone along for the ride. Not because she was scared of Elaine but because she was captivated by Kim's steely composure as she went about her business as though she was not being mimicked by twenty stupid girls.

Kim had waited until bedtime. She'd undressed before them all, cleaned her teeth and washed her face, impervious to the jokes taking place behind her.

As she'd packed away her toothbrush she'd turned to Elaine and smiled pleasantly. "Oh, sorry, Elaine, I didn't see you there."

The entourage had grown silent as Kim made her way to the bathroom exit. She'd paused and turned.

"Is it not a little sad that you give so much thought to someone who never thinks about you?"

Kim had waited for five seconds for an answer before pushing her way through the crowd of silent girls and going directly to bed.

Kim had been thirteen years old and the only person Karen had ever known who was not frightened of Elaine.

"I would trust her with my life," Karen said, honestly.

But as she said the words, Karen realised that it was not her own life she was entrusting to the detective.

CHAPTER 28

"So, what's on your mind, Guv?" Bryant asked as they passed through Dudley.

"Nothing. I'm fine."

"No, you're not. You let me drive and you only do that when you need thinking time."

"It's nothing...I'll sort it."

"I have no doubt about that but you might sort it quicker if you throw stuff at me."

"That'll help?" she asked.

"Not literally. I know what you're like so I absolutely promise to give no useful advice whatsoever. Just speak the problem out loud."

"Tracy Frost isn't the reason Dewain Wright died," Kim said and actually felt a small amount of relief that the words were out there. "She visited the house last night—which is a whole other problem—but she insisted about Dewain so I grabbed the file from the station and took a closer look."

"But she leaked the story so how...?"

"The timing was off. We...I assumed it was her because everything happened so fast. She was breaking it, don't get me wrong, but he'd been dead ten minutes before the first newspaper hit the shops."

"Shit, so someone else let Lyron know that Dewain was still alive?"

Kim nodded her head and then looked out the window.

The constant stopping and starting at the countless traffic lights on the Birmingham New Road was beginning to irritate her. Bryant only needed to take one of them on amber and they'd fly through the rest.

"That kid really got to you, didn't he?" Bryant asked.

Kim didn't look Bryant's way. Yes, Dewain Wright had got to her, because he was one of the bravest young men she had ever met. He had known he was risking his life in trying to leave the gang but he had tried to do it anyway.

"So, what are you gonna do?" Bryant asked. "You don't like loose ends, and with this case..."

"I can't even think about working another case and not only because I promised Karen. I need to be focussed on Charlie and Amy and bringing them home."

Bryant nodded his understanding. "So, you can't work on it."

"I know that, but I'm not going to just ignore the fact that somebody leaked out that the lad was still alive, so causing his death. He deserves better than that."

"God forbid you should allow anything to dangle loosely from one of your cases," he tutted. "But *you* are really tied up at the house."

She looked at him sideways. "Do they pay you extra for repeating everything I say?"

"Nah, I do that by choice."

"Aah," she said, as the penny finally dropped. "I know what you're thinking and I like it."

"I'm thinking nothing at all. Just listening, like I said I would."

She knew now exactly what she was going to do and would address it when they returned.

She turned towards him as they pulled into the prison site. "As usual, Bryant, thank you for being absolutely no use at all."

"Any time, Guv."

* * *

From a distance the scale of HMP Featherstone's door set into the dense brick barrier reminded Kim of a cartoon, as though any entrance to the facility had been an afterthought.

Kim liked to think the architect built it high and built it strong, then took a look and thought, oh, damn it, forgot folks need to get in.

Featherstone in Wolverhampton had never been the poster child for effective incarceration. It celebrated the birth of the Millennium with a survey that found thirty-four per cent of inmates admitted to taking drugs. At least a third could be added for those who didn't admit to it. In 2007 the prison had beat off competition to score the highest percentage in the UK for testing positive for opiates such as heroin.

In recent years three new sparkly blocks had been added, branding it a super-prison and almost doubling the capacity for category C prisoners.

They were met beyond the pixie door by a uniformed officer who looked like she was playing dress-up. Kim guessed her to be no older than twenty-one. Her frame was slight and her face innocent.

Kim knew that looks could be deceptive but they weren't outright liars. She just prayed to God this girl didn't hold the opinion that all the prisoners were decent and misunderstood and that if she treated them with respect they would reciprocate.

They weren't and they wouldn't.

Bryant showed his badge and she took a good look.

She shook her head. "There's no visiting today, it's Monday."

Kim really appreciated the weekday update. She opened her mouth but luckily Bryant was quicker.

"We called earlier and spoke to—"

"Everything okay, Daisy?" asked a male, from the doorway to the rest of the prison.

Bryant was quick to flash his badge. "We have permission. If you call—"

"I've been informed," he said, brusquely.

Bryant continued. "We need to speak to one of your inmates. It's important."

Kim guessed the man to be early fifties. His white shirt was crisp and open at the neck, revealing a severe shaving rash.

"Step through," he said, pointing to the metal detector.

They both emptied their pockets and placed keys, phones and change into the tray. Kim breezed through but a forgotten pen in Bryant's inside pocket prompted a scream from the machine.

"We need to see Lee Darby," Kim offered, reaching for her possessions.

"You'll have to leave your belongings here," the officer said, passing the tray to Daisy.

Kim watched the tray disappear beneath the desk. She protested. "Officer…" she looked closer at his name badge "…Burton. I'd like my—"

"You're not getting past this point with keys, phones and warrant cards."

"Play nice, Guv," Bryant said, disguised in a cough.

Begrudgingly, she accepted this was his play pen, not hers, and sighed heavily.

He reached over the desk and handed them two visitor passes.

"Finally, do you have anything sharp?"

Bryant stepped forward. "Can you take out her tongue?"

"Nature of the visit?" Burton asked, ignoring Bryant's comment.

"Confidential," Kim answered.

Burton appraised her for a full five seconds. Kim didn't blink.

He turned. "I'll show you to the visitors' suite."

"We would prefer to go to him," Kim stated.

Officer Burton stopped walking. "That is highly irregular."

"I understand that," Kim offered. This could not appear to be a planned visit. Kim's one purpose was to establish if Lee Darby was involved in the abduction of his own daughter. First she had to find out if he even knew about Charlie. "But that's what we need and I cannot stress the urgency enough."

Kim began moving forward.

Officer Burton maintained pace. He checked his watch and considered for a moment.

"He'll be in the gym, basketball practice. There will be many other inmates."

"Don't worry about Bryant," Kim said. "I'll protect him."

"Inspector, your safety is my responsibility."

"Okay, Officer," she conceded. "I promise not to move away from you. Is that okay?"

If her plan worked, she wouldn't need to.

He thought for a moment then nodded his agreement.

"So, what's he like?" Bryant asked, as they walked along the corridor. Each stretch of identical hallway was interrupted by the constant locking and unlocking process.

Somewhere in this building a small team of people maintained intelligence on every single prisoner. They knew who they spoke to, who they didn't, which of them were enemies and, more importantly, which of them were friends.

"He's one of our aspirationals," Burton offered.

"A what?" Kim asked.

"We give 'em personality types. Our Lee likes to try and mix above his station."

"How so?" Bryant asked.

"Like everywhere else, there's a hierarchy, a tier system in prison. The bottom layer, the biggest, is made up of petty crime: prisoners in for repeated shop theft, car theft, stuff like that. They're with us for a relatively short period each stretch. They tend to stick together and stay away from the prison politics. Mainly because they're not here long enough.

"Next tier up you've got the career thieves, GBH inmates in for a medium stretch. Our boy likes to try and mix with the big boys. The conversations aren't what you'd call lengthy. Probably just long enough to be told to piss off."

"Not popular then?"

Burton shrugged. "He might be if he stopped trying to get in with the hardest guys. Knocking your missus about is never going to do it. Especially not with him."

"Why not?"

"Because she testified in court and got him banged up, so even his woman isn't scared of him. He's not as low as the paedos, but he isn't far off."

"And he keeps on trying?"

Burton nodded. "Gives him something to do."

"Any other trouble?" Kim asked.

"Few fights but nothing serious. He's added a few months to his sentence and his first stab at parole comes the end of this year."

Burton keyed them into a lobby that housed the door to the gym hall. Kim knew the prison offered many sporting activities, including badminton, bowls, volleyball and football. She also knew that prisoners at Featherstone had approximately ten hours' out-of-cell time each day.

Oh, if only she ruled the world.

Burton turned to her. "Umm...is there no way you could stay out of sight and let your colleague...?"

"Bryant, go talk to that short guy over there. Pretend to know him," she said, poking her head into the doorway.

Bryant offered her a strange look but did as she asked.

Kim stepped inside the room and stood against the wall looking nowhere in particular. Burton sighed deeply but stood next to her.

The scent of a new woman was like cocaine to a drugs dog. She half expected them all to run to her and sit. As anticipated, every pair of eyes in the room turned towards her.

It took approximately four seconds for the men to identify her as a police officer, which killed their interest. All except for one.

Kim didn't look in his direction but peripherally saw him tilt his head and saunter towards her. It appeared that he'd adopted his Sunday-best gangster walk on her account. A slight bounce and then leg drag. It was the funniest thing she'd seen in days.

Burton moved closer.

Lee held up his hands. "'S all right, dude. I know this bitch."

"Hey, watch your—"

"Kim?" he said, finally standing in front of her. "It is, ain't it; Kim Stone?"

She allowed her gaze to fall on him. It remained blank.

"It's me... Lee... Lee Darby. We grew up together. We was mates."

Jesus, he was talking to her as though he actually believed the crap coming out of his decay-ridden mouth. Her recollection was a little different.

Kim tipped her head and frowned. A slight smile hovered over her lips. Oh, go on then, she'd play his game for a little bit.

"Oh yeah, I remember you. We were at Goodhampton together."

He smiled widely. It did his mean face no favours. "That's it. Yeah, I heard yer was a pig but I gorra be honest, I day really believe it."

Kim looked around at her environment as though only just realising where they were having this conversation.

"How'd you end up here? I thought you had it all worked out," she said, shortly.

"Just a blip. Your lot always gerrin' the wrong bloke for shit. I never did nothing. Just wrong place wrong time."

Aah, so it was some kind of mistake that he happened to be on the end of the fist that was pummelling his girlfriend all the way to intensive care. How very unfortunate for him.

"So, what are you doing with yourself when you're in the right place at the right time?"

"A bit of buying, a bit of selling."

Kim nodded her understanding. Anyone who believed him should come see her. She had a nice bridge in London to sell.

"Wife, kids?"

He shook his head. "Nah, cor stand the little fuckers. Do nothing but bleed yer dry. Footloose and fancy free."

He winked at her and the bile actually rose in her throat.

She covered her mouth and coughed. Her sign to Bryant she was done.

Finally she allowed the mask to drop and every ounce of repulsion she felt showed in her eyes.

"Lee, you certainly haven't improved with age. You may not be where you expected to be but you're exactly where *I* expected you to be."

Bryant sidled up beside her. She turned and walked away.

She had detected no deceit in the man at all. Had he been involved in an operation as complex as a double kidnapping he would have carried a more superior air. There would have been a smug self-satisfaction, a delight in his own cleverness.

Kim felt sure he knew nothing of Charlie's existence. No shadow had passed over his face at the mention of kids.

Yes, she could have done it the easy way and questioned him directly but to do so would have alerted him to the fact he had a daughter. A fact Lee would have no doubt tried to use to his advantage at some stage.

Truthfully, she cared nothing for protecting the fragile barrier Karen had constructed around her family. It was a web of lies she would eventually have to confront.

She'd done it for Charlie. Lee Darby was a father the child did not need. She had Robert. For now.

"Where to, Guv?" Bryant asked, as they stepped out into the fresh air.

"Back to the house," she said.

After hitting a bricked-up dead end she hoped to hell there was something in those files.

CHAPTER 29

"Kev, anything?" Kim asked. Dawson had been recalled to the house for a catch-up before the behaviourist arrived.

The frustration was evident on his face. "According to my new best friend downstairs, Inga hasn't brought anyone back to the flat in months. None of the other neighbours speak to her much and all verify that they only ever saw her alone.

"Showed her picture at the local shops. She used the hairdressers for a dry cut a few times and had a couple of take-outs from the Chinese but no conversations. Ran into the team from Brierley Hill who've been assigned the break-in but they're wondering why there's no complainant."

Keeping the force blackout was equally as difficult as blind-folding the press.

Tracking this girl down was proving impossible. For Inga's sake Kim hoped it was proving equally difficult for the kidnappers. The only explanation for the woman darting from the ambulance was fear. She had bottled it. Kim seriously doubted it was part of the plan. It would have made more sense for Inga to wait inside the hospital to be collected or simply leave later but to make a scene outside the hospital told Kim that Inga was now running scared.

"Stace?" she said, turning her head.

"I've sent out begging emails to the phone networks. I've gor acknowledgements and they politely kept the belly laughs to a minimum. I've gor a possible address on one of the families from the last case but the other family is a bit 'arder. Probably change of address and last name.

"Of the list of possibles given by the parents, there's one with a criminal record for petty theft which Robert confirms that he knew about when he gave him a job. The rest are clear except for most of the names on Stephen's list. That's my next job."

"Anything useful about the two mobile phones used?"

"Pay as you go bought from different networks with initial credit included. Both bought with a cloned credit card from Manchester and delivered to a post office box in Ealing."

"Well, that gives us…"

"Eleven months ago, boss," Stacey clarified.

"Damn it," Kim growled. It would have been a long shot anyway but no one was going to recall a person who had rented a post office box that long ago.

"Shows how long they've planned to take these two girls," Bryant said.

"Not these two girls," Kim said. "Shows how long it's been a plan but not specifically who they were going to take. There has to be a link to one or both of these families. There has to be a reason they caught the kidnapper's eye.

"Okay, everyone grab a pile," she said as she took a stack of papers from the nearest box. "I want to know if there are any clues as to why the girls were chosen in the previous case."

Everyone nodded and reached for a portion of old case notes.

"Hey Guv, imagine if this doc tries to profile you," Dawson said, smiling.

Bryant snorted. "For that they could have my sympathies and my house."

"And a well-deserved pay rise," Dawson added.

Kim smiled at them both.

"Shit, Dawson, she's smiling," Bryant observed.

"That'll be me shutting up then."

"Now there's a good idea," Kim said.

She leafed through her own pile, which contained witness statements mixed with call logs, officer reports with possible sightings and the tip calls to the hotline all over the place.

"Oh damn," Kim groaned, as a picture came into her mind.

She darted from the room and returned two minutes later with a framed photograph from the side of Charlie's bed.

"The swimming gala," she said, removing the clipping from the frame.

Kim read it quickly, her heart sinking lower with each sentence. When she'd finished she placed it on the table and pushed it towards Bryant.

"Talks a lot about them being best friends. Amy's father, 'the esteemed prosecutor,' is quoted, as well as 'local business owner,' Robert Timmins."

As the article travelled around the table Kim marvelled at its revelations. The girls were passionate swimmers and they both had wealthy parents. Even without any help at all it wouldn't have taken long to track them to Old Hill Leisure Centre and the lovely picture of the two of them holding up their medals made them easy to identify.

Bryant blew out a whistle. "A perfectly innocent article that pretty much reveals everything." He looked closely at the top of the page. "And this was published in June."

Yes, she had done the sums herself. If this photograph had been the catalyst, they had taken nine months to plan.

"So, what does this tell us, Guv?" Dawson asked. "Are we now not concerned with enemies or family members? Has this information narrowed our search?"

"No, Kev, it's blown it right open."

She could no longer operate under the assumption that a party known to the families was involved.

That scenario at least held the beginning of a trail, and if it was there she would find it, but Kim also now had to face the fact that the choice of girls was random and had been prompted by a newspaper article.

As the possibility of a family connection faded she had to hope that they were dealing with the same crew as last time. Every sentence, fact, contact or witness noted previously had to be re-examined in the hope that somewhere they had inadvertently left her a crumb.

"Okay, everyone back on case notes," Kim instructed. It was time to dig in.

CHAPTER 30

Will checked the charge on mobile phone number three. The first two were placed to the far left of the table and were switched off. He didn't expect a reply. Not yet. That would come later, after the next message.

He lined up the remaining phones, ensuring the top edges were flush with each other. Each phone had a two-inch gap between itself and its neighbour.

Satisfied that the equipment was in order, he returned to the script. He had read this message a hundred times but it had to be perfect. Last time he hadn't taken enough time over the wording. Hadn't savoured it in his own mind enough.

There had been many flaws the last time. He had thought he could do everything on his own but this time he'd had help that had taken two forms. The first had been the most unlikely and had approached him. The second he had courted.

He had found Symes before the couples had been chosen and from the first meeting he'd known he had his man. There were necessary stages of the process and he needed Symes at the end. The man's cold ruthlessness left him free to enjoy his part of the job.

He read the text message again. This time he wanted maximum impact for every word. But what he really wanted was to be there when the message was read.

There was an almost breathless excitement within him that he'd never felt on the night before Christmas. As the middle child of seven, there had been little to anticipate. His first memory was his weary mother handing him the Argos catalogue with an instruction. Put his initials next to something that was under a tenner, she said. He did and she passed the weighty book to the next child in line.

And then the first day at school every other kid would reel off every single present that Santa had brought. He had felt the envy grow inside him. Not only for the gifts but for the belief in a magical myth. He told every kid he could find that Father Christmas didn't exist and explained it was all a fat lie. Girls and boys alike had cried and protested and argued and eventually accepted and then cried some more. And he had laughed, because he had mattered.

His parents had believed in nothing. A tooth placed beneath the pillow had still been there in the morning. Easter eggs came from Asda and were three for a quid.

He wanted the money. He wanted *their* money. He wanted to take something from people who had it all.

Will tried to picture the faces of the families when he ripped apart their lives. Oh, how he wished he could see it for himself, but he couldn't. He would just have to sit here and imagine.

Just one more hour until he sent the text that would change their lives forever.

His thoughts travelled to his colleague. He had expected him back by now with the task complete. There was no choice about Inga's fate. She had acted foolishly and she would have to pay. She knew too much to stay alive. She was a stupid bitch who had succumbed to the nerves and he felt nothing for her fear. Her emotions had proven useful in the beginning but now threatened to derail the whole project.

She had to die and she had to die soon.

And he hoped Symes really took his time.

CHAPTER 31

"Whoever sorted these records should be taken outside for a good kicking."

"Shut up moaning, Kev, and get on with it," Kim snapped. But she completely agreed with him. Their first full day of investigation was nearing to a close. Charlie and Amy had been missing for almost thirty-six hours and it felt like they were getting nowhere.

What was more worrying was that, if the investigation had been carried out with the same level of efficiency as the filing, Kim understood why it had gone so horribly wrong.

"Why do you reckon only one of the girls came back?" Bryant asked.

"Don't know—but I'm willing to bet the answer is in here somewhere."

A soft tap sounded on the door. Helen popped her head in but didn't step over the threshold.

"Marm, there's someone here to see you: a Doctor Lowe."

Kim pushed back her chair and headed to the front door, passing through the haze of deliciousness wafting from the kitchen.

The figure before her was slim and tall, dressed in a pencil skirt, high heels and a power jacket. The woman's chestnut bob was joined together by a blunt fringe.

She turned with a fixed smile that didn't reach the cool blue eyes.

"Doctor Alison Lowe," she said, pleasantly. "You're expecting me?"

"The profiler?" Kim clarified. She struggled with the term "doctor" for people without white coats or scrubs.

"I prefer behaviourist," Lowe said with a tinge of impatience in her voice.

"Of course," Kim answered, with a smile. Woody had made it clear she was to be nice to the seconded experts, yet the expression just did not fit well on her face.

Kim thrust out her hand. Alison appeared startled. Maybe she'd done it too quickly. Truthfully, Kim abhorred physical contact with strangers—unless she was throwing them to the ground.

"Pleased to meet you," Kim said in unison with a brief touching of palms.

"And you are the senior investigating officer?"

She preferred detective inspector, but she'd let it go.

Kim appraised the woman's attire and smiled. "Thank you for coming straight here but if you'd like to go and book into a hotel, get sorted and come back…"

"I already did, Officer."

"Oh, no problem," Kim said, wondering who dressed like this at six thirty in the evening. "Follow me and I'll introduce you to the team. They're all dying to meet you."

As soon as the words were out of her mouth, Kim realised that may have been overkill. But she felt her natural disposition was unlikely to endear her to the woman.

"Guys, this is Doctor Alison Lowe, our consultant behaviourist."

Doctor Lowe used only her toes to navigate her way to the head of the table.

"Please, call me Alison," she said, offering a perfect public speaking voice and a smile that was equally allocated around the room. She placed the briefcase onto the dining table, nudging a coffee mug that Stacey caught just in time.

"This is my curriculum vitae, just to give you a little background on my credentials."

She handed them around the table.

Kim glanced at the CV and idly wondered if Alison had been a child prodigy; one of those kids who finished medical school by the time they were twelve. A degree in sociology, another one in psychology and an impressive amount of capital letters.

What she couldn't see clearly was testimony of practical work.

"So, if you'd like to ask me anything, please do."

Bryant coughed. "Can you give us some idea on the type of cases you've worked in the past?"

Trust him to know what she was thinking and to have the skill to phrase the question infinitely better than she would have.

Alison smiled at Bryant as though she had anticipated the question.

"I assisted on a triple murder investigation in Edinburgh and I assisted on the case of a multiple rapist in Hertfordshire."

Kim was unsure as to what level "assisted" denoted her involvement but this was not a job interview so she chose not to press it. Woody clearly trusted Alison's judgement and Kim trusted his.

"So, where would you like to start?" Kim asked.

Alison moved away from the easy chair and sat at the table.

"I'd like to get an outline of the case so far. I understand there was a similar incident last year."

"That's correct," Kim confirmed.

"If I could have those case notes, also."

Kim indicated the numerous piles of paperwork. "Please, feel free."

Alison looked around the table. "No methodical order, I assume."

Kim was prevented from answering by a knock on the door. Dawson was closest and rose to answer it.

Kim leaned back in her chair and saw Karen.

Karen looked past Dawson to Kim. "Dinner is ready if you have the time."

Her three team members looked at her longingly.

"Go ahead," she said, rolling her eyes. She made a mental note to speak to Karen. It was not the woman's job to feed the investigative team and, although she could understand it gave her a purpose, it had to stop. Eating together produced an intimacy, like family gathering at the table for the evening meal to discuss the day. Her team could not be lulled into discussing anything.

"Feel free," Kim said to Alison.

"I've already eaten, thank you. I'd prefer to get started."

Kim waited until the door closed. "Okay, two nine-year-old girls taken from a local sports facility. The collecting mother's car was tampered with to prevent her arriving on time. Our first kidnapper was dressed as a police officer and was spoken to by a member of the facility staff who was murdered last night.

"Chosen form of communication is by text. Two messages received so far. The content of which is written on the board.

"The girls are best friends and both appeared in a news article a few months ago, where the careers of both fathers were mentioned. And to answer what I'm sure will be your first question there has been no ransom demand as yet."

Alison stared at the board and rubbed her chin.

As Kim outlined what they had so far she realised just how little it was.

She continued. "At this point we're working through lists of potential enemies to the two families but we have to consider that they were chosen due to the article."

"Hmm...that last text message is a little concerning."

Kim nodded her agreement. "Yep, looks like we've got ourselves a psychopath."

CHAPTER 32

Symes necked his second beer, which did nothing to improve his mood.

All day he'd been chasing after this slag and he'd not got one sniff.

He held up his hand for another pint. If there wasn't work to do he'd be downing the spirits but he just wanted to relieve a bit of his anger. Just take the edge off.

He'd argued against involving her in the first place. They hadn't needed the stupid cow and he'd been right. But fucking Will had insisted on it.

One thought did amuse him briefly. He tapped his pocket. She wasn't going anywhere without her passport.

Some of the damage he'd done to her place had been a by-product of his efforts to find the document that would keep her close by. The rest had been to give her an idea of what she'd be getting when he caught her. And he would.

The thing was, Will's assessment of his intelligence had been seriously underestimated. He wouldn't have seen off two tours of Helmand if he was as stupid as he looked.

Symes had researched Inga first. His natural distrust of every living being dictated that you had to know who you were dealing with.

He knew where she went for coffee, where she had her hair done and did her shopping. He knew everything about her. He also knew that human nature dictated that in times of high stress people returned to their places of safety.

She would not be far. She'd been trying to stay alive for almost thirty hours and she was running out of time.

But, he sobered, he had to go back and tell fucking Will that he hadn't got her yet. He could imagine the look that would pass over his face before he turned and stared at his precious screens. It would be a knowing expression, with a hint of disgust and revulsion. And for a minute Symes would be tempted to pummel that look into the back end of next week; but he couldn't. They needed each other—for now.

Even as a kid Will had been a pain, full of sickness and allergies. Symes had been mates with Will's older brother who had held his own against him in a fight. Larry was tough as nails and used to beat up the little shit for fun. He had been invited to join in a few times and the stupid kid had just taken it.

Larry had been put away in his late teens for fencing stolen goods. Somebody had grassed on him, sending him inside, and Symes had a pretty good idea who.

Two weeks into a three-year stretch his mate had been stabbed during a prison riot. Will never even attended the funeral. Fucking family. Symes was glad that his bastard father had died when he was twelve. He was only sorry that it wasn't him that did it.

When he'd seen Will in a Gornal pub eleven months ago he'd been surprised by his friendly greeting and generosity at the bar. They'd met again a couple of weeks later and Will had hinted that he was working on something interesting. Symes's antennae had detected something big.

His colleague was not the easiest person to work with. A permanent sneer shaped his face and just the thought of Will's constant derision set Symes's blood on the hob.

He knew how this worked. If he didn't calm down before going back he'd have no choice in hitting Will. The mist would come and he'd only remember what he'd done later.

From experience there were only two things that would ease the tension from his body. He downed the third pint as he thought of a way he could get both.

He exited the pub and headed to the car parked at the Tesco Express. He drove towards Stourbridge with a smile on his face.

He parked in the high street and entered a bar he'd been in a few weeks ago with a couple of mates. He'd been given the eye and he'd cocked a deaf 'un but now he was listening.

He stepped up to the bar and ordered a Scotch. He saw recognition dawn in the eyes before him.

"Well, hello, big boy. How are you doing?"

The voice was gentle and soft and came from a guy called Stuart who looked slightly displaced in a working man's pub.

"I'm good, lad, yourself?"

"All the better for seeing you."

"D'ya ger a break?"

Stuart checked his watch. "About now if you'd like."

Symes smiled. "Yeah, I'd like. See yer round the back."

He exited the pub and headed around the side of the building. A narrow dark, alleyway separated it from the fishmongers next door. He leaned against the wall and waited.

The heavy metal door to his left opened and Stuart stepped out with a coy smile.

Dressed from head to toe in his uniform of black shirt and trousers, Symes supposed he was a good-looking lad. Almost pretty.

Stuart stood before him, forced close by the narrow space.

"So, big boy, what did you want to talk about?" Stuart asked, running his finger along Symes's forearm.

Symes shook him off and opened his zip.

"Oh my," Stuart whispered, looking down into the space that separated them. His hand travelled down and stroked the erection.

Symes grew even harder. Stuart groaned as he caressed the shaft. He moved closer and sought eye contact but Symes stared over the top of his head.

Symes placed his right hand on Stuart's shoulder and pushed him down to the ground.

Stuart cupped his balls as he took the length of him into his mouth.

Symes smiled to himself. No one gave a blow job like a queer.

He found the heat building inside him. He wound his fingers into the mop of blond hair and pulled the head back and forth as he plunged in and out.

Symes did not look down but sensed Stuart was pleasuring himself at the same time. He dared not look down. The sight of another man on the end of his cock would disgust him.

As the heat built within him everything else receded into the distance. All that mattered was that he reached his destination. He thrust harder into Stuart's mouth and pulled hard on his head. Beads of sweat were breaking out on his forehead. He could see it approaching. He raced towards it, focussed only on crossing that line.

Symes roared as he exploded through the tape.

The effects were immediate. His stress levels were depleting like a leaking bucket but not yet gone.

"Jeez, man, you coulda waited—"

Stuart's words were cut short as Symes punched him in the head. The kid fell onto his side.

Symes quickly zipped up his flies and then kicked Stuart in the back.

Stuart cried out in pain.

"What the fuck you expect, bum boy?" Symes asked. "You fucking faggots are all the same." He kicked him to the stomach. "Yer fucking queer. You're disgusting."

Stuart rolled around on the floor, groaning, his hands clutching his stomach. Just below, his flaccid penis lolled around on the ground.

Symes was disgusted at the sight. Nausea rose in his stomach, which fuelled his anger. He kicked Stuart in the back of the thigh, hard.

"You're a fucking disgrace. Don't yer know it's a fucking sin to do what you just did? It's unclean to suck another man's cock."

Symes kicked again.

Stuart groaned and rolled himself further down the alley to get away.

Symes followed.

"Please...no more..." Stuart begged.

Symes kicked him again. "I should put yer out of yer fucking misery."

"Please...don't..."

Symes stepped over the squirming body so his feet were planted either side of Stuart's torso. He stared down into the terrified face.

"Okay, I'll leave you alone once you say you're sorry."

"Wh...what..."

Symes nudged him in the ribs with his right foot.

"I said, say you're sorry. Apologise for being a dirty, filthy queer and say you're sorry for what you just made me do." He nudged again. "Fuckin' say it."

Symes saw a tear escape from the boy's eye as he repeated Symes's instruction word for word.

Symes smiled, satisfied. The kid had taken responsibility for his actions so he would let him live. He himself had been absolved of all responsibility and was now cleansed.

He straightened his clothes and headed out of the alleyway.

Now he was ready to go back.

CHAPTER 33

Kim paused as she came across a header sheet entitled "Transcript of 3rd text message."

There was no second sheet.

She looked around at the strewn piles. A picture of needles and haystacks came to mind. Her eyes rested on Alison at the other end of the table. The woman was regarding her with a half-smile.

Kim tried to form the same expression but it felt like a reflection from a fun-house mirror.

"Why are you trying to be nice to me?" Alison asked, bemused.

"I'm not trying to be anything," Kim lied.

"Yes you are, and now you're lying." Alison's eyebrows moved closer together. "I just don't understand why."

"What makes you think I'm pretending?" Kim asked.

"I'm a behaviourist, Inspector. I can spot an adopted demeanour a mile away. So why?"

Kim offered the first genuine expression she'd felt since meeting the woman. "I'm not particularly easy to work with, my boss tells me."

Alison looked relieved. "Aaaah, so it's not that you particularly dislike me. You just tend to dislike most people."

Kim admired her perception. "Something like that, but while we're having this chat, I won't lie. Profiling in general turns my stomach."

Alison chose not to correct her terminology. "You don't think that helping to identify criminals through their psychology is a benefit to the police force?"

"I know that it wasn't long ago that criminal profiling was done by measuring body parts. Rapists had short hands, narrow foreheads and were light-haired. Thieves had skull anomalies and thick hair."

Alison smiled. "I think we've moved on a little from that. There are many established profiles in use today that have been scientifically developed: the Myers-Briggs, Guilford-Zimmerman, the Edwards personality profile scale."

Kim put down the piece of paper she was holding.

She knew of all the tests Alison had quoted.

"And they all rely on the subject answering the test questions truthfully. That calls for the criminal to be totally honest and self-aware. That's the first flaw.

"The second is that you only get to question the criminals that have been caught, so you're missing all the ones that got away. The data is incomplete."

"I understand what you're saying—"

"The third problem is that your data is historic. You are predicting what will happen based on what already *has* happened. This type of person will react in this way. Your systems reduce people to predictable machines and they're not."

"But people typically act consistently. Personality traits are ingrained."

"People act differently if going through stress. People make choices and those choices cannot be predicted."

Alison sat forward. "But the comparison of behaviour profiles is a comparison of patterns—and patterns matter."

Kim opened her mouth but Bryant's head appeared around the door.

"Fresh coffee?"

"Bryant, I'd love a nice cup of tea."

His eyes widened. "Guv, you never drink tea."

She turned to Alison. "That's my point. Just because I normally drink coffee doesn't mean that now and again I might not fancy a change."

"But the majority of the time you drink coffee. Clichés are clichés for a reason."

"And there's always an exception to prove the rule," Kim countered. "Each case and criminal is unique so can't be predicted by the historic actions of others."

"So, you see no merit in behaviour analysis at all?"

Kim thought for a moment. "I believe firmly that a good investigation is a mix of observation, deduction and knowledge."

"Aah, the Sherlock Holmes approach."

"Well, not really, because he wasn't real. But there are certain things of which I can be sure. No offender acts without motivation. Different offenders exhibit similar behaviour for completely different reasons. Human behaviour develops uniquely in response to environment and biology.

"Quite frankly, I don't care if our kidnapper has a Freudian fascination with his mother or if he's an anti-social recluse who knits in his spare time, because unless you can give me his address it ain't a lot of help."

Alison surprised her by laughing out loud. "Did you even take a breath?"

Perhaps she had gone in a little hard. She hadn't meant to trash the woman's career choice.

"Look, any help you can offer on potential behaviour based on demonstrated actions would be appreciated."

"Certainly, Inspector."

Kim looked her up and down. "And for heaven's sake, come dressed appropriately tomorrow. A look that severe unnerves the family members. You look like a bloody undertaker." She studied her. "What's with the power dressing anyway? It's a bit late eighties."

"As a woman I have to fight to be taken seriously. My dress code ensures that I will be respected and not disregarded."

Kim knew that respect from a team did not come from a dress code. It came from making good decisions.

"Well, rest assured, Doc, that my team will not disregard you because you're a woman. We'll just do it because you talk shit."

The woman offered her a cold stare.

"Now, that was a joke."

"Oh, got it, Brummie humour."

"Oh no, no, no and talk like that will get you killed. The Black Country is most definitely not Birmingham."

And that wasn't a joke.

"Inspector, I think—"

Alison's words were cut short as a shriek sounded from the lounge. Kim launched herself at the door, trampling piles of paper, and tore through the hallway.

"Text message," Dawson said, handing her Karen's phone. Kim had asked the families not to read the next one but Elizabeth's phone was firmly clamped in Stephen's grip.

Kim held out her hand towards him. "Mr. Hanson, if you—"

"I'll read it, Inspector," he said, wiping his thumb across the screen.

Kim took a step towards him. "Mr. Hanson, please pass me the—"

He stepped away. "She's my child, not yours," he insisted.

As he opened the message on Elizabeth's phone the two mothers gravitated to each other on the sofa. They held hands tightly.

Her team, including Alison, were scattered around the room. Kim would have preferred Stephen not to read the message before she knew what it said but she could not forcibly take his property.

He started to read and a drop of colour left his face with every word.

> How much do you love your daughter? Measure it in pounds. Healthy competition brings out the best in people. The couple that offers the highest amount will see their daughter again. The losing couple will not. These are the rules and they will not change. I will be in touch. Make no mistake. One child will die.

The room erupted into a cacophony of screams and exhalations.

Kim turned her gaze to the distraught mothers and watched as the two women's hands fell apart.

CHAPTER 34

Kim turned to the family liaison officer. "Helen, a word."

Kim strode out of the room, through the hallway and out of the front door. She continued thirty feet down the drive. This was a private conversation.

Helen caught up with her. "Marm?"

Kim turned. "This is what happened the last time, isn't it? A fucking play-off? And you never thought to mention it?"

Kim's fists were clenched inside her pockets.

"I didn't know it would be the same. I didn't know...I just..."

The woman looked distraught but Kim didn't care.

"There's nothing in the case files about this. There's no transcript of the third message."

Helen looked pained.

"Listen, you'd better start being honest with me or so help me God, I'll..."

"It's not in there," she said, finally.

Kim's hands stopped clenching. "Why the hell not?"

"There were only a couple of us that knew about the third text message. We were sworn to secrecy. It wouldn't have looked good had it got out that we knew only one child was coming back and we still didn't come close to catching them. There was only ever going to be one child returned so our investigation gained nothing."

"How has this never been made public?"

"Honestly, Marm. You've got to have been involved in cases where certain information is not in the public interest?"

Kim fumed. "We're not talking public interest, we're talking integral to the bloody case."

"And the senior investigating officer is still my boss, Marm," Helen shot back.

Kim ran her hand through her hair. "Jesus, this just keeps getting better. Is there anything else I should know?"

Helen shook her head.

Kim had two options. She could have Helen removed from the case or she could continue to try to make some use of her.

"Marm, I'm really sorry. I should have told you. The publicity was bad enough but that's no excuse. I should have warned you of what was probably coming."

"Yes, you bloody well should have," Kim raged.

Helen tucked a piece of hair behind her ears. Her fingers were trembling.

"If I let you stay I have to know that you are withholding nothing else from me. Your only priority should be to help bring those girls home."

"Marm, I assure you that I will..."

"Go back inside, Helen. And...make some tea."

Helen nodded and rushed back towards the house.

Kim paced for a moment longer, unwilling to take her anger back inside. She would need to grow another limb to count on her fingers and toes just how many ways the previous investigation had been botched. But those failings were now affecting Charlie and Amy and she didn't like it one little bit.

She would inform Woody tomorrow of the missing paperwork. That was his battle to fight.

Kim's only concern was the safe return of those two little girls.

CHAPTER 35

Kim stepped back into the war room. The mood was sombre.

"Okay, folks, make your calls. It's an all-nighter."

"Already done, Guv," Bryant said. Dawson and Stacey nodded at her. Jesus, her team knew her well. The first full day of investigation was lengthening before her but Kim could not forget that this was the second night the girls would spend away from home. The intensity of the case meant it felt much later in the week than Monday night.

"The priority is to glean anything we can from these files. They're not complete but I'd say it's now far more likely we're dealing with the same crew as last time, so anything we can get will be useful."

Kim checked her watch. It was almost nine. "Alison, feel free to go and we'll update you in the morning."

"I have eyes, Inspector. I can read."

Kim wasn't about to argue.

"Okay, we take turns in getting a couple of hours' rest on the easy chair. Second priority is keeping the coffee topped up."

"Yes, Guv," Bryant offered.

"Right, I'm going to talk to the families," Kim said, standing.

Karen's head was buried in the chest of her husband. Robert stroked her hair.

Elizabeth sat on one of the single chairs with Stephen on the arm. Elizabeth stared off into the distance. The rage from Stephen was palpable.

Helen skittered off into the kitchen as Kim entered the room.

Never had the couples looked so separate and Kim struggled to recall the picture of the two women holding hands.

She sat in the other single chair and faced them all.

"Folks, this development is as much of a shock to you as it is to me but—"

"Did this happen on the last one?" Stephen asked.

"I can't discuss the details of the last case with—"

"I'll take that as a yes, seeing as only one child came back."

"Mr. Hanson, we need to talk—"

"What we need is someone decent to head this investigation."

Three pairs of eyes turned on him. He opened his arms. "What? I'm only saying what we're all thinking."

Karen opened her mouth but Robert was faster. His voice was quiet but firm.

"Stephen, don't ever presume to speak for me. Detective Inspector, I'm not thinking that at all."

Karen moved her head in agreement.

"Please continue, Inspector," Elizabeth said.

"Thank you. The newspaper clipping is useful but I still can't rule out that someone in your lives is involved in this. Please try and think if there is anyone else you haven't mentioned. Even if you think it's irrelevant, please, let me know."

Kim headed out of the room but paused for a second and turned.

"I have to ask that you make no attempt to respond to the text messages. I know that's going to be hard but we have no intention of there being a choice. Okay?"

The responses were not as emphatic as she would have liked.

She turned to Karen. "It's going to be a full house tonight but we'll be as quiet as we can."

Kim headed back to the war room.

It was time to start fighting back.

CHAPTER 36

The makeshift incident room still held the stunned silence from the horror of that message. But they couldn't dwell on it. Kim had to get their focus back on what they were here to do.

"Right, we can't allow this to paralyse us. The kidnappers may be playing a sick game but we are not. Nothing has changed, folks. We want both those little girls home."

"It's horrific, though, boss," Stacey breathed.

Bryant looked pained. "Even making the offer would potentially seal the death of another child."

Kim nodded. The thought was sickening, but no less true.

"Look at the effect of that one text message. The unity between the families has been destroyed. Now it's each to their own. Divide and conquer. The prospect of them working together as a team has been removed. Put yourself in the same position. Are you really going to attach the same level of concern to someone else's child as you would to your own?"

"I can't even comprehend..." Bryant's words trailed away as his mind found the discord between how he would wish to act and how he would act.

"The parents probably will make contact, you know," Alison said, quietly.

Kim nodded her agreement. She wondered which couple would break first.

"Guv, we have to consider the possibility that the girls—"

"Bryant, don't even think about it. The only possibility I'm prepared to consider is that Charlie and Amy are coming home. Alive."

She would not lead this investigation any other way.

Kim took out her mobile phone and keyed in the three mobile numbers used so far. Now they would have her number and that was fine by her.

"What you doing?" Bryant asked.

"I'm sending our friend a little message."

"Do you think he'll check the disposable phones after he's used them?"

"He'll check," Alison offered. "The game's now started. He can't get any gratification face to face. So he'll want any type of adulation he can get. In the absence of press coverage, his validation is very limited."

Stacey turned towards Alison. "Is there any chance that he'll somehow leak it to the press? If he wants that kind of admiration, is it only a matter of time?"

Alison thought for a moment before shaking her head. "I don't think so. Adherence to the plan will be his first priority. His need for respect will come later. Whatever the outcome, this will hit the news and it's going to be big. He's already shown himself to be controlled and patient. He can wait."

Kim didn't look up as Alison talked. She labelled the numbers KN1, KN2 and KN3.

The room fell into silence. The only sound was the soft beep of her phone each time she pressed a key. Her finger hit send.

"What have you asked him, Guv?" Bryant said as three pairs of eyes fell on her.

"I've asked the bastard for proof of life."

CHAPTER 37

Charlie nibbled away at the hair grip she'd taken from Amy's fringe.

As she looked to her left she caught Amy's hand travelling down her forearm.

"Stop scratching, Ames," she whispered.

Since that man had visited them the night before they had spoken only in whispers. Charlie wasn't sure why but it just felt right.

"I can't stop," Amy breathed, but put her hand under her knee.

Charlie knew she couldn't help it. It was what Amy always did when she got nervous. Charlie had first seen her do it before a spelling test when they'd been six years old.

"I still don't understand what you're doing," Amy whispered beside her.

Finally, the plastic covering the wire hair grip dropped off in Charlie's mouth, leaving a thin, sharp piece of metal.

Charlie scooted towards the wall and moved her backpack out of the way. She rubbed the point of the metal against the brick. After a few movements a scratch mark began to appear.

She turned to her friend. "The last time he came he took away some of the rubbish. I was trying to keep count of how many sandwiches we've had. It might help us work out how long we've been down here."

Amy scratched again. This was one long scratch.

"Amy, I need you to remember what sandwiches we've had. Your memory is really good, so can you tell me?"

Amy's hand became busy as she started to count on her fingers.

"There was a cheese one and a ham one and another cheese."

Amy paused for a minute. Yes, those were the ones Charlie could recall, even though they had all been dry and tasteless.

"Oh...and the first one was egg. Do you remember the smell?"

Charlie smiled as Amy's nose puckered up. They had eaten them because they had been starving. She had forgotten about that one.

"Good one, Ames. So, that makes four meals they've given us, maybe two for each day," she said, scratching the marks into the wall. "I think it might be Monday night because—"

Charlie stopped mid-sentence as she heard the sound of footsteps on the stairs. It hadn't been long since the last stale sandwich. He wasn't coming to feed them again.

"Hello, my little pretties. Have you missed me?"

Charlie pulled Amy closer. Their limbs entwined as they tried to form a protective barrier around each other.

"It's okay, Ames, just try not to listen," she whispered.

She could hear her own voice trembling and the sickness was back in her tummy.

"Today I forced a man to suck my dick. Do you girlies know how disgusting that is?"

Charlie didn't know what it was but it didn't sound very nice. Amy's body began to tremble beside her.

"And then I punched his face in. Shall I tell you why? It's because I'm getting impatient. Who I really want to hurt is you."

Amy's whimpering reached ears that were trying to close down.

Charlie could feel the blood rushing around her body and pounding through her veins.

While he was on the other side of the door, talking, they were okay. They were safe.

But then the key turned in the lock.

She heard him laugh as the door opened and he stood, like a giant in the doorway smiling down at them.

A cruel glint lit the expression in his eyes as his gaze passed over the two of them. His next words chilled her to the bone.

"Little girlies, it's time to take off your clothes."

CHAPTER 38

Kim pushed aside the third pile of paperwork. All pages born of a tree that had died for a good cause, and had revealed absolutely nothing useful to her.

She'd read strategy after framework followed by outlines and objectives. All priorities that occupied the very early part of an investigation.

What she hadn't found were the clothes that went on the dummy. The physical actions that had occurred. Severely lacking were lines of enquiry, detailed interview notes, activity logs or even a cohesive logic.

It was almost twelve and not one word had passed between her and the team in the last hour. Every file in the room had been opened and pored over. Except one. The Dewain Wright file.

She pushed her chair back from the table, causing four tired heads to look her way.

"Okay, Bryant, Stace, get a couple of hours' rest. We'll take turns."

Stacey nodded and folded into the easy chair in the corner. Bryant pulled her vacated chair towards him and slipped it beneath his feet. He folded his arms and let his head fall to the side. Alison had been persuaded to return to her hotel room only an hour earlier.

Dawson glanced at them enviously and then nodded towards the door. "Guv, I just need to pop—"

"Kev, we're not at school. You don't need permission."

She pushed herself to her feet and stretched. Something between her shoulder blades snapped and released.

Had the roads been less icy she would have jumped onto the Ninja and gone for a burn to clear her head.

These night-time hours were her enemy on a case like this. Normally she dealt with dead bodies whose exposure to risk and harm was gone. They were no longer in danger. Charlie and Amy were still alive, she knew it. And it was up to her to make sure they stayed that way.

After the text message received earlier, Kim could only wonder at the hushed conversations taking place in the bedrooms upstairs.

Kim was expecting to see Dawson as the door began to open slowly, but instead Helen's head popped into the opening.

"Just to let you know I'm off now."

Shit, Kim had forgotten she was still there.

"Helen, you really—"

Her words were interrupted by a gentle but definite knock to the front door.

Kim frowned at Helen, who stepped back into the hallway. Kim rose and followed. Lucas stood at the door looking to her for confirmation.

Kim nodded and approached. Helen was one step behind.

As the door opened Kim adjusted her gaze down, her eyes coming to rest on a portly woman encased in a full-length jacket that diminished her height further. A thick woollen scarf had lapped itself around her neck. A round, lined face protruded from the layers of warmth beneath a red knitted hat.

This woman had to have taken a wrong turn.

"Are you a police officer?" the woman asked, looking wary.

Or maybe not.

Kim offered the slightest of nods.

The woman offered her hand as though it wasn't past midnight.
Kim ignored it and folded her arms.

The hand was retracted. "My name is Eloise Austen. I have
information."

"About what?" Kim snapped.

The case was not public knowledge. Outside of the house
Kim could count the number of people who knew on one hand.
With a finger to spare.

"Th...the...girls...the abduc—"

"Listen," Kim said, stepping forward. "I don't know how you
got your information or who the hell you are—"

"I know who she is," Helen said from behind her.

Kim looked to the liaison officer.

Helen's expression held distaste, as though she'd eaten something unpalatable but good manners prevented her from spitting
it out.

"She has a monthly show at the Civic Hall. She's a psychic."

"You have to be bloody kidding me?"

Helen shook her head. "Came around last time and managed
to get in the house. Traumatised the parents, saying all sorts of
things that—"

"No, you have to listen," the woman said, looking from one
to the other. "I know things. The girls...the girls...they're alive
but they're underground. They're cold...scared..."

"Oh, Jesus," Kim said, shaking her head. "Tell me something
I don't know." Her stomach felt their fear every single minute.

"There are secrets and lies and deceit and the number 278.
Remember the number 278. And he's not done yet," she said,
urgently.

Kim frowned. "Not done?"

"With the last one. He has plans...there is bitterness...
anger..."

"Come on, Eloise," Helen said, gently turning the woman around. "Time for you to go home now."

Eloise turned her head as Helen edged her forward. She tried to lock on to Kim's gaze.

"Please...you have to listen..."

"No, I really don't," Kim said, turning away.

Cranks and crackpots she did not need.

"He knows, Kim. He knows you couldn't save him..."

Kim's head snapped around. She walked back.

"What did you say? Who knows that?"

Eloise blinked rapidly. "He knows you tried and he loved you so—"

"Helen, get her out of my sight," Kim screamed.

"Look closer, Inspector, someone—"

"Come on, Eloise, it really is past your bedtime," Helen soothed, taking the woman by the arm.

Kim turned away but could still hear the voice behind her, calling something about a blue gate, but she didn't want to hear another word from that woman's mouth.

She strode back into the house and closed the door behind her.

"Who the hell was that?" Stephen Hanson growled from the middle of the staircase.

Great, someone else she didn't need.

"No one you need to worry about," Kim said, stepping away from the door.

"She said she had information," Stephen said, trying to look around her but the door was closed and Lucas had stepped to her side. Mr. Hanson was not going anywhere.

"Please go back to bed, Mr. Hanson."

"And do what?" he spat. "You don't really think anyone is sleeping up there, do you?"

Stephen's voice had risen and Kim thought that anyone who *had* managed to sleep probably wasn't any more.

"Mr. Hanson," she said, reducing her voice to a whisper, hoping he would follow suit. "Please go back upstairs and let me handle this investigation."

His eyes were cold and unyielding as he looked to Helen re-entering the house. "Just as long as you *are* handling it, Inspector."

She took a deep breath and headed for the kitchen wondering how the hell that woman had found out. She'd let Woody know in the morning that his end of the bucket had a leak.

"Sorry for the oversight, Helen. I thought you'd gone home," Kim said, filling the kettle. Instant would have to do for now.

Helen sat at the breakfast bar and rubbed her hands.

"Just tidying around after they finally went to bed. I'll take a nap on the sofa in a while."

Kim took a second mug from the cupboard.

"Milk and sugar?"

"Both," Helen said.

"How were they after the message?" Kim asked.

It took a special kind of person to be around that level of fear and despair without becoming absorbed by it. Family liaison officers were required to offer support, strength and encouragement without the emotional involvement and still maintain the presence of mind to capture anything that might benefit the investigation.

"The couples barely spoke after the text message. There was the odd exchange about cups of tea but it was like watching two tag teams retreat to their corners."

"And the psychic?" Kim asked.

"I know she's in the files somewhere. I wrote that report myself. I mean, it wasn't a lengthy document but perhaps I should have mentioned—"

Kim held up her hand. She realised she couldn't hold every failing of the last investigation against Helen. She'd had a specific role to play which had not included external investigation or the integrity of the case notes.

"I probably wouldn't have mentioned a visit from a psychic either," Kim said, giving the woman a break. There were few police officers who would assign value to the ramblings of a crank.

"Did anyone listen to her last time?"

"Not really. She offered nothing specific but managed to upset the parents a great deal. She kept grabbing the hand of Mrs. Cotton and saying she was sorry."

Kim frowned. "The mother of the child that didn't come back?"

Helen nodded and shuddered. "It was awful."

"You're not a believer of the supernatural?"

"I'm not a fan of anyone who profits from the needs of the vulnerable. Her stage shows focus on dead relatives."

"So, she's a medium?"

"A spiritualist, apparently." Helen smiled to herself. "But to answer your question about the supernatural. No, I'm not a believer. I was raised by my grandmother who was one of the strikers back in 1910."

"Really?" Kim asked.

It was well known that at that time the Cradley Heath female chain makers were some of the poorest in the country, earning less than the price of a loaf of bread per hour.

In August 1910 a group of women did the unthinkable and staged a strike. The move drew international attention to the town.

The ten-week protest resulted in the first recorded minimum wage.

"You didn't live through those times and come out the other side with a belief in anything you couldn't see for yourself. And my grandmother was no exception. Spare the rod and save the child." Helen's mouth was no longer smiling. "Were you raised to believe?" she asked.

Kim shook her head. She had barely been raised at all.

"Parents?" Helen asked.

"Dead," Kim lied. For all she knew, her father, whoever the hell he was, could have been, but her other parent, unfortunately, was not. Her mother still resided in Grantley Care, a secure psychiatric unit for the criminally insane.

Kim took a sip of coffee, eager to bring the conversation back to the present and away from her.

"Kids?" she asked Helen.

Helen shook her head regretfully.

"I always meant to, I suppose. But I just never got around to it. I loved my job and was damn good at it. I chose promotion at every opportunity. I made DCI, you know?"

Kim hid her surprise.

"But with the great restructure four years ago I was offered a choice." She opened her hands expressively. "I still had a mortgage, bills and no one to share them with so it wasn't really much of a choice at all. I took the training required and added the counselling and psychology courses myself. If I was going to help people then I had to understand how they would feel, and more importantly how they would act." She smiled apologetically. "I'm sorry, I'm taking too much of your—"

"Please, carry on," Kim said. There was a loneliness to the woman who spent her working life soaking up the misery of others.

"You just don't notice the years slip away. It's easier for the men. Having a family doesn't impede their career progression at all. For us women it does, however much the force talks of equality. Months of maternity leave add up. Not that there was ever anyone I had to make that choice for." She shrugged. "Never anyone that special. And now…"

"Do you regret it?" Kim asked.

Helen thought for a moment and shook her head. "No, they were my choices and I stand by them." She smiled. "This will most likely be my last major case. I've been retired under the A19 regulation."

Kim knew of the contentious regulation which allowed the police to force retirement on officers below chief officer rank after thirty years of service. It was a regulation brought out in times of austerity and had been used "in the general interests of efficiency" since 2010.

After so many years of service, many officers were ready to retire at fifty-five. Others were not.

"Did you appeal it?" Kim asked.

Helen shrugged. "Unsuccessfully." She drained her mug. "And on that note I'm going to put my head down for a bit."

Kim thanked her again for her help before filling a jug for the percolator. Sleep did not appear to be in her immediate future.

CHAPTER 39

Kim headed back to the war room and closed the door. Stacey's eyes flickered with rapid eye movement and a soft snore coming from the corner indicated Bryant was sound asleep.

Dawson rubbed his eyes and turned another page.

She observed him for a minute and then made her decision.

"Kev, shut the file a sec?" she said, reaching to the floor.

A look of resignation passed over his features. He was obviously too tired to search his brain for what he might have done wrong.

She placed the file on the table between them.

"Relax, Kev. I just want to talk to you about something."

He visibly deflated and glanced at the file.

"It's about the Dewain Wright case," Kim said.

His eyes scrunched slightly, showing just the hint of fine lines at the corners. "I thought we were done..."

"So did I, but it looks like I was wrong about something."

Dawson sat forward. He needed no clarification of the case. It had only ended a few days ago.

It wasn't the first gang-related death they had dealt with and it wouldn't be the last.

Birmingham was listed amongst the top four cities for having serious gang problems, alongside London, Manchester and Liverpool. In some areas of London and Manchester the gangs were becoming more of a cultural transmission of America's Crips and Bloods.

Notable gangs in the area included the Brummagem Boys, the Burger Bar Boys and The Johnsons. Some time ago a TV documentary had witnessed a truce following a bitter feud between the Burger Bar Boys and The Johnsons. Violent crime had fallen significantly in specific postcodes since.

The Hollytree Hoods was not a racial group. It was territorial. And while not in the same league as the Brummagem Boys, The Johnsons or the Burger Bar Boys, it still controlled all the prostitution and drug activity on the sprawling estate that encompassed approximately four thousand inhabitants.

"That kid got to you, didn't he?" Dawson asked.

Kim had finally left his bedside mid-morning on Saturday and by lunchtime he had been dead. Lyron, the gang leader, had been arrested two hours later, once the hospital CCTV showed him removing his mask in the car. The gang had not figured on a camera aimed directly at the parking barrier.

She nodded. "Open the file and check the first two reports."

He took out the two reports and read. The first was a sworn affidavit from Conroy Blunt, editor at the *Dudley Star*, confirming the time Tracy Frost's story had been filed, authorised and sent to print. The second was the death certificate of Dewain Wright.

Dawson looked from one to the other and then back at her. Realisation dawned on his features. "It wasn't her. It wasn't Tracy Frost. He was already dead by the time it hit the shelves."

She nodded. "Make no mistake, she was breaking the story that he was still alive, but the gang already knew."

With no mother and three sisters, Dewain had fallen victim to the seduction technique most often used by the Hollytree Gang.

They held regular parties, inviting all the estate kids as young as twelve and thirteen. They made promises of money, sex, excitement. Everything an adolescent could want.

If the parties didn't work, there were other methods. A common one was to convince kids it was a club or group of friends protecting themselves against the enemy. They identified latchkey kids and told them they weren't loved.

Other kids had been initiated through obligation. The gang would do them a favour, pay a bill, beat somebody up and then demand loyalty as payback.

And, of course, there was the physical beatings or threatening members of the family to get what they wanted.

Getting into a gang was the easy part. Getting out, not so much.

Dawson ran his hand through his hair. "Shit."

"So, Kev, what does that mean?"

"That the person who told the gang is out there, somewhere. Jesus, Guv, we need to find out who it is. That kid died."

Kim smiled. Exactly the response she'd hoped for in the young sergeant. That need to know, to solve it, to finish it.

"Get to it then, Kev. Find out who it was."

He snorted. "You're joking? You're passing this to me?"

Kim nodded. "Take the file. You're out and about. On your travels see what you can find. I won't interfere but just keep me updated."

He sat up straight. "I won't let you down, Guv."

She nodded towards the door. "There's a sofa going spare in the lounge. Go get some rest."

Dawson did as he was told but he took the folder with him.

Kim's gaze travelled up to the picture of Charlie and Amy. Her tired eyes appeared to deceive her as two different faces superimposed themselves onto the photo. Two other children; a girl and a boy; much younger than Charlie and Amy.

Her vision blurred and she blinked the image away.

She had to bring those girls home.

Both of them.

CHAPTER 40

"Okay, guys, I know that wasn't the best night's sleep but let's do a quick catch-up before Alison offers us some insight. I'll go first," Kim said, casting her eyes around the room.

They were all freshened up, ready and wide awake. Almost. But it was the second full day of the investigation and new energy was required.

"Had a visitor late last night, a woman called Eloise Hunter. Claims to be a psychic or medium or something. Stace, I want you to do some digging because she turned up last time."

"Did you have a nice chat?" Bryant asked.

"Not exactly," Kim said.

He grunted. "If she was any good she should have seen that coming."

Kim ignored him. "Stace, anything from you?"

"Nothing obvious in the backgrounds of the families, boss. Karen was off grid for a couple of years but no police record. Still working on it but the Hansons' finances are wrapped up tighter than Kev's wallet."

"Keep at it," Kim instructed. "Anything else?"

"Still nothing from the phone companies but I've got the address of the girl that didn't come back. The other is proving a bit more difficult."

"Probably moved house and changed their name but keep on it. Kev, you know what you're doing."

"Got it, Guv," he said.

"Excuse me, Marm," Helen said from the doorway. "There's a Matt Ward at the door. Says you're expecting him."

"Show him through, Helen. Thanks."

She waited for the door to close. "Oh, fabulous, our second expert is here to assist us." She glanced at Alison. "No offence."

That brought the total number of occupants to four parents, four detectives, two experts, one door guard and a liaison officer. Kim was grateful for the size of the house and its distance from the neighbours. The activity that was resembling rush hour at New Street station would have been difficult to hide in a three-bed semi.

The man who appeared at the door was dour and unsmiling.

He wore plain black trousers and a light blue shirt. His top button was open, she noticed, as he unravelled a grey scarf from around his neck. A heavy black overcoat had already been removed.

Kim guessed him to be late thirties, although the frown added a further ten miserable years to him.

She waved him in, stood and introduced herself and her team. "And this is Consulting Behaviourist Alison Lowe."

Matt offered curt nods at no one in particular as he edged into the room.

Kim sat and pointed to the chair on the opposite side of the dining table.

He traversed the piles of paperwork scattered on the floor, moving with the ease of an athlete at rest. His hair was dark but showed a hint of grey at the temples. The skin that was visible was tanned to a warm golden brown.

"Matt Ward, trained negotiator, just got off a fourteen-hour flight. What do we have?"

Kim raised one eyebrow at his rudeness. She opened her mouth, unsure what was to escape, but Stacey stood quickly.

"Coffee, Matt?"

He offered a change in expression as he turned towards Stacey. Kim wouldn't have characterised it as a smile but perhaps a lower grade frown.

"Short of a double whisky, coffee will do."

Bryant coughed as Matt turned back towards Kim.

She appreciated the direct approach but a modicum of manners would have gone a long way.

She outlined the events in short factual form and ended at the receipt of the third text message and her request for proof of life.

Matt stood to read the printout of the message that had been placed beneath the two shorter ones on the wipe board.

"Hmmm..." he said, re-taking his seat.

He had not once glanced at the photo of the girls.

"Ever come across anything like this before?" she asked.

He shook his head. "When I have something useful to say, I will. Until then I would request you make no further contact with the kidnappers. That's now my call."

Kim opened her mouth to argue but changed her mind. An argument was not going to get these girls back.

The old adage of having only one chance to make a first impression had never been truer. This man was obviously rude, arrogant and obnoxious and she doubted very much that she would ever change her mind.

"Okay, Alison, you're up," she said, glancing across the table.

The behaviourist stood and manoeuvred the easel into position.

Kim stole a glance at their most recent addition, who stared over the top of her head.

She really must remember to ring Woody and thank him for sending such a cold, emotionless present.

Bryant leaned towards her. "Like looking in a mirror, eh?" he whispered.

"Bryant, I suggest you close your damn mouth before I—"

"You can't hurt me. There are witnesses," he smirked, moving out of earshot.

For that remark, she'd happily kill him and do the time.

CHAPTER 41

Alison stood to the side of the flip chart with a marker pen in her hand. "May I have your attention?" she asked, using her projective speaking voice more suited to an auditorium or classroom. Kim looked around. No, it was definitely still a dining room.

"Okay, a few basic facts first. I'm not going to tell you anyone's hair colour or shoe size and, although I know there are sceptics amongst us, past behaviour is still our best indicator of future actions."

Kim could swear that Alison had looked right at her as she'd said the word "sceptics."

"So, by identifying personality traits we can build that into a type which can then offer us a profile. I'm going to refer to our texter as Subject One and I'll deal with him first."

"Ahem," Kim said, consulting her notes. "Could we touch on Inga first? She is our known participant so an insight might be beneficial."

She caught the mild irritation that passed behind Alison's eyes. But Inga was their only identified lead.

Alison thought for a moment and then began tapping the pen into her palm as she spoke. Clearly her "thinking on the spot" tell.

"Caregivers involved with children, especially a single child, normally develop a surrogate mother–child relationship. They are present for many of the child's 'firsts,' so to speak. It builds a pseudo-maternal bond.

"Inga wasn't terminated by the Hanson family, she left of her own accord just two months ago, so we can deduce that she treated Amy well and took good care of her. She was persuaded into doing something against this bond by one of our kidnappers."

"Money?" Dawson asked.

Alison shook her head. "It's unlikely that she was motivated by payment. There are other ways to make money without endangering a child."

"Love?" Kim asked.

Alison nodded. "More than likely. Love is a difficult thing to compete with and money can't buy it..."

"But another kind of love can trump it?" Kim queried.

"Yes," Alison replied. "There's a possibility that Inga was seduced by one of our kidnappers and showered with love and affection, made to feel special, adored. That is a difficult love to compete with. Amy was always someone else's child. It's a step removed."

Kim made a note on her pad. The theory of love trumping love made sense to her but she just wasn't sure which one of their kidnappers would have possessed the warmth to do it.

"Carry on, Alison," Kim instructed. Interestingly the behaviourist had given her something to think about.

Alison threw back the cover of the oversized sketch pad. It was headed "Subject One" and held bullet points. Alison used the marker pen to point to them individually.

"We are clearly dealing with two kidnappers. Subject One, the texter, has already demonstrated his intelligence. He is likely to be cold and meticulous. He exercises extreme control as evidenced by his adherence to a plan. His text messages arrive on the hour, as though pre-planned. He has two young girls captive but is still able to follow a strategy and not rush. Others might wish to hurry things along. The texter does not. His communications are timed to get the most dramatic effect.

"He is reasonably well educated and makes no effort to hide that fact. Even by text message he uses correct grammar and punctuation.

"He enjoys the game. As he sends the message he will picture it being received. He will enjoy the thrill of being in control.

"He has limited capacity for variables and may well act out of character when stressed."

"How will he have reacted to Inga's failure to follow the plan?" Kim asked.

Alison offered her a frown for interrupting but Kim held her gaze.

"He will want her killed, silenced, removed from his view so that he doesn't have to think about the failure, but he certainly won't do it himself."

Kim nodded her understanding and permission to continue.

"If he's known to police it's likely to be for money crimes: embezzlement or white collar theft; a crime that would have tested his intelligence but with an end goal; a reward.

"He is primarily non-violent, which brings me to Subject Two."

"Hang on," Kim interrupted. "Why non-violent? You've already said that he could act out of character if the plan changes?"

Alison took in a deep breath before responding. "I said, primarily: meaning it is not his first course of action."

Kim pushed the point. "But he is capable, yes? I don't want anyone getting the wrong idea about what we're dealing with here."

Alison's gaze did not sweep the room and was directed only at her. "Okay, let me rephrase and say he is less likely to be violent than Subject Two."

Kim nodded her satisfaction.

Alison flicked the page over and pointed.

"From the limited information we have on the accomplice he is the polar opposite of his colleague. The level of damage inflicted on Bradley Evans's head and the photos of Inga's home point to a man who enjoys gratuitous violence. If death was the only motive for Bradley Evans—"

"Brad," Kim interrupted. "Please call him Brad." His name badge indicated that had been his preference.

"Okay, if the only motivation for the violence was death, there are much quicker ways than kicking a man's head around like a football. That was for our kidnapper's benefit. It exposed a higher level of risk but an elevated level of pleasure. The whole incident would have produced more noise than necessary. Brad Evans would have been—"

"Move on, please," Kim said, sharply.

She could feel Bryant's eyes on her. It was a scene neither of them needed to picture.

"Equally there was no real need to destroy everything in Inga's home. He smashed the furniture to pieces and didn't care if someone heard. He felt confident that no one would stop him and that is probably how he lives his life.

"At this point I have no way to tell the source of his rage but it isn't simply because Inga didn't follow the plan."

"What are the chances of negotiation with Subject One?" Kim asked.

"Negotiation will be challenging. It's unlikely you'll get him to speak on the phone and any text messages will need to be well phrased so you allow him to feel that his control is not being diminished or—"

"Thank you for your input and I'll certainly bear your observations in mind."

Matt's sentence was skilfully delivered with professionalism and a polite nod but Kim guessed he'd do it his own way, regardless of Alison's advice.

Kim looked at her own notes. There wasn't much she'd missed.

She stood. "There's something else," she said, simply.

Alison regarded her with a tolerant smile.

Kim continued. "Where's the glue?"

"Excuse me, Inspector?"

"The glue, Guv?" Bryant asked from behind.

She approached the flip chart and ripped off page one. She held it up next to page two.

Matt regarded her with interest.

"We have two extreme personalities here. Who's in charge? Every team, however small, has a leader, a more dominant personality. I'm not sure either of these can be a leader. Their personalities are too extreme. Violent versus non-violent. Methodical versus risk-taker.

"Imagine a see-saw. The seats operate at each end but in the middle is the anchor. It stops each end going too high or too low. I don't think these two personalities could co-exist without a third, an overriding force; an authority."

Alison shook her head. "I think it's obvious that the texter is in charge and Subject Two is the hired help. A clear hierarchy."

She shrugged and looked around the room.

"Except Subject Two is not just a goon," said Kim. "He managed to find Brad Evans, identify a man he'd never met, and kill him without being detected. Yes, he is violent and potentially unpredictable but he has a brain and is not going to be easily controlled."

She lifted the page on the flip chart. It was blank.

Kim tapped it with her finger. "I think you need to label up this one. And call it Subject Three."

CHAPTER 42

Elizabeth tied her hair into a ponytail. The shower she'd taken had been little more than a quick dunk.

Every activity held the promise of distracting her mind for just a minute or two. She craved the luxury of sleep where the images in her mind would be paused for just a while.

It had been uncomfortable enough living in someone else's house before last night, but after that last text message it was positively unbearable.

Since that text message, she had been trying to speak to Stephen. They needed to talk, discuss their options. They needed a plan.

She had wandered around the house until midnight, trying to track him down, but somehow in this vast house he had managed to outrun her.

She felt as though her whole family had disappeared. Her beautiful daughter was God only knew where, terrified. Her son was not with her and now her husband was avoiding her too. She was in the home of her best friend with whom she was now in competition for the lives of their children.

There were moments when Elizabeth had the uncontrollable urge to laugh. So ridiculous was the situation that for a moment she would convince herself that she was stuck in some kind of nightmare and that soon she would wake up in her home with her daughter, her son and her normal life.

And then she would realise that it wasn't a nightmare at all. This was her life and she couldn't now picture what had gone before.

She headed down the stairs and paused as she always did just outside the dining room. She had yet to hear anything but she lost nothing for trying.

The sound of plates being put away told her Karen was in the kitchen. Only yesterday they had been irrevocably bonded by this horror; experiencing what only another mother could comprehend. They had looked to each other for support and understanding—now they couldn't look at each other at all.

Elizabeth no longer knew how to speak to her friend. They were competitors in a sick, evil game.

She needed her husband now more than ever. She took a deep breath before moving to the doorway. Karen was standing over the sink.

"Have you seen…?"

A ping sounded to Karen's phone. Both she and Karen stared at it. Elizabeth had the urge to dive forward and grab the phone with both hands.

Karen lifted the phone and Elizabeth held her breath as Karen's eyes moved across the screen.

She frowned as she read it again, aloud.

> Search well for the gifts I have sent. Dig deep as you picture your child.

Karen looked to her for an answer. "What the…"

She stopped speaking as though she'd realised just who she was talking to.

Karen darted from the room with her phone, leaving Elizabeth numbed by a barrage of questions flooding her mind.

What the hell did the text message mean?

She took out her own mobile phone. There was no flashing light, there was no little envelope and there was certainly no message.

Why had the message only been sent to Karen?

And where the hell was her husband?

CHAPTER 43

"There's something here at the house," Kim said, after edging Karen gently from the room. "Subject One does not use words inappropriately. He said, 'I have sent,' which means there's something here somewhere."

Karen had taken her phone away but the words Kim had read were imprinted on her brain.

She stood at the head of the table. "It'll be outside. There's no way either of them could have got anything in the house." She looked around the room. "Bryant, Kev, Stacey, with me. Alison, help Helen keep the parents in the house." Her gaze fell on the newcomer. "Mr. Ward, please mind the shop. No one is to enter this room."

He nodded his understanding and Kim stepped out of the room, turned right and headed for the utility room and out into the back garden.

The early morning mist had turned into a miserable drizzle that quickly seeped through to the skin.

The area to search was the size of a football pitch. If she divided it into a four-way grid they could search more effectively.

An expanse of grass was divided into two equal sections by a brown barked path that halved the garden. One lawn held a swing set and a sandpit. The other lawn, a raised herb garden.

The entire perimeter was formed of old, gnarly oak trees. In front of them were a selection of storage containers for outdoor tools. To the right sat a play house before a decorative rockery.

On each side of the house was gravel, with bins and storage boxes dotted around.

Kim wiped the rain from around her eyes. "Okay, Stace, take the left side of the house. Kev, take the right. Bryant, take the right side of the garden and I'll take the left."

They all dispersed their separate ways, searching the ground as they went. Kim found nothing and reached the storage boxes just as the thin spots of rain began to fall thicker and harder.

"Guv, I've got a jacket," Stacey cried from between the trees.

"Place it at the corner of the house, away from the parents' view," she instructed. "There'll be more."

None of them were wearing outside clothes and the rain was soaking them to the skin.

She opened the lid of the first storage bin, which held a lawnmower and a strimmer. She picked both items out before ascertaining that it was all clear.

The second, at knee height, looked as though it held more garden tools. She opened the lid and lifted a leaf blower.

"I've got a pair of trousers here," Dawson shouted from around the side.

"Me too," Kim called, as she pulled the leggings from beneath the tool.

Bryant jogged over with a T-shirt that they both knew belonged to Amy. His light blue shirt was darkened with rain and had now melded to his skin.

"Guv..."

"I know, Bryant."

The same picture was forming in both their heads.

"A jumper in the play house," Stacey said, running back to the corner.

They all looked at the pile of clothes as a second jacket arrived with Dawson.

"How the hell did they manage to set up a bloody game of hide and seek without one person in this house seeing or hearing anything?" Kim asked, looking around.

She received no answer.

Kim counted the garments and mentally put them on each girl from what she'd seen in the CCTV. She surveyed the garden as a sickening thought occurred to her.

"Has anyone checked the rockery yet?" she asked, praying that someone said yes.

"I'll do it, boss," Dawson said as he sprinted over.

"That's everything we saw them wearing," Bryant observed, wiping the rain from his eyes.

Kim didn't respond. She was too busy watching the slump of Dawson's shoulders. His back was still as his gaze locked on the bricks. The three of them stood waiting for their colleague.

"Damn it," she said, as the rage began to build inside her. She knew what he had found.

He walked slowly back to where they stood and opened his hands. In them were two pairs of panties.

They stared at the clothes, fully aware of the message they'd been sent.

Charlie and Amy were now totally naked.

CHAPTER 44

Inga felt defeated. Her body ached and she was sure it was only being held together by the grime.

She couldn't remember when she'd last showered. A quick freshen up in the public toilets had left her feeling dirtier than when she entered.

Recalling anything normal that had happened before Sunday was becoming a struggle. She only knew it was Tuesday because she'd heard someone say so.

One day, which she felt almost sure was yesterday, she had walked for miles, pausing only to buy a cheap cup of tea at a market stall, giving her licence to sit and rest. Inga knew that her appearance would prevent even that small luxury today. Her hair was matted despite trying to use her fingers as a makeshift comb. There were dirt marks on her face that could not be shifted by water alone. Her yellow jeans were smattered with the stains of her recent journey.

The overwhelming urge to cry engulfed her, yet the tears wouldn't come.

Everywhere she looked she saw Symes; shorter, fatter, taller... but every male was him until they had passed her by.

They would never forgive her for messing up the plan. She was supposed to be admitted to hospital and wait for her "husband" to collect her. She was then to be taken to the safe house to take care of the girls until the exchange. But she couldn't do it. Amy would have known that Inga was embroiled in the events that had terrified both her and Charlie. And if Amy hadn't worked it out, Charlie would have. And then Inga would have been forced to watch Amy's relief and happiness change to disbelief and mistrust. She knew the child would hate her forever.

Inga felt as though her entire life had happened in the last few days. There was no longer a moment she had lived without fear. There was no movement without trembling.

She had no doubt of what would happen if she stopped running. She had met Symes only once and that had been enough. There had been a detachment in his demeanour that had reminded her of a robot.

He had offered her a smile that held menace, not warmth, as though he knew something she did not. As his eyes had travelled around the café, she had heard one knuckle at a time crack beneath the table.

She felt those hands had been wanting to encircle themselves around her throat from the second they'd met. But while she had been useful the hands had been tied. And now she was no longer useful. Now she was a threat, a loose end, and any protection was gone.

The fear rolled around her empty stomach. If Symes caught her, death would be a welcome gift. This was not a man to offer her mercy. He would torture her and the person she had trusted would do nothing to help.

She had been on her own for many years, but never had she felt so alone.

Her body was battered and her mind was breaking.

Inga knew what she had to do.

CHAPTER 45

Will felt the urge to strike out.

Ever since he could remember, he had been prone to severe blackouts if the order in his brain was disturbed.

When things went to plan his mind remained calm, composed. There was a gentle rhythm that played in the background but an unexpected event released the orchestra in his head. Instruments banged out of time, strings screeched painfully, bringing a cacophony of noise from which he couldn't escape.

He pushed back his chair. The sound of the metal legs scraping on the stone floor reached into the very centre of him like a knife. He paced from one end of the room to the other.

Ten paces each way. Four lengths of the room and the noise began to recede. Another six lengths put more distance between his conscious mind and the noise within.

He should never have agreed to the involvement of other people. He detested being told what to do. He'd always worked better alone.

It was he who had chosen the families, he who had researched their businesses. Did people not realise just how many weeks it had taken to find the right candidates; wealthy families that could be set in competition and then ripped apart?

The first time should have worked. It would have worked if not for an event completely beyond his control.

Symes had been his choice to bring on board. He knew that he'd needed a skill that the man possessed but he'd accepted other help and it was now biting him on the arse.

The source of his stress was not having complete control and it was beginning to piss him off. There were too many people involved.

As a middle child, the natural groupings of his siblings had always excluded him. He was the barrier between the oldest and the youngest and consequently belonged nowhere. He was the butt of their jokes and the bag for their punch. And he had taken it because he had nowhere to turn. His mother said "Boys will be boys."

He had taken solace in planning his revenge. That's where he had found his comfort, his release—as Larry, his brother and most vicious tormentor, had discovered.

He and Symes were more alike than he liked to admit. He knew that as a young boy Symes had been beaten by his army father after being abandoned by a mother to a cruel and unfeeling man.

Although he had been surrounded by his brothers, he had felt as alone as Symes. Both had found escape in revenge, him in psychological torturing, and Symes in the physical suffering of others.

He didn't like Symes, but he understood him.

Five more steps, and the tension in his body began to dissipate.

The clothes had been sent exactly when they were supposed to be. It was part of the plan and it had been executed perfectly. The fact that the parents now had to picture their little girls naked was their early call to action. Empty out the bank accounts.

But some bitch was demanding proof of life. He had decided to ignore the text. Never had they considered responding to any message that was not from the parents.

That had been the plan.

And now he had to change the plan.

Because The Boss said so.

CHAPTER 46

"Satnav says we're 1.2 miles away, Guv," Bryant said, beside her.

She took a sharp left through a residential estate. This was a shortcut that knocked off almost half the distance.

Bryant held the satnav up to his face and spoke to it. "Don't be offended, she doesn't listen to anyone."

Kim ignored him.

"So, was that your proof of life, Guv?" Bryant said as she approached a tiny traffic island. There was no way around it.

"No, that was planned all along and it doesn't prove they're alive," she said, driving straight over the top of it. "This was a prompt to the parents. He wanted them to go looking. He wanted them to find the clothes. He wanted them to imagine them naked."

"Well, that backfired slightly. And why only send it to one parent?"

"Games, Bryant. Our Subject One enjoys the psychological element of it all. He wants to wring every last ounce of misery out of this sick game."

"Aah, well, he didn't quite bargain on you, did he?"

She hoped not. The clothes had been bundled into a bag and spirited away by Dawson to forensics. There was a slim chance that something would be found but for use in court they were hopeless. They had been rolled around in the dirt, grass and goodness knows what else.

"Do you think you should have told them the truth?" Bryant, her external conscience, asked.

It was the first time she'd lied to the parents and she hoped it would be the last, but she wouldn't bet Barney's next meal on it.

She had told them they had found only the jackets and that had been traumatic enough. They did not need to know the rest. Stephen had tried to insist on identifying Amy's coat, just to be sure. But Dawson had already left. Kim had explained to Stephen that she'd been able to confirm from the CCTV.

"What's to gain?" she asked. "The pictures in their minds are horrific enough as it is."

Kim was saved any further explanation as she spotted the door number she sought. She parked the car quickly and knocked.

Time had not been kind to the woman that answered.

Kim knew Jenny Cotton was thirty-six years old and the first thirty-five years of her life had undoubtedly been kinder than the last one.

The light brown hair was tied back in a messy ponytail, exposing premature greying at the temples. Faint lines were visible around a downturned mouth.

"Detectives Stone and Bryant, Mrs. Cotton. Could we have a word?"

The tired eyes registered a stab of hope.

Kim shook her head. "There's no news on Suzie," she said, quickly, to dispel any false hopes immediately.

The case of Suzie Cotton would remain open until they brought her home.

Mrs. Cotton stepped aside, allowing them to enter.

Kim moved through the house to a small kitchen-diner that spanned the width of the property. Immediately Kim saw the absence of life. The room was devoid of character or personality.

It was clean and functional and looked out on to a small garden covered in grey slabs. There was no tree, flower or plant pot.

They had stumbled into a life on pause.

Jenny Cotton stood in the doorway. The light jeans she wore were loose on a size-eight frame. The grey sweatshirt was baggy at the neck and the shoulder seams rested halfway down her upper arms. Flip-flops graced her feet.

Kim sensed that it was a triumph that Jenny managed to dress at all.

Kim suddenly hated the coldness of the visit. She had nothing to offer the woman in relation to the absence of her own daughter, yet Kim wished to glean information, even if it meant forcing the woman to remember the most horrific time of her life.

But right now she had two missing girls and that was Kim's priority. Every day she loved the job she did, but some days she didn't like it all that much.

"Mrs. Cotton, I understand this might be difficult but we need to ask you some questions about what happened last year…"

Intelligent eyes speared her. "Why?"

"Mrs. Cotton, I can't—"

"Of course you can't tell me anything," she spat bitterly. "It's not like I have any right to know, is it?"

Kim remained silent for a moment. This woman was entitled to her anger. Her child had not come home. She couldn't share any details of the current investigation but when Kim's gaze met the sad, desolate eyes facing her she hoped that Jenny Cotton would understand.

There was a sharp intake of breath before the woman closed her eyes and pursed her lips.

She understood.

"Ask me anything you like but please don't pretend to understand. Because you can't."

"You're right, I can't," Kim agreed, softly. "But if you could talk us through your own experience from that first day I'd be grateful."

Jenny Cotton nodded as she sat at a round wooden dining table, indicating that they do the same.

"Don't expect me to remember what happened on what day because I can't. It's all now a blur of activity, inactivity and tears. All I know for certain is that they both disappeared on Monday morning and Emily was found on Wednesday afternoon. God, it seems so much longer than two days."

Kim hated every moment of what she was having to put this woman through but if she was dealing with the same crew this time the information was invaluable. Investigating the first attempt could offer crucial clues. An MO became refined over time. Elements were perfected, lessons learned. Identifying possible mistakes the first time around could offer insight.

"Suzie was taken from the shop halfway between our home and the school. Emily was grabbed fifty metres from her home. I received a text message at eleven and so did Julia."

"Do you have any idea how the girls were identified?"

She nodded. "They did a radio appeal together for Children in Need. They'd raised over five hundred pounds by washing cars. My husband was quoted in the article. He owned a limousine hire service, well, he still does as far as I'm aware."

She smiled sadly. "It's another life. It feels like a past life. Julia's husband, Alan, owned a string of estate agencies. It was not a fair fight.

"I called the police immediately and they interviewed us both at my house. We were all such good friends, so close. Spent almost every weekend together; took holidays together.

"Julia and I held on to each other for dear life. Until the third text message."

"Were you advised not to make contact with the kidnappers?" Kim asked.

"Yes."

"And did you?"

"Detective, if you had children you wouldn't even ask that question. Of course we did.

"Suddenly, everywhere you looked people were trying to hide the private conversations that were going on. Even the police stood in corners whispering."

"When was the deadline?" Kim asked.

"Wednesday afternoon."

Barely more than forty-eight hours after the abduction, Kim noted. They were an hour away from that exact same marker.

"What did you do?"

"We sent an offer. It was everything we could get together: savings, second mortgages, help from family. We received an immediate response that the others had offered more.

"Offers went back and forth until Wednesday morning. We were offering amounts we had no chance of getting but when you're in an auction for the life of your child there is no other choice."

Kim sat forward. There was a cruelty to this situation that repelled her. In a normal ransom situation there were all kinds of emotions but this trade-off strategy offered the parents an element of control: that they could influence the outcome if they could just get enough money together. And if they couldn't...

"When Suzie didn't come home it destroyed me. I lost everything. I couldn't look at my husband because all I could think was that if he'd had a better job we would have got our daughter back."

Kim allowed the woman to talk. It was the least she could do.

"And people grieve at different rates. The first time I heard Pete laugh afterwards the last few feelings I had for him died. I understand that the body reacts and that defence mechanisms kick in, but mine hadn't."

And Kim suspected she was still waiting. This woman was a shadow, existing through time. She had not found a way forward but those around her had.

Kim had a sudden thought. "Mrs. Cotton, do you still have the mobile phone?"

Jenny Cotton moved back her chair and walked to the kettle. "No, Inspector, your lot took it as evidence."

Kim looked at Bryant. He made a note. If the phones were still in evidence there may be something they could use.

Mrs. Cotton stared out of the window; the water overflowing out of the spout of the kettle.

"I used to dream of holidays and perhaps another child." She paused, her hand hovering above the running faucet. "And now all I dream of is being able to bury my daughter."

She turned and fixed Kim with a hard stare. "Can you help me with that, Detective Inspector?"

Kim held the gaze but said nothing. She would not make promises she didn't think she could keep.

"Mrs. Cotton, what do you think prompted the early release of Emily?"

"I'd have thought that was perfectly clear. Julia and Alan paid the ransom."

CHAPTER 47

Kim's finger had pressed the call button before she'd reached the car.

"Stace, work harder on tracking down the Billingham family. They may be far more important than we thought."

"Already started looking, Guv," Stacey answered. "But this is a family that don't want to be found."

Kim was not surprised. "Keep on it, Stace. We're not sure but it's possible they paid the ransom."

She heard the intake of breath on the other end.

"There's nothing in the files to indicate…"

"There's nothing in the files to indicate much of anything, Stace."

"On it, Guv."

Kim ended the call. "So far, we've assumed the crew got panicked because the news broke in the media. We never considered that one of the families actually paid."

Bryant nodded. "And if they did then they had some further contact with the kidnappers: an instruction, a drop point, something."

As horrific as the thought was, Kim had to consider that the actions of the other family had resulted in the death of Suzie Cotton.

CHAPTER 48

Symes smiled. Nothing could spoil his mood today. He had a lead on the loose end that would very soon be tied up.

Yeah, he could go running around the area, chasing after Inga, expending pointless energy re-treading her steps. Or he could remain where he was and wait for her to come to him. And she would.

The stupid bitch had been on the run for almost forty-eight hours. She would be tired, dirty and scared out of her fucking mind.

Her body would be exhausted by the constant moving to avoid danger. Her mind would be drained of rational thought. Desire for self-preservation would be running low.

To catch her was to understand fear.

After two tours of Afghanistan, Symes knew the choices prompted by deep fear. It was a fear that didn't live in the everyday world. It only existed when you were frightened for your life.

Before a bungee jump, fear surged around the body mixed with excitement and adrenaline. But real fear left no room for any other emotion. It worked in from the skin and burrowed until it reached the bone.

It didn't become a part of you. It *became* you. Every breath, every glance, every movement was filled with fear and no amount of breathing exercises would make it go away.

In the army that level of fear was accepted, daily, but Symes had chosen to trick his subconscious. Rather than spend each day trying to live, he'd spent a minute each morning preparing to die.

Every day of his tours he had convinced himself this was his day to die. Every morning he had pictured his own death and every night was thankful to be brushing his teeth.

If Inga feared both himself and the police, it was only a case of what she feared least. And Symes already had that answer worked out.

He smiled and cracked his knuckles.

CHAPTER 49

Inga put one foot in front of the other and hoped for the best. The fear inside was gnawing away at her flesh. Everywhere she looked, people were staring at her. Every male she saw was either Will or Symes. Every shadow had been placed strategically to terrorise her.

The whole world was closing in. Her surroundings were a mass of right angles and dangerous shapes, ready to pounce at any second.

The last couple of days had been a lifetime. She couldn't recall the weeks, months and years that had come before. She couldn't remember a time when every cell of her being wasn't weighted down with fear.

Menace lived everywhere.

Although she'd been on the run for forty-eight hours, these last few moments felt the most hazardous.

Her target was no more than a hundred feet away. She could see it. All that lay between her and sanity was a surging lunchtime crowd, a pelican crossing and a busy crossroads.

She allowed the rushing throng to nudge and push her across the road.

Seventy feet; she didn't take her eyes from the building for fear it would disappear.

She would tell them everything. She would start with what she'd done and then take them to the girls. They would be safely home by tea time; back with their families and she would happily take her punishment.

Thirty feet away she stumbled over a raised kerbstone. She managed to right herself. A couple of males sniggered behind her.

She didn't care. Another twenty feet and she would laugh along with them.

The safety of a police cell called out to her. Whatever her punishment, she was ready to accept it. Nothing could be worse than this.

Five feet away from the entrance, her body began to relax.

The hand on the back of her neck was strong and forceful. It turned her away from the door to the police station that had been almost in touching distance.

"Nice try, yer little bitch, but not quite."

Inga felt herself being carried along by his grip. Her feet were barely touching the ground.

"If you make one sound I'll slit your throat right here."

Inga couldn't speak as she felt the muscly arm land around her shoulders. She tried to scream but the moisture had been sucked from her mouth.

Symes used her stunned silence to shepherd her into an alleyway behind the police station.

She had been so close.

To onlookers it would look like a loving embrace. Only they couldn't feel the strength of the fingers crushing the bones in her shoulder or the fact her feet were barely touching the ground.

The noise of the high street died in her ears.

"We're just gonna go and have a little chat; get yer head straight."

"No, no," she cried, trying to get her feet to land on the ground.

She summoned her last reserve of energy to flail her arms. His grip moved to her neck. The pain seared up into her head. She knew he was capable of breaking it with one move.

"Please...don't...hurt..."

"Yer shoulda thought about that before yer did what yer did."

Inga wasn't too proud to beg. It was now her only chance to live.

"Symes, I'm sorry. I shouldn't have...I just got...scared..."

He chuckled as he opened the door of the van. "Not as scared as you're gonna get."

He slammed the door closed and sprinted to the other side. He pressed a button that locked both doors.

Inga fought the urge to cry. Suddenly the moments she had left were precious. She knew she was going to die and only one thing mattered now.

"The girls?"

He turned to her. His eyes were alive with excitement, the anticipation was shaping his mouth. His gaze was almost trance-like. Every inch of him was in a heightened state, waiting to take her life.

"The g-girls," she stammered.

He threw back his head and laughed. "Because of you, they're dead."

CHAPTER 50

There was an eerie silence to Hollytree as Dawson parked the car in front of the row of shops that marked the entrance to the sprawling estate.

It was commonly known that once beyond the boundary of the shops, you were "in" the estate. Although it was like entering another country, it wasn't a passport that ensured safe passage, but rather an ASBO, prison stretch or possession of illegal substances.

Many other council estates in the Black Country were cleaner, healthier and happier because of Hollytree.

Each community breathed a sigh of relief as a problem family was evicted, but they had to go somewhere and it was never a good idea to put them all together. The result was a gang-ruled community that operated independently of any local authorities.

Dawson acknowledged the irony that Dewain Wright had lived in a flat above one of the shops. At the edge of the estate. Closest to getting out. It's what the poor kid had been trying to do.

Gang culture was not new to Dawson. He understood it better than he would care to admit, but not on the level of Hollytree.

As a child he'd been weighty. There was no underlying hormonal imbalance or obscure medical condition. His excess weight was simply the result of a single, working mother who relied a little too heavily on the ease of the frying pan.

By the time Dawson was fifteen he would have done anything to belong to a group, any group. And he almost had.

There was a day in his teens that still incited a shameful blush to his cheeks and it always would. But it was a day he'd never forgotten.

When he'd turned sixteen he'd enrolled in a gym, prepared all his own food and watched his saturated fats. He would never go back there again.

Dawson accessed the properties using a stairwell at the rear. Although classed as flats the properties were split over two levels. The terrace of each dwelling was separated by a single metal railing and looked on to a maze of rented garages, very few of which were used for storing cars.

He negotiated the outside space that was littered with two rusty barbecues and a collection of mismatched patio chairs. A discarded doll pram sat to the right of the door.

He knocked twice and instantly saw a form darken the patterned glass.

The door was opened by a girl Dawson guessed to be in her late teens. From the photos he knew that he was looking at Dewain's older sister, Shona. Her hair fell in tight, glossy curls around an attractive face that was scowling at him.

"Whattdya want?" she asked, having obviously decided he wasn't welcome.

"Detective Sergeant Dawson," he said, showing his card. Her eyes never left his face. He'd seen the quality of fake ID cards that circulated around Hollytree and most of them looked more authentic than his own.

"May I speak with your father?"

"What for?" she asked.

"It's about your brother," he said, patiently. As irritating as her attitude was, this family had suffered a loss and the police force had failed to prevent it. "There have been developments."

"What, he ain't dead no more?"

"Is your father home, Shona?" he asked, firmly.

"Hang on, I'll check," she said, closing the door in his face. These flats consisted of two bedrooms, a lounge, a kitchen and a toilet. He suspected she knew if he was at home.

A few seconds later the door opened.

Dawson looked up into the face of Vin Wright. The expression was neither pleasant nor hostile. Just set.

"What're you wanting, son?"

Being called "son" narked Dawson. His own father hadn't called him that, not even the night he left to find himself in the Scottish Highlands. For all Dawson knew he was still looking.

But that wasn't the only reason he disliked it. He was a police officer, a member of CID and he was not this man's son.

"Mr. Wright, I need to inform you of a development regarding Dewain. May I come in?"

Vin Wright hesitated before taking a step back.

Dawson knew there was no Mrs. Wright and hadn't been for twelve years, since her death due to complications during the birth of their fourth child.

Dawson stepped into a narrow galley kitchen where Shona was busy placing jars and packets back into the cupboard. A roll of plastic food bags lay on the side. Clearing the debris from the packed lunches for his younger two daughters, Dawson guessed.

A collection of literature displaying headstones and flowers was scattered in front of the kettle. This man was planning the burial of his son.

Vin remained in the doorway, keeping the discussion confined to the small space. Dawson suspected he was not staying long.

And that was okay, because he did not want to prolong the pain of this man for a moment longer than he needed to.

"Mr. Wright, it wasn't the reporter who leaked the fact your son was still alive."

A plate clattered into the sink, causing both Dawson and Vin to look towards Shona. She didn't turn immediately but continued to stare at the object that had slipped from her grip.

Vin's eyes remained on her for a few seconds before turning back to Dawson.

"I don't understand. It was obvious…"

"The times don't match. We have confirmation that the newspapers were only just leaving the printers by Dewain's time of death. Everything happened so quickly we assumed…"

Dawson allowed his voice to trail away as he realised a note of apology had crept in.

Vin heard it too. His eyes held no accusation, just a deep well of sadness. "We all did, son."

"Which means that someone else leaked it."

Vin nodded his comprehension. He'd already worked that out.

"I need to ask you, who other than family members knew that Dewain was still alive?"

Vin rubbed the short, wiry hair on his head. "I don't know, it's all just a blur. This time last week my son was…It all happened so quickly. I got a phone call at work. I called the kids and…"

"Lauren," Shona said, quietly.

Dawson waited. She finally turned.

"We called Lauren. She is…was Dewain's girlfriend. I left her a message but she never called me back." She looked to her father. "Remember, Dad, she never even turned up at the hospital?"

Dawson felt the stirrings of excitement in his stomach. The only call the police had made was to Dewain's next of kin. He knew that they had been instructed not to tell anyone that the boy was still alive until his condition stabilised.

"Do you know where I can find…?"

"I'll write it down," Shona offered, almost running out of the room.

Dawson turned to Vin whose gaze had followed his oldest daughter out of the room.

"Any bother with the gang since Dewain died?"

He shook his head. "Since you lot arrested Lyron for the murder, Kai stepped up. He's not as bad as Lyron. I think they're under instruction to leave us alone."

Dawson doubted that somehow. One death in the family at the hands of the gang didn't keep his three daughters safe. Gangs didn't work that way. Vin Wright would be watching over his girls until the second they were free from the Hollytree estate.

Shona returned to the kitchen and thrust a piece of paper into his hand. "This is where she lives."

"Thank you, I appreciate—"

His words were cut off by the sound of his mobile ringing in his ears.

"Excuse me," Dawson said, turning away.

It was dispatch.

"Finally, I locate a detective," offered the voice at the other end. "Can't get your boss or DS Bryant either. So, I'll have to pass it to you."

He knew he was third out of four on the food chain of their team but he hated being reminded of it.

"Hang on," he said, slipping his palm over the microphone. He turned to Vin Wright. "Thank you for your time and I promise I'll be in touch."

Vin nodded sadly and opened the door for Dawson to step through.

"What's up?" he asked the control room as he stepped around the garden debris.

He stopped dead as the voice uttered the words he'd ached to hear for the last six years.

"We have a dead body and, until we can get hold of your boss, it looks like you're it."

Finally, however briefly, he was the Officer in Charge.

CHAPTER 51

"Go ahead, Kev," Kim said, answering the call.

"Boss, I'm six feet away from the body of a female in her mid-twenties and I don't know if this is our—"

"What colour trousers?"

"Err...yellow."

"That's her," Kim growled, closing her eyes.

She listened as Dawson gave her the details.

"On our way," she said, ending the call.

She turned to Bryant. "We're too bloody late."

After what she'd seen on the CCTV, Kim had no personal feelings towards the woman one way or another. However, Inga had been their only solid lead.

She had been known to both girls, especially Amy. But Inga had betrayed them in the worst way. She had now paid with her life and, although Kim would have preferred to see the woman squirm on the witness stand, she couldn't muster any sympathy for her death.

"Maybe she didn't have a choice, Guv," Bryant offered.

She appreciated his charitable spirit but she couldn't agree.

"There's always a bloody choice. She was no stranger to these kids and still she stitched them up."

"Something made her run, though. Maybe her conscience—"

"Bryant, grow up," she snapped. Just occasionally his optimism got right up her nose. "If it was her conscience, then she'd have continued with the plan and got the girls away at the earliest opportunity. What she did came from self-preservation. She got scared."

"And now she's dead," Bryant said, as though it meant something; that the slate was clean. For Kim it wasn't. Because Amy and Charlie had been subjected to at best a terrifying ordeal, and at worst, a horrific death.

"Bryant, do me a favour and just drive."

Nope, her tear ducts were well and truly dry.

CHAPTER 52

Kim jumped out at the cordon tape, flashed her badge and entered the crime scene. The narrow alley ran between a supermarket and a hardware store on the edge of Brierley Hill High Street.

Dawson stood in her way. His face was drained of colour.

"Boss, it's a mess in there."

"I'm a big girl, Kev," she snapped, pushing past him.

"Ah, Inspector, I thought I heard your soft, warm tone."

Keats was the resident pathologist who just about reached her shoulder. All the hair from his head appeared to have dropped to the lower half of his face in a tidy moustache and a pointy beard.

She took the blue latex gloves he offered that matched his own.

"Keats, trust me when I say I'm not in the mood."

"Oh, dear, has Bryant—"

"Keats, take it from me," said Bryant, appearing beside her. "She really ain't in the mood."

Kim was already assessing the scene before her. She stepped around a forensic photographer to get a better look.

The body appeared to have been placed at an impossible angle. Kim was reminded of the white tape figures used at murder mystery weekends to depict the victim.

The right arm was raised above the head but the wrist pointed the wrong way. The left arm lay to the side of the torso. The shoulder appeared much lower and the hand was facing up.

Inga's face was bloated and swollen. The left eye was obscured completely by flesh that had expanded from her cheek and her forehead. Her right eye stared up to the sky. A trail of blood travelled from the middle of her face to the bottom of her chin. Kim guessed a broken nose was hiding in there somewhere.

Clumps of blonde hair were scattered around as though she were a shedding dog.

"Inspector," Keats said, indicating that she join him at the foot of the body.

Kim stepped out of the way as the photographer knelt to take close-up shots of her face.

"From my cursory exam we're looking at multiple broken bones. I'd say at least four."

"All of her limbs?" Kim asked.

He nodded and pointed to the right leg. The ankle had been turned a full one-eighty.

She took a step closer and peered at the area where the blood trail from the nose ended.

A thin line travelled across her throat from ear to ear. From the width of the wound Kim guessed some kind of garden twine.

She knew immediately that she was not looking at the scene of the crime. Inga had been tortured. There would have been screams that would have alerted someone. This was where her body had been dragged from a vehicle and dumped.

"Cause of death?" Kim asked.

Keats shrugged. "Hard to tell until I get her back for a detailed examination but I thought you might like to see this."

Keats took two steps along the body. He gently pulled at the jacket collar that covered her neck.

"Jesus Christ," Kim said, shaking her head.

She stepped forward and counted. There were seven or eight additional ring marks around her neck.

Bryant appeared beside her and followed her eyes. "Struggle, Guv?"

Kim shook her head. The marks were too pronounced for that. The lines from a struggle would have been less ingrained into the skin as she squirmed.

Dawson appeared on the other side of the body.

"What do you think, Kev?" she asked.

Dawson looked at the rings and then the rest of her body. "He tortured her, boss. Strangling her to the point of unconsciousness and then beating her back to life."

Kim nodded her agreement. "She would have felt every single injury before she died."

"Evil bastard," Bryant murmured before moving away.

Kim had to agree but this was a crime scene she viewed dispassionately. Inga had made choices. She had been party to the abduction of innocent children. Yes, this pitiful figure had felt fear but she was now free of that fear. For two little girls, it went on. She hoped.

Somewhere, they were out there; confused, terrified and alone. Back at the house four parents tried to hang on to their own sanity after being thrust into a cruel game of bidding for the life of their child. And this woman had been instrumental in the cause of it all.

Kim took one last look over the body, committing it to memory in lieu of the photographs. Her gaze paused at the ankle that had been twisted. The fabric of the yellow jeans an inch higher than the other leg.

She bent down and gingerly pushed it higher. Black ink stared back at her. She pushed the denim further. She saw a rectangle with a line through the middle. A dot on either side of the line.

Kim beckoned the photographer. "Close-ups of this," she said, standing up.

"Crude, do-it-yourself job," Keats observed.

Kim nodded as Bryant leaned over and took a look.

"Who called it in?" she asked.

"Guy who delivers snacks to the pub," Dawson called back. "Ducked in here for a piss before his next call. He's just about finished throwing up 'cos there can't be anything left inside him."

"And?"

"Last I can gauge was the pub owner emptied a bin around eleven and our girl wasn't here then."

"Not going to hassle me for a time of death like you normally do?" Keats asked.

"Well, if you can offer better than the two-hour slot I've just been given, feel free."

"I'd say closer to this end of the two hours," Keats offered.

Kim nodded as the mobile phone in her back pocket vibrated. This was a number she knew.

"Stone," she answered.

"Is it her?"

Woody's own social skills appeared to be matching hers right now.

"Yes, Sir. It is."

"So, that's two dead, Stone?"

She began to edge away from the group of people surrounding Inga's body.

"We've been trying to find her since—"

"But you didn't, did you, Stone? Who was on it?"

Kim knew Dawson had done everything humanly possible to track Inga down. No way was that happening. Woody was not going to throw Dawson to any lion.

"Sir, Inga did not want to be caught by either us or the kidnappers. She was involved in the snatch and if I have to choose dead bodies then I'll take hers over Charlie's or Amy's any day of the week."

She heard his intake of breath. "Stone, who was responsible for that part of the case?"

Jesus, he was like a dog with a bone. It was clear he wanted a name.

"Me, Sir. I'm the Officer in Charge and I was out looking for Inga."

She sensed the stress ball in his left hand.

"Of course you were."

Kim growled at the empty line in her ear.

She walked back towards Inga's body.

Keats had caught part of the conversation. "You've been looking for this girl?" he asked.

Kim nodded. "Current investigation."

Keats waited for more of an explanation.

Kim offered nothing as she took one last look at the body.

An attack so brutal normally called for an insane rage—an uncontrollable anger bursting from the hands of the killer—but Kim had the undeniable sense that this had been done for fun.

They headed back towards the car.

"Oh, Bryant, please tell me that's not an Audi up there," she said.

"Yeah, the bloodhound is here."

Too many dog comments came to mind but she kept her mouth firmly closed.

"Don't even think about it," Kim said, holding up her hand as Tracy approached.

"I only have so much patience, Inspector," Tracy said, flicking her long blonde hair.

"Me too, Tracy, and you are severely testing mine."

"And your threat only holds me for so long," she warned.

"Which one?" Kim asked, honestly. She shrugged. "No matter. I'm sure I can come up with another."

Tracy had walked behind them all the way to the car. "You do know that other police officers are far more co-operative with the press. We can be helpful, you know."

Oh that was a good joke and one Kim couldn't let pass. "Bring me a helpful member of the press right now and I'll have a chat, but as it's only you I'll pass, thanks."

"How long have those two girls been missing?" Tracy asked.

In one movement Kim turned and stepped right into Tracy's space.

"Guv…" Bryant warned.

Kim ignored him. "You repeat that question to anyone else and I promise you this will get personal. Shutting you up is worth losing my job."

Kim was careful not to touch Tracy in any way but if the woman did anything to interfere with the safety of Charlie and Amy, Kim would make sure she never knew a minute's peace again.

She stepped away and headed for the car.

"Guv, you were a bit—"

"Bryant, talk to me about the case or nothing at all." She wasn't in the mood for appraisals of her behaviour.

He sighed heavily and glanced back towards the cordon tape. "If this guy is anywhere near our girls—"

"Okay, probably best you don't talk at all," she snapped, getting in the car.

The pictures were already in her head.

CHAPTER 53

"Charl," Amy said, beside her. "I can feel you shaking."

Charlie was trying desperately to tell her body off for the involuntary movements. She could no longer tell if it was due to the fear or the cold. She only knew that now and again her teeth chomped against each other and there was nothing she could do to stop it.

"I'm okay, Ames, just a bit cold," she said, scooting across until the bare skin of her thigh found the bare skin of Amy's.

The wet bathing costume that had welded itself to her body last night had dried against her skin, giving her a chill that reached into her bones. Amy's towel was smaller and was under their bottoms but the cold found its way up through the mattress and the cloth. Her own towel was stretched around them like a shared cape. Amy held one corner and she held the other.

The sound of the key in the lock startled her. She hadn't heard the warning signs. Gradually she was becoming less attentive to what was happening around her. She tried to back further into the wall, holding Amy's hand tightly. Amy stared at the door.

The figure stepped into the open doorway.

Charlie shielded her eyes from the brighter light beyond the doorway. It was the bigger man again. The one who had taken their clothes.

Amy moved closer. "Charl, what's he ..."

"Sshhh ..." Charlie said.

The man had one hand behind his back. He stood with two legs apart.

His left hand came forward. In it was a tiny black and white kitten. Its eyes were sleepy and docile.

Charlie's immediate reaction was warmth. Her gaze fixed on the ball of fur that was opening its eyes and trying to look around.

A sensation formed in the pit of her stomach.

Charlie looked up into the only part of the man she could see. His eyes were crinkled at the corners. He was smiling but she detected no warmth. His eyes were not even on the kitten; they were on her.

The dread in her stomach continued to rise. It was how she felt before a trip to the dentist. But worse. She could hear her own heartbeat in her chest. She wanted to jump up and snatch the kitten from his hands but the trembling was travelling from her head to her toes.

She swallowed deeply, trying to control the involuntary movement of her body. The moisture was sucked from her mouth. Her throat closed around the words that were too frightened to come out.

Charlie watched as the man raised his right hand and placed it around the neck of the kitten.

In one swift movement he twisted the neck all the way around.

Both she and Amy screamed.

CHAPTER 54

Kim listened to the recording a second time. All activity in the room had stopped. All eyes stared at the phone.

The scream was horrific to her ears and Kim thought she might throw up.

She threw the phone across the table and stormed out of the room.

Twenty paces later she was hit by the coolness of the night-time air. She paced around the water feature, her fists clenched at her side. She had the urge to punch her own head in. Her request for proof of life had caused some kind of pain and that was not her job. She was supposed to be protecting these kids. She should have brought them home by now. They were children; terrified and naked and now in pain.

"Damn it to hell," she growled, kicking out.

"Not a fair fight. Tree's done nothing to you."

Kim turned to find Matt Ward leaning against the side of the house.

"What do you want?"

He shrugged. "Just wanted to see you have a good sulk. I've seen better."

"I tend not to show my frustration in front of my team. It's bad for morale."

"Oh, you think they're back there letting off party poppers. They heard the exact same thing you did."

"Thanks for the reminder."

"Except they didn't run out of the room like a spoiled child. Excellent way to support your team, Detective Inspector. They're still in there staring at the phone."

Kim turned on him. Every ounce of her anger was headed in his direction. "You know nothing about me or my team, so piss off."

His expression didn't change. "What's your problem?"

She was stunned by the lack of emotion in his response. "Did you not just hear that, you cold-hearted bas—"

"I heard. And then I heard it again."

"So you know that they've been harmed because I asked for proof of life."

He rolled his eyes. "Oh, get over yourself. I didn't have you down as the martyr type. Of course you asked for proof of life—if I'd been here earlier I would have done the same thing. Get off your cross and listen, because it's not in my nature to make people feel better, but those girls weren't being harmed."

"What do you mean?"

"The screams were horror, not pain. There's a difference."

"How do you know?"

He didn't flinch. "Trust me, I know."

She looked doubtful as he pushed himself away from the wall. "But you're forgetting the most important thing of all."

She didn't bother to ask what that was because he was going to tell her anyway.

"You know now that they're alive. Both of them."

Matt turned and walked back into the house; she watched him go.

She'd already decided she didn't like him. There was a cool detachment from emotion that unnerved her. During their conversation his expression had not altered once.

She didn't like him and she didn't trust him but, damn it, she bloody well hoped he was right.

CHAPTER 55

Jenny Cotton scraped the remains of the microwave lasagne into the bin. Automatically she carried the single plate to the sink and rinsed it immediately. A sad smile crept over her face. There was no need to wash up after herself, not any more. But her hand reached for the tea towel anyway.

The act was symbolic of the last thirteen months. There was little point to anything, but her body had functioned regardless.

Every day she had willed it into action. Every morning she had tried to feel hope. Maybe today, she had told herself, tricking her mind into giving instructions to her limbs.

She stepped into the lounge and tidied the magazines that had lain in her lap. She switched off the television that had remained unwatched. She picked up the mobile phone that had not rung in weeks. Beside it was the other one. The phone that she kept as a last link to her daughter. The one she'd told the detective inspector she no longer had.

Of course the police had requested it back then and had even turned hostile at her irrefutable claim that it was lost. She had given them permission to search the house, safe in the knowledge that it would remain undetected in the bird house on the outside wall.

The messages were still there and she read them often, still searching for clues, but the words never changed and Suzie still hadn't come home.

There was an element of release in not having to keep up the pretence any longer. There was no need to drag herself out of bed every morning and join the rest of the world. There was no need to pull clothes onto her body and comb her hair. There was no need to carry on.

Because now she knew for certain.

The visit from the police had confirmed her worst fears. It had happened again. She'd seen it in the woman's eyes. And if the same people had taken another two girls the truth was staring her in the face.

Suzie was never coming home.

She mounted the stairs slowly, her footsteps the only sound throughout the house. For once Jenny didn't mind. The peace that surrounded her filled her body. There was an acceptance. An end.

She derived nothing from these last moments. She felt no desire to try to wring any enjoyment for this last ounce of time. The pleasure lay at its end.

She undressed and folded her clothes onto the bed. She paused. Should she write a letter of explanation? To whom? Anyone who knew her would not be surprised. The concern of her friends and family had reduced to an occasional phone call born of guilt and responsibility. They had urged, prodded, poked for her to move on and when she'd been unable to they had done it anyway.

Jenny hoped they would understand that she was not running *from*, she was running *to*. Any last hope that had remained in her heart was now gone.

She lowered herself into the bath water and closed her eyes. Only a moment of doubt brought hesitation. What if she couldn't find Suzie in the afterlife? What if her actions propelled her to a darker place and she was then resigned to an eternity of searching?

She shook her head as the fear subsided as quickly as it had appeared. For that she would have to believe in a higher being. And she didn't. Not any more.

She took the razor blade and held it in position. She knew to slice down and not across. A smile began to shape her lips as she felt the pull towards her daughter.

"I'm coming, Suzie, I'm coming," she whispered, as the blade began to reach down.

And then the phone rang.

The other one.

CHAPTER 56

"Okay kids, time to get off home."

A few moans of protest surfaced but Kim cut them off by raising her hand. "No, I need you all rested. I'll draw up a list of priorities ready for the morning and I'll see you all back here at six."

One by one they began to file out of the dining room.

"Including you, Mr. Ward," she said to the lowered head of the negotiator.

"Yeah, just finishing this," he said, without looking up.

Once the room was empty she moved around him to push in the chairs and close the files.

She grabbed her overnight bag from beneath the chair.

"Ahem, I'm sure you've finished whatever it is you're reading, so if you'd like to..."

"Yeah, I'm not leaving. I just didn't want to argue with you in front of your team."

She let out a long breath. "Do we have to do this now? If it's a fight you're after..."

"Nope, just trying to do my job."

Kim banged her fist on the desk. Still Matt didn't look.

"As the senior member of this team I am instructing you—"

"Aah, well, that's your first problem," he said, finally looking at her. "I'm not a part of this team. I don't even work for the police force so don't start with *I'll get my boss onto your boss* 'cos you're pretty much looking at him."

Kim felt her colour rising. "I fight my own battles thanks and this room is seconded by West Midlands Police, therefore as a non-member of my team please remove yourself—"

"Are you going to physically remove me?" he asked with the first hint of a smile she'd seen all day.

"If I have to," she shot back.

They glared at each other across the makeshift desk.

She would not back down.

He held up his hands. "Fine, I believe you." He stood and gathered together the three files from which he was cherry picking. "Okay, I'll move into the kitchen but I'm not leaving this house until those girls are safely home."

Kim nodded and lowered her arms. Great, they could eat biscuits and do each other's nails.

Matt was proving to be the most infuriating man she'd ever met. His arrogance was trumped only by his stubbornness, which was left for dead by his complete lack of emotion.

He paused at the door and turned. "Are you always used to getting your own way, Inspector?"

She thought and then nodded. "Pretty much."

"Well, maybe it's about time you didn't."

"Mr. Ward, I would love to sit and chat about how I value your opinion of me but may I politely ask you to leave what has now become my bedroom."

"Hell, yes," he said, passing through the doorway.

The tension began to drain from her jaw.

A gentle tap sounded on the door.

"What the hell do you—"

"Marm, just letting you know I'm getting off now."

Kim immediately felt bad. She tended to forget about Helen.

"Sorry, I've had no time to catch up today."

"Very little to report, Marm. Each couple still keeping their distance and trying to pretend they're not."

Kim nodded. The fracture in their friendship was not her concern.

"Do you think either couple has made contact yet?"

Helen shook her head. "Not yet. They're all still hoping you're gonna magic these girls back."

Yeah, them and her both.

Kim tipped her head. "Are you aware of the ransom being paid the last time?"

Helen shook her head. "I don't think so. Both families were in contact with the kidnappers as offers were sent back and forth but I don't think money was exchanged. It was just as much of a shock to all of the parents when Emily was found."

That was what Kim suspected. She wanted absolute confirmation from the second family but her gut said it had ended for some other reason.

"Jenny Cotton is sure that the other family paid," Kim said. And she could understand why. Their daughter had lived and hers had not.

Helen was not convinced. "I would have known. There would have been a distinct change in their demeanour. You can't keep hope like that to yourself."

Kim turned in her chair. "What do you think prompted the release of one child?"

A brief hesitation preceded the woman's words. "The SIO thought..."

"Helen," Kim said, narrowing her eyes. "I'm not asking the SIO. If he told me I was female I'd run to the bathroom and check. I'm asking you."

"I think it was something that went wrong on their end. I've wracked my brains for anything that happened at the house but there was nothing."

"Okay, thanks, Helen. We'll catch up better tomorrow. Get some rest."

The sixteen-hour days were taking their toll beneath the blue eyes.

"Will do, Marm. Same to yourself," she said, backing out of the room.

"Hey, Helen, just out of interest, which couple do you think will crack first?"

Helen appeared back in view. "Elizabeth and Stephen," she said, without hesitation.

Kim didn't ask for clarification of the conviction behind her opinion.

She didn't need to. It's what her gut said too.

Kim waved her out. "See you in the—"

Her words cut off as her mobile phone began to ring. It was a number she didn't recognise.

Helen remained in the doorway.

"Detective Inspector Stone."

Silence met her ears. She waved at Helen to leave.

"Hello, who's there?" she said.

Nothing.

Jesus, she hated crank callers. "If you've got nothing better to do with your time I suggest you take up—"

"Inspector," said a small voice that was familiar to her but that she couldn't quite place.

"Who is this?" she asked, narrowing her eyes.

"It...it's Jenny Cotton. I'm...err...I think..."

Kim was already on her feet. "Mrs. Cotton, has something happened?"

"It's the phone, the other phone...I have a message..."

"Mrs. Cotton, don't do anything," Kim said. "I'm on my way."

CHAPTER 57

Elizabeth sat on the edge of the bed, exhausted.

From her toes to her neck she held the tension of the day. But her mind raced. Her emotions were skidding and colliding like a stock car race.

She missed her children deeply. She ached for the warm gentleness of Amy and the cheeky mischief of Nicholas. She felt that both children had been taken from her.

Stephen entered the room from the en-suite. He placed his clothes on top of the chair that was right next to the suitcase.

She moved around the bed and picked up his jeans.

"We have to at least discuss it," she said, quietly.

Stephen fiddled with his watch but said nothing.

She reached for the sky blue shirt. "Stephen, we can't just pretend it never happened. We've avoided it for twenty-four hours but we have to talk about this."

She held the shirt to her body to fold it. The awareness of her betrayal surged through her as each word left her mouth.

He sighed. "You want us to live in their house, eat their food, sleep in their bed and discuss how much we can pay to kill their daughter?"

Elizabeth clutched the shirt tightly. "You read the message. It's theirs or ours."

She had known Charlie since she was four years old and loved the child like a niece, but not like a daughter. Elizabeth's affection for Charlie was one step removed.

Her own child had a less fervent disposition. Amy's sweetness was calm and unruffled. She allowed Charlie to lead in everything they did; content that the two of them were together.

Wherever they were, Elizabeth prayed that they still were together. She was honest enough to admit that Charlie was the stronger of the two. Only last week at the ball pit an older boy had crashed into Amy, sending her flying to the ground. Elizabeth had been busy tending to a small cut on Amy's elbow, but not too busy to see what Charlie had done next.

She'd waited for the boy to stand at the top of the slide. He had beaten his chest like Tarzan and Charlie had launched herself into him full force and sent him tumbling down the slide, head first. Then she had shouted, "Sorry."

God forgive her, Elizabeth hoped Charlie was protecting Amy the way she always had, despite what she had to say next.

"We have to at least discuss it, Stephen," she whispered, hating every syllable that left her mouth.

She was talking about sealing the fate of one child to secure the release of another. Her own.

But she had no choice.

"I need to know how much we can offer."

There, the words bubbling in her throat had finally been set free. She knew she could never take them back.

"You can't seriously be considering it. You'd really do that, to them?"

"And you wouldn't to get Amy back?"

Stephen's overriding concern for the safety of another child unnerved her. She loved her husband but was not blind to his faults. Why had no offer been sent already?

She turned on him. "You're prepared to let our daughter die?"

He swallowed and looked away.

She threw down the shirt and walked towards him.

"Do you think they're not down the hallway right now having the same conversation?"

Stephen dropped his head into his hands.

Elizabeth suddenly felt alone. They were supposed to be a team. Both fighting for the life of their daughter. But her husband had already left the ring.

She talked down at the top of his head. "Robert has probably made calls to his bank manager, his accountant and anyone else he can think of. He may have made an offer already, for all we know."

Stephen pushed himself up from the bed and moved away.

She followed him. "Stephen, what the hell is wrong with you? We have to try and save our child."

He turned on her. "By killing someone else's?"

Elizabeth took a step back. The words were there but no emotion showed in his eyes.

"Stephen, I don't... I mean, what..."

He turned away from her again. "I just can't get my head around what we're having to do. It's barbaric."

There was a lack of depth in his tone that belied his words.

"How much, Stephen?" she asked. "How much can we raise to secure the life of our daughter?"

Stephen's evasion was not going to work.

He sat back on the bed. His eyes darted around the room as they always did when he was getting irritated.

"Stephen, answer me. How much money is Amy's life worth to you?"

His eyes flashed. Good, she wanted any emotional response that was real, that was him.

"I don't know. It's complicated."

"No it's not. You know our assets."

"Elizabeth, it's late," he said, avoiding her gaze.

"Come on, Stephen. There's the savings account."

"Liz, stop, please. You don't understand the finances," he snapped.

She moved closer. "Don't patronise me. How quickly could we raise a second mortgage on the house?"

"Liz, stop. This is insane."

"If we sell the cars and jewellery as well we've got to be close to—"

"Liz, I'm asking you one last time to stop what you're doing."

Elizabeth froze, realising he hadn't given her one decent answer.

As he stood by the window she could see the tension hardening his shoulders. It would have been sensible to leave him alone. But she couldn't.

She stepped in front of him, forcing him to look at her. His eyes were filled with rage.

"Tell me, Stephen, what value do you place on our child?"

She saw the control in his eyes snap a second before his fist punched her in the mouth.

CHAPTER 58

The five-mile bike ride from Pedmore to Netherton had been fraught with patches of ice. More than once the rear wheel had weaved almost beyond Kim's control and the hill leading up to the house had been like a ski run, but she killed the engine exactly nine minutes after receiving the call. Although she had left her details with Jenny Cotton, Kim had never expected a call.

The woman was already standing in the doorway, clad in a white towelling robe, phone clutched in her hand. The frozen expression on her face had nothing to do with the temperature.

Kim removed her helmet and guided the woman inside, closing the door behind her.

"Thank you for coming... I didn't know what else..."

"It's okay," Kim said. "You did the right thing."

Kim wasn't surprised Jenny still had possession of the phone. If she was honest, she wouldn't have handed it over either.

Jenny moved mechanically, numbed into a state of shock. She stumbled into one of the dining chairs.

Kim reached out and steadied her, forcing her to take a seat.

She herself needed a hot, sweet drink but the woman before her appeared to need it more.

Kim stepped into the kitchen and filled the kettle. After a few attempts she located mugs, coffee, sweetener and milk.

"I was so close," the woman whispered as the kettle switched off.

Kim turned.

Silent tears were falling onto Jenny's cheeks as she stared down at the phone in her hand.

"To what?" Kim asked, but her gut gave her the answer before Jenny did.

"To peace," she said, raising her gaze.

Kim set the coffee mugs on the table and sat down. "It's not the answer," she said softly.

"It is when you no longer know the question."

Kim thought it was Albert Einstein who had said, "Life isn't worth living unless it is lived for someone else."

A prime example of that sat before her. This poor, defeated woman had tried to exist without her child, but had been unable to move in any direction.

Kim reached across and gently touched her hand.

"Have you read the text message?"

The woman nodded and clutched the phone to her breast.

Kim held out her hand. "May I?"

With reticence the hand came forward. Kim plucked the phone from the woman's grip and scrolled to the most recent message.

It hadn't come from a number already used. She had the numbers above each text on the board in the war room. The texts and the numbers were burned into her memory.

The message was short and simple.

Do you want to play again?

Kim closed her eyes. At worst they were looking at the cruellest of jokes, an attempt to extort money from a woman still lost in her grief. At best, this was a mother being taunted into bargaining for the body of her child.

A vision of Eloise being frog-marched from the Timmins' garden appeared in her mind. She had said that he wasn't done with the others. Was this what she had meant? Just as quickly,

Kim pushed away the thought. Every crackpot had to stumble across lucky coincidences now and again.

Kim was a police officer and she dealt in fact.

She stood and pushed her chair under the table. "I have to ask you to let me take this phone."

Jenny Cotton looked horrified. Her eyes darted to the phone and Kim could feel the urge in her to grab it back and cradle it.

She used her right hand to wring the fingers of her left. "Is there a chance, any chance at all that you can bring the body of my daughter home?"

Kim was loath to make promises that she didn't feel she could keep but one look at the face, so close to the edge, reached down and squeezed at her gut.

"If they have her, I'll find her."

CHAPTER 59

Kim realised there was no way out of her current predicament.

She was cold, the coffee pot was empty and she had a lot to think about. She needed water and there was an arsehole in the kitchen.

She didn't relish the idea of another battle but life without coffee was not an option, especially after midnight. There were many things she could function without: love, yes, sex, normally, food, often but coffee—never.

She grabbed the coffee pot forcefully and strode out of the incident room. Damn it, she was not scared of anyone.

She entered the kitchen with a set expression but paused. Matt's head was in his hands and his breathing was deep and even.

Her footsteps were light as she headed to the sink. She turned the faucet to the bare minimum and held the pot in place as water dribbled in.

"Thanks for your consideration but I wasn't asleep."

Kim groaned inwardly. She turned. "Really, your snoring would tend to disagree."

"I was practising the art of deep mind meditation, whereby your conscious mind remains alert while your subconscious has a rest. It's especially helpful when dealing with difficult people."

"Yes, living with yourself must be quite a trauma."

"Oh, good response, Inspector."

Kim headed out of the kitchen.

"The dickhead in charge of negotiation on the last case should be taken out back and shot," Matt called after her.

Kim stepped back into the kitchen. "Why?"

"Because he went at it like a market trader. No strategy, just positioning and posturing."

Kim took two further steps in. "Go on."

Matt sighed and rubbed the bridge of his nose.

"A few years ago there was a tiger in Bolivia."

"A tiger?"

"Sorry. A tiger kidnapping is where a hostage is taken to persuade a loved one or family member to do something."

Kim took a seat.

"A five-year-old boy was taken to persuade his father, a judge, to release the kidnapper's brother from prison. His brother was a political activist and responsible for the murder of seventeen people on a city bus. This was exchange of life for life, not money. It was an impossible choice and obviously one the judge was powerless to execute."

"What happened?"

"The boy's body was found two days later on a riverbank, which is what happens when a negotiator operates with a complete lack of respect for the process. If we were dealing with an express incident..."

"Express?" Kim asked. It wasn't a term she'd heard before.

"It's where a small ransom that a family can easily pay is demanded. At the outset it is understood that money will be paid and that the child will be freed and the only negotiation is the cost."

"Are these gangs ever caught?"

Matt shook his head. "Rarely. They are adept at what they do. And as long as you work the negotiation right, everyone wins."

Kim heard something in his voice that caught her attention.

"Does it ever go wrong?"

He stood and turned to the sink. "Now and again."

It was the first flicker of emotion Kim had witnessed from Matt but something about this case was puzzling her.

"We have no demand for an amount, so how can you start negotiations?"

He turned back with a glass of water.

"On this occasion I'm not bargaining for the money. I couldn't give a shit who pays what amount of money. I'm bargaining for life. Despite what the text message says about one life. I want them both," he stated.

"Have you seen this before?" Kim asked. "An auction situation?"

He shook his head. "No, I've had a double before, two brothers, but it was a flat-out demand."

Kim was not heartened by this news. "So, how do you propose...?"

"The first thing I need to do is gauge their expectations. There has been no demand for an actual sum but there must be a figure they're hoping to achieve. I'm also going to be looking to see if they have a preferred family. They may be interested more in the Hanson family and the Timmins are along purely to help boost the price, or vice versa. Every response I get will tell me something and help to direct the course of action to take next."

"So, it's a fluid plan?"

"It has to be until I get some reactions."

"Wow, you almost smiled then," she observed. "Be careful, you'll have me thinking you have some level of emotional capability."

His face returned to the set position. "As your opinion means nothing to me I won't be losing sleep but, to address your point, my emotions could get those girls killed."

"Surely you could still do your job if you smiled now and again?" she asked.

"Perhaps, but if I'm in a good mood then I might concede something I shouldn't because the sun is shining or I had a good night out. Equally, if I'm in a negative mood—because you're around, for argument's sake—it may prompt unnecessary irrational behaviour. It is a fact that pissed-off negotiators use more competitive strategies and co-operate less." He raised both eyebrows. "So, please stay out of my way."

Kim stood. "Trust me, that won't be a problem." She moved towards the door. "Oh, and just to add to your stress, Jenny Cotton—that's one of—"

"I know who she is," he said, shortly.

"She's received a text message, asking if she wants to play again."

He sat back in his chair and rubbed at his chin. "You're joking?"

Kim shook her head. "I have the phone."

"You don't seriously think that kid is still alive?"

Kim took a breath and shook her head. The sickness still rolling in her stomach stemmed from the knowledge that the contact might help them find the two that were. She was using the death and misery of one family to try to save two more.

"You need to reply," he said.

She opened her mouth to respond.

"Just say yes and see what comes back."

It was what she'd planned to do.

Kim headed out of the room with the coffee pot. At the door she paused.

"So, just for my interest, what's going to be your opening gambit?"

"It's what I was working on when you stepped into my bedroom."

"Well, any time is good for me. I'd hate you to be rushed by the fact we've got two kids missing."

"Inspector, I can assure you that I never rush. But just for my own interest, if you could get the crew leader on the phone what would be *your* opening bid?"

Kim thought for only a split second.

"Bring them back now unharmed and I'll let you live."

He stared at her for a full ten seconds and she returned the gaze without flinching.

"Yep, now I can see why they sent for me."

CHAPTER 60

"Charl, I feel sick…" Amy said, clutching her stomach.

Charlie knew what she meant. The sandwich earlier had been warm and had smelled funny. Neither of them had eaten it all, both far too sickened by the thought of the limp kitten as he'd dangled it by the neck before closing the door.

Every time she closed her eyes she saw that beautiful black and white face staring back at her. So sleepy, so warm, so trusting.

Charlie had the sudden longing for stew. Her mum had cooked it in the past and every time Charlie said she didn't like it. It was a mess of vegetables and meat pieces in a gravy filled with little white beads that her mum said was pearly barley or something. It was another reason why she was always pleased that winter was over. No more stew.

But right now the thought of it brought tears to her eyes.

"I th-think we've b-been here three d-days," Charlie said, counting the scratches on the wall. "So, I think it's T-Tues…"

"Charl, you're stuttering again," Amy observed, putting her hand on Charlie's arm.

"J-just…the…c-cold, Ames," Charlie said.

Amy took the towel from around herself and wrapped it around Charlie then moved her hands quickly up and down her arms.

That simple act prodded the tears that lived permanently behind her eyes.

"I'm s-scared, Ames," she said, using the corner of the towel to wipe at her face.

"Me too, Charl, but I won't let anything hurt you. I promise."

Charlie couldn't help the tears that cascaded over her cheeks. The sobbing started in her stomach and worked its way up to her throat. She had tried to stay strong for her friend and now she had let her down.

Amy rubbed some warmth into her legs. "We'll be okay, Charl. As long as we're together. Our parents are out looking for us right now. They'll find us, I know they will."

"You h-have to get b-back in here," Charlie choked out. Amy couldn't be without some covering for long. Their bathing costumes were no defence against the damp, cold room.

Amy scooted next to her and they huddled beneath the towel.

"Do you th-think they will find us, Ames?"

Amy chuckled and the sound dried the last of her tears.

"Don't you remember when we went to Great Yarmouth?"

Charlie thought for a minute.

Amy nudged her. "We saw that clown and we followed him because he was holding Olaf balloons and then we didn't know where we were. We walked around for ages looking for our parents and then we just sat and waited for them to find us. The fair was closing and it was starting to get dark but they found us."

Charlie knew it wasn't the same thing. "B-But that time they knew where we were. Th-They knew where to find us."

Amy shrugged. "But they wouldn't have gone home until they did," she said simply.

Charlie wondered if Amy realised that they had switched roles and she was now the strong one.

She had opened her mouth to respond when she heard the familiar sound of footsteps.

"Charl…no…not again…"

"Evening, girlies," he said.

Neither of them spoke, listening for the sound of the key in the door.

"I saw a friend of yours today. You both remember Inga?"

Amy stiffened and nodded towards the door.

"Answ—"

"Yes," Charlie shouted. After seeing what he'd done to the poor kitten she didn't want to make him angry.

Amy's hand dropped her side of the towel and moved towards her forearm. Charlie put her hand in the way.

"Cover your ears," she whispered but Amy shook her head and stared at the door.

"Well, girlies, you'll be pleased to know she's dead—"

Amy's cry cut him off. Charlie could imagine him smiling on the other side of the door.

"Ames, don't listen," Charlie said again. She moved her hands towards Amy's ears but Amy pushed them away.

"Yeah, she's a goner and I made her suffer a lot more than I did with Brad. I hurt her real bad, girlies, before I finally broke her neck."

Amy began to shake her head.

"She cried, and begged, and screamed every time I belted her. She was pathetic but you know why she had to die, don't you, girlies?"

They were both silent but for the sound of Amy's nails raking the skin of her arm.

"She had to die because she let us down. She was part of it, you see. She helped us get to you two. Told us everything about you, where you'd be. She did it because she never cared."

Even in the dim light Charlie could see that Amy had lost every spot of colour from her cheeks. Her free hand was rubbing her stomach as her widened eyes continued to stare at the door.

"He's lying, Ames. Don't listen," Charlie said. She had known Inga since she was five years old and she didn't want to believe. But how else would they have known about her and Amy?

"And, do you know what she said to me before I killed her? She said she never liked either of you and she hoped you were dead."

Just at that second, Amy threw up.

CHAPTER 61

A cold air accompanied her team as they entered the war room. A light smattering of snow overnight had frozen to a thin crunchy carpet.

"It's bloody making up out there now," Bryant blustered as he passed behind her. They were now paying the price for a warmer-than-average February.

"Get coffee and let's get started," Kim said as overcoats landed on the easy chair in the corner.

Stacey stood at the coffee machine. "Matt, would you..."

"I'm fine, thanks, Stacey," he said, nodding towards the mug he'd been nursing for the fifteen minutes since Kim had allowed him into the room. They hadn't spoken once.

"All right, folks; new day, new energy," Kim said as her team took their places around the table. It was now Wednesday and she was sure that the lengthening gap from the snatch on Sunday was on all of their minds.

"Stace, you first."

Stacey opened her mouth but stopped as the dining room door began to open. Kim was on her feet immediately. No one entered this room without her permission.

The six-foot-high frame of Detective Chief Inspector Wood-ward stood in the doorway. Kim's blood ran cold and she lowered her hand to the table for support.

Please, God, don't let them have found the bodies.

"Just here for the briefing, Stone. As you were."

The relief almost buckled her back into the chair but she managed to remain upright as she introduced her boss to Matt and Alison. Both shook his hand and nodded.

Woody retreated back to the corner of the room and stood against the door. His body was spirit-level straight and his arms crossed at the chest, covering the sports insignia on his light blue T-shirt. Thank goodness he hadn't come in uniform. Although casual wear looked out of place on Woody, it suited the environment he was currently in. She had no doubt he'd be home to change before heading to the station.

She turned her back on him and nodded for Stacey to resume.

"Got the address for the other family, Guv. It wasn't easy."

"Send it to Bryant's phone," she said.

Stacey continued. "Still nothing from the phone networks. One has even blocked my emails as spam so I'm guessing he's got nothing for us. Can't find a lot on the psychic. Got a couple of bad reviews but, hell, even the Rolling Stones get them. Local folks love her shows at the Civic but other than that I can't find any money-making schemes: no books on Amazon, no audio books, CDs, anything. She charges a fiver entrance fee and donates half of that to the RSPCA. No Facebook, Twitter or any other following. Nothing malicious that I can—"

"Hang on," Kim said as her mobile phone vibrated. It was an email from Keats who also appeared to have swallowed the early worm. It was hard to believe they had visited Inga's crime scene only yesterday.

"Kev, post mortem is at nine."

He nodded his understanding. He would attend.

"Anything else, Stace?"

Stacey shook her head.

Attached to the email were the crime scene photos. She opened the first one and passed the phone to Alison. "Just scroll through to the picture of the tattoo." Someone in the room had to know what it meant.

She turned her attention back to her team. "Got a call from Jenny Cotton last night. She's received a message too."

A wave of surprise travelled around the room.

"Mr. Ward has the phone in case any other messages come. The text is short and direct, asking if she wants to play again."

"Jesus, that's cruel," Bryant said, shaking his head.

"Is it a prank?" Dawson asked.

Kim shrugged. "No way to tell. The message didn't come from any of these numbers but as he's used a different one each time that doesn't help us."

Stacey leaned forward. "Do you think it is the same guys we're dealing with?"

Kim sighed. "She's kept that phone for thirteen months just hoping it would ring again. The fact that it has at the exact same time our two girls are missing isn't coincidental. Doubtful that it's a random prank either. No one knows about Charlie and Amy."

Dawson caught her eye. "Guv, do we think..."

"No, Kev, we don't. If Suzie Cotton is still a factor in this the best we can hope for is recovery."

The room silenced. They all knew what she meant. For Jenny Cotton, even that would be closure.

"Horrific," Alison said, handing the phone back to Kim.

Kim nodded her agreement. "I think we can safely assume this to be the work of Subject Two. Any further thoughts?" she asked the behaviourist.

"If he's known to the police it will be for brutal, violent crimes. He could be a slaughter man or in a profession linked to killing of some kind. You could even be looking at ex-services."

"A soldier?" Bryant asked.

"Go on," Kim encouraged.

Alison nodded. "It's well documented that until recently the most effective weapon in the armed forces was hate. Soldiers were instilled with hatred towards the enemy, to remove the inhibitions of taking a life. If you hate the owner of that life it is easier to destroy.

"Rage and aggression are the staples of military life but to produce an effective killing machine you have to dehumanise it. You have to remove empathy, understanding, forgiveness. Otherwise an enemy pleading for his life might garner a moment's hesitation, which is long enough to get control of a weapon and kill an entire squad.

"It's all very clever until the soldier is released back into society. The mind-set instilled is not a temporary state. It's an altered set of beliefs. But suddenly, where is the enemy? Where is the guidance? Where is the rest of the team united in one clear goal?

"Society then tells soldiers that what they did was wrong. Violence is wrong, killing is wrong.

"You can't just suddenly wipe a mind clear because you now want that person to exist in a 'normal' society. The hatred doesn't go away. It just has no clear target."

Kim looked around the room. For once Alison had their attention.

"Continue the assumption," she said. This man enjoyed killing, as evidenced by the bodies of both Brad and Inga. And he had learned that somewhere.

"If Subject Two was in the services he would have been in his element and probably wouldn't have left of his own volition."

"We're dealing with a fucking machine," Dawson offered.

Alison shrugged. "Not exactly. He will have vulnerabilities but they will be deeply buried and only in relation to his own feelings. Back in civilian society, this individual is now on unfamiliar territory. He will possibly be confused, bewildered and abandoned. Unfortunately, these emotions will feed his anger."

Alison turned to Kim. "If I'm right, the girls have much more to fear from him."

Kim hadn't needed confirmation of that.

"But won't he feel anything, hurting innocent children?"

Oh, bless Bryant's eternal optimism. He did like to think that everyone had boundaries that could not be crossed. That he could maintain his naiveté in the job that he did was a constant mystery to Kim.

Alison shook her head. "Not any more."

Kim turned to Dawson. "Once you're done with the post mortem, continue your other line of enquiry."

Dawson nodded, grabbed his jacket and headed for the door. Woody stepped aside but left the door open.

"Inspector . . . a word," Woody said, stepping out of the room.

Bryant muttered a few notes from the death march under his breath as she left the room.

Kim caught up with the chief inspector as he reached his car parked on the other side of the water feature.

"You do know that Baldwin is calling me for updates almost hourly."

She was tempted to say she would pass that along to the kidnappers but closed her mouth just in time.

"You know what's at stake here?" he asked.

"The lives of two nine-year-old girls called Charlie and Amy."

"And...?"

"Sir, with all due respect you are now wasting your valuable time. And mine. There is no greater motivation to me than to see those girls safe and well. Nothing else can inspire me to work faster, harder or more thoroughly than I am doing and if—"

"I can see that, Stone. I've just witnessed the balls you currently have in the air and I have nothing to add in terms of your running this investigation."

She offered him a conciliatory smile. "Sir, you worry about the politics and I'll worry about the girls."

He hesitated for one moment before opening the driver's door. "Just bring them home, Stone," he said, shutting the door.

She turned and headed back into the war room and picked up her phone which had been passed around the room.

Her thumb hit the screen, which illuminated the last photo taken at the crime scene. Kim tipped her head as she enlarged it to full screen.

She paused. "Stace, you got this email from Keats?"

"Yeah, it just pinged..."

"Get the photos on the screen. Full size."

As she tapped a few keys Kim moved to stand behind Stacey.

"Scroll to the last one."

Stacey did so.

Kim pointed to where the Chinese symbol filled the screen. "Do you see that?"

Stacey peered closer and shook her head.

"Zoom in."

The symbol grew in size.

"There are lines from one side to the other," Stacey noted, looking closer. "Jeez, lots of them."

"Look at the top right-hand corner."

Bryant was now behind her looking at the screen.

"Dried blood," Bryant said, scratching his head. "I don't get…"

"That is the Chinese symbol for mother," Matt said, from her left.

Kim hid her surprise that he knew that. She peered closer. "And the dried blood indicates she has recently tried to scratch it out?"

They all stood back and stared until Kim broke the thoughtful silence.

"Stace, I want you to focus all your energy on Inga. I want to know everything about her. I think this dead woman still has something to say."

CHAPTER 62

Karen picked up the brown teddy bear Robert had brought to the hospital the day Charlie was born. The stuffed animal had suffered every indignity over the years. He'd been covered in vomit, dragged around by his ear and the stuffing had been all but squeezed out of him.

In recent years he'd been relegated to the top of the bookcase to make way for the more vital necessities of a nine-year-old, but he still remained in view.

Three weeks ago Charlie had been unwell with a sore throat and a cough. Somehow the bear had made it from the bookcase to the pillow.

Now Karen sat on the edge of the bed, the bear clutched to her torso.

This room was her place of safety; where she could be surrounded by Charlie and all her treasures. Everything in the room had a memory: a picture frame from Jamaica covered in shells; a mirror with battery powered built-in lights above her dresser; a brush and comb set bought during a day out in London.

Here in this room she could feel the presence of her daughter; as if Charlie was only down the hall in the shower.

It was the one place in the house not invaded by strangers. Her home no longer felt like her home. It was a battlefield, a hotel, a fortress; and yet the feeling of displacement didn't come from the unusual activity in her house, but rather because of what was absent. Namely, her little girl.

She hugged the bear tighter as a wave of physical pain surged through her. That heartache could translate to physical pain was a revelation to her. Throughout her childhood, the foster homes, the children's homes, the beatings, the abuse—never had she felt the pain that coursed through her now.

"I love you, my angel," Karen whispered. "Stay strong. Mummy will get you back."

The tears stung before they fell yet somehow it eased the pain, just a fraction, to speak out loud to Charlie.

"Hey, sweetheart, I thought I might find you here."

In the doorway stood the only person with whom she could share this room.

She patted the bed beside her. Robert sat and pulled her close.

She knew what other people saw when they looked at her husband. A tall, well-built man with more than a sprinkling of grey. His nose was sharp for his face and he had ears that stuck out just a little too far. They saw the first few age spots on his hands and the absence of them on hers.

But they didn't see what she did. If they paid more attention to his eyes they would get it. In them lived love, strength, compassion and a generous nature. And she saw it every day.

"We'll get her back, sweetheart, I promise. Every hour the team is making progress."

His voice was gentle, warm and assured. She closed her eyes against his chest, allowing herself a minute in this safe place.

"Poor bear," Robert said, picking at its left ear. "Do you remember that one time we had to wash it after she'd fed it a jam sandwich?"

Karen nodded against the warmth of his chest.

"We tried everything to wrestle it from her and when she understood what we wanted she became even more determined to hang on to it."

Karen smiled.

"Eventually we decided on a game of Twister because we knew she couldn't keep hold of it. You snuck away from the game and spirited the bear to the washing machine.

"Half an hour later she wandered into the kitchen and screamed when she saw him bobbing around through the portal. She thought we'd tried to kill him."

"I remember."

Robert sighed. "That night I lay awake wondering if we'd caused her any permanent psychological damage through the trauma of seeing her bear treated that way."

As always, her husband had eased her pain.

"And you call me over-protective?"

"You're my family and I love you."

She felt him stiffen against her. He held some traditional views and felt it was his job to protect them both. He felt he had failed.

Karen took his hand. "You couldn't have prevented it, Rob. Neither of us could."

Her thumb rubbed the inside of his palm.

He stroked her hair. "We have to get her back, Kaz."

She nodded her head. She knew what was coming.

They had talked late into the night. Their thoughts had formed circles and they had talked themselves dry. Loss had fought with betrayal, friendship with priority, survival against integrity. And at ten past four they had reached a decision.

It was time to send a text.

CHAPTER 63

Kim spent most of the journey second-guessing the decision to issue a press blackout.

She knew they were on borrowed time with keeping it out of the press. The broken appointments and days away from school would soon start to attract attention. Never mind the threat from Tracy Frost. People would talk. Friends would start calling. Extended family would pop round and before they knew it they would be the lead story on Sky News.

Despite the blackout being in place before she had taken the case, Kim knew that if it proved to be the wrong move she would be the scapegoat and her career would be over.

Most detectives were able to recall the case of Lesley Whittle, not only for the horror of what had happened to the seventeen-year-old girl but also as a testament to what happened if you got it all wrong.

Lesley had been taken from her home in Shropshire in 1975. The kidnapper was already known to police as the Black Panther due to wearing a black balaclava during post office raids.

Nielson had committed over four hundred burglaries and three fatal shootings before he kidnapped the girl and placed her in a drainage shaft at a park in Staffordshire.

A news blackout had been implemented initially but the investigation was bungled from the outset and two attempts to engage with Nielson's demand for fifty thousand pounds failed.

Lesley's body had eventually been found hooded and tethered to the side of a shaft by a wire noose. It had never been proven whether she had fallen from the ledge or if Nielson had pushed her. She'd weighed only ninety-eight pounds and her stomach and intestines were completely empty.

The chief superintendent who led the investigation had been demoted to a uniformed beat officer.

If that was the treatment given to a chief superintendent, Kim knew she'd be lucky to get a night job guarding a scrap-yard.

The decision to maintain the blackout was based on the balance of gain from public awareness against the detriment of false leads. There would be a staggering level of press interest, attracted by the juicy story of the abduction of two young girls, with countless reporters searching for a story, an interview with the parents, the back stories and past. Both families would have their entire lives laid bare for the world to see, consume and judge. Kim knew that would be a heartily unpleasant experience for Karen alone, never mind the others.

But there was very little benefit to the case by making it public. There was no area of the investigation that could be enhanced by the press intrusion.

"How much further?" Kim asked, growing restless. Time spent sitting in the car was not solving the case.

Bryant glanced at the satnav. "Just under two miles."

They had long left the built-up hub of the industrial towns and travelled through the first layer of the green belt where rows of houses were strung together, punctuated by the odd shop or pub, but with back gardens looking out on to fields. Now though, they were passing into Kim's worst nightmare.

The road was flanked by grass on both sides and mobile phone signals were intermittent.

The unease began in her stomach. Being this far away from civilisation made her nervous. She felt comfortable amongst sprawling housing estates and derelict steelworks. She enjoyed breathing in the mixture of pollutants that reassured her that thousands of other people were fighting to occupy the same space. She was used to waking to car horns and revving engines, not birdsong; shadows formed by tower blocks, not trees.

The satnav stated their destination was to the right.

"Is she having a laugh?" Kim asked. A normal postcode covered twelve properties. Out here, that could cover a good few miles.

"We're looking for number four Larksford Lane," Bryant said.

They passed a gate with a number five fixed to it.

"I don't know which way the numbers run so I'll have to carry on."

A quarter mile later they spied a number six.

Bryant drove past and reversed into the paved driveway. He didn't rush the manoeuvre. They hadn't passed a car for miles.

He drove back to number five and then slowed to ten miles an hour. A six-foot-tall hedge lined the pavement.

Eventually they were back at a double gated property that stated loud and proud that it was number three.

"Okay, how to go from mildly amused to severely aggravated in about ten minutes," she said, as Bryant turned the car again.

This time they crawled the distance. Kim inspected every inch of the hedge. She understood they were looking for a family that didn't want their home to be found. They had moved house and changed their last name from Billingham to Trueman.

"There," she pointed.

A waist-high gate no more than three feet wide separated the two squared-off edges of the hedge barrier. There was no mailbox and no house number.

Bryant drove partially onto the pavement and parked the car.

Through the gate the privet hedge continued wrapping itself around them imposingly. Kim felt like she was in a maze.

Ten feet in they were greeted by a single wrought iron gate that was the respite between two brick walls. The top of each wall had been finished off with a colourful mosaic of broken glass. Anyone trying to scale the wall would be better off trying to catch the business end of an angle grinder.

The wrought iron itself was finished with one-foot-high spikes—ornately crafted and in keeping with the design of the gate; but spikes all the same.

"Sociable folks," Bryant observed as he pressed the intercom fixed to the right-hand wall.

"Mrs. Trueman?" Bryant said, as a voice filled with static acknowledged their call.

"Who are you?" the voice said, neither confirming nor denying.

"I'm Detective Sergeant Bryant and Detective Inspector Stone is beside me."

"Please hold your identification card up to the camera."

Bryant looked around for a camera as he removed his ID card from his pocket.

"Where's the bloody thing?" he snarled.

Eerily a voice said, "It's on the entryphone next to the push button."

Bryant looked closely. "Jesus, it's tiny."

Kim followed his gaze. The miniature CCTV camera looked like a screw fixing.

"And the other one," said the voice.

Kim passed her card and Bryant held it up.

"That's fine, now what do you want?"

"We'd like to come in and speak to you," said Bryant, shortly.

Like her, he was beginning to lose patience with the game of hide and seek.

"I'd like to know what this is about, Inspector."

Kim leaned forward. "It's a matter concerning your daughter, Mrs. Trueman, so please open the gate so we can speak properly."

There was a definite click from the centre of the gate. Bryant pushed on the handle. It remained secure.

"Guv, I am seriously gonna lose—"

A second thunk sounded from the top of the gate and a third from the bottom.

"Triple electronic dead bolts?" Bryant said. "What's she got in here—Lord Lucan wearing the Hope Diamond riding around on Shergar?"

Kim sighed as she closed the gate firmly behind her. "No, Bryant, just her child."

The three locks clicked back into place.

They stepped into a property set in approximately two acres. The path from the gate led between two symmetrical lawns.

To the left, in front of the kitchen window, was a single swing. The wall encircled the property, as did the glass.

As they neared the front of the house a heavy oak door was pulled back by a petite brunette wearing jeans and a man's T-shirt. The garment was spattered with lime green paint.

"Mrs. Trueman?" Bryant asked, holding out his hand.

She returned the handshake but there was no smile. She stepped back and allowed them in, taking a careful look outside before closing the door behind them.

Kim spotted five doors and a stairway leading from the space but the woman didn't point to any of them.

"You said this was about my daughter?"

Kim stepped forward. "Mrs. Trueman, we need to speak with you about Emily's abduction."

"Have you caught them?" she asked, clasping her hands.

Kim shook her head and the woman's face dropped.

Her hands met and wrestled each other. "Then what?"

"We're looking at the case again, Mrs. Trueman, and we'd like your help."

No way could Kim allow this woman to suspect that the same thing had happened again. The anxiety that radiated from Julia Trueman could shatter her into a million pieces.

Emily's mother pointed to a door. Their footsteps echoed in the hallway. There were no house sounds: no television, no radio and no chatter. The silence of the house was thick and oppressive.

The door led into a small sitting room. Plump sofas faced an open fire. The wall behind was stacked floor to ceiling with books. A picture window looked out on to the rear of the property. A gravel drive ended at a dense wooden gate that rose as high as the wall.

Kim guessed the drive led on to a lane that met civilisation a few miles down the road.

Mrs. Trueman sat on the edge of the single seat. They took the sofa.

"Yesterday we spoke with Mrs. Cotton. She—"

"How is she?" the woman asked quickly.

"I take it you don't speak any more?"

"How can we?" the woman asked. "I kept my daughter and she lost hers. How can I even look at her? We were like sisters. I miss her. I miss them both."

She glanced behind them to the wall that held the door. The wall that faced the single chair.

Kim's eyes rested on a blown-up framed photograph of the six of them at a table surrounding a huge dish of paella. Their faces were reddened from sunburn.

"Our last holiday together," Mrs. Trueman said, quietly. "Suzie was a beautiful child. I was her godmother as well. Jennifer and

I were friends since school. But everything was destroyed during those few days."

Kim was about to ask about the ransom but the woman fixed her with a look.

"Inspector, do you know what kind of person you are? I mean, do you really know?"

"I like to think so."

"And so did I—until one text message made me question everything. What these people did was unforgivable. We all turned into something from our own worst nightmares. Desperation and fear do horrible things to a person."

Kim wanted to ask the one question that mattered to her but felt they were travelling in that direction anyway.

"Our friendship counted for nothing against the lives of our children. My best friend was suddenly my enemy. We were locked in this surreal battle and only one of us could win."

"Did you pay the ransom?" Kim asked, quietly.

The woman looked at her, her face stripped bare. Her eyes held the terror of that time. And the shame.

"No, we didn't. But we were going to," she said, honestly.

Kim and Bryant exchanged a glance.

"So why was Emily freed and yet Suzie was not?"

Mrs. Trueman shrugged. "We don't know. We've asked ourselves that a million times."

Kim wondered who the hell had made that decision and why.

The door to the room opened gently and a head popped round.

A little older and considerably paler than her likeness on the wall, but Kim recognised Emily. Her mouth closed as her gaze took in the presence of strangers. Instantly her eyes were troubled as she looked to her mother.

Mrs. Trueman stood. "It's okay, Emily. Have you finished your history lesson?"

The girl nodded but her gaze had returned to Kim.

Although Mrs. Trueman tried to block the path of her daughter, she curled around her mother and entered the room.

"Emily, it's nothing to worry about. Go back upstairs and start—"

"Have you found Suzie?" the girl asked, hopefully.

Kim swallowed and shook her head. The girl's eyes filled with tears but she bravely fought them back.

It had been thirteen months since her ordeal, but clearly her best friend was never far from her thoughts.

"Emily, please go upstairs. I'll be up in a minute to mark your work."

Emily hesitated but a guiding hand on her forearm prompted her to do as her mother asked.

"She doesn't go to school?" Bryant asked.

Mrs. Trueman closed the door and shook her head. "No, Emily is home schooled. It's safer."

"Could we spend a few minutes with her?" Kim asked, softly.

Mrs. Trueman shook her head vehemently. "No, that's impossible. We don't speak about it, to her or anyone else. It's best she forgets."

Yeah, that didn't seem to be working out too well. Every waking minute locked inside a fortress with no interaction was a constant reminder of the reason why.

"Did Emily get counselling?"

Mrs. Trueman shook her head. "No, we decided we just needed to put it behind us. Children are resilient and bounce back. We didn't want some psychotherapist putting feelings of guilt into her head, telling her how she should be feeling. That wouldn't have helped anyone."

Kim idly wondered whose feelings of guilt the woman was trying to bury.

"So, I'm sorry but I can't allow you anywhere near her. You'll bring it all back."

From what Kim could see, it had never gone away. For any of them.

Mrs. Trueman remained by the door. "Now, if you'll excuse me, I have to get on."

Kim stood and suddenly had a thought.

"Did they give you a drop point?"

If this family had been prepared to pay they would have had to know how.

Mrs. Trueman hesitated.

"Please, you have to understand that we need your help right now."

"And you have to understand that I know they're still out there."

"I get that, but they're not coming back for Emily."

"I hear the words, but I don't believe them. There is no guarantee you can give me that I will accept."

Kim sighed heavily.

"But I will tell you if you assure me that you will leave us alone from this point on."

Kim could see she was never going to get to Emily alone so she had to take what she could get.

She nodded her agreement.

"The money was to be dropped on Wednesday at twelve into a grit bin on Wordsley High Street." She frowned. "But you should know that. You still have my old phone."

Damn it, Kim realised too late that she had slipped up. If they were investigating the old case like she'd said, she would have already checked the evidence—which was still in storage as the case had never been solved.

"I was just checking that was the last communication you had," Kim said, quickly.

Mrs. Trueman nodded her confirmation.

The second she left this house she'd be instructing Dawson to pick up the phone.

Kim took out a card and placed it on the hallway table. "If you think of anything else that might help please give me a call."

It was on the tip of her tongue to tell her that Jenny Cotton was desperate to bury her daughter. But she didn't.

Bryant headed to the car but Kim stepped back.

"Look, I understand you want to protect your child but this is too much. You're stifling her. She needs to be around other people. She needs to run and laugh with kids her own age. She needs to build positive memories before she can let go of the bad."

The woman's face was set. "Thank you but I think I know what's best for my daughter."

Kim shook her head. "No, this is what's best for you. She'll develop into a nervous, anxious kid who's frightened of everyone she meets."

"Inspector, I'm keeping my child alive."

Kim looked around at the complete absence of joy.

"Yeah, but it's not much of a life, is it?"

The heavy oak door started to close in her face, but not before Kim saw a shadow pass by the top of the stairs.

CHAPTER 64

Emily closed her bedroom door quietly and sat on the bed.

She should be opening her geography book next but she couldn't face it.

Although she was schooled at home her mother was a stickler for keeping proper school hours. She was at her desk by nine o'clock with four equal lessons throughout the day.

What she missed about school was the racket: the chatter, the shouting and squealing.

Out here in their new house there was nothing.

The wall and the hedge deadened the traffic noise from the road. She never heard sounds from their neighbours whose houses were a ten-minute trek from her own. She had no clue if there were children her age anywhere close by.

Even the house was silent. On weekdays her mother moved around downstairs cleaning and tidying but there was never anything in the background. No radio, no television. It was like her mother was constantly listening to the sounds of the house, waiting for anything out of place.

Only with the deafening sound of tyres on gravel did the house come alive. When her father returned from work her mother's anxiety was released and for a few hours each evening they would pretend to be normal.

Emily missed a lot of things from her old life, but mainly she missed her friend.

She reached beneath the bed and took out the half-filled scrapbook. The first page was a printed-out picture of Emily and Suzie beaming above a heading of "Our Travels."

The scrapbook held page upon page of the two of them on holidays, in go-karts, on fair rides, in the sea and their last one at a Justin Bieber concert.

She looked at the blank page opposite, still not able to believe there would be no more. That the memories she had were all she was ever going to get.

She stared at their last picture, hard. Suzie had been so proud of her "belieber" T-shirt. All the way home from the NEC arena in Birmingham they had laughed, swooned and argued about who was going to marry their idol. They eventually decided they would share him; much to the entertainment of their mothers in the front seats.

Three days later they'd been snatched.

Emily looked into the eyes of her friend; so full of fun and mischief. So different to when they'd been pulled from each other that last time. Suzie's face began to blur before her as Emily's finger touched the face that still lived in her dreams.

She constantly remembered the ordeal, as though it had happened last week. During the day she suffered the guilt of having lived when Suzie had died. At night the fear returned in her dreams. Especially of that last day.

She remembered the man's arms around her stomach as he pulled her away from her friend. She remembered the feel of his bony chest against the back of her head as he'd pulled her across the room. She remembered the sensation of trying to grip Suzie's cold hand. She had thought that if they both held on tightly nothing could force them apart. But she'd been wrong.

A punch to the side of Suzie's head had sent her tumbling to the ground and Emily had been unable to hang on. Within a second she had felt herself being grabbed around the waist and lifted. She had screamed at Suzie to wake up but she'd remained where she was on the ground. And she'd never seen her friend again.

The vision hit her in the stomach anew and the tears began to fall.

She wiped a droplet from the face of her friend and clutched the book to her midriff as the sobs ripped through her body.

"Oh, Suzie, I'm sorry, I'm sorry, I'm sorry."

CHAPTER 65

"What's bugging you, Guv?" Bryant asked as they got back into the car after leaving the Truemans' house.

"Piss off," Kim said, aggravated he knew her that well.

"You look like a kid on Christmas morning who got a stocking full of coal. Actually, that probably wasn't..."

His words trailed away as he started the car.

"It's all about logic," she said. "My brain is happy to dismiss something once it understands the logic and yet there's something that won't go away."

"Like what?" he asked.

"Maybe I should have listened," she said, staring out of the window.

"Well, that'd be a first, but you're gonna have to narrow it down."

"Eloise."

He switched the engine off. "You've got to be kidding me. You're considering changing a lifetime habit for a crackpot, psychic, medium...whatever she is?"

Kim realised how ridiculous it sounded but Stacey's findings about the woman were not what she'd been expecting. She'd anticipated the woman would be a self-serving, manipulative charlatan preying on the vulnerabilities of others. At the very least a book or two.

"She told me that he wasn't finished with the others and last night Jenny Cotton got a message asking if she wants to play again."

"Coincidence," he said, dismissively. "Did she offer anything else?"

"Yeah, the number 278. She repeated it and told me to remember it."

"Anything else?"

Kim shook her head. She would not share the third observation about Mikey.

She remembered Eloise's words as Helen had dragged her away. "She did say something about someone close to the..."

"I think you're giving it too much thought. She's some kind of crook and we're just waiting for the punchline."

"But what did she have to gain?"

Bryant shrugged. "Involvement on a high profile case would have done ticket sales the world of good. Maybe an occasional appearance on *This Morning*. Who knows?"

"But that's the problem. Why hasn't she gone to the papers or the radio trying to make something out of it? Why is there no money-making scheme here at all? Until I understand it I can't forget it."

He glanced sideways. "That look ain't budging." He sighed. "You can't seriously believe she has anything useful to offer us to find Charlie and Amy? And if she did say anything, can you honestly tell me you'd believe her, let alone act on it?"

Kim counted about three questions there and the answer was no to every one of them. And yet Eloise had said that the other game wasn't over and the things she'd said about Mikey...

Damn it, no one could have known about that.

CHAPTER 66

Dawson checked the address on the paper in his hand. Yep, it definitely said 42 Rosemary Gardens. And that was the address he was looking at right now. The house lay in a cul-de-sac that branched off the Amblecote Road in Brierley Hill. The differences between this and the properties on Hollytree were not synonymous with the one mile that separated them. Relatively speaking, this house was on another planet.

Dawson wondered if Shona was having a bit of a laugh at his expense. Sending him on a wild goose chase. Girls who lived in Rosemary Gardens didn't voluntarily enter the Hollytree estate and if they did they needed to be locked in their rooms.

After his conversation with Dewain's family, this was his logical next step. He hoped to leave here with a lead on who had informed Lyron that Dewain was still alive. Someone had leaked it to the gang leader and the boss was entrusting him with the task of finding out who.

He'd worked his own cases before but this was not like an armed robbery of a petrol station or a GBH or even a domestic assault. This was a case that had affected his boss deeply. He'd heard that she had even pinned Tracy Frost to the wall in a gym somewhere. He had no idea if that was true and he knew he'd never hear it from her. But it wouldn't have surprised him. There was something in that kid that had resonated with her. He had no idea what it was.

But when they had stood beside Dewain's bedside, observing the artificially induced movement of his chest, he had seen her right hand touch lightly on the boy's wrist as it lay motionless above the crisp white sheet.

This was a case she would have worked herself if she hadn't been trying to save the lives of Amy and Charlie. And she had passed it to him. He could not let her down. He would not let her down.

He approached a spacious front porch that displayed a selection of green, leafy plants in jardinières. The doorbell sing-songed in his ears.

The front door opened to reveal a girl in her late teens. Her legs were clad in Fair-Isle leggings covered by a slip of a black skirt. A plain pink T-shirt dropped off her left shoulder. The aroma of Reckless by Roja Parfums reached out towards him. He recognised it immediately as the fragrance he had bought his fiancée for her birthday. She had joked that he only ever bought her expensive gifts when he'd done something wrong. And that perfume had been *expensive*. Too bloody expensive for a teenager, he mused.

"Lauren Cain?" he asked, holding up his badge.

She didn't look away from his face to acknowledge the identification before opening the door, just stepped back and stood in the doorway.

"Come in," she said, with a smile, and a tilt of the head.

Dawson stepped in, taking care not to brush against her, and stood just inside the hallway as she closed the door behind him. He had the sudden, inexplicable desire to open the door back up.

"Go through," she said, pointing to her right, exhibiting impeccable manners.

He entered a lounge that stretched the entire length of the house. A spacious garden preceded a view down into the basin of Lye and across to the Clent Hills.

"Sit down, Officer," she said, tipping her head.

As he did she looked him up and down and made no secret of it.

He quickly assessed her. A square nose kept her face the wrong side of pretty but Lauren was a girl who made the most of what she had. Her hair was dyed an attractive blonde and her make-up had been perfected. More obvious was the sex appeal that hit him before her perfume.

Despite the abundance of chairs she sat right next to him on the sofa. Her knee rested against his. He moved it away.

"I need to talk to you about Dewain."

Her eyebrows lowered briefly in a calculated, questioning look.

Irritation surged through him. "Dewain Wright. Your ex-boyfriend. The one that died last week."

If she heard the edge to his voice she ignored it.

She squeezed his upper arm as though he was a toy she didn't quite know how to work.

"Nice muscles," she said, tipping her head to the side.

"Thank you," he said, moving his arm away and shuffling as far as he could to the left. "Can you tell me what you remember about the day Dewain died?"

He'd deliberately asked an open question to see if she admitted to receiving the text message from Shona.

She sat back against the sofa and crossed one leg over the other. Her ankle brushed his shin.

Dawson stood and moved towards the fireplace. This girl was not getting the hint.

"I don't really remember it all that well. Sorry. Are you married?"

"That's not really your business," he replied, tersely. He needed to ask his questions and leave this teenager to her little games. "How did you find out about the attack?" he pushed.

She shrugged. "I honestly don't recall."

Dawson could see from her expression that she was no longer trying.

"Lauren, I need you to—"

She stood. "I don't have a boyfriend, you know."

"Did you know he was in a gang?" he asked, ignoring the suggestion in her voice.

She rolled her eyes as she took a step towards him. "Duh, of course."

Dawson took a step back. "Was that the attraction?" he asked, openly.

She shrugged. "I don't really..."

"Remember," he finished for her.

Her expression didn't change. She regarded him coyly and tipped her head as though they were playing kiss chase in the playground.

"Were you told he'd died after the knife attack?"

"I think so." She nodded. "Yeah, definitely told he was dead."

Thank goodness she remembered something.

"And you got a text message from Shona?"

"Yeah, I got something from her. An hour or two later, I think." She took another step forward, twirling her hair. "My parents won't be home for hours."

It wasn't so long ago Dawson had been a teenager full of raging hormones, but he couldn't remember the girls acting like this. Back then he would have loved it but right now it just turned him off.

This flirty, over-sexed girl was nothing more to him than a witness. A person of interest in a crime he needed to solve.

"Lauren, I have a fiancée and a child and what I need from you are answers."

"Doesn't bother me," she shrugged. Dawson realised too late that he had allowed the conversation to divert from the death of

Dewain but there was a determination in this girl's eyes that was beginning to unnerve him.

"Did the text message tell you Dewain was still alive?"

She shrugged. "I think so. I'm on the pill," she blurted out, leaning towards him.

Okay, enough was enough. The potential for this situation to become hazardous to his career progression was sounding warning bells in his head.

He stepped past her and headed towards the front door.

She followed closely behind. "I can tell my parents you did, you know," she hissed. Clearly, Lauren had finally got the message. Her sudden mood change was more suited to a toddler refused sweets.

The precariousness of the situation was not lost on him. He was alone in a house with a kid who had all but pinned him to the floor and he had done everything by the book. At nineteen years of age he didn't need parental consent to question her but what he did need was a witness. For his own safety.

Dawson waited until he was outside the door before he turned and asked the only question that mattered.

"Tell me, Lauren, did you tell anyone at all that Dewain was still alive?"

She smiled at him coyly and he could recite the words before they even left her mouth.

She couldn't bloody remember.

CHAPTER 67

Karen emptied the water from the sink and reached for the cream cleaner. Her beautiful kitchen had always reached levels of laboratory standard cleanliness but she now felt that open heart surgery could be performed on her worktops without any fear of infection.

The house had settled into the afternoon routine that had quickly cemented. The guard sat at the front door with little to do. Helen wandered around in the background eager to fetch and carry for anyone who moved a muscle.

There were times when Helen's presence irritated her; not the woman herself but her constant attempts to try to make life easier for them all. Karen didn't want the distractions removed. She wanted to pick up plates, mugs, glasses. She wanted to do anything that occupied her mind or her body, even if only for a second.

Any distraction from the questions in her head was a welcome relief. She knew that Stephen, and to some extent Elizabeth, felt that the press blackout was the wrong move. So far she had managed to persuade the two of them to trust Kim but she didn't know for how much longer. Stephen was not an easy man to convince.

Yet Karen still felt they were right to trust Kim's judgement. Their paths had crossed throughout their childhood and the surly, dark-haired girl had been an enigma to them all. She didn't want friends; in fact, she actively avoided forming any kind of bonds.

Just like prison, personal circumstances and reasons for being in care were rarely shared and it was only much later that Karen had learned of Kim's tragic past. That the young Kim could function carrying all that baggage was astounding.

But there was another reason Karen trusted the forthright woman and Kim didn't even know.

Twelve years earlier Karen had been living in a squat on the outskirts of Wolverhampton. She hadn't had a job in two years and had lost her flat. The derelict pub had been raided by twelve police officers and three social workers for the seven children living inside. She had recognised Kim immediately and had kept her hand up to her face.

One woman, Lynda, had slammed the bedroom door shut and refused to open it, threatening to throw her two-year-old son out of the window if anyone entered the room. While the rest of the police officers had cleared the building, Kim had stood at the door and kept Lynda talking.

She had promised Lynda that no one would touch her son and they would be kept together until his health had been assessed.

Eventually, when the building was clear, the whole team was assembled outside the last door. Karen could hear officers urging Kim to let them break the door down but Kim would not get out of the way.

A further forty minutes of reassurances passed before Lynda opened the door. Two social services women rushed forward to take the child but Kim stood in their way.

"I gave her my word," was all she said.

Karen had seen and heard it all, because she'd been in the room when Lynda locked the door. Upon being freed she had hurried past, unnoticed.

She had been mortified to reflect on her own life in the face of the woman's success. Kim was a bloody police officer and she was scum in a squat.

The next morning Karen had walked into the job centre and refused to leave until they found her some kind of work.

"Oh, I'm sorry, I didn't realise you were in here."

Although Karen knew the voice, she turned to see Elizabeth backing out of the room.

"Can we not even be in the same room now?" Karen asked, sadly.

It had been such a short time since they'd stood in this room, holding each other, comforting each other. Sharing a pain that only the two of them could understand.

"It's just…"

Elizabeth's words trailed away. It was just what? That a few days ago they had been closer than sisters. And now they were in competition for the lives of their children.

The surreal nature of the situation hit Karen hard. No matter the outcome, they would never recover from this.

It would never be a memory fondly recalled over dinner on a balmy Saturday night.

They stood in opposite corners of the room with more than the breakfast bar between them.

Karen wanted to say something, anything that would take them back to the night she had trusted her best friend with the biggest secret of them all. Only Elizabeth knew that Robert was not Charlie's father.

For the first time she looked at her friend closely.

"Your lip is swollen," she said, angling her head for a better view.

Elizabeth turned an inch away. "Oh, I fell over in the bathroom."

"On what?" Karen asked. She didn't even try to hide the disbelief in her voice. They had known each other for too long.

"I just slipped on..."

"You've *slipped in the bathroom* before, Elizabeth. I remember it."

Elizabeth took a step backwards. "No...I didn't..."

"You said you wouldn't let him do this to you again."

"It's just the situation. I pushed and..."

"Robert hasn't hit me and we're feeling it just as much as you are."

Karen hadn't meant the words to come out that way. In her head they had sounded so different. Out of her mouth it sounded like they were competing for levels of distress and pressure.

Finally their eyes met and Karen saw the tears form as Elizabeth gingerly touched her lip.

Normally she would have crossed the distance between them and comforted her. But even that felt like a betrayal of her own daughter. How could she consort with the enemy? The notion stabbed at her heart but whatever the outcome, they would never be able to look at each other and not know each other's innermost thoughts. What each of them would be willing to sacrifice for the sake of their own child.

Her darling Charlie was her world. Karen would offer her own life and the life of anyone else to save her child. Including Amy. And she knew that Elizabeth felt the exact same way. No friendship could ever endure that knowledge.

And as they stared across the kitchen table, they both knew it.

Karen turned back to the sink.

There was nothing left to say.

CHAPTER 68

Kim looked up and down Wordsley High Street. The grit bin was positioned on the corner.

"What time is it?" she asked.

"Eleven fifty-five."

Kim walked along the street. The left-hand side was a string of shops including a café, butchers, jewellers and a mini market.

The opposite side of the road held a row of new town houses.

She walked back to the middle of the road and continued to look both ways. She tuned out the crowds on her side of the road, rushing in and out of the shops.

What made this road useful to the kidnappers?

"Bryant, when were those houses built?"

"Only recently. They're mainly studio apartments."

Kim started to get a picture in her head. "So, back then it was an empty space?"

"I think so. What you seeing, Guv?"

"I'm seeing nowhere on that side of the street for officers to lie in wait. There's nothing there so anyone hanging around would have stuck out like a sore thumb. The only viewing point is over here. I'm missing something so . . ." her words trailed away as she spotted the last piece of the puzzle. "And here it comes."

Bryant looked to his left. A double decker bus ambled along the street and stopped right in front of the grit bin.

"Jesus, nobody would have been able to see a thing. He could have been waiting just around the corner. He would have heard the bus pull up."

Kim nodded. "A few people to get off to do their shopping and we're talking at least a minute to open up the bin and pick something up."

"Simple but clever."

Kim ran the twenty feet to the top of the road. She caught the number of the bus as it turned the corner.

"Bloody hell, Guv, what was that about?" Bryant asked, catching her up.

"The front of the bus. Damn it, the bus number was the 278."

CHAPTER 69

"Jesus Christ, Symes, did you have to do that much damage?"

Will had read the newspaper article twice, which held considerably more detail than the television reports.

Symes shrugged and smiled. "I got the job done and I'm happy in my work. What's your fucking problem? Dead, ain't she?"

Will shook his head and turned away. There was no point trying to explain to the moron that he was taking unnecessary risks. The more violent the crime scene the greater the chance of him leaving behind something of himself for them to analyse. He was just thankful the idiot hadn't raped her. With the leisure centre kid Symes had used only his feet, judging by the online news report. And his Tesco trainers were common enough to be untraceable. But still, it was unnecessary.

He wheeled himself over to the phone table.

He switched on mobile phone number one and was not surprised to see a missed call.

He switched on phone number two. Another missed call from the same number.

He switched on phone number three to see he had a voicemail and a text.

He put the phone on loudspeaker and hit the play button.

The voice was calm and pleasant.

"Matt Ward, negotiator. Give me a call and we can resolve this. I can help you get what you want."

Will deleted the message. He didn't need to speak to any negotiator. He had stated his terms and the onus was on them.

"You wouldn't think about it, would you?" Symes asked.

"Think about what?"

"Changing the plan, making a deal—'cos *we* have a deal, remember?"

Will did remember. It was something he'd agreed to so he could keep Symes away from the girls. For now.

He could not risk the idiot damaging the merchandise until they had the money. And after that, well . . .

"We have a deal," Will confirmed.

He scrolled to the only incoming message he was interested in. It had come from one of the parents.

The game was finally on.

With a smile he opened the text message and read. His eyes widened in surprise as he read it again.

He turned to Symes who was waiting eagerly.

As he handed over the phone, he said, "Well, I wasn't expecting that."

CHAPTER 70

"This really gonna do us any good, Guv?" Bryant asked, bringing the car to a stop.

"Bryant, I have no idea," she said, honestly. She only knew that something was compelling her to speak to the woman.

The dwelling was an unassuming bungalow at the top of a slope on a small residential estate. A blue, ten-year-old Fiesta sat in the uncluttered driveway.

"Wait here if you like," Kim said, opening the car door. It was mid-afternoon and the woman could be off trawling the Wednesday markets for all Kim knew.

She had no idea what she was going to say, anyway. Bryant had been right when he'd surmised that she probably wouldn't believe a word that came out of her mouth. And yet she was here all the same.

"With all due respect, Guv, the last time I waited in the car you attempted to force entry into a leisure centre so I think I'll tag along."

They walked single file beside the Fiesta and knocked on the door.

"If I ask her nicely do you think she'll give me the lottery numbers for Saturday?"

"Shut up," she snapped.

She listened closely for any sound of movement. There was none. She knocked again and leaned down to open the letterbox.

The front door led into a small hallway from which she could see a couple of plain white doors but nothing beyond. She listened keenly for sounds from the house. Silence.

She knocked again, harder, and moved to the left-hand side of the door. She pressed her face against the window but could see nothing through the heavy net curtain.

"Knock again, Bryant," she said, stepping backwards. The window to the other side of the door was equally obscured.

Kim looked at Bryant and they both looked at the car.

"I'm going round the back. Try next door," she said, nodding to the adjoining property.

"Guv…"

"Just do it, Bryant," she growled.

The side of the property was unencumbered. A roll of logs rose a foot from the ground to mark the boundary to the property on the left.

The back door was a single panel of distorted glass. Kim could make out shapes but nothing else. The window was bare and looked into a small, bright kitchen.

Kim could feel the frustration building in her stomach. "Come on, Eloise, where the hell are you?"

"Guv, neighbour last saw her yesterday afternoon with a couple of bags from Aldi."

"Look in that window," she said, stepping back. His extra couple of inches might see beyond the immediate area.

Bryant looked in and cast a glance over the area. He began to shake his head and then stopped. He adjusted his position and pressed his face against the glass.

"Hang on, that might be…"

"What?" she said.

He beckoned her towards him. "I'm gonna have to lift you up now; press your face against the glass and look to the far left."

Kim looked around for something to stand on but saw nothing. "Go," she said.

Bryant formed a circle with his arms around her thighs and hoisted her so her head was a good twelve inches higher than his own. She did as he asked and saw the sliver of a wingback chair. At the top was a clutch of grey.

"Put me down," Kim said.

She headed straight for the door and knocked loudly. "Keep watching and see if she moves."

She knocked again on the glass door.

Bryant shook his head.

"Okay, we're going in," Kim said, looking around the garden for something heavy.

"Hang on, Guv," Bryant said, taking a handkerchief from his pocket.

He tried the door handle, which opened.

Bryant shrugged in her direction, looking a little too pleased with himself.

"Not one word," she said shortly, stepping past him.

Kim traversed the small kitchen in three strides. The wingback chair was beside a small round table that held a mug of something cold and a copy of *Pride and Prejudice*. Beside the mug was a bowl of different coloured crystals.

Kim moved to the front of the chair. The woman's eyes were closed and her mouth was slightly open.

Her frame looked less portly clad in a thick cardigan, her legs covered by a shawl. Kim nudged her gently.

"Eloise," she called.

No response.

Kim shook harder and called louder but the head simply lolled to the side.

"She's not asleep, Guv," Bryant said from behind.

"Damn it," Kim said, stepping back.

"Looks peaceful enough," Bryant said, tipping his head. "Might have been a stroke or something while she was sleeping."

Kim shook her head. "I should have bloody listened to her. What would it have hurt?"

She stepped away and sighed deeply. Only a couple of days ago this woman had tried to tell her something and she'd been too damn stubborn to listen.

She turned back to the body. "Best call an ambulance," she said as Bryant took out his phone.

She took in the sight before her of a poor old woman who had died alone. From the bookcases behind it looked as though books had been her companions. Clearly a lover of the classics, Kim spied a Tolstoy, a few more Jane Austen novels and the full works of Dickens on Eloise's shelves. A photograph of two dogs graced the windowsill but Kim could see no other evidence of their presence.

"Looks like she was quite…"

Her words trailed away as she studied the picture before her. There was something not right with this scene.

Bryant ended his call. The ambulance was on its way.

"Come and stand here," she said, tipping her head.

He did so.

"Anything strike you as a bit strange?"

He looked from the curly grey hair down to the flowery slippers protruding from beneath the blanket.

He shook his head. "Looks quite comfy and snug to me."

"Precisely," Kim said, stepping forward. She looked to the right of the woman and then the left.

"Look at the shawl, Bryant. It's covering her hands."

Bryant looked to where both hands disappeared below the covering.

He looked at her quizzically, then looked back at the old woman's hands. "I don't get what…"

Bryant stopped talking as he realised what Kim was referring to.

"Shit, yeah, I see your point. It's like she's been tucked in."

That's how it looked to Kim. The shawl had been placed across her and then tucked into her hips on both sides. It was possible that she'd done it herself, that she'd smoothed the fabric behind her own hips and then burrowed her hands underneath, but it was unlikely when she had a drink to hold and a book to read.

Kim moved forward and put her legs astride the feet of Eloise. She placed her hands on either side of the armchair and leaned in close.

"Damn it," Kim said, as her eyes registered a speck resting at the woman's mouth. "Bryant, there's a dark blue fibre on her lip."

The shawl was red and navy.

She reached forward and gently moved the lower lip.

"Jesus Christ," she cried, jumping backwards.

"Bloody hell, Guv…"

Kim recovered from the shock quickly, her mind racing. She reached in again and placed two fingers to the soft skin of the neck.

She turned to her colleague in wonder. "Bryant, put a rush on that ambulance. Our victim is still alive."

Bryant hesitated for just a second but took out his phone.

"Eloise, if you can hear me, it's gonna be okay. There's an ambulance coming and we're not going to leave you."

There was no response.

Kim placed a gentle hand on her shoulder, her heartbeat still up a gear.

Bryant finished the call.

"They're just two minutes out," he said, shaking his head.

Although she'd never seen it, Kim knew that asphyxiation victims could fall into a coma before death. Whoever had smothered her had thought they'd done enough, but this lady had held on to a thin sliver of life.

"So, you think our killing machine found out about Eloise and got worried she had something to say?"

"No way, Bryant. Subject Two has been busy out killing and Subject One would need to have stayed with Charlie and Amy. I think this was the work of Subject Three."

As she heard the sound of sirens in the distance, Kim realised that Eloise hadn't shouted anything to do with a blue gate. She had been trying to warn her that she was going to be too late.

Kim had to wonder if she'd meant for herself or for the girls.

CHAPTER 71

They watched as the ambulance pulled away.

Kim had the urge to throw the car into gear and follow, simply because no one else did.

As the ambulance exited the road a squad car entered. Officers would secure the property, enabling them to leave.

She had already called the scene in to Woody, who'd assured her he would dispatch a small forensics team to the house. She updated him on the state of the investigation. When she finished, the silence on the other end of the line had been heavy.

Woody's disappointment paled against her own.

Two small huddles of neighbours had gathered in the small street but no one had bothered to approach.

"Look at 'em," Bryant said. "They're all just relieved it's not them."

Eloise would arrive at the hospital as she had left her home. Alone.

"Did Woody offer anything useful?" Bryant asked, pulling away from the kerb.

She shook her head. "Can't really blame him," Kim said. "Charlie and Amy should be home by now."

"Bloody hell, Guv, give yourself a break. No one could be working harder to get those kids back. You're living and breathing—"

"They're just kids, Bryant. Little girls. Wherever they are they're terrified, confused, possibly hurt, God forbid even worse." A picture of their clothing came into her mind. "I need to get them back. I need to keep them safe," she said.

"Keep, Guv?"

She didn't realise she'd said that. A vision of Mikey came into her head. "I meant make them safe," she said, blinking Mikey away.

"We're going to find them, you know," Bryant said, staring forward.

"How can you be so sure?"

"Because you're not gonna rest until we do."

Kim couldn't fight the smile that tugged at her lips. And there it was. The simple truth that dispelled all doubt.

"Okay, Bryant, get me back to the house, now."

CHAPTER 72

"So, what's that tell us, Doc?" Kim said, fixing her gaze on Alison. An aerial view of the Black Country had been taped to the wall. Plotted on the map was the snatch site, the start and end of the bus route, and the drop site, all marked out in red pins.

The impatience in her voice stemmed from the knowledge that the girls were not coming home tonight.

Her own timeline was beginning to blur. She was sure their last briefing had taken place at least three days before instead of first thing that morning. She reminded herself it was still Wednesday.

The vision of Eloise being taken away from her home would not disappear from her mind. Kim could kick her own arse for not even allowing the woman a minute. She resolved to call the hospital later. Just for her own peace of mind. Maybe if she'd just given Eloise a chance to speak she could have prevented this somehow.

The case was affecting them all. Her team surrounded the table in various states of disarray. Bryant's tie had dropped a few levels. Dawson's shirt was crumpled and the red lines in Stacey's eyes were like an Ordnance Survey map.

But tonight they had more work to do.

The blue pins noted the two snatch sites of Suzie and Emily and the point at which Emily had been found.

Yellow was for where Inga had been found.

Alison stood and studied the map for a minute.

"I'm no expert on geographic profiling. Much of the data comes from the premise of how a killer will interact with a crime scene or where and how a body was disposed.

"It's assumed that if a body is found at a site different from that of the murder the killer generally lives in that area. Alternatively, if the body is left at the murder scene it's possible the killer is not local."

She covered her mouth briefly to stifle a yawn. The late nights were getting to her too, Kim thought.

"A crime scene close to a major road can indicate the murderer is not familiar to the area. If the crime scene is a mile or more from a major road, this suggests the killer is local."

Alison continued to speak while staring at the plot points.

"But some things remain a safe supposition. One is that each criminal has their patch. Organised killers stay close but disorganised killers roam more. And most people have an 'anchor point.'"

She turned and faced Kim. Her expression said, *That's all I've got.*

"Thanks, Doc," Kim said. It wasn't a lot but that wasn't Alison's fault. There would be a pattern in there somewhere. It was just finding it.

"Matt, any contact with the kidnappers?"

"Trying," he answered, without looking at her. His focus was on the dots.

"Care to elaborate?"

"No."

Kim felt the irritation growing inside her. Her spelling of team didn't include the letter "I." Obviously Matt spelt it differently.

"Stace, I want you to draw a circle around all those dots and look at any recent criminal activity in that area. There might be something that jumps out. I still want to know what brought the incident to a close the last time. Why was Emily released without any payment and not Suzie? We have two murders and an attempted murder clearly carried out by someone else. And who the hell is Subject Three?"

Everyone nodded their agreement.

"I want everyone thinking about who this third person could be."

"Difficult when we don't know who the first two are," Bryant offered.

That was the stumbling block in her mind every time. If even one of the kidnappers was known to them they could work off known associations but they didn't even have that.

"Kev, anything from Inga's post mortem to help?"

"Clothes are a bit of a history lesson: traces of engine oil, wood preserver and rodent shit. In total seventeen broken bones, thirty-eight points of contact with either a foot or a fist and nine circles around her neck."

Kim noted that Dawson didn't need to refer to his notes to read off the statistics.

The numbers told her that the woman had worked hard to avoid the inevitable.

Her killer was a monster with no empathy for human suffering. He was volatile, with no regard for human life. He was taking unnecessary risks and there could only be one reason to have such a man on the team.

The realisation hit her in the stomach.

"They're not coming back," she whispered, looking around the room. "That's the purpose of Subject Two. His job is to kill the girls."

All eyes fell on her. In her gut she knew it was true. It was the only reason to have such a liability on the team. Subject Two had to have a necessary purpose. It was his job to clean up the mess.

"I would agree," Matt said.

"So, what's the point of the auction?" Bryant asked.

"Drives up the price," Kim said. "There's a difference in fighting for your child and doing so before someone beats you to it. It injects a note of speed, desperation."

Matt turned to Bryant. "Imagine a guy running a ten-thousand-metre race on his own, secure in the knowledge he'll come first. He'll run the race. Put another eight guys on the track with a hunger to win and our guy is going to dig deep. He'll find reserves of energy he didn't even know he had."

"So, this is all just to push up the price?" Stacey asked.

"And then they'll take both," Kim said. "They'll each be given a different drop-off point and time. And they'll take the lot."

Matt nodded his agreement.

"That's a heck of an assumption," Alison said, doubtfully.

"Said the profiler," Kim noted, as Matt's police-issue phone sounded the receipt of a text message.

The room stilled and all eyes bored into him.

"It's them," he said.

Kim followed his eyes as they moved across the message.

He raised his gaze to meet hers. "Damn it. This is not good."

CHAPTER 73

Holding her rage in check, Kim gathered all the parents in the lounge. Helen stood at the window. Matt leaned against the door frame. The rest of the team had remained in the incident room.

Her gaze passed over them all individually. She lingered on Elizabeth's lip for a few seconds. Elizabeth looked to the floor.

"Who made contact with the kidnappers?"

The faces of Elizabeth and Stephen dropped. They looked at each other before turning their gaze accusingly on their friends.

"I did," Robert said, calmly. There was no apology in his voice. He was just stating a fact.

"How could you do that?" Elizabeth cried.

He turned to her and met her gaze. "How could I not?"

Stephen crossed the space at speed but Matt inserted himself between them quicker.

Robert didn't flinch.

"You devious bastard," Stephen spat over Matt's shoulder. "How the hell could you do that? You fucking know—"

"Stephen, calm down," Robert said, cutting off his words.

Robert knew what? Kim wondered. Judging by the puzzled expression on Elizabeth's face, she was wondering the exact same thing.

Stephen allowed Matt to push him gently to the other side of the room and Karen turned to him, eyes blazing. "If you can't control your temper then please leave my home."

Kim could see that Stephen's rage was not yet spent, so quickly said, "If we can all calm down, the problem we now have is that the kidnappers won't deal with the negotiator. We have just received a text message stating they would prefer to respond to the parents' request."

Robert nodded his understanding. "I'm sorry but I just—"

Kim held up her hand. His apology was sincere but wouldn't help. They could only move forward now with what they had. Kim's only surprise was that it was Robert and not Stephen who had broken first. Her gut told her there was a reason for that but she left it for now.

"Have you received a text message back?"

Robert nodded. "Fifteen minutes ago."

"Which said?"

"Not an option."

Kim was confused. She assumed that Robert had offered a monetary value.

"What did you ask?"

Robert met her gaze squarely. "I asked how much for both."

A small sob escaped from Elizabeth's lips and Stephen's head snapped around. Karen stared forward with no reaction. She had known.

Everyone looked at each other for a moment.

"Okay," Kim said. "Matt is going to work with you both on how to communicate with them. He'll be negotiating through the two of you."

"That's the most ridiculous thing I've ever heard," Stephen exploded.

An exasperated sigh travelled around the room.

"Why is this all on us? What exactly are you doing to get our daughters back?"

Kim was now weary of his questions. She didn't get this much shit from Woody.

"Mr. Hanson, my team and I—"

"I don't want to hear about how hard your team is working. I want to know where you are in the investigation. I want to know when you will concede defeat and go to the press. Will they have to come home in body bags before...?"

"Outside, now," Kim snarled.

She almost felt the rush of air as every head whipped around towards her.

She stormed past Lucas and threw the door open. Stephen followed closely behind, matching her pace.

He started speaking before she'd stopped walking. She'd wanted more distance between the house and the sound of her voice but she stopped walking. Here would have to do.

"Detective Inspector, I do not appreciate—"

"I couldn't care less about what you appreciate but don't you ever speak about your daughter or theirs like that again."

"My thoughts are—"

"Best left in your head. Now, listen to me carefully. I have had enough of you second-guessing my every move on this case. It is distracting and I will not be pushed around like some women, Mr. Hanson. Do we understand each other?"

His look was defiant. "No, Inspector, we do not."

She stepped closer, into his face. "Then let me spell it out for you. I am not your wife and I will not put up with your bullshit. If you do anything else to disrupt this investigation, including hitting your wife, Karen won't be the only one asking you to leave." Kim stepped even closer. "Only I'll be doing it with handcuffs and a police escort." She paused, her face an inch from his. "Now, do we understand each other?"

He stepped back, giving her his answer.

She had tried to be empathetic to his plight but Stephen's constant badgering had pushed her one step too far.

"Inspector, you should know that I don't think you're capable of running this investigation."

Kim bit her tongue and followed him towards the front door.

Stephen disappeared back into the lounge. Bryant blocked her entry into the house.

"Guv, a minute," he said, closing the door behind him and coming outside.

"Bryant, whatever this is, it can wait."

"No, it really can't."

"What?" she snapped, eager to get back to the war room.

"You're losing it, Guv," he said, turning to face her.

"Who the hell do you think—"

"Okay, I'll rephrase. You're losing it, Kim. Because I'm telling you as a friend. You're not eating, you're not sleeping, you're snapping at everyone and you just brought one of the girls' fathers outside for a verbal kicking. Talk to me."

She glared at him. "You do know there is a line and you are seriously close to overstepping it?"

Bryant shrugged. "Yeah, deal with me later but for now will you just bloody well let it out?"

"There's nothing to let out and you need to back the hell off. If you dare undermine me in front of—"

"Never gonna happen and you know it—but if it helps to take it out on me, do it. I can take it. But you've got to release it somehow."

"There's nothing—"

"For fuck's sake, Kim," he snarled.

Kim was stunned. Bryant rarely cursed and hardly ever shouted. And he'd never done either at her.

"I know exactly what you're doing. You're taking everyone's frustration and turning it on yourself. Every negative feeling is your responsibility because those little girls are still out there.

You're trying to shoulder the fears of a dozen people and, as strong as you are, you just can't do it."

Kim felt the familiar rage building. "Take your analysis and shove it up your arse. How dare you presume—"

"I'll dare because no one else will and you need to be told that it's not your fault."

Kim knew this was her opportunity to tell him how she was feeling. And Bryant would find some way to make her feel better. He always did.

But as well as being her friend, he was a member of her team. And she would not allow any of them to see her fear. Two people were dead and a third was fighting for her life. Charlie and Amy were still out there, frightened and at risk.

She couldn't allow herself to feel better.

Not until she brought them home.

CHAPTER 74

Elizabeth waited until the bedroom door closed behind them.

"What the hell was all that about?"

Stephen walked past her without meeting her gaze.

"She just wanted to have a quiet word about—"

"Not that, Stephen. I know what that was about. She took you outside to smack your arse—and quite rightly too. That's not what I'm talking about."

He shook his head. "Then I have no idea what you mean."

Elizabeth sat on the other side of the bed. She was happy to have her back to him.

"Why haven't we made an offer, Stephen?"

Her heart was hammering in her chest but she would not let this conversation go. She wasn't frightened of a repeat performance with his fist. The real fear came from the realisation that was trying desperately to dawn in the back of her mind.

"We hadn't finalised . . . we were discussing . . ."

"Robert and Karen talked and discussed, then took action and tried to save Amy and Charlie. Why haven't we?"

"It was an empty gesture on his part. Robert knew they would not accept—"

"Don't you dare do that, Stephen. Don't you even dare try and denigrate what Robert tried to do so you can feel better about yourself. At least he tried."

"Jesus, Liz, anyone can send a text message."

"Then why didn't we?" she asked, simply.

Every response knocked a nail into her heart—she knew where they were headed. Elizabeth didn't want to hear the words but she had to.

"How much do we have in the savings account, Stephen?"

"Liz, I don't know. I'd have to go online..."

"Amy has been with kidnappers for three days and you haven't checked our bank account once."

She felt his agitation from the other side of the bed.

"There's nothing in there, is there?"

"Don't be ridiculous. Of course—"

"Stop lying, Stephen. I know there's nothing there. What about the house?"

Stephen said nothing.

"Have you taken out a second mortgage on our home?"

"Liz, let me explain..."

She stood. She wasn't even angry any more. She felt dead inside.

"So, we're broke. We have no money and you couldn't find the balls to tell me the reason we didn't make an offer was because we *couldn't*."

"Liz, sit down and we can—"

"Robert knew, didn't he? He knew that we couldn't play the game to save our daughter's life—which is why he tried to save both."

Stephen stood and approached her. His expression was desperate.

She held up her hands. "Don't touch me."

"We can get through this."

Elizabeth smiled sadly as she moved away. At that moment she realised that she no longer loved her husband—but her heart didn't have the capacity to hate him. It was already mourning the loss of her child.

In all their years she had deferred to him. She had agreed that she could complete her law degree later. She had supported every promotion. She had spent every late night without him.

She'd even understood when he'd done it the first time. His gambling debts had wiped out their savings. She'd believed him when he'd said it would never happen again.

All through their marriage Elizabeth had consoled herself that every partnership was a balance sheet. There were assets and debts on both sides but now that she added up her net worth she realised the company had gone bust.

"No, Stephen, you're wrong. I can't ever come back from this. Our marriage is over, regardless of what happens next."

He took another step towards her. She held up her hands and met his gaze. She did nothing to hide the repulsion she felt.

He took a step back.

"Feel free to stay...Amy is still your daughter, but you will sleep on the sofa."

His head dropped like a pathetic, abandoned puppy. She felt nothing.

She held out her right hand. "Now, give me the car keys. I'm going to fetch my son."

CHAPTER 75

Julia Trueman finished loading the dishwasher. Alan had returned home for dinner, showered, changed and left for his monthly meeting with the regional managers of his estate agency.

It was now the only time he ever left them in the evening.

Their dinner had been a subdued affair. Emily had been distracted and quiet. Every question asked had been answered with barely a full syllable.

Alan had glanced at his wife a few times and she had shrugged in response. She had chosen not to share the visit from the police with her husband. It was over. The kidnap was in the past and she wanted it firmly left there.

In spite of her ordeal, Emily was not a sullen child. She remained reasonably well balanced, not prone to sudden mood changes, so Julia guessed she'd been unnerved by the visit from the police. She knew Emily still missed her old friend. The photo album the two of them had built was never far from her bed. And she had little opportunity to make new friends.

Julia knew the social aspect of her daughter's life had been stunted by herself and Alan. Emily didn't attend school and was not allowed to join any social networking sites. People could be traced through those sites. Julia knew. She had checked.

Although Julia had heard what the female officer had said, she chose to completely ignore it.

When Alan left the house Julia switched off the television and went to check the alarm in the kitchen. All four sector lights winked at her. The quad screen showed no activity. She sighed with relief and headed to the snug.

The small room was her favourite in the whole house. Not least because she could keep watch on the front door.

She glanced along the bookshelves and settled on a Val McDermid novel. She paused before she sat, wondering if she should check on Emily one more time.

The child had claimed a headache and retired for an early night.

Julia had already checked her once since Alan had left.

The room had been dark but the low hum of Emily's iPod had confirmed that she had fallen asleep to the two thousand songs on the device.

Julia never bothered to remove it. Although the songs wouldn't run out, the charge on the iPod would.

No, she resolved. She had to give her daughter some space.

In the first few weeks after the kidnapping, Julia had slept in Emily's bedroom. The house had been sold cheaply to get a quick sale. Their current property had been on Alan's books for a while and he had shown it to her. The remoteness, the privacy and the brand new CCTV system had made the decision for them both.

Once they moved in she had returned to her own bed but woke almost hourly to check on her daughter. It was the same with the CCTV. Since they moved to this house, sitting before the monitor during daytime hours had become an addiction, a compulsion in the early days. Now she limited herself to every couple of hours.

She sat down and opened the book. There was an anxiety in the pit of her stomach that reached upwards to her throat.

She tried to read a couple of pages but the words were jumbling together like a foreign language. The sentences made no sense.

Julia told herself that it was because of the police visit earlier. She closed the book. She knew it wasn't that. When her thoughts rested on Emily the anxiety reacted like a poked wasp nest.

She stood. It was no good. She had to go and check one more time. She would risk that expression of exhausted tolerance on her child's face.

She mounted the stairs, forcing herself to remain calm. Tomorrow she'd do better. It reminded her of giving up smoking. She'd give up after the next one but this one, she had to have.

Emily's door was exactly as she'd left it.

Julia pushed it open gently. The evidence before her said that everything was as it should be but the wasps in her stomach said otherwise.

The shaft of light from the hallway illuminated the sleeping form of her daughter.

Justin Bieber sounded from the pillow.

She moved closer to the bed and touched her daughter lightly on the hip. Her hand was swallowed by the plush quilt.

Julia's heart beat loudly in her chest, drowning out the faint sound of the music.

She reached over to turn on the bedside lamp. Instantly, the room illuminated, telling her eyes what her heart already knew.

Emily was gone.

The scream from Julia's mouth filled the house.

CHAPTER 76

"Okay, guys it's almost ten and we've been at it for fifteen hours. Time to call it a night."

Kim rubbed her forehead. There was little else they could do at this stage.

Everyone began tidying up their work area.

"Leave it. I'll do it later."

Bryant gave her a look which she ignored. The last few hours had been spent poring over the old case notes, re-reading witness statements and trying to find some kind of geographical link.

"You coming, Matt?" Bryant asked from the doorway.

"Nah, got detention," he said.

Bryant smiled and hesitated. She knew he was looking her way but she didn't look back.

Everyone took a moment to bid Matt goodnight. Bloody traitors. He had gradually been wheedling his way into the team; making a fresh pot of coffee here, fetching a takeaway there. It might work on her feckless team but it wouldn't work on her.

"So, what's your strategy?" she asked, as they faced each other across the table. "And don't say it's none of my business 'cos it bloody well is."

"Well, since you asked so nicely I'm going to tell you."

"Really?"

"Yeah, you need all the help you can get. I'm going to get Stephen to make an offer first thing in the morning."

"You do know they've got no money?"

"You caught that too?"

"Hard to miss. Obviously Robert knew as well, which is why he started trying to negotiate for both girls. I can't hold that against him even though he pissed on your chips."

"But see, you're using emotion again and not logic."

Kim felt the familiar irritation growing inside her. "I'm acknowledging his generosity, not giving him a gold star."

Matt shrugged. "You're getting a bit close; a bit involved."

"Don't be bloody ridiculous," she snapped.

"Really? Why did you take Stephen Hanson outside?"

"I didn't appreciate his reference to body bags in front of the others."

"Nothing to do with him slapping his wife around?" Matt asked.

"The family dynamics of each couple are nothing to do with me."

He tutted. "You know, I hear the words but I just don't feel the conviction behind them. You're getting attached."

"I'm not, but even if I was, would that be such a bad thing?"

He thought for a moment and then nodded. "Yes. You were right to take Stephen outside for what he said but Stephen is an easy man to confront. He's an arsehole and you don't like him. But would you have had the same conversation with Robert?"

"Yes," she said, immediately. And she knew it to be true. She never got too close to anyone, as demonstrated by the contact list on her phone.

"Hmmm...we'll agree to differ on that one."

Kim offered a mock yawn. "And now I'd like to go to bed."

She looked pointedly at the door.

Matt gathered up his folders and left the room without speaking.

She didn't appreciate his observation, not least because it echoed Bryant's words to her earlier. She was not emotionally involved in the case. She was driven and determined to bring

Charlie and Amy home. And she would not allow herself to think otherwise.

The dining table resembled an explosion in a printing factory. She began tidying Bryant's pile first.

"Err...we appear to have a problem," Matt said, coming back into the room.

She rolled her eyes. "I told you..."

"There appears to be a man in my bed."

"Excuse me..."

Matt closed the door but still spoke quietly as he placed his folders back on the table. "Stephen Hanson is sleeping on the sofa so I'm guessing his wife knows about the money."

She looked at the folders and then back at him. "I've spotted at least four sofas, five armchairs and a giant bean bag. I'm sure..."

Her words trailed away as her phone began to ring.

It was not a number she recognised. Her first thought was of the kidnappers and a fresh phone, but the number began with the area prefix.

"Stone," she answered.

Silence greeted her at the other end.

Kim cast a glance at Matt, who had stopped messing with his papers.

"Stone," she repeated.

Still nothing but the line was active. Behind the silence was the background hum of traffic.

"Hello," she said, softly.

"Is that the police lady?"

The voice was soft, young and scared.

"This is Kim Stone."

"It's Emily...Emily Trueman. I've run away."

"Oh Jesus," Kim said. Matt was watching her intently. "Emily, where are you?"

"I caught a bus. I think I'm in Lye."

"Tell me what's around you. What can you see?"

"There's a pub called The Railway. There are three men standing outside smoking. There's an Indian restaurant on the corner and a pizza takeaway on the…'"

"Okay, Emily, I need you to go into the pizza place and stay there."

Kim knew the takeaway well. It was brightly lit and busy on the corner of a four-way intersection. The Railway pub was tiny but decent enough.

"I don't have any money," Emily said.

"Just tell them you're lost and that the police are coming to get you. Can you do that for me, Emily?"

"I th-think so."

"Listen, you must do what I tell you. Don't move from inside that shop. I'm coming to get you but you must stay there. Do you understand?"

"Yes."

The voice was small and frightened and Kim realised that despite everything Emily had been through, she was dealing with a ten-year-old who was younger than her years. On the Hollytree estate alone she knew of five kids that age who were the proud owners of ASBOs, but it was dark and late and the girl was away from her mother for the first time in months.

"Don't worry, Emily. Everything is going to be okay. We'll sort it all out when I get there. Now go to the pizza shop and I'll be there in a few minutes."

"Okay," Emily said.

Kim ended the call and turned to Matt. Her options were seriously limited.

"Do you have a car, because you're coming with me."

CHAPTER 77

Dawson counted seven clutches of youths watching him as he drove through the roads that traversed the estate, before pulling to a stop at the tower block that loomed imposingly over the centre of Hollytree.

Kai would definitely know he was coming.

As he walked towards the entrance to Highland Court he glanced up at the camera protruding from the building. Hollytree had twenty-seven strategically placed domes; all of which had been vandalised, painted and smashed too many times to count. As a consequence the council had conceded defeat and no longer made any repairs or replacements to the CCTV.

Dawson had experienced no hesitation in donning his stab vest before he'd left the Timmins' house. The heavy garment offered no real protection if someone was serious about causing him harm. A knife wound to the neck or thigh would finish him off just as efficiently. But somehow it made him feel better.

He pressed the lift button with hope but no expectation. Kai Lord lived on the thirteenth floor. The top.

His body breathed a sigh of relief when the lift opened before him. It had been a long day.

Dawson was not surprised to see another group of youths as he stepped out of the lift. But he was shocked that they stood aside to let him through.

As with the other micro gangs he'd spotted during his journey, this one was also comprised of a mixture of colour. Hollytree Hoods had never been a racially motivated gang, it was territorial and controlled the area on and around the estate. But the commonality was obvious as he stepped through the middle of them. They all wore the colours of the gang. Some had the bandanas on their heads, others around their wrists and one had threaded it through the belt loop of his jeans.

He heard teeth being kissed as he knocked the door. He turned and met the gaze of a short ginger-haired lad whose stance was a bit too gangster to be gangster. The self-satisfied smirk confirmed that the sound of disrespect had come from him.

Dawson shook his head and turned back to the door as it opened.

The expression of Kai Lord showed no surprise, as Dawson had expected.

As he quickly appraised the man before him, Dawson found himself immediately thinking of a Staffordshire bull terrier. Kai was not tall but he was solid. His jeans dropped low enough to display the Armani band of his shorts. His upper body was naked and Dawson could understand why. His brown skin only accentuated his well-defined six-pack and pectorals.

There was neither a frown nor a smile on Kai's face as he stepped away from the door.

The hallway was small and windowless but the light from the lounge lit the way.

Dawson stepped into a living space that was dominated by a grotesquely large television. He counted three games consoles stacked beneath with an assortment of joysticks and controllers that littered the floor.

Rather than a conventional three-piece suite, Kai had opted for five leather La-Z-Boy chairs formed in an arc around the huge screen.

The smell of marijuana was present but not overpowering.

Kai sat back and relaxed in the middle chair. "What you wanting, blud?"

Dawson remained standing. He was not this gang leader's friend.

"How well did you know Dewain Wright?"

"He was fam, ya get me?"

"Did you know he wanted out of the gang?"

"Kinda."

"Did he ask to be let out?"

Dawson knew there were few ways to leave gang culture. The most successful was to "age out." Get a job, a girlfriend, marry, have a kid. It worked more for peripheral members than core players but Dewain had been a teenager and nowhere close to "ageing out."

"Nah, kid been acting booky for a while, innit?"

"Booky?"

Kai waved his hand in the air as though it was obvious. "Weird. Losing his colours. Not coming around. We see the signs, man," he said, knowingly.

"What signs?" Dawson asked.

"Of wanting to leave the crew. Do it gradual, like, and no one gonna notice."

Dawson knew of this method but it had to be planned and taken slowly. Very slowly.

"But Lyron noticed?"

"Woulda been shit if not. Bang weren't gonna do it so Lyron decided a shank was best."

Dawson was pleased he knew enough to understand that a bang was a punch and shank meant stab.

He was surprised at the openness with which Kai spoke. But he supposed Lyron had been arrested for murder and wouldn't be back any time soon.

"When did you know Dewain was still alive?"

Kai shrugged. "Dunno, blud."

"Were you at the hospital?" he pushed.

Another shrug.

"So, you were an accessory to the murder?" he pushed. "You were part of the fight in the corridor that caused the distraction so your 'blud' could get in there and finish the job?"

Kai was unmoved and shrugged again.

"Jesus, you guys are all as bad—"

"Nah, mate, you're wrong there," Kai said with the first hint of emotion. "Lyron was a dick who ruled by blood in, blood out. Not me, man."

Dawson knew that meant you committed a crime to get in and only by blood did you leave. And Dewain had paid in spades.

"You did all right out of Dewain's death, eh?" Dawson asked.

Beneath the affable exterior he saw the irritation flash through the narrowed eyes.

"Job was going spare, innit?"

"Who told him, Kai?" Dawson asked. "Who told Lyron that Dewain was still alive?"

Kai remained silent. No shrug and no answer.

Dawson sighed heavily and shook his head. He was getting no more. He glanced out of the window and could see that three groups had converged beneath the street lamp right next to his car.

He turned to the gang leader. "So, do I leave this place alive?"

Kai smiled and shrugged. "You don't come for me, I don't come for you. Ya get me?"

Dawson nodded his understanding and headed towards the hallway. The stench of marijuana faded and was replaced by a stronger smell that he recognised.

Of course. Why had he not realised before? Dawson cursed his own stupidity.

He knocked three times on the only closed door in the hallway. "Lauren, you can come out now. I'm done."

He took the stairs back down in an effort to clear his head.

As affable as Kai was, Dawson could not afford to forget that Lyron had been told by someone that Dewain was still alive. Lyron had finished the job and would be imprisoned for a very long time and now Kai was king of the castle. Nice promotion.

The gang of four that had been outside Kai's door were now beside his car, a restless energy emanating from them that he hadn't felt before. He offered them a look before he sensed the tension in the air.

Dawson turned his head and looked up to the thirteenth floor. The silhouette of Kai was outlined against the window.

The shadow turned and moved away—just as the first powerful blow landed on the back of his head.

CHAPTER 78

Dawson gasped out loud and tried to reach his car door.

The second blow caught his right temple. Instantly a veil dropped over his vision, like a curtain of the night sky, complete with stars.

He felt a jab to his right kidney with more than just a fist. He suspected he'd been struck with a knuckleduster as four points of pain exploded through his body. He heard the groan escape his lips as his body ached to fold. He fought to remain upright as the blows continued to land.

Dawson knew if he gave in to his body's instinct to bend at the waist he would be making life even easier for his attackers.

He brought up his arms around his head as another fist landed behind his ear. "Get the fuck off," he managed to spit out, as he twisted and turned trying to avoid the blows.

"Shut the fuck up, pig."

"Kai gave you … instruction to …"

"Fuck Kai, man. This is for entering our patch at all."

A foot caught him behind the knee and he fell to the ground. Again, he tried to protect his head.

A shoe landed somewhere near his ribs but the vest helped shield him from the blow.

"He's vested, man," the kicker shouted.

"Shank him, man, shank him," another cried.

He raised his head and saw a blade attached to one of the hands. Real fear seeped into his stomach. What part of his body should he try to protect? His rage grew with his inability to fight back. He hated gang fights. He'd take any of them one on one but this was far from a fair fight.

He could hear feet scuffling around his head as they moved around his body.

"Get outta the fucking way, man," he heard.

The one with the knife was trying to get closer to him but the others aiming punches were getting in the way.

He twisted and turned and bucked his body as his mind tried to prepare for the blade. Every limb was thrashing out to stop that knife making contact.

His mind screamed that this could be it. Any second he could feel a blade slice into his flesh.

"Hey, you little bastards, get away from him," a woman's voice called.

"Fuck off, bitch," one of them sneered.

The voice was familiar but Dawson couldn't place it. However, the kicks had paused for just a few seconds and for that he was grateful. His body sang from the respite.

A light shone towards them as the woman spoke again. "In about three seconds I'm going to be able to identify every one of you."

The voice was strong and confident.

"Jackpot, I know that's you at the back."

Dawson heard the rustle of clothing as they all turned and scarpered away. A stray foot landed on his hand in the process.

He couldn't help the cry that escaped from his lips.

He felt a hand rest beneath his elbow. "Hey, are you okay?"

Dawson's gaze travelled over the high heels, up the trousers that clung to shapely calves and a thick jacket.

"Oh, Jesus, not you," he said, without thinking.

Tracy Frost tipped her head, raised an eyebrow. "You're welcome," she said, pulling him to his feet.

Instantly he realised how his response had sounded; he was grateful that Tracy had happened along when she had.

"Sorry. I didn't mean to sound like an arsehole. Thank you for getting them off me."

"Look, one good turn deserves another. I remember a time I was grateful for your help and your discretion. So now we're even."

"I think you may have just saved my life."

She tutted. "Don't be stupid. If they'd wanted you dead I'd be on the phone for an ambulance right now." She turned him towards her and looked him up and down. "But I think you'll live."

Despite the pain raging around his body, Dawson's brain was fully functioning and he realised that the bloody reporter had been following him. And although he was grateful that she had been there, she was not getting anything from him.

"Listen, Tracy. I don't care how much you just helped me. I'm not going to talk to you about anything else."

The statement took her by surprise but she recovered quickly. "Great, that's a wasted night following you around, then, eh?"

"You weren't here for me, were you?" he asked. A smile began to form before the pain in his jaw stopped it dead.

His right hand immediately rubbed the affected area.

"Yeah. I thought you'd be easier to tap than Pearl."

He frowned. "Pearl?"

Tracy shrugged. "It's what we call your boss at the office. You know, clam, closed, impenetrable. Probably one of the nicer names, if I'm honest."

"Hey, hang on," Dawson said, feeling his body stiffen. "You don't know her. She's—"

"Don't bother," she said, holding up her hand. "Not really going to believe a word you say so you'd best save your breath," she said, turning away.

Dawson conceded the point, but was suddenly struck by a realisation. "Okay, and your secret is safe with me."

"What secret?"

"You weren't on Hollytree for me," he said. "You were here because you want to know what happened to Dewain. It's because you actually do give a shit."

She sighed heavily. "Okay, you're half right. I do want to know what happened to Dewain but make no mistake. It's only because I want the story."

The words were too forced. An edge of ruthlessness injected for effect.

He tried the smile again as she headed off into the darkness.

He called loudly enough for her to hear. "Like I said, Tracy. Your secret is safe with me."

It didn't really matter why Tracy had been there. He was just thankful that she was. He had the feeling that he'd just cheated death.

CHAPTER 79

Six minutes after Kim had received the call from Emily, Matt parked on double yellow lines outside the pizza parlour.

Kim launched herself from the passenger seat before the car stopped moving. The queue at the counter was three people deep, while people who had already been served milled around eating their doner kebabs.

Kim pushed her way to the front, ignoring the shouts of protest.

"Police; where's the girl?" she asked the manager.

"Over there," he said, nodding towards the fruit machine. Kim looked where he had pointed. Two girls shrieked as the machine spat out two pound coins.

Emily wasn't there.

"Where?" she shouted. Everyone in the place turned and looked.

The manager looked over the heads waiting to be served and then shrugged.

"Shit, she's gone," Kim said, as she rushed past Matt. He landed outside beside her. "Damn it, where is she?" she cried, looking right and then left. The takeaway sat at the bottom of Lye High Street. There was the road they had travelled along from Pedmore. Surely they'd have seen her if she'd gone that way. But Kim hadn't really been looking, as she'd expected Emily to be at the takeaway.

Another road headed up towards the Merry Hill shopping centre. The road opposite headed straight to the Stourbridge ring road.

"Shit, where do I look?" she said to herself. There were four possible directions of travel.

"Calm down," Matt instructed.

"How can I calm down when I'm missing a ten-year-old girl? I need to call her mother. What if she's been taken...?"

"Think logically. She's old enough to get this far and she managed to phone you. So, if she moved of her own free will, where would she have gone?"

She stood still and looked in each direction. Emily had been in the takeaway. The manager had seen her. What had prompted her to leave, and where would she have gone?

Kim looked across the road to The Railway pub. Two men stood outside the entrance, smoking. The rest of the road, as far as she could see, was lit only by street lights and a petrol station just past the vet's office.

Over the road was an Indian restaurant which was dimly lit. No other lights showed beyond, so Kim ruled out Emily going in that direction.

Along Lye High Street a couple of shop windows were illuminated.

"You check the petrol station and I'll go this way," she instructed.

Luckily, Matt decided not to argue with her and headed away.

Kim walked slowly along the high street, checking in shop doorways as she went. Her heart beat louder with every passing step. She knew she should have phoned Emily's mother as soon as she put the phone down, but she had been sure she would be with her in just a few minutes.

If her actions had harmed Emily in any way Kim would never forgive herself.

She stepped across the road to check the doorways there and passed a darkened street leading to a car park at the rear of the shops. Kim felt sure Emily would not have gone down there. Even she herself would have hesitated.

A shadow loomed up behind her from the doorway of a convenience store. She turned. It was the proprietor closing up.

"Have you seen a little girl?" she asked, looking past him into the shop.

He shook his head and edged away from her.

Two males were swearing at the cashpoint. She approached them.

"Hey, you seen a young girl hanging around?"

She could see that they were only late teens. One looked her up and down and the other shook his head.

A couple were sitting in a car on the double yellow lines. They appeared to be having a domestic. Kim knocked heavily on the window, scaring them both to death.

The female in the driver's seat wound down her window, her mouth ready with abuse.

"What the—"

"Have you seen a young girl wandering around on her own?" Kim asked.

The woman shook her head, anger forgotten.

Shit. It could only have happened in the last few minutes. How could no one have seen a ten-year-old girl wandering alone at this time of night?

Emily, where are you? Kim silently cried.

She took a breath and continued walking. Another few feet and a bright light shone across the road and onto her boots.

A wave of hope surged through her. The double window displayed the welcoming bright lights of a mini market.

Kim immediately knew that if *she* was on the move, that's where she'd go.

She darted across the road and glanced in the window. The cashier was not at the front desk.

Please be here, Emily, she prayed, opening the door.

A bell sounded somewhere at the rear of the shop.

A woman in her early fifties appeared, dressed in navy blue trousers and a black zipped-up fleece jacket.

"Have you seen a little girl?" Kim blurted.

"And who are you?" the woman asked.

Kim could have cried with relief. Emily was there or the answer would have been a simple "no."

Kim had never been happier to show her badge.

"Detective Inspector Stone, the girl called me earlier to come and get her."

"Follow me," she said.

Kim headed to the rear of the shop and through the door marked "Staff Only."

Emily sat in the corner of a small staffroom that held some tea and coffee provisions and a few lockers.

Kim charged towards the girl and grabbed her hands. "Emily, why did you leave the takeaway?"

The poor girl was pale and trembling uncontrollably. Her palms were ice cold.

"I had to," she said, looking at Kim through terrified eyes.

Kim lowered herself to Emily's level. She hadn't sounded like this on the phone.

"Emily, what happened?"

"It was him," she said, as the first tear fell. "I saw him. I saw the man that took me."

CHAPTER 80

Kim kept her hand on Emily's shoulder as they entered the takeaway. The crowd had thinned and only two people stood at the counter.

Matt was searching the area looking for a "blue booted car" which was the only description Emily was able to give.

Although Kim had been doubtful, Emily had insisted it was him and that their eyes had met. She had been sure that he had seen her and that's why she had run. If he was still in the area Kim hoped Matt would find him but she wasn't leaving this girl alone for a second.

Kim suspected it was a fruitless search. The man Emily had seen already had a good ten- to fifteen-minute head start.

If Emily was correct about the direction of travel, he'd crossed the traffic lights and headed towards the Stourbridge ring road. And that led just about anywhere.

Kim caught the eye of the takeaway manager and nodded towards the restaurant section that was cordoned off at night. "May we?"

He nodded in return and flicked a light switch so that the furthest point in the corner was illuminated.

"Thank you," she said, opening the black tape to let Emily through.

She would have preferred to stay at the rear of the shop but the woman had made it clear that she needed to close up and lock the building.

Kim seated her and took the chair opposite. "Why did you run away from home?"

Emily stared down at the table. "I just couldn't stand it any longer. It's like a prison. I can't move without Mum asking me what I'm doing. In the last thirteen months I've left the house six times. Once to see the doctor, two dentist trips and a few times to get new clothes."

Kim sympathised with her. There were inmates at Featherstone with more freedom than this kid.

Emily glanced towards the window anxiously.

"He's not coming back, Emily," Kim said. "Nothing will hurt you while I'm here. I promise."

Emily smiled and nodded. "I know, but I just keep seeing his face now."

Kim guessed that Emily would not feel completely safe until her parents arrived and removed her from the area.

Kim leaned forward and spoke softly. "Why did you call me?"

"Because I heard what you said to my mum. It won't make any difference but I know that you got it. And I know you asked if you could talk to me so I took the card you left on the table."

Kim was drawn to the sadness of this girl. But she knew what she had to do.

"Emily, you know you have to call your mother."

She nodded and her lower lip trembled.

"She's not going to be angry. She's probably very frightened right now."

"It's never going to change, is it?" Emily asked, sadly.

Kim said nothing. She suspected the child was right.

Kim held out her hand. "If you give me your phone..."

Emily shook her head. "I don't have one. Mum says you can get the internet on them so I'm not allowed."

Kim took out her phone. "What's the house number?"

Emily read it off and Kim dialled immediately. It was engaged. She pressed the call button repeatedly. On the fifth she got half a ring.

"Hello?"

Kim heard the anxiety and fear in just one word.

"Mrs. Trueman, it's Kim Stone. We met—"

"Please get off this line. My daughter is—"

"With me," Kim said, quickly.

"Wh-what?"

"She's safe, Mrs. Trueman. Nothing has happened to her."

"Thank God...oh my...thank...oh..."

Kim handed the phone to Emily.

Kim guessed she could hear her mother's sobs on the other end of the phone. The tears began to roll down her cheeks.

"Mum, I'm sorry. I didn't mean..." Emily nodded and listened and then nodded some more. "I know, Mum. I love you too."

Emily handed the phone back to Kim.

"Inspector, I'm o1 my way. Please don't let her out of your sight."

"Not a chance, Mrs. Trueman," Kim said. She explained exactly where they were and ended the call.

Matt appeared behind Emily and shook his head. As she'd suspected, the man Emily had seen was no longer in the area. Matt took a chair and sat a metre away from the table.

Kim turned back to Emily. "Your mum loves you very, very much. She's only doing what she thinks is right."

"I know. That's why I can't be angry with her. It's not her fault."

Kim's insides clenched with anger. No, it was the fault of the bastards that had abducted the two of them and probably still had two more.

"You can talk to me," Emily said, quietly. "It'll be a bit until my mum gets here."

Kim was desperate to but she couldn't. She smiled at the child. "I can't, sweetheart. I don't have permission from your parents to ask you any questions..."

"But I can," Matt said, pulling forward his chair.

"No, Matt...I can't allow—"

"I wasn't asking your permission. I'm not governed by police rules and if your sensitive nature can't take it I suggest you step away."

Kim sensed that whatever she did, this man would not do as she asked.

Emily watched the exchange between them.

"Emily, cover your ears," Kim said, leaning closer to Matt. "I can't stop you speaking to her but if you say one word that upsets her your balls will be hanging from—"

"I have no intention of upsetting her," he hissed back. "But not because you're threatening me, but because I'm not an insensitive pig."

Kim drew away from him. Fine, as long as he got the message.

She motioned for Emily to uncover her ears. He leaned forward and spoke gently. Kim hid her surprise at his tone.

"Emily, I'd like to show you a picture of a man. I think he might have been the man that abducted you. Are you okay to look at it?"

It was the sketch that had been compiled from Brad's description of the fake policeman. The picture had meant nothing to the Hansons and the Timmins.

Emily swallowed and looked at Kim. Kim reached across the table and touched Emily's arm. "You don't have to, sweetheart."

"Could it help you find Suzie?"

Kim swallowed and looked away. Did this young girl hold out hope that her friend was still alive?

"Don't worry, I know she's dead, but she should still be brought home."

Kim felt the emotion gather in her throat before she nodded. "It might, Emily."

"Please, show me the picture. Suzie would have done it for me."

This child was not as young as she'd thought.

Matt took the sketch from his pocket and opened it up. Looking at it, Emily sucked in her breath and turned her face away.

"Is that the same man you saw earlier?"

Emily nodded her head but wouldn't look again, just clutched at Kim's hand. Matt folded up the paper and put it away.

"Okay, Emily. I'm not going to show you again. Was this the man that snatched you?"

"Yes, he had a ginger kitten. He said it was poorly and needed a hug. I cuddled it and he put tape over my mouth and put me in a van. He grabbed the kitten and threw it out the door and then tied me up. He drove for a bit and then he threw Suzie in."

She closed her eyes. "I was happy when I saw Suzie 'cos she was my best friend and I didn't feel so scared any more."

Kim sat back and listened, feeling the occasional flex of Emily's fingers as Matt gently asked questions. Her memory of her time in captivity was remarkably detailed.

"What happened on that last day?" Matt asked. She knew what he was after.

"The big man came in and grabbed my hair. Suzie tried to hang on. She was screaming...we were both screaming but he punched her and she fell backwards. I looked back. I screamed her name but she didn't move."

Kim stared down at a crumb that hadn't been wiped from the table.

"He put me in a van, drove for a while and then he took me out. He spun me around a few times and then pushed me to the floor.

"I heard the van drive away but I didn't see it because I'd got a blindfold on and I was dizzy."

Matt leaned forward. "Emily, can you remember anything else at all about that day? Did you hear any noises or see anything that might tell you where you were?"

Emily shook her head. "I was too scared. I didn't know what they were going to do with me. I was crying and..."

"It's okay, Emily," Kim soothed. The young girl had remembered so much. Unfortunately not a lot that would help them.

A sudden rush of air caught Kim's attention.

Julia Trueman headed towards them at speed. Her eyes were red discs in a colourless face but her gaze rested only on her daughter.

Kim moved out of the way. Matt followed.

An attractive man with short blond hair followed closely behind. His expression was not as fraught as his wife's but there was no doubting the concern etched into his features.

The family joined together and hugged and cried and hugged some more.

"There's more in there," Matt said to Kim, quietly. "Perhaps with more time..."

"Inspector, thank you so much," Mr. Trueman said, extricating himself from the hug.

Kim held up her hand. "She called me, Mr. Trueman. She wanted to help."

Mrs. Trueman straightened. Her eyes were full of fear but her mouth was set. Julia probably blamed her for Emily running away. If she hadn't visited and started asking questions, none of this would have happened. Kim suspected she could be right.

Kim knew she had to give it one last try. With her eyes she motioned the two of them to the side, leaving Matt to distract Emily.

"Look, I understand how difficult this is for you but it would be helpful if Emily could talk to us some more. She's begging to help and I think she remembers details that might help us but are not at the forefront of her mind." Kim took a deep breath. "If we could consider hypnotising..."

A small cry escaped the mouth of Mrs. Trueman. Her husband placed a reassuring hand on her arm.

"Inspector, we've worked very hard to distance Emily from the events of the past. I don't think..."

"And how's that working out for you?" Kim asked, gently. "I don't mean to be rude but the kidnapping might as well have happened last week for Emily. She loves you both very much but she is not a happy child."

"But what if we allow her to help and they come back for her? After all, they were never caught."

Kim heard the mild accusation in the woman's voice and let it pass. Julia was entitled.

Kim knew she had only one option left.

"Because they've done it again, Mrs. Trueman."

"Oh, God, no," she said, covering her mouth. Her husband swore under his breath.

"I can't give you any details. There's a press blackout so I must ask you to keep this to yourself but two young girls were taken on Sunday."

"And you think it's the people who took Emily?" Mr. Trueman asked.

"We're pretty sure it is," she said to Mr. Trueman and then rested her gaze on his wife. "If you allow us to work with Emily I swear to you that I will not rest until these people are caught."

Kim hadn't noticed Emily close by until she stood between her parents.

"Please, Mum, let me help. I'd do anything to bring Suzie home."

When Kim saw the look of agreement that passed between the parents she could have hugged the life out of the brave little girl.

Mrs. Trueman nodded. "Okay. Let us know what you want us to do."

Kim thanked them before they headed out the door.

She stepped to the corner of the restaurant and called Woody's mobile. He promised to have a qualified professional in place by the morning.

"Well, I just earned myself a cup of coffee. Want one?" Matt asked.

She hesitated and then nodded. She could just about stomach a coffee with him even though it was not where she wanted to be.

She would prefer to be driving the streets looking for the man that Emily had seen but she knew he was long gone by now.

More importantly, had he seen her?

CHAPTER 81

Kim turned her gaze on Matt. "So, are we gonna bond now and swap life stories and reach a mutual respect?"

"Jesus, it'd take more than a cup of coffee."

Kim took a sip. For a takeaway pizza place it was good coffee.

"I saw it, you know," she said, with a half-smile.

"Saw what?"

"Emotion. A little bit seeped out when you were talking to Emily but don't worry, it was barely noticeable."

"See, you couldn't do it, could you? I buy you a cup of coffee. All I ask is a ten-minute ceasefire, but you just couldn't do it."

She conceded the point. "Fair enough. What's your history? Were you a police negotiator?"

He nodded. "Yeah, for the Met."

"But you're not any more?"

"No."

"Jesus, and I thought my social skills were lacking."

"Sorry. I'm not good on small talk."

The similarities were beginning to freak her out. Damn it, she hated when Bryant was right.

Kim realised Matt was most animated when talking about his work. Asking him about it would mean more talking for him and less effort from her.

"Did the Met send you overseas?"

He nodded. "I was tasked to go to Mexico. The granddaughter of a member of the House of Lords had been kidnapped. She was back home forty-eight hours later."

"Do all cases go so smoothly?"

He shook his head. "Each gang is different. The primary reason for child abduction in South America is to fund terrorist organisations. Although it's a business, you can never lose sight of the type of person you're dealing with."

"Go on," Kim prompted. She was intrigued and it was good to give her mind a rest from the case for ten minutes. "Please, just talk."

He took a sip from his coffee. "The first decision you make is, adversary or partner. Are you going to battle—or co-operate? As I said to you before, there are not many parents who will encourage an adversarial strategy when you're negotiating for the life of their child.

"Gangs will normally offer a straightforward presentation of demands. A technique is adopted based on the information available."

"Such as?"

"There are many. Our kidnappers have used the auction approach, a bidding process to create competition. Brinksmanship is when one party sets out terms that are not negotiable. There's a bogey, where you pretend an issue is of little importance but can be used later.

"There's Flinch, where you show a strong physical reaction to an offer like a sharp intake of breath. Effective over the phone but not so much by text message. There's highball, lowball, nibbling, snow job and the old favourite of good guy, bad guy."

"Which works best?"

He thought for a moment. "It makes no difference, as long as you stick to the rules. The gangs know the techniques better than we do. They expect them. There is an underlying agreement that if everyone plays the game properly, both sides will win."

"So, the kidnapper can guess the tactic you're going to use?"

Matt nodded. "The key is in remaining true to the strategy. Gang members don't like surprises. If you change it part way through they get nervous, and that's not a good thing."

"Does it always go to plan?"

He shook his head.

"No, there was a case in Panama. There were two of us working to secure the release of the five-year-old son of a government official.

"Unfortunately reports of a recent inheritance had been greatly exaggerated. We adopted good guy bad guy and in two days had negotiated them down by a third. The system was working well. I was bad guy giving them barely anything, and the local guy, Miguel, was offering bigger concessions.

"We took it in turns to answer the phone and continually worked down their demand. We knew that the boy was safe. His parents had received an email with pictures of him chasing a chicken in just his underpants.

"See, that's what they do. They take the child to a remote village and leave them with family members where they're fed and play with other kids. Their business is not murdering kids. It's normally to fund an ideal in which they believe."

"What happened?" Kim asked.

"We were so near to the closing. We knew it and they knew it. Another day and an agreement would have been reached.

"Miguel took a call while I was out of the room. He changed the plan and made them a final non-negotiable offer."

"Why?"

Matt sighed heavily and shrugged. "Trying to inject an element of surprise thinking it would unnerve them into giving in; trying to impress the family, save them some money."

"What happened?" Kim asked. The dread had already formed in her stomach.

"They ended the call and didn't ring back. Ethan's body was found six hours later."

"Jesus."

Matt twirled the empty coffee cup with his left hand. His right hand had formed a fist.

"How long ago was this?"

"Four and a half days."

"Oh, Matt, I'm—"

"Don't," he said, raising his hand. "Keep your sympathy for the poor kid."

Kim nodded her understanding. "Is there ever any effort to catch these gangs?"

"Sometimes a half-hearted operation to stake out the drop point but twenty-four per cent of the population in Panama lives in poverty. Volume of crime far outweighs the number trying to fight it."

Kim was silent for a moment. "So, what should we expect next?"

"A prompt. They'll more than likely want to remind the parents of their potential loss, just to get them to dig a little deeper. They may send the voicemail of the scream to the parents or something like a personal plea from the children—that's why they're still alive."

Kim understood.

"Once you get that prompt, you're living on borrowed time. The girls are no further use. Just like Inga." He paused. "You know, don't you, that this can't go to the end game? On the day of the drop the girls will already be dead."

Kim swallowed deeply and nodded.

She knew.

CHAPTER 82

Kim stepped back into the dining room and sat at the table, which was still littered with papers from the day's work.

Matt had stopped off in the kitchen to write notes.

She marvelled at his ability to adapt to a new investigation so quickly. His last case had culminated in the death of a child and here he was, just days later, tuned into another.

She looked at the picture of Charlie and Amy. She wasn't sure she'd be able to adapt quite so soon.

Kim still didn't like the man but there was grudging respect for him that she had to acknowledge, if only to herself.

She stood and stared at the map. This was the key. It had to be.

Everything else they had uncovered meant nothing. The only thing that counted was where they were now.

Negotiation was not going to work. The best she could hope for was a delay, but the only way the girls would live was if she could find out where they were before the day of the drop.

She resolved to freshen up in the downstairs bathroom, make coffee and study it again.

The ting of her mobile sounded from the table. She grabbed it to see one new message, and frowned when she saw it was from Bryant. Her grimace deepened when she saw what it said.

Come outside

It was midnight and not the time to continue their earlier discussion. That would take place once the case was over. So, what the hell did he think he was playing at?

She grabbed her jacket and headed through the hall.

"All right, Marm?" Lucas asked from his post.

Kim nodded and opened the door.

Bryant stood twenty feet away, to the right of the water feature. Her gaze travelled to his hand which held a dog lead. Attached to the end was Barney.

Bryant unclipped the lead and Barney hurtled towards her. She dropped to her knees and opened her arms. His warm, furry body bucked and turned within her arms.

"Hey, boy, how are you doing?" she asked into his fur.

She grabbed his head in her hands and looked into eyes that were alight and excited. She kissed his head and held him close. "It is so good to see you," she said, scratching the point on Barney's back that caused a little growl in his throat.

Bryant had closed the gap between them. "If you won't talk to me . . . talk to him," he said, holding the lead towards her.

Kim shook her head. She didn't need the lead. Her dog never strayed from her side.

She walked around the side of the building with Barney hopping at her heels and nuzzling her dangling hand with his nose. She lowered herself to the ground and sat on the path that ran alongside the house. Immediately the dog was against her, nestled in the crook of her arm.

He turned and deposited one huge lick to the side of her face. She laughed out loud and hugged him close. "I've missed you too, boy.

"Check," she said, and the dog moved a few inches and sat. She had taught him to sit still on her command. She started at the top of his head and used her hands to feel every part of his body.

Any weight gain or loss was difficult to assess through his thick, glossy coat. As she went she checked for any areas of matting fur that were inevitable with a border collie.

Barney stared straight ahead as she checked his welfare.

He was rewarded with a head rub. "Good boy, you're fine."

There was no doubt he was being taken care of.

He snuggled back into position against her torso. Her arm snaked around him. "I know, boy, I miss you too."

For a moment she was barely aware of the cold, hard slab seeping in through her trousers. There was no cold wind biting at her neck. Just Barney and the comfort he brought.

"He's right, you know," Kim whispered into Barney's ear. She nodded to where her only human friend waited around the front of the house. "I'll never tell him that but I *am* scared, boy; terrified I can't bring these girls home alive."

A message on the wind whispered that she may already be too late.

And even if she wasn't, what had these bastards done to those two girls? She knew they were terrified and, even worse, naked. Of all the things they had done, that was one that sent her blood boiling around her veins. The indignity of stripping those children bare to up the damn price. It was a level of depravity that went beyond any case she'd worked.

Kim rested her head back against the wall and closed her eyes. Just for a few minutes she allowed Barney's warmth and closeness to comfort her, and she could almost feel the despair seeping out of her and into the cold ground. His warmth circulated around her body as her hand stroked rhythmically and then burrowed into his fur.

Kim allowed herself a whole ten minutes of Barney's healing company. It was ten minutes that she cherished.

She opened her eyes and sat forward, kissing him on the nose. "Thank you, my lovely friend."

She stood and dusted off her behind. Barney walked alongside her to the front of the house where Bryant was pacing around the water feature.

He'd been right to speak to her earlier. She now knew that she had been snapping and shouting at everyone around her, even the parents. Stephen Hanson was one of the most insufferable men she had ever met. But his child was missing and for a moment she had forgotten that and she shouldn't have. And only Bryant had the balls to tell her.

Barney stood between them, looking from one to the other.

Kim coughed. "Listen, about earlier…"

"You're welcome, Kim," he said with a lopsided smile. "Now let me get Prince Barney home and I'll see you in a few hours."

Kim smiled and nodded and then watched until her only two friends in the world disappeared from sight.

She re-entered the house feeling more hopeful than she had in days.

She would get these girls back if it was the last thing she did.

CHAPTER 83

"Ames, you gotta stop doing it. Your arm's bleeding," Charlie said. Amy's scratch marks were turning into open sores.

"I can't help it, Charl. They're just so itchy all the time. I have to scratch them."

"You've got to try and help it, though. Those scratches are going to go bad ways." It was what Daddy always said to her if she picked a scab or messed with a sore. She'd never seen what "bad ways" was but it didn't sound nice.

She had tried to occupy Amy's mind by making her walk around the room with her. Together they had strolled around the tiny space while hanging on to the towel that now smelled as bad as they did. That movement was the only thing that stopped the chattering of their teeth and the cold from biting into their bones.

After their last meal Charlie had scratched an eighth stick into the brick. A stick for each meal. She had noticed that it was taking much longer to do than the first time. Her strokes were not as forceful and she would lose the groove she'd made. Once she had even forgotten what she'd been trying to do, even though the pin was right there in her hand.

But that was nothing compared to the marks on Amy's arms. Charlie knew she had to be clawing at her skin when they did eventually manage to fall asleep. The faint red lines had turned into deeper red marks that had coloured the whole of her forearm but now the nails were breaking the skin.

Charlie wished that she could stop her friend from hurting herself, but she didn't know what else to do.

The walk around the room had tired her muscles and what she really wanted was to rest.

"Charl, are we ever going to get out of here?"

Charlie remembered that one of the days Amy had been so sure that they would. And now she was not.

"Yeah, Ames, course we are," she said, as her friend snuggled against her. Amy's head fell onto her shoulder and Charlie rested her own head on top of her friend's.

Charlie felt her body slump with exhaustion. She silently sent out the prayer she did every time she closed her eyes.

I pray that Mummy and Daddy will find us soon and take us home and keep us warm. And please God stop Amy from scratching her arms. Amen.

As her body began to crawl towards sleep the fear began to ebb, just a little, as the peaceful darkness moved towards her. Amy's rhythmic breathing beside her lulled her own body along the same journey.

A sudden banging on the door brought them both to sitting positions. Amy clutched both her hands tightly. Charlie had no idea if she'd been asleep for hours or if she'd fallen asleep at all. She only knew that the fear was back and it was ripping at her tummy.

"I just wanted to tell you little girlies, goodnight. I've enjoyed our late night chats but this will be our last. I can't wait to see you both tomorrow.

"Because then I'm gonna make you scream."

Amy cried out and Charlie pulled her close, unable to speak. The fear had paralysed her throat because a part of her had realised the truth.

Tomorrow they were going to die.

CHAPTER 84

Most of the team filed in one by one. By five fifty-nine there were five of them in the room.

Kim looked behind Stacey. "Dawson?"

Stacey shook her head.

Kim checked her phone even though she knew that she would have seen any message. She scrolled down to his number and pressed to call. He was not going to mess her about on a case like this.

The ringing of his mobile phone sounded in the hallway. A second later he appeared at the door. Kim ended the call.

"Bloody hell," Bryant and Stacey said together, staring at his face. Alison and Matt offered no words but their expressions of surprise mirrored her own.

"What the hell happened to you?" she asked.

His left eye was dark and swollen, his bottom lip was split at the centre and a bruise was spreading nicely across the right side of his jaw.

He sat down gingerly, which told Kim those were not his only injuries.

"A few of Kai's friends weren't happy to see me."

"Can you identify them?" Kim asked. She'd go and fetch the bastards herself.

He shook his head. "Too dark." He held up his hand. "I'm fine—help came from an unlikely source, which I'll tell you about another day."

His expression implored her to move on.

"Kev, have you been to the—"

"Guv, honestly. I'm fine."

Kim knew his eagerness was born of pride. Few men wanted to sit amongst their colleagues and strangers explaining how they got a good kicking but Kim was pretty sure he'd been ridiculously outnumbered.

She would check on him later but for now she would respect his wishes and move on.

"Okay, folks, let's get started."

Stacey peeped out to the right of her computer screen. "Guv, before we start I've got some stuff on Inga. Not sure it'll 'elp but the family hails from East Germany. Her father is credited as the last but one person to be shot trying to emigrate to the West; two years before the wall came down. Her mother was half British and the two of 'em came 'ere in '91.

"Nothing for a couple of years and then in '93 Inga Bauer was voluntarily surrendered to the care system when she was eight years old by 'er mom. She remained in the system until she became an adult."

"What happened to the mother?" Kim asked.

Stacey shrugged. "I can't find anything: no marriage certificate, no death certificate and no registered name change."

"So, she just left her there?" Bryant asked. "Jeez, that's rough. A kid belongs with its moth—"

"Okay," Kim snapped. "Doesn't help us a lot right now . . . but thanks anyway, Stace."

Stacey nodded in return.

"Kev, did you pick up the phone from evidence?"

He shook his head and turned his hand upwards. "It's not there, Guv."

Her head snapped around. "What do you mean, it's not there?"

"It's not even listed on the contents page."

Kim had to consider that Julia Trueman had lied to her and had never handed the phone over in the first place. Just like Jenny Cotton.

It wasn't something she could afford to dwell on right now.

Kim continued. "Matt feels that there will be some kind of prompt today to up the ante. Once that's been received, the hourglass turns. After that it's only a matter of hours before Charlie and Amy are killed."

"Really?" Stacey asked as Bryant swore under his breath.

Matt sat forward. "There comes a point when the girls have served their purpose and they become nothing more than a liability, whatever the outcome."

Everyone nodded their agreement. They understood.

"The key is in these maps," Kim said, taking over. "We don't need to be geographic profilers. We all know the area so we can all use common sense. These maps will help us pinpoint a location. Speaking of which, Emily Trueman ran away last night." Kim held up her hands to stem the expressions of concern. "It's okay, she's safely home now, but while she was waiting for us to get there she is sure she saw the man that abducted her the last time."

"Seems a bit of a coincidence, Guv," Bryant offered. "First time she's out in thirteen months and she sees the guy that took her?"

Phrased like that, Kim could see his point. She wasn't convinced herself but Emily had been so sure.

"Just consider the possibility while you're looking for clues in the dots," she advised.

"Guv, do the points from the previous case confuse matters 'cos there's nothing to suggest they'd use the same location again?" Dawson asked.

"And there's nothing to suggest they wouldn't. Especially as they were never caught. Stace, you got anything to help with what prompted the end of the incident last time?"

"Guv, all I got was an RTA on the Kidderminster expressway, a traffic light outage on the Thorns road and the grand opening of a new supermarket."

"Okay, we'll just have to worry about that later. For now, focus on the maps. The answer is there. Put yourself in the mind of the kidnapper."

They all nodded and looked at the printouts.

Kim could honestly look at the dots no more. She reached for the percolator which had been emptied with their arrival drinks and nudged Bryant as she passed behind. He coughed. Yeah, he knew that was her way of saying thanks for what he'd done the night before.

"Kev," she said, looking towards the door.

Dawson put down the sheet and followed her.

"So, how's it really going with the Dewain Wright case?"

He looked troubled. "Didn't get much sleep last night."

She put the percolator on the side and leaned against the sink. "Tell me about it."

Kim stood and listened while he told her the details of each of the interviews he'd carried out. She didn't interrupt and by the time he finished she heard the first movements from upstairs.

"I just don't know where to take it next. What do you think?"

Kim had listened to every word and she knew exactly who she'd be talking to next but that wasn't what this had been about.

"I think you should give it a little space. Stop scratching at it, trying to force the answer because it's just burrowing further under your skin." She tapped her forehead. "Let it germinate in here for a while. It'll come."

"You sure?" he asked, looking younger than his years.

She nodded. "I'm sure."

"You know, Guv, I did something once. I'm not proud…"

"Kev, we've all done stuff," she said.

He sighed. "I won't say what it was but I did it to fit in. I get why these kids end up in a gang. I hate it but I get it. Even the kids themselves know all the clever recruitment techniques but they still do it anyway. They just want to be part of a crew."

Dawson shook his head with despair and Kim got the feeling this side investigation had taken him somewhere he didn't want to go.

She was considering her next words carefully when Matt suddenly appeared at the door.

She gave him her full attention and nodded for him to speak.

"Okay, Detective Inspector, I'm ready to send some texts."

CHAPTER 85

Kim stood at the edge of the banister as the couples made their way down the stairs.

"Can I have you all in the lounge?"

Elizabeth sat at the end of the sofa with Nicholas on her lap. Stephen took up residence against the wall beside the window.

Karen took a seat on the arm of the chair occupied by her husband. They didn't speak or look at each other but somehow their hands met and held.

Matt was staring at his pad until Nicholas started to cry, unhappy at being held by a mother who was loath to let go.

Matt glanced at her. She got it. He needed their full attention.

"Elizabeth, would you mind if Helen took Nicholas to the kitchen?"

She hesitated then nodded. Helen swooped in and lifted the baby up. From the way she held the child Kim could tell she wasn't a natural, a bit like herself. At least Helen had the right end.

When he had their full attention, Matt spoke.

"Okay, we're going to start negotiating with these bastards."

Robert nodded his head but Stephen looked stricken.

"We have no intention of handing over anything but we're playing for time."

The relief on Stephen's face made Kim wish he'd been left to suffer for longer. Just a bit.

"We're getting ever closer to getting back your girls but we have to play the game or they will know." He turned to Stephen. "I want you to start with a lower offer of—"

"Yes, let's stay as close to the truth as we can," Elizabeth said, bitterly.

Matt ignored her. "Your initial offer should be for £894,000. I want to see his response to you. I then want Robert to send a much higher offer of £1,750,000."

Kim knew that Matt's strategy was to find out if the kidnappers reacted to both offers in the same way. If they did it would prove that both families were being strung along and their theory about the return of the girls was correct.

Both families listened earnestly to Matt as he spoke and explained how the wording for each text should be different.

"So, what exactly is the strategy?" Stephen asked.

Matt ignored him and passed a piece of paper to Elizabeth.

"This is what I want you to send, word for word."

Stephen moved to stand behind his wife and read it over her shoulder.

Elizabeth ignored him and continued to read.

"Will somebody tell me what the hell you're hoping to achieve?" Stephen fumed.

"Stop it," Elizabeth snapped.

"I have a right to know. She is my daughter."

Karen stood and moved towards him. "Stephen, calm down, please."

He stepped away. "No, I am not going to be treated as though I have no say."

Kim stood with her arms folded. Every gaze in the room was upon Stephen. Kim was in awe of the man's ability to become the main attraction in a situation that was far more important than him.

"Stephen, shut up."

The words from Robert were not loud or angry. They were calm and decisive.

And they got Stephen's attention.

Kim stepped forward. "Folks, this is not helping to—"

"Please tell me to shut up again, Robert," Stephen said. His face had darkened with unspent rage.

"Jesus Christ," Matt hissed.

Robert exhaled heavily. "Stephen, this is not a competition. Our daughters need us to be strong."

Kim saw a slight stiffening in Elizabeth's back as she shot a warning glance at her husband.

Kim looked at all four parents and knew what was coming.

Shit. She stepped in between the two men. "If we just take a minute—"

"You haven't worked it out yet, have you?" Stephen raged, looking around her.

"Stephen," both women shouted together.

Stephen was impervious to anything other than his own fury.

"Charlie isn't even your fucking child," he blurted. "Your wife had a fling with an old boyfriend—and now you're going to ruin yourself for a child that's not your blood?"

A cry escaped from Karen's lips and even Matt looked up.

Robert's face remained frozen for five seconds before his eyes fell to the face of his wife.

The room had stilled. Elizabeth's face was filled with horror, her eyes fixed on her friend.

"Karen...?" Robert asked.

All eyes were on her. Her face lost colour and slackened. Her hands clung together.

Karen's hesitation answered the question in his eyes. She took a step forward. "Robert...I..."

Robert turned and left the house.

CHAPTER 86

For ten seconds the room stood still.

Matt broke the spell. "Give me the phones," he snapped. Everyone looked at him. "Your children don't need this fucking soap opera. Let me take the phones."

Karen stared into the hallway and Elizabeth looked to her.

Kim nodded her agreement. The atmosphere was too fraught for him to do his job.

"Let Matt take the phones and get the ball rolling."

She took Elizabeth's phone from her hand and retrieved Karen's from the coffee table, then passed them to Matt. He left the room without speaking.

"What...all I did was tell the truth," Stephen said to no one in particular.

"It wasn't your truth to tell," Karen said brokenly, before she turned and left the room.

Bloody hell, Kim thought. She did not get paid enough for this. For once she agreed with Matt. This domestic drama was not going to help get Amy and Charlie back.

Kim guessed that Karen had entrusted the information to her closest friend who had in turn shared it with her husband. And Stephen had chosen the worst possible moment to share it with everyone. Worse, he had shared the information only because of his inability to secure the release of his own child, as a way to lash out.

That was the trouble with a secret. Everyone thought they could trust someone. And it was the perfect example of why Kim would never trust anyone with hers.

Helen had wandered back into the room and stood on the periphery. Stephen's expression was unrepentant. There was no point in wasting her breath.

Kim strode towards the kitchen door and paused at the sound of Elizabeth's voice.

"I'm so sorry, Karen. Stephen should never have—"

"How could you?" Karen screamed. "You were the only person I've ever trusted with that and you tell *him*. How could you do that to me, Liz? How could you..."

Kim passed in front of the door, unnoticed by both.

She didn't break her stride. This was not going to help get their girls back.

CHAPTER 87

Kim and Bryant sat outside the premises in Stourbridge High Street. It wasn't what she'd been expecting. There were no vinyl letters on the glass about empowerment or smoking or losing weight; just vertical blinds at the window and a brass name plate.

The Trueman family were due to arrive any minute.

Kim glanced in the passenger rear-view mirror, keeping watch for approaching vehicles.

"They're here," she said, opening the passenger door.

A white Range Rover had inched gingerly down the street and parked three cars behind them.

Kim approached the vehicle, offering what she hoped was a reassuring smile to the three occupants.

"Thank you for allowing this," Kim said to Julia and Alan Trueman. "And thank you for being so brave," she said to Emily.

"Is it going to hurt?"

Kim smiled and shook her head.

"No, but I'm going to ask the hypnotherapist to explain it to you so you feel comfortable with what's going to happen."

Kim led the way into the building followed by the family. She could feel their apprehension.

The lobby led into a small office, where a woman in her mid to late fifties sat behind the desk. Her greying hair was tied back in a bun, held in place with a pencil. Clear blue eyes peered from behind oversize glasses. A bulky man's watch on her wrist was at odds with the delicate crystal that hung around her neck.

"We're here for Doctor Atkins," Kim said.

The woman smiled warmly. "You've found her, but she prefers to be called Barbra."

Kim shook her hand and introduced the whole group. "You are expecting us?"

"Not quite as many of you, Inspector, but yes."

"Is it a problem?"

"Not out here but in there, yes. But we'll get to that in a minute."

She stood and moved around the desk, her eyes on Emily.

"I assume this is the young lady I'm going to be working with today?" She took Emily's hand and guided her to the sofa. "Are you frightened, sweetie?"

Emily nodded. "A little bit."

Kim noted that Barbra held on to the girl's hand.

"There's nothing to be afraid of. It doesn't hurt and I'm not going to take you anywhere that you don't want to go, okay?

"Think of it this way. Imagine hearing the first line of a song but you can't remember the title or the singer. You know the information is in there but you just can't bring it forward in your mind."

Emily nodded her understanding.

"That's all we're going to do. The only thing you'll feel is completely relaxed and at ease and afterwards you'll feel like you've just had a great night's sleep."

She turned to the rest of them. "Any questions?"

Mr. Trueman stepped forward. "Have you done this before, I mean, with victims?"

Kim noted Julia's look towards her husband. Their "victim" was listening to every word.

Barbra nodded. Kim saw that she hadn't let go of Emily's hand and understood that she was maintaining contact to build a trust between them.

Kim also noted that one of her fingers was resting on Emily's wrist, monitoring her heart rate without the girl knowing. Kim instantly liked Barbra's style. A terrified patient was unlikely to respond positively to the procedure. Kim could see from Emily's body posture that she was beginning to relax. Her shoulders had eased into the sofa.

"Yes, Mr. Trueman, I've done this many times before. I've assisted victims of crime in recovering lost details, sometimes going back decades."

"Is there any chance of lasting effects from hypnotism?" asked Julia.

Barbra shook her head. "This isn't a stage show. All we're doing is turning over a few stones of the mind to see if there's anything hidden underneath. The only lasting effect is that any memory we bring to the fore is likely to remain there." Barbra turned to Emily. "I need you to understand that, okay?"

Emily looked to her mother who in turn looked to Kim, alarmed.

Kim stepped forward. "Emily already recounts the whole experience with accuracy. We're only looking for any forgotten or suppressed details."

Mrs. Trueman nodded, somewhat appeased.

Barbra waited for a few seconds and, when no further questions came, she squeezed Emily's hand and stood.

"Okay, I'm ready to start but I can't allow you all in the room. That's too much pressure for Emily. I'll allow two."

At the same second Bryant stepped back and Julia stepped forward.

Kim glanced towards Mr. Trueman. His face showed the battle with his protective instinct for his child, but he gestured in her direction. Kim nodded her thanks.

Barbra held open the door to the treatment room and motioned for Julia and Emily to enter. She hung back and spoke so that only Kim could hear.

"What are we looking for specifically, Inspector, a description of the offender or...?"

"Location," Kim said. "Anything that might help me identify where she was held."

Barbra nodded and entered the room. Kim followed.

"Okay, Emily, if you take a seat in the big chair for me. Mrs. Trueman, feel free to sit beside Emily."

Kim closed the door and remained standing in the corner. She took out her phone and held it up.

"May I record the session?" she asked, looking from Julia to Barbra. Both women nodded.

The big chair that swallowed Emily was formed of soft, tan leather and the position rested somewhere between flat and upright. Julia took the seat to the right of her child and Barbra sat to the left.

"Okay, Emily, I want you to get comfortable. Sit in a position that makes you feel relaxed."

Emily adjusted her position and nodded.

The light from outside was muted by vertical blinds and facing the chair was a row of black and white prints of various city skylines.

"Good girl, now all I want you to do is look at any one of those pictures on the wall. It doesn't matter which one. Just choose the one that appeals to you the most and focus on it."

Emily nodded and chose to stare at New York.

"Now, I want you to take nice deep breaths, slowly and evenly. Breathe in through your nose, one, two, three, four, five. And let the air just escape from your mouth. Good girl. In through your nose, one, two, three..."

Kim noted that Barbra's voice had dropped to a mild, undulating tone that was little more than a whisper. She could see Julia's left hand trembling. She caught her eye and smiled, grateful for the woman's co-operation.

Kim glanced back to Emily just as her eyes fluttered and closed.

"Okay, Emily, I want you to think back to the day you were taken. You were placed in the back of the van, talk me through the journey."

"Me and Suzie...crying...scared..."

"Were you able to see anything?"

Emily shook her head. "Dark."

"Was the journey smooth or bumpy?"

"Smooth, then bumpy. Tried to hold on but bounced around. Suzie hit head."

Kim started making mental notes. They were probably taken onto rural roads.

"Go forward, Emily, to when the van door was opened."

"Head...covered...bag..."

Emily's eyes fluttered and Julia's jaw clenched.

"They covered your face?"

Emily nodded.

"Can you hear anything, Emily?"

"No...quiet..."

"Can you smell anything?"

"Squelch...feet..."

"Are your feet in mud, Emily?"

Emily nodded. "Lots."

"Are you being taken into a building?"

Emily nodded. "Cold...stairs...walls...cold..."

"Are you being taken downstairs?"

"Hand...here..." Emily touched the back of her neck. "Pushed down."

Julia closed her eyes and bit her lower lip.

"Walls...wet...cold..."

"Okay, Emily. Are you and Suzie in a room?"

Emily nodded.

"Are there any windows?"

Emily shook her head and wrinkled up her nose.

"Smell..."

"Is it a bad toilet smell?"

Emily shook her head. "Old..."

"Okay, Emily, can you go forward to when you were taken out of the room?"

Emily nodded but her breathing altered.

"Grabbed...my hair...Suzie...screaming...holding on..."

Kim saw Julia's right hand move to her mouth and bite down. She knew it was taking every ounce of determination for the woman to keep quiet.

Kim moved silently across the room and rested her right hand on Julia's shoulder.

"Go on, Emily," Barbra said, quietly.

"Let go...had to let go...Suzie punched in the face...by man...fell backwards...not moving..."

Barbra swallowed. "Are you going back up the stairs?"

Emily nodded. "Quickly...pushing...tripped..."

"Are you being taken back outside?"

"Yes...pushing...stumbled..."

"Do you feel the squelch, Emily?"

She shook her head. "No...grass..."

"Can you hear anything?"

"Yes...machine...shouting...far away..."

Barbra glanced her way. Kim nodded.

"What does it sound like?" Barbra asked.

"Shouting but far..."

"Is the noise close by?"

Kim looked down to check the phone was still recording.

Emily scrunched her eyes and shook her head.

"Is it further away in the distance?" Barbra asked.

Emily nodded.

"Are you being placed back into the van?"

"Thrown...quickly...bumpy...couldn't hang on...stopped...
faster...something hitting the van...thrown against the side..."

"Emily..."

"Left...left...right...left..."

"Where are you now, Emily?"

"Pulled from the van...being turned and turned and turned..."
She rubbed at her upper right arm with her left hand. "Hurts...
squeezing..."

Emily's face contorted with the memory of the pain.

Barbra looked to Kim. That was all they were going to get.
They were seeking information regarding the location and Barbra
had taken her through arriving and departing.

Kim nodded for Barbra to bring her round.

"Okay, Emily, I want you..."

"He said...something...twirled...and turned...and
pushed...and...*See you again, sweetheart*..."

Julia cried out and Kim closed her eyes.

She finally understood why they'd allowed Emily to live.

They had planned to snatch her again.

CHAPTER 88

"I knew it. I knew it," Julia exclaimed on the pavement outside the building. "Everyone thought I was just being neurotic." She turned to her husband. "Even you thought so, but I knew it wasn't over. I knew as long as they were still out there Emily would be at risk."

Bryant shook his head, still reeling from the news.

Emily was nestled between her mum and dad. The revelation had clearly unnerved her. She stared dazedly to the ground.

Kim had nothing to say. The actions taken by Julia—moving house, the name change and keeping Emily home from school—had probably saved her daughter's life. Kim couldn't help feeling a pang that she had accused the woman of stifling her child when her actions had actually been necessary.

Both parents held on to their child protectively.

"I'd give it all up," Alan said, quietly. "I'd give my business away and live in a shack to protect my family."

Alan Trueman clearly felt responsible. His financial success had brought the attention of kidnappers who felt he was lucrative enough to snatch his child and had been planning to do it a second time.

Kim couldn't imagine what that would have done to this small family.

"There is no fault here," Kim said. "The blame lies solely with them," she said truthfully. "And although I know you have Emily well protected I'd be happier if you would allow a police presence at your home. Just for a little while."

The Truemans looked at each other and nodded. Bryant stepped away and took out his phone to make the call.

"Was there anything in there that will help you catch these people?"

Kim felt the anxiety radiating from them. No level of police presence would make them feel safe until the kidnappers were caught. And even then they would never view the world the same way again.

Kim nodded to Alan and looked down at Emily. A fresh fear was showing in her eyes.

"Yes, Mr. Trueman, your daughter was very brave and we now have additional information."

She touched Emily's shoulder. Emily looked up at her.

"I promise you I'm going to find these people and make sure they never hurt you again, okay?"

Emily nodded and moved closer to her father. "And you'll try and bring Suzie back home?"

Kim met the gaze of the brave little girl. There was no false hope that her friend was still alive. Like Jenny, she just wanted to put Emily to rest.

Kim nodded. "I promise I'll do my very best."

She thanked them all again and headed towards Bryant.

A second person was already standing beside the car.

And this time Kim knew she was in trouble.

CHAPTER 89

"I'm running it today, Detective Inspector," Tracy said as she approached.

"Tracy, f—"

"Now, now—if I'm not mistaken that was the surviving child of the last abduction you lot messed up," Tracy said smugly.

If ever there was a time that Kim wished Actual Bodily Harm was not against the law it was right this second.

Tracy's blonde hair flowed out of a beanie hat, with ears. Kim idly wondered how anyone so heartless could wear a hat with ears.

"I'm thinking this story has got legs..."

"Yeah, use yours and piss off."

"Guv, let it go," Bryant advised.

Tracy ignored her jibe. The woman was used to it. "I'm thinking the first feature would be the fuck-up of the last case, then the fuck-up of this case and end with a feature on you, the star of the show," she said, snidely.

Kim had no problem with a negative news article. If anything happened to those girls she'd write it herself.

"How about you just act like a real person and just leave it alone?"

"That wouldn't be very reporterly of me, would it?"

Bryant guffawed beside her.

"Is that even a word?" Kim retorted.

"Listen, you appealed to my better nature and it worked for a few days, but not any more."

"You don't own a better nature. You reacted to my threat to expose what you're really like and that still stands."

"Ha, good luck with that one. My editor will forgive me murder if I bring this home."

Kim knew her threat had run dry. She opened her mouth to speak but Tracy held up a gloved hand.

"Listen, I'm doing you a favour by letting you know my plans. At least you've got a fighting chance."

"Wow, thanks a bunch," Kim hissed.

"You've had time, Stone. I'm just doing my job."

"You intend to defy the blackout?" Bryant asked.

She nodded and looked back at Kim. "Do your worst, Stone. In the meantime we'll sell a gazillion newspapers."

Kim dared not speak, knowing anything she said would be twisted, turned, quoted and exaggerated. And that was exactly what Tracy was goading her to do.

"That'll be 'no comment' then, Inspector," Tracy said before stomping away.

Kim watched helplessly as the Audi fired up.

"Do you think she means it?" Bryant asked.

It was only by default that Tracy Frost had not been responsible for the death of Dewain Wright. Another ten minutes and she would have been.

Kim took a deep breath. "Oh yeah, she means it."

And the minute she did the girls would be dead. The kidnappers had done nothing to incite press attention and, just like them, they did not welcome it.

The Cotton family had been destroyed by the loss of their daughter, Suzie. And Kim had two families about to face the same fate.

CHAPTER 90

Will put the phone back in his pocket and tried to stay calm. Had Symes not been dozing on the sofa, he would have paced.

He would have walked circuits of the room until the rage left his bones.

They'd had a fucking plan and changes were being made to the game.

It was a game of chess, of strategy, of waiting, of timing, of anticipating every move and having three moves ready for each eventuality. There was a finesse to the game that was to be respected.

You didn't change the game halfway through and start to play draughts.

You didn't start jumping each other's pieces in an effort to get to the end of the board and get crowned. There was no finesse, no beauty in what he'd just been told to do.

And he fucking well hated it.

Will knew he was still rattled from last night. Waiting at a set of traffic lights he'd turned his head and seen her. The one he'd been searching for since he'd let her go. For a few seconds his mind had muddled and he'd wondered if he was just transposing her face onto another young girl, standing idly in a takeaway.

And then he'd seen the fear in her eyes and he had known.

He had jumped the lights and parked the car on the petrol station but when he'd got back she'd gone.

He had been about to start looking when a silver Astra had screeched to a halt on double yellow lines outside.

Remaining in the area had almost been worth the risk, but not quite. That one little girl had always been his golden goose. And right now he needed one of his plans to pay off.

Tapping into her family bank account would have produced millions but the family had hidden well. Finding their new home had not been too difficult. He'd had help. But getting to her had been a more difficult prospect.

He tried to console himself that he still had his own little game—only that was lunch-money compared to Emily Billingham.

But the frustration of seeing Emily again was still in his veins.

"Symes, wake up," he said, turning.

The oaf continued to snore loudly, his mouth wide open.

Will wheeled across and hit him in the arm.

Symes was upright and awake in less than two seconds.

"The parents need a push."

Symes was confused. "I thought that was later."

The big guy had obviously paid more attention to the plan than he'd thought.

"There's been a change. Parents need a reminder of how much they love their little cherubs."

Symes's face lit up.

Will shook his head. "No, you can't have them yet."

The plan said the reminder was supposed to be a psychological prompt that would open the purse strings.

The plan said it was supposed to be their voices pleading with their parents to do whatever the kidnappers asked.

But the plan had changed.

There was a sigh inside him. It had been much easier the first time. It had been just him and a simple motive. Make some money.

Symes wanted them dead.

The boss wanted them alive.

And Will no longer cared.

Symes put his hands together and cracked his knuckles.

He hated it when the master plan changed. Because now he had to adapt his own, secret little game.

He turned to Symes and hissed, "It's time to make them scream."

CHAPTER 91

As Kim returned to the house after the hypnotherapy session with Emily, she almost collided with Helen, who was carrying a tray of cups to the kitchen.

"How's it been?" Kim asked, walking alongside her.

"Karen's trying desperately not to break down. Elizabeth is busying herself with Nicholas and Stephen's been out of sight all morning."

Kim didn't blame him. She was surprised Karen hadn't physically kicked him off the premises but, unlike Stephen, Karen's priority still lay with the return of her own child and theirs.

"Anything from Robert?"

Helen shook her head. "Karen's tried to reach him at the office but he's either not there or 'not there,'" she said, making quote marks with her fingers.

Kim wasn't surprised. To find out that he was not Charlie's biological father was bad enough, but to find out in front of a room full of people, most of them strangers, was horrific.

She entered the incident room to a wall of silence. "What is it?" she asked, closing the door.

All eyes turned to Matt.

"We have the prompt—and it doesn't sound good."

Kim's mouth dried as she sat.

The mobile phones sat on the table.

"Go on."

Matt found the message and played the recording.

Kim stared at the wall as she heard a child's voice crying "No" repeatedly. The child started to sob and then there was a scream.

Kim now understood what Matt had known before. The scream was different. This one was pain.

Kim was incredibly thankful that Matt had taken the phones from Elizabeth and Karen.

"Is it the same recording on the other one?"

Matt shook his head and reached for the second phone, Karen's.

He played the message.

Charlie's voice instantly filled the room. "Get away from me... don't touch..."

Kim could hear the fear in the voice but there was no crying. Then there was a scream.

Both messages punched her in the stomach but the second with a little more force.

Karen's girl was a fighter, obviously holding back tears, determined not to give her captor the satisfaction. Kim liked to think it was what she herself would have done.

"There's something else. A second text message sent to both phones. A demand for two million and no less."

Kim raised an eyebrow at Matt. "Why?"

"The change in strategy is unsettling. Something's happened to prompt a shift in tactics. It's not a good sign."

The rolling in her stomach did not disagree.

"Could there be some kind of problem with where they're holding the girls?" Stacey asked.

Kim shook her head. "They would have allowed for that. It's more likely been caused by something that's happened here," she said, thoughtfully.

It had been a busy morning.

Stephen had been a dickhead.

Robert had walked out.

And Emily had been to the hypnotist.

Kim had no idea which of these events had led the kidnappers to panic but there was one thing she knew for certain.

The hourglass had turned.

CHAPTER 92

"Okay, guys, we learned from Emily the following. When they were taken out of the van it was muddy and quiet. The building had a bad smell—I'm guessing mould.

"On the day of the release Emily heard shouting in the distance and a machine. The van left the property across grass and, from Emily's description of the journey, I'm thinking a dirt track road barely big enough for a vehicle. She heard something hitting the side of the van; I'm assuming it was tree branches."

Kim looked at each face in turn. "I know it's not a lot but I want you to work backwards from where Emily was dropped."

Dawson coughed.

"What?"

"Guv, aren't we taking one hell of a gamble to think that they're in the same place as the last time?"

She opened her mouth to respond but Matt beat her to it.

"It's a reasonable assumption that if the location was working for them the first time there's no reason to think they wouldn't use it again. They know the area so it makes sense."

Kim stared at the dots until they began to fade into the page. She knew the clue was in her own logical mind, if only she could just locate it and throw it to the ground.

Her gut told her that the kidnappers' new strategy was a desperate move, one that had been put into motion after the recent developments had occurred here. But last time there had been no changes that could have been the catalyst for Emily's release.

Kim was disturbed from chasing her own tail by the sound of a text message tinging to a phone somewhere in the room.

Everyone stopped and looked up.

"It's me," Matt said, lifting a phone.

Kim recognised it as the old Nokia that belonged to Jennifer Cotton.

No one moved a muscle as Matt's eyes travelled from left to right.

"He wants fifty thousand, same place as before. At six tonight," Matt said, looking directly at her.

"Surely, that's good news?" Dawson asked, looking from her to Matt.

"It gives us nothing," Kim answered. "The text could be a hoax. It could even be a diversion to split our resources. The real demand is for the two million. I told you that we had to assume that Suzie Cotton was dead and that has not changed."

"Guv, are you really saying that we ignore this?" Dawson asked.

Kim let out a huge sigh as a picture of Jenny Cotton swam past her eyes.

Yes, God forgive her, she was.

CHAPTER 93

Kim could feel the dissention in the room. Secret glances were being shared across the table.

"Focus on the maps, please," she said, without looking up. "The clock's ticking."

Every time she tried to study the map her brain screamed only one question.

What the hell had occurred to prompt the release of one girl? Something had to have happened where the girls were being held.

"Stace, get me more info on those old news—"

"Marm, got a sec?"

Helen's face was peering around the door.

"Come in, Helen," Kim said.

The woman had earned the right to step over the boundary. In another life Kim would have been calling *her* Marm.

Helen moved towards the table, a puzzled frown shaping her features. "You asked me to let you know if I remembered anything about the day Emily was released; well, there's just one thing that just came back to me. I mean, it probably doesn't mean anything but . . ."

"Go on, Helen."

"Well, I remember stepping outside for some air and there was an officer standing outside. His radio was on. There'd been an accident. Kidderminster way, I think. It was West Mercia but it must have been bad because we were getting traffic tailbacks and congestion as far back as Lye. I mean it's probably nothing but…"

Her words trailed away and Kim could see the anxiety in her jawline. Every one of them knew they were running out of time.

"Thank you, Helen," she said, as the woman backed out of the room.

Kim looked to Stacey. "The traffic accident report."

Stacey started tapping keys. Kim stood behind her as the news article opened.

The first screen covered the basics. A man injured, etc.

"Go to full report," Kim said, feeling an excitement build in her stomach. Stacey opened it and Kim read quickly.

The half-ton lorry had careered off the dual carriageway, breaking through the barrier. "Aah, shit," Stacey said, reading along with her.

"Give me an aerial view."

Stacey tapped again. The screen zoomed into the area.

Kim tapped the screen. "Right there, look at the terrain. The ground slopes away from the field into a ditch. That means they would have needed a crane to get the vehicle out of the field. And there would have been a lot of—"

"Sirens," Bryant answered, joining them. "There'd have been fire service, ambulance and police converging. Would've made quite a racket."

Alison moved to her left and stole a glance. "Subject Two wouldn't have been spooked by that level of noise. Subject One definitely would have been. It wouldn't have been part of the plan, and so close to the drop time he might have panicked."

Kim agreed with the behaviourist, but it still begged the question of why Emily had been released before the money had been received and why Suzie had not been released at all.

Stacey busily tapped away, zooming in and out of the map.

"The two closest properties are either side of the dual carriageway. The sounds would have been heard further away but loudest here."

Kim knew they were on to something. With so much activity the kidnappers couldn't have run the risk that someone was going to knock on the door.

"Stace, I need you to carry on looking for clues. If we get no joy at either of these two properties we'll need to start working our way out. But it's here. I know it."

"Got it, Guv."

It felt like someone had injected a shot of adrenaline into the whole room.

"Okay, Bryant, Dawson, get your coats. It's time to find these children."

CHAPTER 94

Karen held tight to her husband as the footsteps thundered past. He had been home for almost half an hour and she'd been unable to let him go. No one else knew he was back.

Robert also looked towards the doorway of the kitchen but they didn't break apart. She turned to face him.

"Rob..."

He shook his head. "It could mean anything, sweetheart. How many times have we seen them rushing in and out of the house?" He stroked her hair gently. "We have to do this. We have to know what's going on and we can only do that if we get the phone back. We have to save our daughter."

Karen felt the relief flood through her body as he said those words. For the few hours Robert had been gone her world had held no meaning. Her beautiful daughter was missing and her husband had left her as well. In her heart she had known he would return; he would forgive her anything. Not immediately, she knew that. There would be many tears, explanations and apologies. He would need time to understand her deceit, but his love for the two of them would not be broken.

The fact that he had come back had calmed some of her fears.

Despite what he was proposing.

"But..."

"It's the only way, Karen," he said, gently. "But you have to help me do it."

Karen took a deep breath and nodded.

Robert stepped away from her and picked up two plates, gesturing for her to step to the side.

She covered her ears as the plates were hurled to the ground.

CHAPTER 95

Stacey almost jumped out of her skin.

"What the hell...?"

She was on her feet immediately but Matt beat her to the door. Alison pushed her chair back.

Stacey ushered him out of the way. "Stay here," she said to both of them as she opened the door. She didn't feel the need to state that she was the only police officer in the room.

"You're a fucking liar, Karen. How the hell did you think I would feel?"

Robert's voice bellowed along the hallway. Stacey headed towards the kitchen.

The two of them stood on opposite sides of the breakfast bar. A pile of crockery lay in the corner.

Robert's face was dark with rage as Karen sobbed into her hands.

"I'm s-sorry I lied to—"

"Sorry," he screamed. "You're fucking sorry? Ten years of my life you've stolen with your lies—and you're sorry? To let me believe that child was mine—"

"Mr. Timmins," Stacey said, stepping forward into the room. "Please calm down."

His look was filled with disgust. "Don't tell me to calm down," he cried, sweeping his arm along the surface.

Utensils and coffee mugs crashed to the ground.

"And where the fuck is that selfish bastard?"

Robert came striding towards her in the doorway. His size forced Stacey to step back but she held up her arms. He slapped them away and shouted over her head.

"Stephen Hanson, stop hiding. Show yourself like a man."

Matt appeared behind her. "Mr. Timmins, calm down," he urged.

"Will everyone stop telling me to calm down? Where the hell is that arsehole?"

Elizabeth appeared at the top of the stairs. Robert started heading towards her. "Is the cowardly bastard up there with you?"

Matt was trying to get up the stairs in front of him but Robert kept pushing him back.

Helen stepped in from the lounge and looked to Stacey.

"Is Mr. Hanson outside?" she asked, as Robert continued his journey upstairs.

Helen shook her head.

"Come on, Elizabeth, tell me where he is. I want the pleasure of kicking him the fuck out of my house."

"I swear to you, he's not with me and Nich—"

"I'm right here," Stephen said from behind Elizabeth.

Stacey thought that even Elizabeth looked surprised. Wherever he'd been, it hadn't been with her.

"Robert...please..." Elizabeth said.

Everyone began moving towards the stairs. Robert was almost at the top, but Matt was trying to get there first.

"How could you do it, you spineless bastard? Just to divert the attention away from the fact that you're broke and even your damn wife didn't know."

Stephen stepped around his wife. Only three stairs separated them.

"It's not me you should be angry with. It's that slut of a wife that lied to you."

Robert's fist flew forward, missing Elizabeth by an inch, but hitting Stephen smack on the nose.

Stephen reeled backwards. He must have thought the placid Robert would never actually strike him.

Finally, Matt managed to get between them and held the two men at arm's length.

Stacey was halfway up the stairs when she heard Alison tell her to be careful.

Stacey stopped dead and turned around to see Lucas and Helen at the front door.

Robert, Stephen, Elizabeth and Matt were at the top of the stairs. She was in the middle and Alison was at the bottom.

Two questions jumped into Stacey's head immediately.

Who was guarding the war room—and where the hell was Karen?

CHAPTER 96

Kim had barely driven a mile when her phone rang. She passed it to Bryant. "Put it on loudspeaker."

"Boss, we have a problem," Stacey said, breathlessly.

Great, because she needed another.

"What is it?" she shouted, as Dawson leaned forward to hear.

"It's all kicked off here. Robert came back, plates were smashing. He was screaming at Karen and then punched Stephen in the face."

Kim knew that they had not yet reached the problem. This was the lead up and the punchline was waiting.

"I left the room first to find out what was going on but it all got a bit crazy…"

"Stace, get to the point," Kim said. But she had a feeling she already knew.

"The phones are gone. During all the fracas Karen disappeared. Helen is looking for her now. But the two mobile phones are missing from the war room."

"Shit," Kim shouted. A bloody diversion so they could get the phones—there was only one reason for that. "They want to take control and they're going to see the text with the two million demand," she said.

"And offer it, probably," Dawson added.

"And thereby seal the fate of the girls," Bryant said.

Kim realised that the parents also had access to the screams of pain that she had chosen not to share.

Now they had the problem.

"But why, boss?" Stacey protested. "They might honour the—"

"Stace, once the kidnappers engage the parents in an offer, they no longer need the girls."

CHAPTER 97

Will stared at the text message and a slow smile began to spread across his face. The planning and execution that had led him and Symes to this moment had all been worth it. They were about to get paid.

Both of them.

Now the parents had accepted the terms, it was a straightforward drop. He saw no reason to change the drop plan he'd had last time.

Will felt the victory of the game in his blood. Two million pounds and neither of his partners wanted a cut. They each had their own motivations for their part in the crime. He already knew Symes's incentive: he just wanted to hurt, to cause pain and eventual death. The vision of snuffing out the life of two little girls had carried him through the week.

About the boss, Will wasn't so sure.

He had made two separate deals—he had to double-cross someone. He had promised Symes their death and he had promised the boss their lives.

Will had to decide which double-cross worked best for him.

Symes was here with him now. The boss was not.

"Is it time for me to get paid?" Symes said, pacing back and forth across the room.

Will hesitated for the briefest of seconds.

"Yes. This time you can do whatever you want."

CHAPTER 98

"Err...just to mention, Guv, this isn't the way to Kidderminster."

"Thanks for pointing that out, Bryant, but you saw the aerial view. The noise caused by the accident would have been heard for more than a mile in every direction. We have to narrow it down. Emily said the noise was in the distance so the location of the accident is the wrong place to start. But Emily also said something else," Kim said, bringing the car to a halt.

"I don't get it," Dawson said, from the back seat.

Bryant was looking around. "This is where Emily was found," he said.

The road was an entrance to a new residential estate built on the edge of the green belt just outside Harvington.

"And what she said was left, left, right, left."

"You sure?" Bryant asked.

Kim took out her phone and began to play the recording. She forwarded closer to the end. Ten seconds later Emily's voice confirmed Kim's words.

Realisation dawned on Bryant's features. "We're going to track backwards from where they dumped her."

Kim nodded. "Kev, get Stacey back on the phone. As we move keep telling her where we are. She can let us know if we're warm or cold in relation to the target area."

Dawson took out his phone.

Kim started driving slowly.

"I get what we're doing," Bryant said. "We're gonna go right, left, right, right, reversing Emily's memory, but we don't know if it's first right, second right, third right."

Kim could hear Dawson explaining to Stacey what they were about to do.

"Where they dropped Emily isn't important," she explained. "The most important thing was not being seen. They won't have used main roads or residential streets so they can be ruled out."

"Aaah, got it."

"All set, Kev?" she asked.

"Set, boss."

Kim continued to drive until she saw a narrow lane on her right. She turned. Now she needed a left that was rural.

The next four left turns were residential. The fifth road was flanked by bushes. She took it.

The lane stretched for a third of a mile before hitting the village of Belbroughton.

"Too populated," she said. "This isn't the way."

She turned the car around on a pub car park and went back looking for another left turn.

Kim continued along for another quarter mile, but her gut told her something didn't feel right.

"Boss, Stacey says we're almost three miles from the crash site and moving further away."

"Shit," Kim said, stopping the car.

She had made a mistake. Eloise's warning rang in her ears.

Damn it, she was going to be too late.

CHAPTER 99

"C-Come on, Ames, you gotta s-stay with me. He'll be back in a m-minute."

Amy held her right hand in her left. The tears coursed over her cheeks. "It hurts so bad."

"I know, Ames, b-but we gotta stay strong."

Charlie knew Amy's little finger was broken. It looked the same as when she'd hurt her own in netball.

The pain coursed through her right foot where the man had stamped down on it. Amidst the pain she had heard bones crunch beneath his heavy boot but she had not cried, even though it was killing her to keep the tears at bay. It was hurting so bad now but she had to focus on the plan.

"Ames, it's g-getting worse. We have to go th-through with it."

Fresh tears sprung from Amy's eyes. "I can't, Charl, I can't..."

"You c-can. I can't do it b-but you can."

Charlie knew they had to try.

"I know your hand is hurting b-but they're g-gonna hurt us some more."

Amy cried harder and Charlie scooted closer.

"Okay, listen. I'm g-going on a picnic and I'm t-taking an apple," Charlie said. The game always calmed Amy down.

"Banana."

"Ch-cherries."

"Doughnut."

"Eggs."

"Err . . . frankfurters," Amy said.

"G-Gingerbread."

"Hot dogs."

The tears were slowing down. Charlie continued the game with one ear listening for the sound of footsteps.

"Ice cream."

"Jelly."

"K-KitKat."

"Lemonade."

"Mars bars."

"Nuts."

"O-oranges."

Amy's answers were coming much quicker.

"Poppadums."

"Q . . . I always get Q," Charlie said.

"That's 'cos you always start the game, Dumbo," Amy said, wincing.

Charlie tried to laugh and then stopped as she heard a door opening in the distance.

Amy heard it too. Her eyes widened. Her hand began to scratch skin.

Charlie put her hand on Amy's arm. They were out of time.

"Ames, you gotta be b-brave and do wh-what I said."

Amy shook her head and clutched Charlie's hand. "I can't . . ."

"You m-must." Charlie squeezed Amy's hand. "Promise me, Ames. P-Promise me you will."

A tear fell from Amy's eye. "But you'll . . ."

"I'll be right behind you b-but please just do what I say."

Charlie fought to keep the lie out of her voice. If Amy knew she couldn't run she'd never do what she asked.

But this way, one of them would live.

CHAPTER 100

Kim took a moment to think. She trusted Emily's memory, but knew she was missing a crucial piece of the puzzle.

"Of course," she cried. She started the car and backed into the driveway she'd blocked.

"What?" Bryant asked.

"I've assumed Emily was facing the same way as the driver," Kim said, beginning the journey back to the start point. "The poor kid had been thrown into the back of the van and was being tossed all over the place. That's why we're heading away. Emily was obviously facing the opposite direction."

Bryant frowned as Dawson repeated what she'd just said to Stacey.

"So, let me get this straight. We have to do the opposite of what we've just done because Emily's left is our right."

"Precisely," Kim said, cursing herself for the wasted time.

Minutes later she was back at the start point. "Okay, same again," Kim instructed.

She drove forward as Bryant called out what he saw.

"Houses, houses, private drive, turn."

Kim turned left.

The road had a pub on one corner and two terraced houses on the other corner. Beyond that, a hedge rose up on both sides.

Kim drove slowly as Bryant continued to call out.

"Turn," he shouted.

She took a sharp right and the road narrowed. She was now on a single track road. Hope began to build in her stomach. This was more like it.

"Kev, you getting this?"

"Yeah, Stacey said we're moving towards—"

"Turn," Bryant cried.

Kim took a left onto a single track road with tufts of grass breaking through the tarmac. She hit two potholes in a few seconds.

A branch caught the driver's side door.

"Guv, I think we're getting close," Bryant said.

Oh yes, she knew they were. According to Emily those potholes had been there thirteen months ago too.

"Kev, how far away from the crash site?"

"Just over half a mile."

Kim continued to look for the next turn.

"Guv," Bryant shouted.

She followed his gaze and brought the car to a quick stop. A sawn-off log blocked the road.

Kim looked to Bryant.

"Now, we're getting close."

CHAPTER 101

Symes didn't always take such care before killing. But this was different. The week had been torture, picturing their pure little bodies bending to his violent will; but in some strange way he had enjoyed the painful anticipation. He'd only had one fear. That Will would back out of their deal.

But yesterday Will had given him the go-ahead to take his pay and he was enjoying the luxury of knowing that it was now within his control. A wash and shave had been the order of the day. Symes knew that once he entered the basement he would not return for some time.

He had spent hours imagining how it would feel to break their small bones with his bare hands. He imagined it would be like snapping a chicken wing.

Of course, there would be the violence he craved of kicking and punching but he knew he needed to exercise an element of control. After waiting so long it could not be over in minutes. He would take hours, possibly days. He knew how to take someone to the point of death before bringing them back again to prolong their agony and his pleasure. He would do this until he became bored.

Symes unlatched the door to the stairs that led to the basement.

He would walk into that room knowing he was the last person they would ever see.

CHAPTER 102

"Okay, let's go."

They all exited the vehicle.

One side of the road was hedged but flat.

"Kev, you still got a signal?"

He nodded.

"You take the field."

He pushed himself through the hedge, leaving her and Bryant. The other side of the road was a different story. The grassy earth sloped down away from the road and then rose steeply into the hillside.

"Jesus, Guv, Bear Grylls, I ain't," Bryant said, trying to keep up with her.

Kim ignored him and focussed on her footing.

The grass was dense and slippery. The imminent darkness hovered behind a sun that was waiting to set.

Hang on girls, she silently prayed. Just a little bit longer.

CHAPTER 103

Charlie heard the sound of footsteps coming down the stairs.

"Ready, Ames?"

Her friend looked terrified but nodded.

Charlie heard the metal key slide into the lock. The door opened and Charlie felt her stomach flip. Amy was nestled behind her, waiting.

His right leg drew level with her body.

"Hello again, my little—"

Charlie heard no more as she lunged forward, her mouth open wide.

She grabbed at his ankle with her hands and sunk her teeth into his calf.

"What the fuck—"

She bit down as hard as she could. Through his jeans she could feel the mound of flesh in her mouth.

He cried out loud and raised his leg.

"You fucking little bitch..."

Charlie could see from the corner of her eye that Amy was rooted to the spot. Please, Amy, do it, she willed silently.

The man shook his leg but Charlie wouldn't let go. He leaned down and grabbed her by the hair, prised her teeth off his leg. He swung her around so she was in front of him.

"Run, Amy. Now," she screamed.

Amy gave a little cry as she edged slowly past.

"Go," Charlie cried.

She bucked violently so that he had to use two hands to restrain her and could not reach for Amy.

Amy sobbed and edged closer to the door.

"You fucking little—"

His words turned to a low growl as Charlie sunk her teeth into his left forearm. And this time she had flesh. She could taste the blood on her tongue.

"Get off me you—"

He was screaming and trying to get a grip of her at the same time but she refused to let go. She closed her eyes to the pain and gave another burst of energy, felt her teeth driving further into his arm.

The man cried out again and punched her on the side of the face.

Agony coursed around her whole head but she saw the shadow of her friend edging out of the room.

"You're gonna fucking regret that, you rabid little dog."

Charlie turned her face to the door and cried, "Run, Amy, run."

CHAPTER 104

Kim reached the crest of the hill and swore. The muscles in her legs burned from trudging through the knee-length grass.

"Oh, great," she said, as Bryant puffed his way level with her.

She surveyed the landscape and saw what had been hidden by trees on the aerial view.

Buildings lay to the east, north and west of her view. Only the one straight ahead had shown up on the screen.

"Jesus, which one, Guv?"

Kim shook her head. She only knew that as soon as they left the safety of the long grass they would be visible to all three properties.

"Damn it, if we go for the wrong one…"

She didn't finish the sentence. Bryant knew that any stupid move at this point could get the girls killed or bundled into a van and taken to another location. If that were to happen the girls would be lost.

Bryant chewed his lip.

Kim felt her own heart rate increase. A simple mistake right now and two families could be destroyed forever.

She closed her eyes and utilised every sense she had.

The wind howled around her ears, carrying a light rain that landed on her cheek. She had only one chance to find the girls before time finally ran out. She'd made a call and she hoped to God it was the right one.

She focussed hard. *Come on, girls, send me something. Please help me to find you.*

She opened her eyes, took two steps and stopped.

"Bryant, what's that?"

Bryant followed her gaze. Three hundred metres away at the bottom of the hill, moving from the right, was a blob on the landscape. It was heading in their direction.

They both stared as hard as they could.

Two hundred and fifty metres away, and they looked at each other. Bryant spoke.

"Guv, it looks like a kid."

Kim's own thoughts exactly.

Bryant's legs began to move forward at the same time as Kim's. She managed to catch him before he left the safety of the long grass.

"Get down," she said, grabbing him by the arm.

"Guv, what the hell—"

"Sshh, buzz Dawson."

Bryant took out his mobile phone and Kim raised her head to steal a quick look.

The figure was two hundred metres away and heading right for them.

"What the hell are we doing, Guv? That's one of our girls."

He looked at her as though she'd lost her mind.

Kim popped up her head. One hundred and fifty metres. She snatched her head back down. The long dark hair blowing in the wind told her it was Amy hurtling towards them in nothing more than a blue bathing costume.

"Guv, let's go get her."

"Just wait a minute." She looked up again. Seventy-five metres. And finally she saw what she'd been waiting for.

"Go, when I say so," she said to Bryant.

The sound of panting and sobbing reached their ears. Bryant crawled forward in the grass. She put a hand on his arm. "Wait."

The sound of the child's exertion grew closer. Amy was tiring. The run had been all uphill.

"Guv, I've gotta—"

"Wait," Kim hissed, attuning her ears.

She could now hear the sound of the grass being trodden underfoot.

"Get the fuck back here, you little—"

"Now," Kim screamed and they both erupted from the long grass. Amy was twenty metres west of them. Her pursuer was just three metres behind.

Both stopped dead in surprise.

"Get her, Bryant," Kim shouted.

The man had already turned, but Kim lunged forward and tackled him to the ground.

He squirmed beneath her but she punched him in the right temple. He struggled, trying to shake her off, but she pulled on his hair like a horse's mane, arching his whole head backwards. Kim punched him again in the right jaw.

He bucked and she fell to the left. His desperation to escape added strength to his movements but her motivation was equally strong.

He turned on his side and she struck out with her foot and got a good firm kick in his groin.

"Now stay down."

Bryant appeared beside her. "Here, Guv, let me."

Kim ignored him and rounded on her victim. She knew she was in the company of Subject One. His diminutive height and weedy torso told her she had just tackled the man who sent the texts. This man was not capable of inflicting such a level of violence on Brad and Inga.

That one still had a child.

"Where the hell are they?" Kim screamed into his face.

"Fuck off," he spat.

Kim would have liked to hang around and invent new methods of torture to make him talk but she didn't have the time. Charlie was still down there somewhere.

She looked up the hill to see Amy standing alone, dwarfed by Bryant's overcoat.

"Bryant. Don't let him get up."

Kim sprinted back up the hill. She had known that if they made their move too soon, anyone pursuing the child would have turned back around. And she'd wanted them both.

She knelt before the girl who trembled uncontrollably.

"Amy, it's okay, you're safe now. No one is going to hurt you again."

Kim could see that at least one finger on her right hand had been broken.

"Can you be brave for just a little bit longer?"

Amy nodded.

"Okay, sweetie. I have to go and get Charlie and I need to know where she is."

"She bit the man. She waited for him to come and she bit into his leg. She told me that I had to be the one to run 'cos of her foot and I didn't want to but she made me promise."

"It's okay, Amy. Charlie was right. Did the man hurt her foot?"

Amy nodded. "Stamped on it."

"Okay, Amy. You're doing great. Where was she when you ran?"

"Downstairs... there are rooms... the walls are cold."

Kim looked down the hill. There were four separate buildings. "Amy, can you tell me which building you were in?"

Amy looked where Kim pointed and nodded towards the building to the far right. From the side view it looked like the farmhouse.

"Okay, sweetie, can you tell me what the man looked like?"

"Big," she said, looking up. "Bigger than you. No hair, smooth face."

Amy closed her eyes and trembled violently.

Kim placed a hand on her arm.

"You've done great, Amy. You're a very brave girl."

Dawson came sprinting over the brow of the hill.

"Don't let Amy out of your sight," she instructed as he got closer. "Get an ambulance en route and the fire service to move that log but no calls to the Timmins' house, got it? Not even to Stacey."

Dawson nodded and knelt beside Amy.

"Guv, you can't go down there alone," Bryant said.

Dawson was needed to keep Amy safe and Bryant had to guard their kidnapper.

Charlie was on her own. There was no choice.

Kim turned away from Dawson. She didn't know how long back-up would be. She was unarmed and completely blind to the location.

But there was a psycho somewhere in that building with a nine-year-old girl.

Kim turned on her heel and ran.

CHAPTER 105

The darkness was beginning to fall around Kim as she stopped at the first building. It was a windowless structure with no features. She guessed it would have been used as a cow shed.

The doors were metal and rusted, a padlock securing them.

She skirted the side of the building and came alongside a white van parked beneath a roof structure without walls.

Kim entered the main farmhouse, the doors having been left open by Subject One after chasing Amy. The smell of damp hit her immediately.

The door to her left was a two-panel stable door that led into the kitchen. She stepped inside, careful not to make a sound.

The cupboard doors that remained were all hanging off. Spaces gaped where appliances had once lived. Cobwebs hung from every corner. Rodent droppings sat in piles.

The walls were a mural of black and green damp patches.

Kim edged out and headed into the next room. She guessed this would once have been a small lounge but had more recently been used as a control room.

The window had been covered with a single navy curtain nailed into the wall above.

The area held a table on the left housing a row of mobile phones. On the window wall was a desk with three computer monitors. A sofa took the rest of the available space.

Kim took a step closer to the desk. All three screens were showing white noise. Damn, the cameras had been smashed so she couldn't see exactly where he was. She was going in completely blind.

She stepped out of the room. Next was another wooden door. Kim opened it carefully but the metal handle clattered as it left the latch.

She was immediately confronted by stone steps that led down into darkness.

She placed a hand on each side of the wall and felt the elevation of each step with the back of her heel.

When she felt no more steps she took her mobile phone from her pocket and hit the screen. It provided a small shaft of light against the total blackness.

She pointed it to the left and then to the right.

She was halfway down a corridor that appeared to run the length of the house. To her left was a brick wall but to her right the corridor appeared to turn a corner.

Kim turned to her right and shone the phone at the floor.

She gingerly stepped over the glass that had been smashed from the light bulb above and turned as she heard a sound from the left. The light from the phone found nothing. Kim suspected it was a rat.

She stepped past an open door. She shone the light around. The space was barely bigger than a prison cell.

One corner held a collection of juice cartons and sandwich packets. The other held a mattress and a bucket. The stench reached her out in the corridor.

She moved two steps forward and aimed the phone ahead of her. Two feet more and she'd be round the corner.

"One more step and I'll slit her fucking throat."

Kim stilled. A small cry escaped from the lips of the child. Kim closed her eyes. Thank God, Charlie was still alive.

Although she'd never met him, Kim knew what this man was capable of.

Trying to appeal to an empathetic streak wouldn't work. He no longer possessed one.

This man was not a psychopath. He was a product; moulded and programmed to kill. The war had taken advantage of a man with a propensity for violence and enhanced it, destroying any last traces of humanity.

Kim considered her options. At the moment he didn't know he was dealing with a woman.

"I can smell you, bitch," he said.

Great. But his voice was only a couple of feet away and he sounded amused. That was good. Anything that distracted him from hurting Charlie was good.

His own arrogance prevented her making a decision as he stepped into the light. Kim was instantly struck by his size. She guessed he was carrying eighteen stone of muscle in his six-foot-four height.

Charlie was clutched in front of him, a knife at her throat.

Her left eye was swollen shut and her bottom lip was split.

Her other eye was wide with terror.

Symes laughed out loud. "They send a slag to get me. It's a fucking joke."

Although his voice was filled with mirth, Kim could tell he was insulted.

She lowered her gaze. "It's okay, Charlie. We got Amy and I'm gonna get you out of here."

He laughed again. "No, she fucking ain't, kid," he said to Charlie. "I'm gonna slit your throat like I was promised and then I'm gonna kill her, so she's talking shit."

He took another step towards her. His right leg was stiff. Kim guessed that was where Charlie had bitten him. A trail of blood travelled along his forearm.

Despite his size, if they had been one on one, Kim knew she could have taken him. If there hadn't been a child and a knife between them.

"I'm not alone," she said.

He looked past her.

"Brought your imaginary friends?"

Kim tried to keep her voice low and calm.

"The place is crawling by now. It's only a matter of time before they're down here."

Symes looked unconcerned. "I don't need long."

She was keeping her thumb on the phone screen to prevent the area from going dark. She wanted to try to make eye contact but his gaze was fluttering around.

Kim assessed the distance between them. Without any kind of distraction she couldn't chance lunging for Charlie. His hand was poised and steady. Ready to cut the child's throat.

"What do you hope to gain?" she asked.

She knew she was not going to talk him into handing over the child but she had to play for time.

"You know it's over. We've got the other one; the planner."

"How the fuck you know he was the planner?" Symes asked, pulling Charlie against him.

He didn't like her assumption that he was not the mastermind behind the operation.

"Give us the information and we'll do a deal," she offered. "He's going to prison for the rest of his life but you don't need to. We can—"

"Fuck off, slag. You think I give a fuck about doing time? Gimme a fucking break."

"But what are you—"

"A promise is a promise. Don'cha get it, yer dumb bitch? I *wanna* kill her. I'm *gonna* kill her and—"

"Guv, you down there?"

Symes's eyes travelled to the direction of Bryant's voice. It was all that she needed.

Kim held up the phone, shining it right into his eyes as she lunged forward and grabbed Charlie by the arm.

She threw the child behind her and reached forward for the knife. As her hand made contact with the handle Symes pulled up the blade.

The flesh of her right hand tore open. The light on her phone died.

Footsteps sounded on the stairs.

She felt herself being pushed backwards and stumbled over Charlie.

In the darkness, Kim had no clue what was happening.

Until Symes put the key in the door and locked it.

CHAPTER 106

Symes threw Charlie into the far corner. She whimpered and curled into a ball.

"What your friends gonna do now?" he asked.

The phone was still in Kim's hand. She touched it and the screen lit up again.

She could hear Bryant hammering on the steel door. He would need specialist equipment to get through it. By then they'd all be dead.

And the man standing in front of her knew it.

He looked from her to Charlie and back again.

"Eeny, meeny, miney, mo . . . who's first?"

"Was it ever about the money?" Kim asked, desperately. She had to get his attention away from Charlie. She could feel the blood dripping from her gashed hand onto her jeans.

He paced the area between them to make sure she and Charlie stayed apart.

"Nah. You gotta get it, slag. I like to kill. I enjoy it. The more violence the better. And now I've made my decision."

He came to stand in front of her. She could hear Bryant banging on the door and shouting but her colleague had no way to close the ten-foot gap between them.

So near and yet so far, she thought, as Symes raised his foot and stamped down on her injured hand.

The pain shot up through her arm. The darkness swam before her eyes.

His next blow caught her in the ribs and she fell sideways, the phone sliding from her hand.

His foot caught her square in the jaw. Pain exploded into her head.

"I'm gonna leave you alive, just so you can listen to the show."

He kicked again and hit her left elbow.

"Stop it," Charlie screamed.

"Don't worry, your turn is coming, little girl."

In the darkness Kim tried to crawl out of reach. She knew what he was doing. He was disabling her from all angles so she would be unable to move. Just as he had with Inga.

His next blow caught the top of her left thigh. A slight roll had prevented his foot from shattering her knee.

She fought to think through the pain that was consuming her from every direction.

Another blow landed on her right ankle.

By the light of her phone she could see the pleasure in his eyes. He was just getting warmed up.

Kim thought of the people who were now crawling all over the property. And not one of them could help her.

She felt like the appetiser before the main meal. When he was done with Charlie, he'd return to her for dessert.

He stood back and admired his handiwork. Kim couldn't identify one body part she could move with ease.

She was powerless to fight. The agony flooded her body but she would not cry out. Only the sound of Charlie's soft whimpering from the corner forced her to hold on to consciousness.

The nausea rose in her throat. She coughed it down and her whole body reacted to the movement.

She had no weapons. He had the knife and she could barely move an inch.

Symes turned his attention to the far corner. A growl of anticipation sounded from his throat.

Kim blinked the threat of darkness from her eyes. If she succumbed to the pain for even a minute the child would be dead.

Symes started moving away and Kim could not follow.

He moved towards his prize; his payment for a job well done. Kim was powerless to stop him.

And then the phone light went out.

CHAPTER 107

Kim could hear voices on the other side of the door but they couldn't get through. Charlie cried out from the corner.

Kim tried to focus as a thought tried to form, something Alison had said.

She put every ounce of strength into the one thing she could move. Her mouth.

"Soldier, what the fuck do you think you're doing?"

She sensed the stillness that fell in the room.

"You think we got time for this, soldier?"

"B-but…"

Kim seized the advantage. A sudden hope infused her and dulled the pain.

"Is this what you trained for, soldier?"

She moved a few inches across the floor. Her body screamed for her to stop but she refused to listen.

"Since when did we hurt little girls, soldier?"

Another few inches.

"I'm…I'm…"

"When did we train you to do this, soldier?" she shouted to hide the slow movement of her body along the floor. The pain travelled all the way to her voice but she fought to keep it firm. She hoped the repetition of the title, "soldier," would confuse him just long enough.

"You think your squad would accept you now?"

"But...I'm not...not any..."

"You're always a soldier," Kim barked.

"I don't...see..."

"Of course you see me, soldier," Kim shouted. In the darkness her eyes could just make out his stance. He stood, legs apart, two feet away from Charlie.

Just another few inches.

"Stand down, soldier, and return to your barracks."

"But...you're not...real..."

Kim pulled her left leg back and shot one good kick to his right calf. He toppled to the ground, falling forward.

Kim heard Charlie shuffle out of the way.

The fall brought him back to his senses and his focus was back on Kim.

"You fucking bitch," he screamed. She could hear the anger in his voice as well as the pain. But she knew the blow wouldn't incapacitate him for long.

Kim tried to crawl away, heard him crawl right behind her. Her knees crunched on the broken glass from the smashed light bulb.

His hands lunged for her ankles. She fell forward onto the ground, face first.

Within a second his knees were astride her. He threw her onto her back.

Kim tried to wriggle beneath him but his weight forced her down. She bucked again and he laughed.

She felt the cold metal rest at her throat.

"I'm gonna enjoy every second of this—and then the kid gets it."

Kim could feel the puddle of blood beneath the palm of her right hand.

She lifted her hand from the floor and opened the palm wide, splaying her fingers, stretching the gash.

She smacked her hand down to the ground and felt the glass shards from the light bulb embed in her wound. The nausea was strong and immediate. A hundred knives danced in her palm.

She swallowed frantically as the pain tried to take control.

Fireworks exploded in her eyes as his face suddenly lit up. Charlie was holding the phone, blinding him with sudden light.

Symes's eyes were wide open, trying to adjust.

Kim raised her right hand from the ground and smashed her palm into his eye. The glass shards sticking out of her palm pierced his eyeball.

He screamed like a wounded animal. The knife clattered to the ground as his hands rose to his eyes.

Charlie was quicker than Kim and grabbed the knife from the floor.

Kim scooted over and grabbed her, forming her body around the child like a shell.

Symes rolled on the floor, screaming.

Suddenly, the metal door swung open. And in that moment Kim could have cried.

"Jesus Christ, Guv," Bryant said, shining a torch right at her. A spare key hung from the lock.

She held up her hand against the light to shield her eyes.

Nuggets of glass fell from the wound.

Bryant stepped back into the corridor.

"Paramedic, down here now," he screamed. Blood continued to drip from her hand.

Dawson was the first body to appear. He immediately hauled Symes to his feet. Bryant offered her a hand, but she ignored it and pushed herself to a standing position.

Symes tried to lunge towards her but Dawson held him firm.

She staggered one step towards him. "And all they sent was a bitch, eh?"

"You fucking wait," he spat as a mixture of blood and intraocular fluid rolled over his cheek. "I'll fucking get you."

She took a last look at his one good eye.

"Kev, get him out of my sight."

Dawson shoved him roughly against the wall. Symes cried out in pain.

"Oops," said Dawson, pushing him into the corridor.

Kim turned to Charlie who sat shivering against the wall.

"Charlie, it's okay. He's not coming back. I promise."

The little girl nodded, the disbelief showing in her eyes. There was little Kim could do to reassure her right now but over time she would come to believe it.

"You were so brave just then. Your parents will be very proud."

"Guv, can we call?" Bryant asked.

Kim shook her head as a paramedic entered the room. Not until they had Subject Three.

"See to her foot," Kim said, pointing at Charlie.

Bryant passed the torch to the second paramedic who shone it down towards the child.

Bryant stepped forward and picked up Charlie like she was nothing. "There are ambulances upstairs. He needs to take a look at your hand."

Bryant carried the child up the stairs.

The paramedic took her hand gently. The other shone the torch onto the wound.

"I'm gonna need to get you to the hospital. There might be nerve damage."

Kim shook her head. "Take out the glass and wrap it up."

"No, you need X-rays. You've taken quite a beating."

Kim pulled her hand away. "Do it, or I'll do it myself."

There were still unanswered questions.

He offered her a look of disapproval.

"You'll have to sign a disclaimer."

She looked down at her hand and raised one eyebrow.

He smiled. "Yeah, okay, fair enough."

Kim stared at the wall while he used tweezers to prise out the glass. Most of the pieces had embedded themselves in Symes's eye.

"Can you go quicker?" she asked. The feeling was returning to parts of her body and she still had work to do.

"I'm trying to do it gently," he snapped.

"Well, don't. Just get it out and clean it up," she snapped back.

By the time Bryant returned, her hand was covered in gauze and bandage and was three times the size.

"You have to get to hospital as soon—"

"Yeah, yeah; are we done?"

The medic closed his case and shook his head. "She's all yours," he said to Bryant.

"Cheers, mate," Bryant responded.

Kim eased herself slowly to her feet. The pain sent a dozen reminders around her body.

"You look a bit banged up, Guv."

"I'll live," she said, heading for the corridor.

"Err . . . do you want any help up the stairs?"

"Oh, Bryant, please ask me that question again."

"Got it. I'll go first."

She silently thanked him. If he was ahead of her, he would not see her struggle.

Kim knew she had to get back to the Timmins' house, but there was a final piece of the puzzle that had to be resolved.

She reached the third step up and paused.

"I can't," she said.

"I told you to—"

"Not that," she said, shaking her head. "I can't just leave."

The remains of another child were here somewhere and out there was a mother who dreamed of their return.

She stepped back down into the corridor. Bryant followed and lit the area with the torch he'd taken back from the medic.

"Guv, what are you hoping to find?"

"Get the keys," she said, pointing to where they still hung from the open door.

Bryant removed the keys and Kim headed to the left and the dead end. There was a second metal door.

"Open it," Kim said. Her gut churned in response as the key turned in the lock.

She took the torch in her left hand and shone it around the silent room.

The shaft of light rested at the top right-hand corner.

Kim closed her eyes for the briefest of seconds and sighed heavily. There was a mother who was about to get her wish.

They had found the body of a little girl.

Jenny Cotton would be able to bury her daughter.

CHAPTER 108

Kim waited for her eyes to adjust to the darkness and approached the shape in the corner.

Her heart stopped for the briefest of seconds.

"No fucking way, Guv," Bryant whispered behind her.

Yes, she had seen it too. The figure in the corner had moved.

Kim stepped forward slowly, her eyes refusing to blink.

"It's okay, Suzie, you're safe," Kim murmured.

The tiny form forced herself further into the corner, her head turned into the wall.

Kim pushed at Bryant's torch so that it was aimed in Suzie's general direction but not shining directly upon her.

Although a year older than Amy and Charlie, this huddled shape looked so much younger.

She wore a pair of black leggings and an oversize shirt that dwarfed her upper half. Her light brown hair had been cut short, hacked close to her head.

Like the room next door, a bucket was placed in the corner. The floor was littered with drinks cartons and wrappers.

Kim felt the tears sting her eyes. The child had been down here for thirteen months.

She swallowed the emotion in her throat.

"Suzie, the bad men have gone. They've been taken away. They are never going to hurt you again."

No response.

Kim felt Bryant step into the room behind her but she waved him back out.

She moved a couple of inches closer.

"There's no need to be frightened any more. I promise you're safe."

No response.

Kim's heart ached for the terror this child had experienced. She had to give her something familiar.

She moved closer again. "I met your mum, Suzie. She misses you so much."

Suzie shook her head into the wall.

"Are you angry with your mum, Suzie?"

Another shake of the head.

Kim took another few inches. She had to make the child look at her, to let her know she was safe. But Suzie hadn't budged from the safety of the corner.

Kim cursed her own stupidity. How many times had the child imagined that door opening, praying for her release?

"Are you scared to look at me?"

Kim took the lack of response as a yes.

"Do you think I'll disappear?"

No response.

Kim realised the child thought she was imagining the intrusion and if she opened her eyes it would disappear. Kim bit her own lip to fight back the tears. She wanted to run to the corner and gather the child in her arms but she couldn't risk adding to her terror.

"Suzie, I'm going to reach out and touch your right foot. If you feel the weight of my hand you'll know that I'm not in your imagination and I'm real, okay?"

No response.

Kim touched the girl on the ankle. The contact acted as a catapult, as Suzie launched herself from the corner and into Kim's arms.

Kim closed her arms around the small, fragile body and closed her eyes.

The tears were loud and wracking but Kim was pleased there were tears.

"It's okay, sweetheart. Those men are never going to hurt you again. I promise you."

Suzie nestled further and Kim stroked her hair.

The rage was burning inside her.

Kim rocked the child back and forth and whispered reassurance into her ear.

The tears began to slow.

"Suzie, are you hurt?" Kim asked, gently.

Suzie shook her head no but Kim could feel the bones of the painfully thin body in her arms.

The child had been given enough to survive and, to judge from the facilities available in the house, that had not included one proper meal.

"Okay, sweetie, we need to get you out of here."

Suzie huddled closer.

Kim took her gently by the arms and prised her away.

"Don't be scared. I promise everything is going to be okay, Suzie, but I need to get back up those stairs and I could do with some help."

Suzie nodded slightly so Kim moved gently away.

"Okay, if you hold my hand I think I can make it."

Again the child nodded and Kim realised that she hadn't spoken once.

That was not something to be tackled here and now. She was alive and the rest could come later.

Bryant mounted the stairs ahead of them.

The staircase was narrow so Kim climbed it sideways, not letting go of Suzie's hand.

"Well done, Suzie. You're doing great. Now when we get outside there will be a lot of people, but don't worry about it. None of them are going to bother you."

She felt the hand tighten within her grip. She kept talking to give the child something to hang on to.

She remembered the sirens and noise herself when she was six years old and being removed from their flat. She had wanted Mikey's hand to hold. But she couldn't because he was dead.

She pushed the thought away and focussed on easing Suzie's fear.

"Almost there, sweetie," Kim said, as they walked through the house.

Voices were coming from the control room. The evidence collection was already in progress.

Kim gripped the girl's hand tightly. "Remember what I said. No one is going to bother you, okay?"

Suzie nodded as they stepped out into the cold.

The darkened sky was ablaze with flashing blue lights.

Suzie's eyes widened as she looked at the activity; two ambulances and three squad cars produced quite a display.

Kim turned to Suzie and used her hand to tip the girl's chin to look into her face.

"Suzie, this man here is my friend and I would trust him with my life. He's going to take you straight to your mum."

The girl clutched her hand even tighter and Kim's bandaged hand instinctively stroked the top of her head.

"I promise you'll be fine, sweetie, but we need to get you home."

The child would need to be checked over soon. She was severely undernourished. They would also need to question her at some stage but nothing trumped seeing her mother. Bryant was taking her home.

Reluctantly, Suzie allowed Bryant to take her hand and guide her up the hill to where Kim had parked the car what seemed like three days ago.

Dawson materialised beside her and followed her gaze.

His head snapped around. "No way, Guv. That is not Suzie Cotton."

Kim allowed herself a smile. "Yes, Kev. It is."

Their gaze met and held for a moment. He began to shake his head. "Guv, I..." He rubbed at his chin. "I mean...how the hell did you know?"

"I didn't; but I couldn't just leave her here anyway."

His smile widened. "You really..."

"Where are we?" she asked, glancing around.

He turned towards the vehicles. "Our kidnappers have been read their rights. Will Carter has already been taken to the station. Symes is in the first ambulance with three constables for company. And the girls are with a WPC in the second ambulance just about to leave."

She watched as Bryant and Suzie crested the hill and disappeared from view.

She thought of Jennifer Cotton who was soon to receive a gift. The woman's life had ended with Suzie's disappearance but now it was going to re-start. Kim marvelled that they had both managed to hold on, such was the bond between mother and daughter.

Kim was jolted by the notion. Suddenly everything fell into place.

"Dawson, go nick a squad car, now," she said.

Finally, it was time to get Subject Number Three.

CHAPTER 109

The squad car pulled up on the Timmins' drive. Kim hadn't spoken during the journey as she pulled together every last strand.

"Boss, do you want to tell me what's going on?" Dawson said.

She shook her head. "You'll be busy."

She stepped out of the car and the front door opened. They had not returned in the manner they'd left; rushed, panicky and full of fear.

Four anxious parents stepped out of the house. Karen and Robert were clutching each other's hands. Elizabeth was a step behind hugging Nicholas closely. Stephen walked to the far left holding his phone, alone. Their expressions were united in a mixture of both fear and hope.

Kim allowed the smile to form on her face.

"We have them both."

Her statement was followed by a collection of screams and cries. Kim wasn't sure what came from whom.

"Amy has a broken finger and Charlie has an injury to her foot and face, but other than that they're alive and well and incredibly brave."

Kim made eye contact with Karen as she said those last words.

"They're on their way to Russells Hall for treatment so I suggest you get on your way." She turned to Dawson. "My colleague will escort you on the blues."

"Everyone in mine," Stephen said, pointing to a black Range Rover. In the throes of their euphoria the fractures in their relationships would pale. For now.

As they filed past her, Kim couldn't help addressing one last issue.

"Hey, Stephen," she said, smiling. "Do you like me now?"

He paused and looked at her. Gone was the aggression and hostility, now replaced by relief and joy.

"Oh yes, Inspector, I like you very much."

Kim watched as they huddled into the car. Stephen and Robert took the front seats, while Elizabeth put Nicholas into the baby seat.

At the last second, Karen hesitated before climbing in beside Elizabeth.

She ran back and threw her arms around Kim, pulling her close.

"Thank you for everything, Kim. I owe you my life."

Kim returned the hug briefly and then pushed the woman away.

"Just go and be with your daughter."

Karen didn't need to be told twice.

Dawson stood beside her. "Boss, I've got the answer. I know who ratted on Dewain."

The sadness in his face told her he'd arrived at the same conclusion as her.

"I knew you would. Get these parents to the hospital and then go and make the arrest. It's all yours."

"Thanks, boss," he said, heading towards the squad car.

"Oh, and Kev," she called, as he opened the car door.

He turned.

"I don't know what you did back then, but you're in a crew now, okay?"

His smile widened as he offered Kim a mock salute.

She waited until both vehicles had disappeared before she entered the house.

Matt stepped out of the kitchen.

Alison stood at the bottom of the stairs.

Helen stepped out of the lounge.

Kim turned and closed the front door.

There was one more loose end to tie up.

CHAPTER 110

Stacey appeared in the hallway and looked her up and down. "Bloody hell, boss, are you okay?"

Kim held up her good hand and smiled. "I'm fine, Stace."

The detective constable stepped forward. "I found Karen but she'd already sent the..."

"Stace, it's fine. We got them all."

Kim turned left into the lounge.

Helen followed with her hand at her throat. "You said the girls are okay? Oh, my goodness, I'm so relieved."

"Of course you are," Kim said, tipping her head. "It's what you wanted all along."

Helen frowned and Kim itched to smack the pleasant, homely face.

"You've failed, Helen. I know exactly what you wanted and you are not going to get away with it."

Matt now stood in the doorway. Alison and Stacey were right behind. Their confusion was obvious.

Helen looked from one to the other.

"Kim, what on earth are you talking about?"

"That'll be Marm to you, Helen—and it's time to drop the act."

Helen shook her head dumbly but Kim could see the workings behind her eyes. She was trying to fathom where it had all gone wrong.

And Kim was happy to share.

"It was clear to me early on that your boys were not working alone. Their personalities were too extreme to function without an overruling authority—and what better than a maternal figure to keep the boys in check?

"The first kidnapping case was devised by Will on his own. It was his plan but it all went wrong because of the road traffic accident. A couple of months after that you were informed that you would be forcibly retired. You appealed and failed. Now, empty your pockets."

Helen's eyes darted from her to the spectators in the doorway.

Kim took a step that caused pain to echo all around her body. She didn't feel like wrestling the phone from her grip but she would if she had to.

"Kim, have you lost your mind? I'm a family liaison officer," Helen protested.

"Helen, I will empty them for you."

Helen dug into her back pockets and pulled out an iPhone.

"The front ones," Kim said, wearily.

Helen slowly put her hand into her right pocket and brought out a second phone. A Nokia.

"I keep two phones…"

"It's not your phone. It belongs to Julia Trueman, aka Julia Billingham and you stole it from the evidence room." She looked behind her. "Stacey, take the phone."

Stacey strode across the room and snatched the phone from Helen's hands. She pressed a few keys and then nodded.

"You contacted Will on the phone he'd used to try and extort money from their family. I'm betting you told him you could make sure it went right this time. That you would be in place to make sure nothing went wrong. And then I played right into your hands by requesting your involvement on this new kidnapping.

You knew that anyone leading this case would have asked for the same thing.

"I wondered why that second message was so long in coming. The girls had been gone for almost twelve hours but it was to give you time to get here and assess the situation."

"Kim, you're mistaken. I haven't done anything. I haven't hurt—"

"What about Inga Bauer? You know, I couldn't work out what could have happened to persuade Inga to turn on these girls. At first I thought it was love—and in a way it was, wasn't it, Helen? But not from the men. You were the one who courted her for months, found out that she'd been abandoned as a child and that she craved maternal love, and that's exactly what you gave her. You manipulated her need for a mother; her desire to be loved unconditionally. You gave her that love and then took away her life."

The expression on Helen's face didn't change. There was no sliver of remorse for what she had done.

"And even Eloise had you running scared. You were terrified that she might say something to incriminate you. Once she hinted that there was bitterness close to the investigation you couldn't escort her from the property quickly enough.

"You knew she'd let you into her home if you offered to listen to her, so you did your own dirty work and tried to make it look as though she'd died in her sleep."

Helen stepped back and visibly paled.

"Well, she didn't die, Helen," Kim spat. "And she will identify you."

Helen's head began to shake slowly, as though her brain couldn't compute the complexity of just how badly she'd miscalculated.

"And the clothes had to get here somehow, didn't they?" Kim fought down her rage. "You walked around this property placing those items for the parents to find. How the hell could you do that?"

Kim was in no mood to give her the time to answer.

"But the final clue. The nail in your coffin was your timely mention of a forgotten memory. And that was your intention all along, wasn't it? It was your plan that you would save the day. Your sudden memory would be the key to unlocking the location of the girls. And then you'd be the hero, wouldn't you, Helen? What police force could retire an officer so instrumental in the safe return of two young girls?

"You subjected Charlie and Amy to a week of the most horrendous terror, just so you could be the hero and keep your bloody job. Did you think your co-conspirators would just walk away from the farmhouse when you told them to? Were they supposed to leave the girls there alive so they wouldn't be caught and identify you?" Kim asked incredulously. "You really thought that's what they would do?"

Finally the mask of bewilderment dropped to reveal a genuine expression of disbelief.

"The girls were never in any danger," Helen protested.

"Jesus, you just don't get it, do you?" Kim stormed. "They were going to *kill* the girls. Will's only motivation was money and Symes had been promised their lives."

Now she frowned. More miscalculations. What had she expected from Will; loyalty, trust?

"No...no...no..."

"Why, Helen?" Kim said, taking a step towards her. "Were you really so badly affected by your retirement that you resorted to this?"

"You should know, Kim," Helen said, quietly.

"Know what?"

Helen finally met her gaze. Her eyes were cold and hard.

"I gave everything to this job. I gave it my life. I devoted every waking hour to the police force. I did whatever I was asked.

"I have no husband, no family; only this job—and I was about to lose that. I was owed. I asked to stay on and I was refused, yet they advertise for new officers every year.

"I've been discarded at the point where I can have nothing else. I'm too old for children. My looks are gone. In two months' time I'll be a nothing. I'll be the woman wandering around the supermarket eager to strike up conversation with anyone who'll listen.

"You asked for proof of life for those girls, but where's the proof of mine?"

A half-smile played on Helen's mouth.

"You'll see, Kim. You're so much like me. You've given every ounce of yourself to this case. Do you even remember where you live? Do you have a loved one, a child, even a pet? I'm betting not, because you're allowing yourself to be swallowed by the job and in twenty years' time when you're the same age..."

Kim stepped right into her face. "I will never feel bitter and twisted for the choices I make and I would never endanger the life of young girls or torture families because I didn't get my own way, you evil, psychotic bitch. And, I have a dog."

Helen's rage showed on her face. She lunged forward, hands outstretched, aiming for Kim's throat.

Kim sidestepped the attack easily and Helen fell to the ground.

Kim looked down at the pathetic figure who had almost cost two girls their lives.

"Better practise that before you get to prison 'cos they're gonna love you in there."

CHAPTER 111

Dawson stood at the front door and hesitated before he knocked. He understood gang culture more than he cared to admit and it had cost him a memory that was ingrained in his brain.

Two days after his fifteenth birthday a group of lads a year older had suddenly stopped calling him "lard-arse," "pie-face" and every other name reserved for fat kids. Instead, they had offered him a seat in the common room and a smile. He'd been invited to meet them in Cradley Heath High Street after school. It had been the happiest afternoon he'd ever spent in class.

They'd been waiting for him outside the market, full of smiles and back slaps. For a whole ten minutes they had chatted around him but he'd felt part of their gang, their crew.

Then suddenly he'd noticed the ringleader, Anthony, nod towards an old woman walking with the aid of two sticks. Two of the four kids had strolled towards the woman and kicked the right stick out of her hand. As she'd stumbled and tried to keep her balance, Anthony ran by and ripped the handbag from her right shoulder.

Dawson had followed his instincts and started to run too. By the time he'd reached the woman she was lying on the ground. Something had forced him to look into her face, terrified she'd banged her head and died. He had looked down into eyes that were filled with terror. And in that brief second he knew that woman's life would never be the same again.

It was only when he'd reached the safety of home that Dawson had finally understood why he'd been asked along. He was fat. He couldn't run as fast as the others so anyone chasing would have caught him first.

The shame had burned within him for months but had lessened in line with his BMI. But not the memory of the fear in the old woman's eyes. That had stayed with him for good.

He understood why Dewain Wright had been part of the gang, but he'd been betrayed in the worst possible way.

Dawson took a deep breath and knocked three times.

The door opened slowly.

Shona Wright stood before him with real fear in her eyes.

"May I speak with you and your father?"

There was no attitude and no swagger this time.

He followed her to the lounge where two little girls sat cross-legged on the floor. A mini picnic had been laid out while they watched the television.

"Rosi, Marisha, go to your room," Shona said, ushering them out.

Vin sat at the far end of the sofa.

Shona stood in front of the closed door.

Dawson looked from one to the other and finally settled on Vin.

"I know what you did to your son," he said, simply.

Vin stared at him for the longest minute before dropping his head into his hands.

"Dad...?" Shona said from the door.

Dawson looked to the girl's father to see if any explanation was forthcoming. The broad shoulders were shaking gently and tears fell to the ground.

He turned to Shona. He could see that her mind had accepted the truth but her heart had not yet caught up.

Dawson sighed and spoke quietly. "Shona, it was your father that contacted Lyron. He told him that Dewain was still alive."

"Don't be ridiculous," Shona spat. "You lot are bloody mental." She tapped her temple. "Bloody stupid."

Dawson looked at her father. She followed suit.

She stared at his slumped shoulders, waiting for him to refute the words. Her head began to shake slowly from side to side. But Dawson could see that it was starting to sink in.

He gave them a moment to digest what he'd said.

He had originally thought that Lauren was responsible for passing on the information that Dewain was still alive, and even more so once he'd discovered she was now with Kai. The girl was not bright enough to have done so deliberately and didn't care enough about Dewain to have done so by accident.

Lauren was a girl who just wanted to live on the wild side. Her suburban shackles had been loosened by a foray into gang culture on Hollytree. As one cheap thrill was murdered there was another waiting to take its place.

Dawson had realised the real culprit when he'd returned to the Timmins' house after the girls had been found. Stephen Hanson had offered to take Nicholas from his wife while she climbed into the car. She had refused and clutched her son closely to her body. With one of her children missing, the grieving mother had held even more tightly to the one she still had.

"He did it for you girls, Shona," Dawson explained. "While Dewain was alive you were all in danger. They would never have left you alone. Your lives would have been more horrendous than ever. The whole family would have been targeted and your father knew that."

The sobbing from the corner grew louder.

"He was never gonna recover, Sho," Vin cried, raising his head. Mucus and tears mixed together and streaked his face. The voice was tortured and hoarse. "My boy was gone. Kept alive by machines and tubes. His brain was dead, they said."

Vin howled and Kev would swear it was the sound of a breaking heart.

"I begged and begged to be moved but they wouldn't move us, Sho. We weren't high risk and Lyron would have found us wherever we went. I couldn't risk losing you all. Oh my boy, my brave, brave boy…"

Shona fought with the emotions storming around inside her. She ran to her father and knelt on the floor. His arms immediately encircled her and they sobbed together.

Right now, this minute, Dawson felt no triumph in the conclusion of this case. Vin Wright had been faced with an impossible choice. Trapped in an environment where he was powerless to protect all his children, he had sacrificed his only son.

He spoke softly. "Mr. Wright, I'll be in the hallway for a minute, but then you know what I have to do."

"I know…son. I know."

The words were strangled with emotion. For once Dawson didn't flinch at being called "son."

Dawson possessed enough self-awareness to know that tomorrow his sympathy would be replaced by pride. It was a case and he'd solved it. A crime had been committed and the perpetrator would be punished.

So, he was in no doubt he'd feel better tomorrow. But right now, he felt like shit.

CHAPTER 112

Kim stared hard at the plate.

It was a look that persuaded most of her colleagues to bend to her will. Unfortunately it didn't work on biscuits.

The recipe and instruction list had been taken from a website for kids and she had followed it to the letter. She was sure she had.

The website also contained pictures sent in by twelve-year-olds who were proud of their end result. Kim would not be photographing hers.

The title of the product said "rock cakes" but hers did not look like rocks, they looked like oversize Frisbees. The dollops of mixture once placed in the oven had spread, as though trying to crawl away and escape.

Cooking was her nemesis. She had tried complex dishes that took more concentration than a Mensa quiz and the end result had spilled across the plate like a liquefied stew. She had tried simple dishes like a Victoria sponge that most kids had mastered at school. Still no joy.

Erica, her foster mother, had been a wonderful cook and had made complex dishes look simple. For Kim it was the other way around but, for the memory of the only person she'd loved as a mother, she would always continue to try.

Woody had insisted she take a few days' leave until her hand started to heal. Luckily there had been no nerve damage and only twelve stitches to sew her hand back up.

"Please tell me you haven't been cooking again," Bryant said, entering the kitchen. "You can't cook a ready meal with two hands so at fifty per cent…"

"Bryant," she warned.

He placed a pizza box on the countertop.

"Want one?"

"Yeah, good one, Kim. I'll pass."

She took two plates from the cupboard, still clumsy with her left hand.

"Look how considerate I am. Bought you one-handed food."

Kim took a piece of pizza and put it onto her plate.

"Please tell me something… anything. I'm going out of my mind."

"Actually there is something Woody asked me to pass on," Bryant said with a smile.

"Go on."

She was desperate for news on the case.

"You're getting a commendation."

Kim rolled her eyes. "Oh, how fabulous for me."

Bryant took out his notebook.

"Damn it, Dawson won."

"Won what?"

"The sweep on your response to that news. He got it word-perfect. To be fair, he even had the eye roll. Look, it says here, 'eye roll.'"

Despite herself Kim laughed out loud.

They all knew her well enough to know her response. Commendations from her superiors did not lull her off to sleep at night but served only as a buffer for the next time she got a complaint or failed to follow procedure or didn't adhere to an order.

"The office looks like the Chelsea Flower Show by the way. There are baskets from the girls, bouquets from the parents and Suzie's mom even sent a kidney."

"A what?"

"Nah, I'm just kidding, but I'm sure she would if you asked."
Bryant shook his head and lowered his face. "Jesus, Kim, I wish
you'd been there when she opened the door. I'll never forget the
look on her face. There were tears—and I'm man enough to admit
that some of them were mine."

Kim smiled. That was what lulled her to sleep at night.

"Suzie's since been checked over and although it's gonna take
some time to build her back up slowly, she'll make a full recovery."

Kim took a moment to enjoy that news.

"Seriously, Kim, if you hadn't insisted on—"

"Have you spoken to the others?"

He nodded. "Karen and Robert are drawing up adoption
papers. They're pretty sure that Lee will give up parental rights
for a small fee. And they're happy to pay." He smiled. "They'll
get through this. As unlikely a couple as they are, they love each
other and Robert would die for that child."

Kim thought of the brave little girl with the wild blonde hair.

"They have a lot to be proud of."

"I spoke to Elizabeth this morning. She's asked Stephen to
move out but she hasn't given him a date. If he plays his cards
right I think she'll forgive him."

Kim nodded her agreement. "Perhaps, but he'd better get ready
for the change. I suspect she is not the person she was ten days ago."

She pushed her plate away and stood. She took a pack of
Colombian Gold from the cupboard. It was empty. She reached
for a fresh pack.

Bryant stood. "Do you want me to…?"

Kim shot him a look. "Bryant, it's hard to floss my teeth at
night. Do you wanna hang around for that?"

"Ugh, no thanks. Fine, I'll just sit here and watch."

Kim took a pair of scissors and then placed the packet in the
crook of her elbow. Three cuts with her left hand and it was done.

"You know, if I was stranded on a desert island do you know the one thing I'd want with me?" Bryant said.

"What?"

"You."

Kim laughed as she shook the coffee into the filter. She turned and fixed him with a look.

"So, are you being deliberately obtuse or what?"

He smirked. He knew what she wanted to hear.

"Okay, Symes is singing like a canary. You were right about him not being involved in the first one. He didn't even know Suzie was there. If he had we both know that Suzie would be dead. That was Will's own little project.

"Symes hasn't requested a lawyer and seems happy to do his time. I think there's a part of him that craves prison life—the regimentation, the structure. He is one seriously disturbed individual."

Oh yeah, Kim knew that all too well.

"Oh, and the sight in his left eye is permanently gone."

"I'm crying on the inside. What about Will Carter?"

"He's blaming all this one on Helen. And won't comment on anything to do with the last one."

Kim clenched the one fist that would move. "Thirteen months he had that child down there. Honestly, if I could choose one of them to torture it would be him. How could he watch her like that for all that time?"

Bryant nodded his agreement.

Kim suspected that Will had thought Suzie was dead when he left to release Emily. Only when he returned did he realise the child was still alive. There was no evidence to suggest Will was capable of hands-on murder.

Because of his intention to take Emily at a later date, Kim had to wonder if he'd decided to keep Suzie alive to play the same parents off again. And when he'd been unable to snatch Emily a second time he had kept Suzie alive as another way to make a few quid.

His refusal to talk probably meant that they would never know. "What about Helen?"

Bryant's jaw tensed but he kept his voice light.

"Oh, she's claiming mental distress, post-traumatic stress, and diminished responsibility. She's quoting the entire gamut of mental health disorders all brought about by the stress of the job."

"You're kidding?"

"Nah, she's got a fancy QC—but ours will be better."

They would have to be, Kim thought.

"And that's about it," Bryant shrugged.

That was plenty.

"Oh, except for the fact Kev is strutting around like he discovered the meaning of life after wrapping up the Dewain Wright case. Vin will plead guilty, by the way, no trial."

Kim accepted the news sadly. She wanted to hate the man but couldn't. She abhorred the decision he'd made but in a twisted kind of way she understood it. Vin Wright had made seven separate requests to the council to move, but he'd been short of points to get transferred to a decent estate. It was a decision he would have to live with for the rest of his life.

Silence fell between them.

"She was wrong, you know. Helen. Stacey told me what she said to you and she wasn't right."

Kim nodded her understanding. The parallels the woman had drawn between the two of them had stayed in her head. And she didn't like the fact they had managed to settle there. Her left hand reached down and met the soft warm head of Barney. She knew Helen had been wrong but maybe not completely, which was something she was going to have to think about. But not now and not with Bryant.

"Oh yeah, and did you mean what you said to Suzie about trusting me with your life?"

Kim guffawed. "Kids; they're so gullible. They'll believe anything."

He smiled. "Yeah, that's what I thought." He stood. "Almost forgot. Matt was in for his last debrief today. He asked me to give you this."

It was a folded piece of paper.

She placed it on the breakfast bar and walked Bryant to the door.

"I'll be round in a couple of days to make sure you're not eating your own cooking."

"Yeah, be sure to bring something nice."

He laughed as he walked down the path.

She closed the door and headed back to the kitchen. The smell of fresh coffee filled the room.

She looked at the unopened note from Matt, sure it was nothing good.

Every conversation between them had been a battlefield, each gaining an advantage or trying to get the last word, like a tennis match stuck at deuce.

Matt Ward was not an easy man to get along with. Every moment in his company had been a challenge; a fight.

He was exhausting and difficult, just like her.

Kim opened the note and read:

I'll pick you up at eight. No negotiation. Be ready.

Kim stared at the note for a full minute and then took a glance at the clock.

She sipped the rest of the coffee before pushing herself to her feet and smiled as she headed for the shower.

She had never refused a challenge in her life.

Tonight she was going out.

CHAPTER 113

The carrier bag rested on Kim's right forearm as she stepped quietly into the room.

The silence was broken by a rhythmic beeping sound that travelled from the index finger to the machine. An intravenous drip fed nourishment in through a tube.

Kim placed the bag onto the chair at the side of the bed and moved closer.

"Good evening, Eloise," she said, gently.

She had no idea if the woman in the bed could hear her. Her body offered no response.

Her frame looked smaller than it had in the garden. The gentle face more ravaged by age. A mop of grey curls framed an expression that was peaceful and calm.

Kim found it strange that this woman had no one. She looked like she should have been a mother to someone.

All week, Kim had been surrounded by aspects of parental love.

Jenny Cotton had been unable to move on with her life, paralysed by the loss of her child. Elizabeth Hanson had settled for less than her due to give her children a stable life. Karen Timmins had lied to the world to protect her child.

Even Vin Wright had sanctioned the life of one child to protect the lives of three more.

Helen had used that magical bond of motherhood to manipulate a young woman into acting against her own instincts. That need had been abused and twisted by a despicable person.

It was further proof to Kim that some people were not meant to parent children. She placed her mother at the top of that list.

All week the memories had threatened her but her resolve had kept them at bay. She would not visit her past; the place would tear her apart.

She knew that somewhere, some time, it would catch her. The shadows that loomed would take form.

But not here and not today.

"Eloise, I wasn't too late," she whispered. "I got them back. All of them."

She stood silently for a moment, stroking the skin on the woman's thumb. "And if Mikey's with you, tell him... tell him... I miss him every day."

She sat, reached into the bag and took out a paperback. For a moment it nestled in her lap.

She imagined the rest of her colleagues, all celebrating a job well done. She silently applauded their efforts. They deserved their moment of victory. Together they had saved the lives of three young girls.

Kim allowed a smile to form on her lips.

All three children were at home, safe in the embrace of their families.

And that knowledge was enough for her.

Kim let out a long, satisfied sigh, the smile still playing around her mouth.

"Okay, Eloise, I chose *Great Expectations*. I hope it's one of your favourites."

Kim turned the page and began to read.

LETTER FROM ANGELA

First of all, I want to say a huge thank you for choosing to read *Lost Girls*. I hope you enjoyed the third instalment of Kim's journey and hope you feel the same way I do. Whilst Kim might not be the warmest of characters, she shows passion and drive and a real hunger for justice.

If you did enjoy it, I would be forever grateful if you'd write a review. I'd love to hear what you think, and it can also help other readers discover one of my books for the first time. Or maybe you can recommend it to your friends and family...

Each story is intended to entertain and take the reader on an exciting, interesting journey. There are some subjects in the books that are difficult to stomach but I aim to treat each situation with respect and sensitivity and not sensationalism. I hope you will join both Kim Stone and myself on our next journey, wherever that may lead.

If so I'd love to hear from you—get in touch on my Facebook or Goodreads page, Twitter or through my website.

And if you'd like to keep up-to-date with all my latest releases, just sign up at the website link below.

Thank you so much for your support, it is hugely appreciated.

Angela Marsons

www.bookouture.com/angela-marsons
www.angelamarsons-books.com
www.facebook.com/angelamarsonsauthor
www.twitter.com/@WriteAngie

ACKNOWLEDGMENTS

I have always been interested in how circumstances can affect behaviour. How differently would we act under extreme pressure? Do we remain true to the person we think we are or does some inherent primal instinct take over?

I could find no better platform to explore this than writing about probably the most instinctual urge to protect, especially a child.

I hope I have done the subject justice.

I can never find the words to express my gratitude to my partner, Julie. Her honesty and belief has guided me throughout my writing journey. She is my sounding board, my first reader, my harshest critic and my most ardent supporter. Twenty years of rejections always elicited the same response of "their loss," before the inevitable encouragement to "crack on with the next." Everyone should have a Julie.

As ever I would like to thank the team at Bookouture for their continued enthusiasm for Kim Stone and her stories.

Oliver Rhodes is a true magician and both his and Claire Bord's passion for the books and the authors at Team Bookouture is both heartening and inspirational.

My editor, Keshini Naidoo, is incredibly talented, knowledgeable and adds more to the books than she will ever understand.

Kim Nash continues to hug, shelter, protect, encourage and support the entire Bookouture family and offers the warmest shoulder in the world.

Thank you all for everything. You inspire me to be the best I can be.

I would like to acknowledge my fellow Bookouture authors. Every one of them is talented and unique and contributes to an environment of fun, support and understanding. My book buddy Caroline Mitchell started her journey along with me and is always ready with words of wisdom, helpful advice and incredibly funny pictures. Lindsay J. Pryor is brilliantly talented and full of warmth. Renita D'Silva has one of the most beautiful souls I have ever met. All are my exceptional writing colleagues but have also become very dear friends.

My sincere thanks to my Mum and Dad who tell everyone they meet about my books, whether they are interested or not. Their enthusiasm and support is amazing.

My eternal gratitude goes to all the wonderful bloggers and reviewers who have taken the time to get to know Kim Stone and follow her story. These wonderful people shout loudly and share generously not because it is their job but because it is their passion. I will never tire of thanking this community for their support of both myself and my books. Thank you all so much.

And finally a warm thank you to the lovely Dee Weston, my safety blanket who continues to offer me support and friendship in times of need.

ABOUT THE AUTHOR

Angela Marsons is the *USA Today* bestselling author of the Detective Kim Stone series, and her books have sold more than three million copies and have been translated into twenty-seven languages. She lives in the Black Country, in the West Midlands of England, with her partner and their two Golden Retrievers. She first discovered her love of writing at junior school when actual lessons came second to watching other people and quietly making up her own stories about them. Her report card invariably read, "Angela would do well if she minded her own business as well as she minds other people's." After writing women's fiction, Angela turned to crime—fictionally speaking, of course—and developed a character that refused to go away.

For more information you can visit:
AngelaMarsons-Books.com
Facebook.com/AngelaMarsonsAuthor
Twitter @WriteAngie